OF DUST AND STARS

JENNA WOLFHART

For those, once again, who dream of a better world.
Fight for that world.

Author's Note

This series is intended for adult readers and will contain dark elements. To see a full list of potential triggers, visit www.jennawolfhart.com/books/content or scan the QR code below.

THE FAE OF AESIR

ELITE FAE

All the common fae
powers, as well as
additional magical
abilities related to
their bloodline.

COMMON FAE

Immortal life-span.
Enhanced senses,
strength, and speed.

LIGHT FAE

Power over fire.
Power over light.
Ability to create shields.

SHADOW FAE

Power over mist.
Animal communication.
Telekenesis.

STORM FAE

Power over wind.
Power over rain.
Power over lightning.

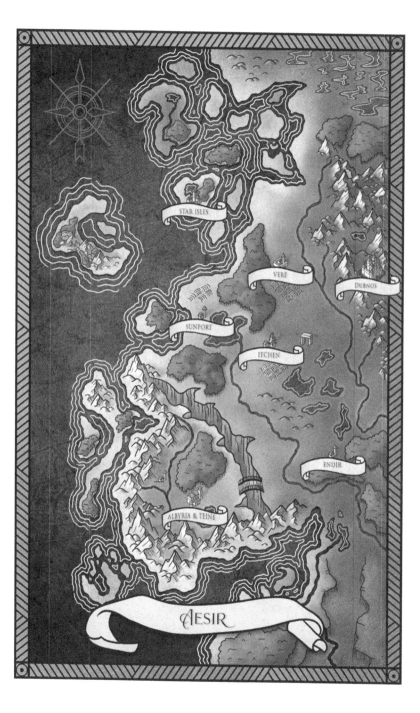

THE STORY SO FAR

In case you need a refresher...

In book one, Tessa Baran defied cruel King Oberon by stealing his powerful gemstones from the chasm. He caught her and punished her by choosing her to become his next mortal bride. Once he took her from her loved ones, he terrorized her and tricked her into believing he'd killed her sister.

Eventually, she escaped with the help of Morgan, one of Oberon's guards, who secretly works with the Mist King—Kalen Denare.

Kalen found her in the mists and took her back to his kingdom in the mountains. There, he offered her a deal. If she would sneak back across the barrier and kill King Oberon with the Mortal Blade, he would find a safe haven for her people, and he would help her find her family, currently lost somewhere in the mists.

She agreed.

They traveled together, dodging attacks from

dangerous monsters and enemies from the Kingdom of Storms. When they got trapped in a castle in Itchen, they grew closer. But half of the God of Death's power was also trapped in that castle. She offered Tessa the life of her sister in exchange for her release.

Tessa denied her and tried to destroy her as a way to stop the god from muting Kalen's powers any longer. It was the only way she could help him fight the storm fae, who had been attacking them for days.

It worked. Kalen got his powers back, and they survived.

Soon after, a letter arrived from Kalen's kingdom. Tessa's mother and dearest friend had made it there safely, against all odds. Eagerly, she returned to Kalen's homeland to reunite with them, only to discover the note was faked.

Kalen had betrayed her. According to Morgan, her family was trapped in Oberon's dungeons, and Kalen had known about it the entire time they'd been traveling together.

With vengeance in her heart, she stabbed him with the Mortal Blade, and then returned to Albyria where she stabbed Oberon as well.

Unfortunately, she soon discovered the blade was a fake. Oberon didn't die, and neither did the Mist King.

King Oberon then threw her into the dungeons, where she discovered her sister was still alive. That night, when she slept, Kalen visited her dreams.

"Hello, love," he said. "Surprised to see me?"

In book two, Tessa and Kalen reconciled in their dreams. He told her he once made a vow to his mother to destroy anyone who brought back the gods. She also learned her own father had dabbled in the dark magic and that Kalen had been forced to kill him.

Meanwhile, Oberon prepared her for their wedding ceremony once again. His eldest son, Ruari, encouraged Tessa to fight back. So when Oberon took her before his court, she revealed that he no longer had access to his powers. Oberon retaliated by pulling his power back into his body, breaking down his protective barrier and letting in the mist. But his power fought back against him in an explosion of fire. The entire city was consumed by flames.

Tessa fled to Teine with her family, and she discovered writings left behind by her father—evidence that she was a descendent of the God of Death.

Not long after, Kalen and his Mist Guard arrived to save her. The Mist Guard led the mortals of Teine to safety while Tessa and Kalen hunted down Oberon. They investigated the Tower of Crones and found Oberon had left behind his previous mortal brides. When one of them touched Tessa's arm, she gave Tessa a vision. Oberon had been in love with Kalen's mother, Bellicent Denare, and when she got killed, Oberon turned to the God of Death in order to save her. The God of Death agreed and gifted Bellicent with eternal life—by putting her soul into the bodies of others.

After this discovery, Kalen took Tessa to the city of Endir where the other mortals were taking refuge. But Tessa's mother did not trust the Mist King and she attempted to flee with several others. She was slaughtered by the shadowfiends, leaving Tessa bereft. To help her overcome her grief, Kalen trained her to fight.

Meanwhile, Morgan had taken an injured Oberon and a weary Bellicent Denare to a hidden cave in the mountains. There, Bellicent suggested Oberon transfer her soul into Morgan's body, and Oberon reluctantly agreed. Panicking, Morgan contacted Kalen and asked for his help.

After receiving Morgan's plea for help, Kalen, Tessa, and the Mist Guard left Endir to find Oberon and Morgan. During the journey, Tessa finally remembered her childhood horrors. Her father had known she was a descendent of Andromeda (the God of Death), and he'd left her in the mists to fight the monsters on her own, hoping it would spark her powers to life.

And then Oberon appeared, regretting everything he'd ever done. He dosed the Mist Guard with valerian fog and stole Tessa away to lock her and the necklace in a vault beneath Albyria—to protect the world. When she woke, she fought him and stabbed him with the Mortal Blade. But he had been carrying the gemstone necklace that held the God of Death's essence, and so it was destroyed as well. Andromeda was finally released, and then the comet heralding the return of the gods streaked through the sky.

Tessa searched for Kalen in the mists, but she could not find him.

Where did he go? Did he believe Tessa brought back the gods? If so, did that mean he would soon be forced to kill her?

In book three, Tessa believed she was the one who brought back the gods and that Kalen would be forced to kill her. She soon discovered him in Albyria, where he was searching for her, and that she wasn't the one responsible for releasing the gods, so nothing could keep them apart. However, she and Kalen formed a marriage bond that would supersede all other vows relating to the two of them, just in case.

Bellicent appeared. She was in Morgan's form and no one knew. However, Kalen still didn't trust her, and he locked her in the dungeons.

The Mist Guard then made a plan to save humanity from the gods. Kalen, Tessa, Toryn, and Fenella journeyed to the Kingdom of Storms to create an alliance. Val, Alastair, and Niamh sailed to the human kingdoms to find out what the humans knew about the gods.

There, they learned how the humans had banished the gods previously. They also learned of a prophecy where Tessa won by using her power against the gods, as well as channeling Kalen's power. And if she did not do so, humanity would be doomed.

While Kalen and Tessa were in the Kingdom of Storms, the remaining gods awakened. The fae fled to Dubnos while the enemy gathered their army. The gods' army then attacked them. Tessa found a way to channel Kalen's power, using it against the enemy. Dubnos won, but they knew the victory was only temporary.

Not long after the battle, Ruari (Oberon's eldest son) informed Kalen that Bellicent had escaped the dungeons and went to Gailfean. Because of Kalen's vow, he was forced to confront her there. Tessa went with him, but it was a trap. Andromeda appeared. She shoved her sword into Kalen's heart and told Tessa she would let him die unless she made a vow never to use her power against the gods. And never to see Kalen again.

Tessa was then taken prisoner. She was trapped in Malroch, the storm fae city on the coast, and there was nothing she could do to stop the gods from destroying humanity.

PROLOGUE
FIADH MacCAIN

THOUSANDS OF YEARS AGO

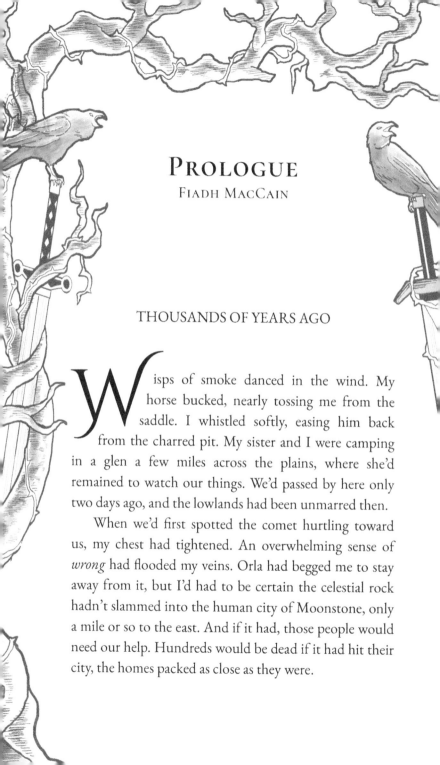

Wisps of smoke danced in the wind. My horse bucked, nearly tossing me from the saddle. I whistled softly, easing him back from the charred pit. My sister and I were camping in a glen a few miles across the plains, where she'd remained to watch our things. We'd passed by here only two days ago, and the lowlands had been unmarred then.

When we'd first spotted the comet hurtling toward us, my chest had tightened. An overwhelming sense of *wrong* had flooded my veins. Orla had begged me to stay away from it, but I'd had to be certain the celestial rock hadn't slammed into the human city of Moonstone, only a mile or so to the east. And if it had, those people would need our help. Hundreds would be dead if it had hit their city, the homes packed as close as they were.

Thankfully, it hadn't. The blasted thing had charred one of their wheat fields.

As I turned my horse around to return to camp, my skin prickled on the back of my neck. I paused and glanced over my shoulder. The ground seemed to pulse with ash, where a collection of gemstones glistened beneath the fading light of the sun.

I dismounted and slowly approached. These gemstones looked nothing like those found in the mountains of Aesir. I tipped back my head to search the sky. They must have come with the comet.

They must have come from the stars.

Unease rolled through me. At least a dozen of them were a deep red color, as vibrant as freshly fallen blood. They made me feel as if my skin wanted to jump off my body and flee across the sea, back to the fae lands, where comets did not fall from the stars and blast the ground with dread and rot.

Suddenly, my horse whinnied and took off across the plains, his thunderous hooves loud in the uneasy silence. I cursed and started after him, but knew I'd never catch up. He'd flee to camp, where Orla would see to him. I'd have to walk the entire way back.

"Blasted animal," I muttered with a sigh—though I could hardly blame him. When I looked upon the wreckage of the comet, I wanted to run, too.

Distant shouts drifted toward me from the gates of Moonstone. I shielded my eyes against the sun and spotted a party headed this way. The humans had noticed the comet, too, and they were coming here to investigate. I ought to warn them to stay away. Their senses were dull

compared to the fae, and they might not feel that heavy
weight of *wrongness* oozing from the ash.

But I could not. I took a step back. If they questioned
me, they'd want to know where my camp was. Then
they'd discover Orla. My sister, the murderer, who had
killed a fae lord in cold blood. King Ovalis Hinde of
Talaven would not protect Orla. He would send her back
to Aesir for the fae to deal with her as they saw fit.

And the punishment would fit the crime, no matter
that Orla had been driven by desperation. That bastard
lord had whipped her so many times I'd lost count. Just
thinking about her back's shredded flesh made my blood
sing with anger.

Yes, a voice whispered on the wind. *You will be perfect.
Come to me, child of dust.*

Frowning, I turned back to the charred pit. The
specks on the horizon had grown larger, but the humans
still weren't close enough to spot me yet. So who had
spoken?

I gazed around the wheat fields that rolled gently
toward the distant city. There were no trees or caverns or
rocky ledges for anyone to hide behind, and there were no
signs of anyone else near me.

Come closer, the voice whispered again.

My heart clenched as my eyes lowered to the charred
pit, and the gemstones glowed ever brightly. The light
within them pulsed like a heartbeat.

"That's impossible," I said, shaking my head and
wishing my horse had not charged off across the
lowlands. I needed to get away from this place as quickly
as I could.

Do not be afraid, child of dust. I can help you and your sister, Orla. All you must do is take the crimson gemstones and run. Before the humans see you. Hurry now.

I shook my head, my chest tight. This was some kind of trick or mirage. Hands clenching, I started to move away, but my feet wouldn't respond. A desperate hope had flared to life inside me, the gemstone's words rattling around in my head. Orla. The voice had mentioned Orla. It said it could help her.

"How? What can you do for Orla?" I asked.

I am from the stars and have power beyond anything you could imagine. I can save your sister. All you must do is prevent the humans from getting their hands on us, do you understand? Doom will come upon you if they do. They have already begun to turn against your kind. This would clinch their win.

Her words were true. Whispers had been swirling through Star Isles for years. The humans had grown bolder under the rule of King Ovalis Hinde, and he'd begun to look further than the shores of Talaven. He saw the riches and powers of the fae and coveted them. Rumors of war spread through the city streets like rats.

If this voice was right, and she held some kind of star-gifted power...the lord we'd run from was terrible and wicked and cruel, but what about everyone else? All our friends and cousins and aunts and uncles? When Orla and I had run, I'd accepted I might never again see them in this lifetime. But they still lived. This world still held them.

If war erupted between Aesir and Talaven, they

would be in grave danger. Star Isles sat right on the coast-line. Talaven would attack it first.

I couldn't risk this voice being right.

I rushed forward, and ashen dust sprayed into the air. My hand closed around the crimson gemstones a moment later. Unbidden power throbbed against my palm and set my teeth on edge.

Hurry. The human king will see you if you don't move quickly.

Tears filled my eyes, though I didn't know why. I clutched the gemstones to my chest, and I ran.

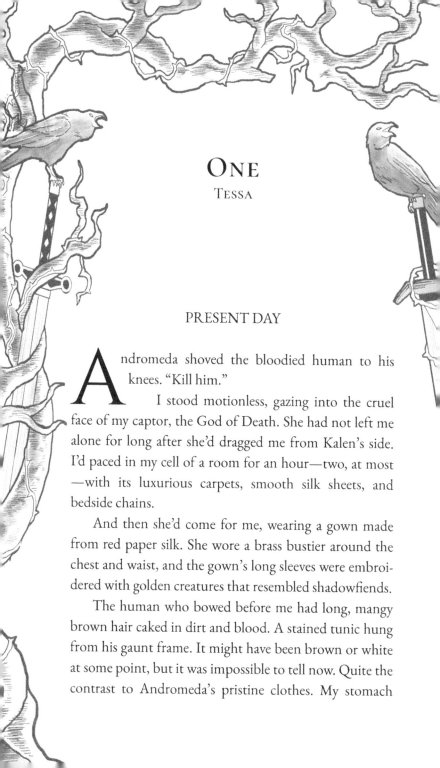

ONE
TESSA

PRESENT DAY

Andromeda shoved the bloodied human to his knees. "Kill him."

I stood motionless, gazing into the cruel face of my captor, the God of Death. She had not left me alone for long after she'd dragged me from Kalen's side. I'd paced in my cell of a room for an hour—two, at most—with its luxurious carpets, smooth silk sheets, and bedside chains.

And then she'd come for me, wearing a gown made from red paper silk. She wore a brass bustier around the chest and waist, and the gown's long sleeves were embroidered with golden creatures that resembled shadowfiends.

The human who bowed before me had long, mangy brown hair caked in dirt and blood. A stained tunic hung from his gaunt frame. It might have been brown or white at some point, but it was impossible to tell now. Quite the contrast to Andromeda's pristine clothes. My stomach roiled, but not from his stench or the sweat dripping down his cheek. Andromeda's words echoed in my ears like a death knell.

"Do it yourself." I stepped back and lifted my chin in defiance.

She smiled. Even though we stood in a cavernous Great Hall, empty save for the three of us, the walls closed in tight. Her presence seemed to expand with every moment that passed, making the room smaller and smaller, like Oberon had once seemed to do. But after seeing the gods, I realized just how small he'd always been.

Andromeda would have crushed him beneath her pointy boot if he'd still been alive.

The room itself had once been a hall for merriment and official courtly business, based on the emerald tapestries that lined the stone walls and the oak tables shoved into the far corner. A rich, golden carpet softened the floor beneath us, though the human's blood soaked through the threads. Andromeda did not seem to notice or care. It wasn't her hall or her carpet. Why should stains matter?

"No, I will not do it myself," she said. "You will."

"You cannot make me."

"You have a gift, and you *will* use it."

"A gift?" I fought the urge to laugh and instead kept my expression as cool as steel. Andromeda had broken me down, but after I'd sobbed and screamed and cursed the skies that first hour I'd been in captivity, I'd vowed to myself—and to Kalen, wherever he was now—not to let my emotions control me. If I was going to beat the gods, I would have to keep myself from falling apart again.

"My power is far greater than anything you could imagine," she said. "So yes, it most certainly is a gift."

"I don't need to imagine. I've used your power, and I know exactly what it can do."

She narrowed her deep black eyes. "And yet, you hold yourself back from it. I can sense your hesitation, my daughter."

I flinched, despite myself. "My mother's name was Ula Baran. And she—"

"Ah yes, Ula Baran," the God of Death cut in, her top lip curling back. "The woman with so much hate in her heart that she forsook her own daughters and left them in the arms of her greatest enemy, the Mist King."

I looked away.

"Is that not how the story goes?" she asked. "My spies tell me she fled into the mist, leaving you and your sister with the fae king she'd always hated with every fiber of her being. She thought escaping would be her salvation. Instead, it was her doom."

"Do not talk about my mother," I said, my voice cracking.

I understood what Andromeda was doing. She was trying to get into my head and manipulate me into doing whatever she asked. What better way to break me down than by reminding me of the pain that drenched my past like the blood on this carpet? She would know I still grieved for my mother, that I still felt betrayed by her actions. But Andromeda was not human. She didn't know what forgiveness was.

The God of Death could not understand love.

After a moment passed, I met her gaze and said, "No

matter what you say to me, I will not kill this man for you."

The human sagged forward, pressing his forehead against the stained carpet.

"I see." Andromeda's boots scuffed the carpet as she came closer. "You believe this is a request and not a command. But I'm afraid, dear daughter, that you have no choice in the matter. Kill the man, or I will send my brother to cast a plague on Dubnos. I was going to leave the shadow fae to their own devices, but if you force my hand..."

Ice froze my veins. "Leave them be. They've been through enough."

"All right. Kill the human, then."

My hands clenched. "Why are you doing this?"

"Because I need you to accept and use the power I've given you. This is the only way I know how to make you do that."

"What are you going to do with him?"

"The human spy, you mean?"

"Are you..." I nearly choked on the words, bile rising in the back of my throat. "You and the others...are you...?"

I couldn't say it. I could barely even think it. It was as if my mind wanted to wrap bandages around the truth to protect me from the horror of it. But the memories bled through. In my mind, I could even hear the voices of the elders when they'd lectured the children of Teine on the horrors of the Mist King. Their words were so loud it was as if they were in this very room.

The Mist King decided to invade the Kingdom of

Light after burning down human cities in the lands beyond the sea, mimicking the ancient myths of the five banished gods: powerful beings who fed upon the burned flesh of fae and mortals alike.

But Kalen had never done such a thing. Those warnings had only been stories and nothing more, a way for Oberon to control us. But I couldn't say the same for the gods. The humans were the entire reason they were here, as far as I could tell.

Andromeda had the indecency to smirk. "You're asking if I plan to roast the flesh of this man and feed him to my brothers and sisters."

The spy whimpered.

"Aren't you?" I asked.

"No. The idea of feasting upon flesh disgusts me, cooked or not."

I blinked. "What?"

"This is the problem with lore, Tessa Baran. The years erode the truth, leaving nothing behind but a smudged portrait of the real history. We will not feast." She placed her boot on the man's back and shoved him face first onto the carpet. "Now kill him."

My blood roared in my ears. "I don't understand. You and the other gods, you came here for the humans. You even said yourself that they're all you care about. You need them to survive. What do you want from them if not their lifeblood?"

For a moment, Andromeda didn't answer. She merely stood there with her hands clasped in front of her brass bustier, her hair stirring around her shoulders from a breeze that touched her and nothing else. I'd feared the gods from the moment I'd learned they were real, knowing what they wanted and what they were capable of. But this feeling—the *unknown* of it all—took the breath from my lungs.

What could they want from us? The fear held me motionless as I awaited her answer.

At long last, she cocked her head. "Perhaps I will tell you once you've proven yourself to me. As it is, I do not trust you with that knowledge."

"Prove myself by killing this innocent man?"

Her smile returned, curving her red lips. "This man is not innocent. He is a spy from Talaven, and I'm growing bored of this conversation. Kill him, daughter, or I will allow Sirius to loose his plague on Dubnos. Either way, there will be death on your hands. It's up to you who lives."

"Plague? Is Sirius not the God of Beasts?"

Andromeda looked at me for a long moment before answering. "No, Callisto is the God of Beasts. Curious that you were given incorrect information about that, too. Now kill this man."

My heart pounded painfully in my chest. "I said I wouldn't do it."

She stared at me for a long moment, then shook her head with a laugh. "You won't do this for the people of Dubnos? Well then. I'll make you a better offer. One I know you will not refuse. Do these trials for me, become one of us, and I'll release you from your vow."

The world around me vanished as I stared into the cruel eyes of the God of Death. Her words echoed in my ears. *I'll release you from your vow.*

My breath shuddered from my lungs. Surely I hadn't heard her right.

She arched her brow in question. "Well? What will it be?"

I shook my head, still in disbelief. When I found my voice, I said, "Now I understand where Oberon learned his cruelty."

"Oberon." Andromeda scowled. "Do not speak his name to me. He's the reason things have gotten as bad as they have."

"Gotten as bad as what?"

"No more questions," she suddenly snapped. "Make your choice. I have things to do, and I'll have no more of this stalling."

I tried to think, my mind desperately grasping for any thread it could pull—anything to stop this. But there was nothing. The glint in Andromeda's eyes was harsh and angry, her patience fully spent. If I didn't do what she demanded, or I tried to keep her talking, she would send the plague into Dubnos. This wasn't a bluff. She didn't care about the fae.

But if I gave her an excuse to attack them, she would surely take it. Her beasts and the storm fae already had once.

What was more, she'd given me a way out—a way to reunite with my mate. The need for him burned through me like the fires of Albyria.

"How many trials?" I asked. Instantly, I hated myself for it.

She smiled. "Three. Or four. However many it takes."

I ground my teeth and turned away. This was the first,

so only two or three more. But what would she make me do next? Surely it would be much worse than this.

Please, I thought, not daring to speak the words aloud. *Don't make me do this.* But outwardly, I was a mask of calm. The only thing that might give away my despair was the flutter of my heartbeat in my neck.

Swallowing, I lifted my hand. The man sobbed, his entire body shaking like a leaf. Pain and anger raged through me and filled my head with the roar of my heart. Everything about this was wrong. I knew I would hate myself if I gave in to Andromeda's demands, but I didn't see a way out of this. The God of Death did not bluff. If I didn't kill this spy, she'd destroy Dubnos. Thousands of innocents would die.

That didn't make this all right, though. This man did not deserve this fate.

A tear threatened to spill down my cheek, but I blinked it back.

I thought of Kalen, of Nellie, of Fenella, and of Toryn. None of them would survive unless I killed this man.

I bowed my head. "I am so sorry."

And then I brushed my bare fingers against his face.

D arkness surrounded me.

I blinked, and the darkness cleared. A pile of dust sat by my feet, and Andromeda stood beaming, hands clasped, smile bright. She looked like a proud mother. Bile rose in the back of my throat.

Turning away from the dead man's ashes, I tried to understand what had happened. One moment, I'd been touching his skin, the next, I was standing here...it was as if I'd lost several moments.

My mind had done this once before. It had hidden the dark moments from my childhood deep inside me to protect me from the harsh truths of my world. But I couldn't forget this, and I couldn't avoid what I'd done. I had killed his man.

I'd done it to save others, but that did not make it right. And I refused to lose myself and forget.

"Well done, my daughter," Andromeda trilled.

I tensed. "I am not your daughter."

"You will be once your trials are done."

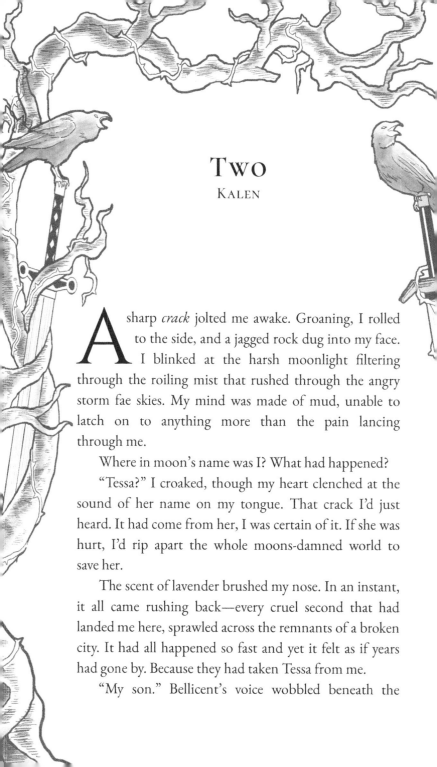

Two
Kalen

A sharp *crack* jolted me awake. Groaning, I rolled to the side, and a jagged rock dug into my face. I blinked at the harsh moonlight filtering through the roiling mist that rushed through the angry storm fae skies. My mind was made of mud, unable to latch on to anything more than the pain lancing through me.

Where in moon's name was I? What had happened?

"Tessa?" I croaked, though my heart clenched at the sound of her name on my tongue. That crack I'd just heard. It had come from her, I was certain of it. If she was hurt, I'd rip apart the whole moons-damned world to save her.

The scent of lavender brushed my nose. In an instant, it all came rushing back—every cruel second that had landed me here, sprawled across the remnants of a broken city. It had all happened so fast and yet it felt as if years had gone by. Because they had taken Tessa from me.

"My son." Bellicent's voice wobbled beneath the

crunch of boots on crumbled stone. She came to stop a few feet away, but she did not dare come any closer. "How are you feeling?"

"Get away from me."

Pain split my skull as I rolled onto my front and slammed my fists into the rock. More pain shot through my fingers, but it was nothing compared to the rage burning in my veins. My mother and the gods had taken everything from me.

Everything.

I lifted my eyes to Bellicent's face. Her skin was as pale as the silver of her hair—of *Morgan's* hair. She had stolen so much from everyone, all to escape death long enough to drag the gods back into this world. Long enough to doom us all.

But for the first time in my life, I struggled to care about my mother. Tessa had been taken from me. There was no telling what Andromeda would do to her.

"Where is Tessa?" I said, slowly pushing to my feet. After what Andromeda had done to me, there was weakness yet in my limbs, but the rage fueled me enough to keep me standing. I would not rest until my wife had returned to my side.

Bellicent pressed her lips together. "She is gone."

"Where?" I asked through clenched teeth. The vow I'd made with my mother tugged at me, but my desperation to reach Tessa shoved it down.

"It doesn't matter. She made a vow, my son. You can never see her again."

The anger filled my head with a roar. I strode toward her, but the lightness in my head made my feet stumble against the rocky surface. Slowing to a stop, I spoke with all the fury I could muster. "You will not keep her from me. Not even the God of Death can hold me back."

Her silver eyes swept across my face, then narrowed. "No, my son, please. You *didn't*."

"Didn't what?" I snapped.

She shook her head, then let out a bitter laugh that filled the eerie silence of Gailfean's rubble. "I would recognize the feral glint in your eye anywhere. It's the look of a fae bonded in marriage. You promised yourself to that mortal." Her voice dropped to a whisper. "Get out of here now, Kalen. The gods will not stand for this."

The tone of her voice was like a lick of fire down my spine, but with it came the glimmer of hope. "My bond with Tessa. It can override the one she made with Andromeda, can't it?"

"A part of it...perhaps yes." Her eyes darted to the darkness just behind me. "Which is why you must run. If one of them discovers you two are bonded, the gods won't—"

Whorling shadows suddenly consumed the space between me and Bellicent. Powerful wings thundered to the ground, and a god landed in a crouch before me. When he stood, a creeping dread pulsed from his towering frame. He wore full plate armor, except a helm, and his hands were free. They were so large he could easily snap even the strongest fae's neck. Hair as black as onyx curled around his pointed ears, and his eyes glowed red, like blood.

As he swept his gaze across me, he frowned. "You."

That single word sounded like a curse, or like a promise of death.

"You," I repeated back to him in a snarl. His power did not terrify me, nor would I cow before him. Not like my mother, who had knelt and splayed her hands across the ground.

He curled back his top lip, revealing his sharp teeth, each chiseled to a point. "You cannot hide something as big as a marriage bond from Andromeda."

"Please," Bellicent said, her voice wobbling. She still bowed before the god, though she had not dared to lift her head. "Perseus, leave him be."

Perseus. The God of Fear.

I glanced at his bare hands and took a step back from pure instinct. Out of all the gods, he was the one I wished to face the least. I'd heard stories of what his curse could do. I would see my worst fears come to life, every single horror my mind could conjure. I knew, without a doubt, so many would be about Tessa.

I lifted my sword from the ground and angled it toward the god. In my state, the weapon wobbled, but I did not back down.

The god frowned. "Weapons are useless against us, Mist King."

My mother climbed to her feet and started toward him. "Leave him be. I made a deal with Andromeda, and she swore to spare his life. I—"

Perseus's hand snapped out, and he gripped Bellicent's throat. His fingers dug into her skin. Her eyes went wide as she loosed a strangled cough and clawed at the god's hand. With an impassive expression, Perseus tugged her against his chest and snapped her neck. Then he released her, and her body—Morgan's body—hit the ground. Horror and revulsion churned my gut.

For a moment, I couldn't speak. All the love I'd once felt for my mother had been twisted and corrupted by the thing she'd become. Bellicent Denare had changed from the vibrant, bold, and powerful fae she'd been. In her place had been a cowering creature willing to sacrifice everything to be close to the gods.

But that did not blunt the sword of pain that sliced through my heart. I'd harbored a secret hope that we could find a way to break the vow and get her back to who she'd once been—that I would one day be able to look at her and see the mother I'd once known before her relationship with Oberon had driven her to the gods.

None of this had been her choice.

I lifted my eyes to the god's cruel face. "She had a deal with Andromeda."

"I am not Andromeda."

I should have seen it coming, but I didn't. There was no warning, no twitch in the god's form. The sword slid from his scabbard, and the blunt end slammed into my skull. The shadows that consumed my mind were darker than any night sky.

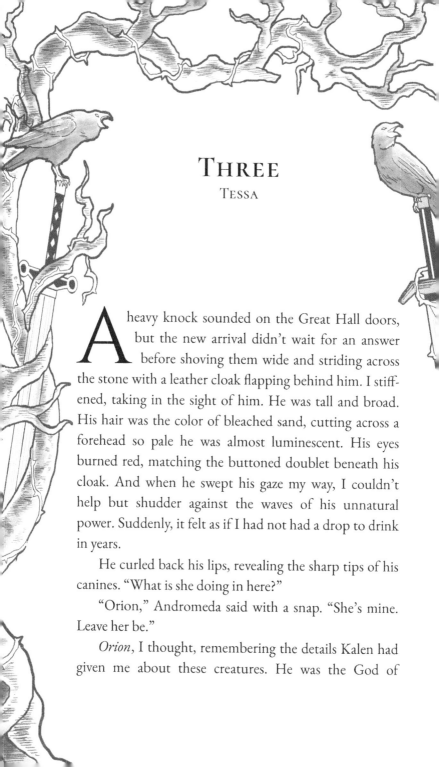

THREE
TESSA

A heavy knock sounded on the Great Hall doors, but the new arrival didn't wait for an answer before shoving them wide and striding across the stone with a leather cloak flapping behind him. I stiffened, taking in the sight of him. He was tall and broad. His hair was the color of bleached sand, cutting across a forehead so pale he was almost luminescent. His eyes burned red, matching the buttoned doublet beneath his cloak. And when he swept his gaze my way, I couldn't help but shudder against the waves of his unnatural power. Suddenly, it felt as if I had not had a drop to drink in years.

He curled back his lips, revealing the sharp tips of his canines. "What is she doing in here?"

"Orion," Andromeda said with a snap. "She's mine. Leave her be."

Orion, I thought, remembering the details Kalen had given me about these creatures. He was the God of

Famine, which meant he could starve every human in Talaven if he desired it.

Dragging his gaze away from me, he scowled. "You should kill her and be done with it. She threatens our entire plan just by being alive. If she—"

"I said leave her be." Andromeda's voice was as hard and cold as steel, cutting down Orion's objections. She drew herself up to her full height, and despite her shorter statue, she seemed to tower over her fellow god. And then to me, she said, "Tessa, you're dismissed."

I cast a quick glance between them, then moved toward the open doors, where I expected to find guards or storm fae soldiers waiting for me. But the hallway was empty.

"You have earned an hour of freedom," Andromeda called after me. "As long as you don't cause any trouble, you might earn an hour more. Return to your room when the next bell strikes."

My heart thumped against my ribs, just from that small morsel of freedom she dangled in front of me. If only I could escape Malroch, I could flee to Dubnos and reunite with Kalen, gods be damned. I might be able to do it, too, despite what I'd vowed. If my marriage bond with Kalen superseded everything else, nothing stood in my way.

As I walked away from the Great Hall, my mind churned. The temptation to run was almost overwhelming, echoing loudly in my ears. I ground my teeth and tried to *think*, steadily putting one foot in front of the other so that if anyone saw me, they wouldn't guess just how close I was to throwing all caution to the wind.

I steadied my breathing and kept walking.

A few months ago, I would have charged out of this castle, racing toward the gates of the city without a single thought to the consequences. But rashness had never been my friend. I'd learned that lesson the hard way. The gods were likely having me watched. If I tried to run now, only moments after being given my first taste of freedom, Andromeda would stop me. With force. I wasn't strong enough—yet—to fight her.

This was a test, I realized. If not one of the actual trials, it was still a test. Andromeda wanted to see what I would do with this sliver of freedom. And if I was right and I *did* make it through the gates, I'd show my hand. She'd realize Kalen and I had a marriage bond.

Right now, she didn't know. If I were to use my secret against her, I'd have to wait until the right moment. I'd have to be certain I could escape without getting caught. I needed to bide my time.

I release a tense breath and moved down a stairwell toward the ground floor of the castle. Torches lined the curving walls, illuminating the steps and chasing away the shadows. My every instinct warred against my choice. I hated the idea of spending even a moment longer away from Kalen. When I'd left him, he'd still been bleeding out on the rubble. I needed to see him, I needed to hear his voice and know that he still breathed.

But for now, there was nothing I could do but play this game. I would have to wait for nightfall and find him in my dreams.

O
utside, a wall of mist surrounded the city of Malroch, though the skies overhead were clear and full of beaming sunlight. When I stepped foot on the cobblestone road that wound away from the castle, then down into the port-side city sprawled across the shoreline, I tipped back my head and drank in the warmth of the sun.

I loved Dubnos and the moonlight and the stars, but a part of me would always unravel beneath the sun. The tension in my shoulders loosened, and weariness released its grip on me—as much as it possibly could while I was trapped in a city full of monsters.

As if in answer to my thoughts, the sound of heavy footsteps snapped my attention away from the sky. I turned just as a towering figure clad in plate armor thundered across the drawbridge into the castle. Most of his body was hidden beneath the mass of plate, but his onyx hair glistened beneath the sunlight. He paused as he passed through the gates, and his crimson eyes latched on me. Suddenly, I felt very afraid. A shudder went down my spine.

"The God of Fear," a voice piped up from behind me.

I jumped and whirled, coming face-to-face with a human woman who...no, she couldn't be human. She had slightly pointed ears and horns peeking through a curtain of red hair, though her build was more like mine. Half-fae, then, perhaps. She wore a simple drab shift, like the other maidservants I'd seen. I was surprised she was bold enough to speak to me. Andromeda likely wouldn't be thrilled by it if she were anything like Oberon. And she *was* like him—just worse.

"That's Perseus?" I asked.

"Couldn't you tell? He reeks of fear."

"I thought they could only use their powers through touch."

"For some of them, yes." She smiled tensely. "Perseus carries with him an aura of fear, just like Callisto feels like violence. It's extremely...unnerving." Suddenly, she blinked and quickly said, "But don't tell them I said that. Please."

"Not a word," I assured her.

"Also," she said, dropping her voice to a whisper, "we Maidservants, you know we listen. And Perseus has just returned from Gailfean. I thought you should know."

My muscles tensed. Gailfean. *Kalen.* "Why are you telling me this?"

"Because you need to return to his side," she hissed.

I searched her flashing eyes, taken aback by the intensity of her words. She seemed more than just a bystander, a maidservant caught up in the games of the gods. But my need to find out what I could about Kalen drew my attention to the drawbridge—just for a moment—and when I turned back to the girl, she was gone.

Frowning, I tossed aside my curiosity and hurried after Perseus. If he was returning from Gailfean, the God of Fear would likely meet with Andromeda and give her an update. She'd want to know where Kalen was. Did they let him go? And if they did, would Kalen attempt to come here? He'd sounded defeated when I'd agreed to Andromeda's vow. Did he suspect, like I did, that our bond with each other was more powerful?

As much as I wanted to return to his side, I hoped to the sun above he would stay away.

Because Andromeda would kill him.

With that thought in mind, I took the curving stone steps leading into the North Tower two at a time and ducked inside the door. I quietly shut it behind me, my eyes readjusting to the dimly lit interior. Voices drifted toward me from around the corner. I'd recognize Andromeda's melodic timbre anywhere. She must be speaking to Perseus about what he'd found in Gailfean.

I strained to hear them, but they were too far away for me to make out their words. If I rounded the corner, they'd see me.

Sighing, I looked around. There were a few coats of arms hanging along the walls, but nothing more substantial to hide behind. Even if there was, it would do me little use. I needed to get into the next corridor.

That only left *up*. I tipped back my head. The ground floor had a high hammerbeam ceiling with carved hanging pendants in the shape of winged horses. Every so often, short vertical posts painted a brilliant gold mortice into the arches, though the spaces between each post were fairly substantial. One could hide up there in the rafters. *Could*, I repeated to myself, *if one were stealthy enough.*

A heartbeat passed before I flared my wings. I had to hear this conversation.

I beat my wings as quietly as I could and lifted into the air. Soon, I reached the beams overhead. I grabbed ahold of the wood, crouched, and folded my wings into my back, straining to listen.

Only silence greeted me. No sound of alarm had been raised.

Breath shaking, I leaned forward, grabbed the next beam, and swung into the arch where the corridors met. Halfway down the hallway, Andromeda and Sirius—*not* Perseus—were deep in conversation. Seeing Sirius again with his crimson hair, his towering form, and his glowing red eyes made my soul buckle with fear. The last time I'd seen him, he'd gotten into my head and showed me the future the gods craved. I'd seen exactly what destruction they would loose upon my world.

He whispered to Andromeda, and the scowl on her face sent a tremor through my belly. And her words, at long last, were loud enough for me to hear, though just barely. "If this is some kind of joke to provoke me, I'll have you locked in a sarcophagus for a hundred more years."

Sirius stiffened and turned my way. I pulled back, digging my fingers into the wood to hold myself steady. A beam blocked me from view, but my breathing was ragged, and my heartbeat thundered like a Gailfean storm. With my legs bent awkwardly beneath me, my muscles shook, spasming in pain. But I didn't dare move. If he saw me, I'd never hear the rest of their conversation.

"What is it?" Andromeda demanded. "Answer me, Sirius."

"Nothing," he said. "I'm just tired of being the go-between with you and Perseus."

I clutched the beam tighter. Now, without his wicked

rage bearing down on me, Sirius sounded less like a rotten, hollow thing and more like a weary father who wanted to put his feet up on the table and drink a barrel of ale.

"Don't try to change the subject. Is it really true? Swear to me, Sirius."

The God of Pestilence sighed. "I'm afraid so. Your new toy and the Mist King have a marriage bond. Her vow to you can't keep her away from him, though she must not have realized it. Otherwise, she'd be long gone by now."

I fought the urge to suck in a breath. Perseus had discovered the bond when he'd been in Gailfean. But if he had, then...I closed my eyes and ground my teeth, hating the first thought that entered my mind. If they knew about the bond, then—

"Did Perseus kill him?" Andromeda asked.

"No, he let him live."

She huffed. "And the gemstones? Did he find them?"

"Two of them. They were right where you thought they'd be. We're ready now to—"

A bell clanged from somewhere in the tower, drowning out the rest of Sirius's words. My relief was a churning sea within me, and I nearly choked on it. But I forced myself to focus as the bell rang. If the sound of it covered their voices, it would hide my movement in the rafters. I took the opportunity to unfold myself and swing around the corner. Every muscle in my body ached, but I didn't slow until my boots landed on the stone floor just out of sight.

And then, with silent steps, I fled to my room.

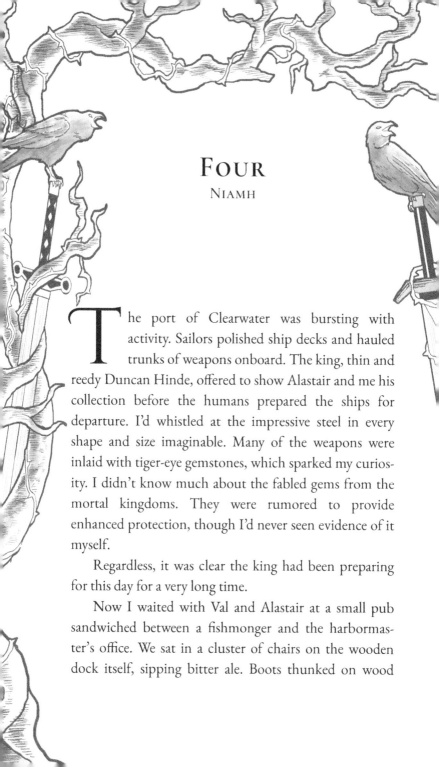

FOUR
NIAMH

The port of Clearwater was bursting with activity. Sailors polished ship decks and hauled trunks of weapons onboard. The king, thin and reedy Duncan Hinde, offered to show Alastair and me his collection before the humans prepared the ships for departure. I'd whistled at the impressive steel in every shape and size imaginable. Many of the weapons were inlaid with tiger-eye gemstones, which sparked my curiosity. I didn't know much about the fabled gems from the mortal kingdoms. They were rumored to provide enhanced protection, though I'd never seen evidence of it myself.

Regardless, it was clear the king had been preparing for this day for a very long time.

Now I waited with Val and Alastair at a small pub sandwiched between a fishmonger and the harbormaster's office. We sat in a cluster of chairs on the wooden dock itself, sipping bitter ale. Boots thunked on wood and soft waves rushed against the bank beneath us. The sailors' ruckus had drowned out most attempts at conversation, but the din was beginning to die down. With most of the ships readied and fully loaded, it was as if Clearwater had taken a deep breath, then held it in anticipation.

Val stared at the nearest ship, which would carry the king across the choppy waters—and us. He'd donned it *The Sea Fae's Curse*, which rankled my ass. For one, there was no such thing as a sea fae. Two, if anyone were cursed, it was these damn humans with their vision comets. Now that I'd spent some more time with the man, it was clear these visions had haunted him since he was old enough to know his left toe from his right. Half the time, he wandered around muttering to himself about knife edges, wings, tranquility and bounty—which made little sense to me—and someone named Fiadh MacCain.

When asked about it, he merely waved his hand and said, "I've shared all I can. Any more, and it could break the knife's edge."

Val tapped her finger against her full tankard. She hadn't touched her drink, which told me all I needed to know about her state of mind. "Are we sailing straight to war?" Her voice was tight; her cheeks were pale. I wanted to soothe her worry, but I wouldn't lie to her, either.

"Hopefully, no. The king has planned a route to Sunport, which is far enough south that it should have avoided getting swept up in the war. But I can't promise you there won't be surprises. The gods can fly."

"But so can the little dove," Alastair cut in from

where he had been quietly observing the busy docks. "She knows we're coming. And she'll do everything in her power to distract the gods from the Bantam Sea, especially with you on board one of the ships. You're her family."

"That's exactly what I'm worried about," she said with a sigh. "I don't want Tessa to put herself in danger trying to save me. She's already done that far too much."

"If only the damn king hadn't thrown our communication stones out the window," Alastair muttered.

Scowling, I nodded my agreement. When we'd contacted Kal, the mortal king had taken the opportunity to snatch our remaining stones. He'd chucked them right out the tower window. Something about the fucking knife's edge again.

"Too much communication could snap the fragile threads that bind the past to the future," he'd said.

I'd gone hunting for them on the rocks below the tower window, but the wind had blown away whatever shattered residue they'd left behind.

I understood why Duncan Hinde was the way he was, but I didn't much like it.

The king suddenly appeared, as if my thoughts had summoned him. He approached the table in his swirling emerald robe and sandaled feet, flanked by a score of armored guards. He didn't go anywhere outside the castle without them, which always made me wonder if there was something he'd seen from the comet. A future he wanted to avoid.

"Val," he said with a polite nod. He always addressed

her first. "You and your companions may board the ship now."

We'd been assigned to sail with him on The Sea Fae's Curse. Some might take that as an honor. I, on the other hand, knew it for what it was. He wanted to keep an eye on us. Even with his comet, he hadn't anticipated our arrival in Talaven. Something about the comet's potency faded over time. But I knew it unnerved him. Our being here hadn't been part of his carefully constructed plan.

Deep down, I knew that should worry me, too. As much as I hated how the human kingdom had secretly woven their threads, manipulating and watching and twisting fate into what they wanted it to become, I understood why. They'd done everything in their power to protect the world from the eventual return of the gods. And, if they were right about Tessa, it had worked. She was fated to stop them.

But if our arrival wasn't on the cards, did that mean the knife's edge had cracked?

I didn't want to think about what that might mean if it had.

Val stood and followed the king, and I let her lead the way. Alastair fell into step behind her, jaw clenched. I knew him well enough to read the tension in his shoulders and the way he rubbed his right earring. Everything I'd noticed, he'd noticed, too. We hadn't spoken about it, too wary of the ears all around us. But he knew.

I gave him a nod as we approached the ship. He nodded back. We might be sailing into familiar waters, but there would be storms ahead.

As we walked across the gangplank, I spotted another

ship leaving the harbor. Several more were easing away from the port. Brine thickened the air even as a soft breeze soothed the heat beaming down from the persistent sun. I gazed across the rippling blue expanse, awestruck for a moment at how far I could see. Somewhere beyond the horizon stood a land consumed by mist and shadow, now under threat by immortal beings intent on destroying us all. And suddenly, it felt like that darkness was racing toward us, even though the sky remained clear.

Despite the heat, a shiver raced down my spine.

"What's wrong?" Alastair asked.

I shook my head. "I think I just feel uneasy about what the king said we—"

The furthest ship away from the port tipped to the side, the sea bucking beneath it. A tentacle twice the size of The Sea Fae's Curse surged from the depths. Its skin was a deep reddish pink, and dozens of suckers dotted the arm that slammed down on the ship. Men screamed; wood snapped.

The ship cracked in two.

I gripped Val's shoulder and pulled her to my chest, watching in horror as tentacle after tentacle curled around the shattered ship and dragged the humans down into the sea. Every time one of the warriors tried to swim away, another tentacle appeared and sucked him under.

In only moments, the only signs of life were floating bits of debris.

I tugged Val back across the gangplank to the relative safety of the docks. If the giant octopus went after another ship, I wanted her nowhere near it. Alastair followed, then so did the king. His face was so pale, he might have been dead.

He met my gaze, his lips parting. And in his shock, he let something slip.

"Something's gone wrong," he whispered.

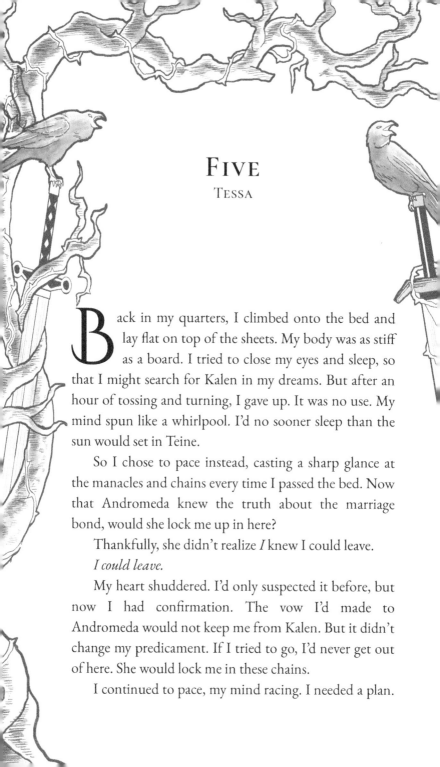

FIVE
TESSA

Back in my quarters, I climbed onto the bed and lay flat on top of the sheets. My body was as stiff as a board. I tried to close my eyes and sleep, so that I might search for Kalen in my dreams. But after an hour of tossing and turning, I gave up. It was no use. My mind spun like a whirlpool. I'd no sooner sleep than the sun would set in Teine.

So I chose to pace instead, casting a sharp glance at the manacles and chains every time I passed the bed. Now that Andromeda knew the truth about the marriage bond, would she lock me up in here?

Thankfully, she didn't realize *I* knew I could leave.

I could leave.

My heart shuddered. I'd only suspected it before, but now I had confirmation. The vow I'd made to Andromeda would not keep me from Kalen. But it didn't change my predicament. If I tried to go, I'd never get out of here. She would lock me in these chains.

I continued to pace, my mind racing. I needed a plan.

I needed to find a way to escape *and* a way to rid this world of these immortal beings. At least I knew Kalen was alive. That was what mattered most. And when we finally reunited, we would end the gods once and for all.

As the day grew late, I watched the procession of the sun with rapt attention from the window. I'd heard stories about sunsets, of course, but I'd never seen one. Back in Teine, the sun had merely crept from one side of the sky to the other, over and over, until constant daylight drove us into our windowless rooms for a brief respite.

In Dubnos, only darkness and shadowy moonlight filled the sky. There'd been nothing quite like this, the streaks of orange across the deepening dark, the pink flares that spiralled across the clouds, the glow it cast upon the coral-lined streets. If only Kalen were here to see it.

Stomach twisting, I crossed the room and climbed back into the bed. Sleep had eluded me earlier, but I had to find him. I had to speak with him. I had to be sure he was all right. Taking a breath, I closed my eyes and tried to sleep, but I tossed and turned for a good long while before I finally drifted into the dark.

I found myself in a dreamscape entirely of my own making. It was so familiar to me now that a sense of homesickness swept over me at the sight of the swaying grass, the sweep of mist curling through the trees, and the sound of the birdsong. But as I waited there, my unbound hair flowing in the breeze, an understanding settled over me. Kalen's absence was as loud as the birds. He wasn't here, and he wasn't coming.

I was alone in my dreams for the first time in a very long while.

Where is he? Perseus had let him live, but I knew Kalen would come here if he could.

My anger was thick and hot on my tongue, and my fury fuelled me as food never had. After forcing myself to wake, I leapt from the bed and paced. I could not rest until I found a way out of this.

Hours passed. My mind conjured nothing but anger. A knock sounded on the door sometime later, breaking me out of my reverie.

"What is it?" I asked the closed door.

A moment later, it opened to reveal Andromeda again. She swept into the room. This time she wore a golden silk gown that whispered around her sandaled feet. A matching necklace glittered at her throat, but the gleam of it was nothing compared to the flash of her teeth when she smiled. I tensed, half-expecting her to mention the marriage bond.

But she merely gave me a quick once-over. "Come."

My first instinct was to argue or make a cutting remark. I bit my tongue instead. "Where are you taking me?"

"Nervous, are we? The guards told me you've been pacing in here for hours. Come. Break bread with us."

"Break bread," I repeated, resisting the urge to recoil. "You're inviting me to dinner with you?"

"With all of us." She moved toward the door, then waited for me to follow.

I steadied myself and forced my feet to move. If I was going to convince her to trust me, I needed to spend more time in her presence. I needed to do what she asked without complaint. But deep inside, my bones turned to liquid. The last thing I wanted was to eat a meal with the gods, despite what Andromeda had told me about the blood drinking rumors. If they were to serve me something I did not want to eat, would I even know it? A lump of nausea lodged itself in the back of my throat.

Andromeda laughed when I fell into step beside her. "You look thrilled about my invitation."

"It's not that," I tried. "I just—"

"Don't want to consume flesh and drink blood? I can assure, the meal will be quite standard. For your tastes, at least. I find the food of Halen Mon a bit unsavory myself."

Curious, I glanced at her. "Halen Mon?"

"This rock where you live. Your *world*."

Interesting. I'd never known a name for it until now.

"If you're speaking truths," I said, "then what is it that gods eat?"

"In our natural forms, nothing. But in these bodies, we require the same sustenance you do. We just...think it all tastes a bit odd for the most part. Particularly things like cheese." She wrinkled her nose. "How strange and gross you humans can be."

"Cheese," I said flatly. "Is this...some kind of joke? Did you think it would be amusing to trick me into believing you avoid flesh and also...cheese?"

She cocked her head. "You humans have such a strange sense of humor if you think that would be amusing."

"Well, *I* don't think it would be amusing, but you might, especially if you actually are the cannibalistic gods that history calls you."

"Your history has been written by the victors," she said quietly. "Besides, would we really be cannibals if we consumed your flesh? We are not you, and you are not us. Thank the stars."

"So then, what are you?" I asked.

She looked at me suspiciously. "That is a very difficult question to answer, and I'm not certain you're ready to hear the answer."

"Perhaps if you told me, I'd be more willing to go along with whatever it is you want from me. Like your trials."

Rather than answering, she took a sharp turn around the next corner and led us into the Great Hall, where the previously empty space had been transformed. Several candelabras hung from the hammerbeams on thick, rusted chains. Hundreds of flickering candles splashed light onto an oak table that had been polished to a shine. An array of food spread across the center of it: richly buttered potatoes, savory pies with browned flaky crusts, honey-glazed carrots, and a platter of meat that I didn't want to look at too closely.

Andromeda had assured me the gods didn't feast on flesh, but...I wasn't taking any chances.

But the most impressive thing about this feast wasn't

the food. It was the four gods lounging around the table, their deep crimson eyes all turned my way.

I swallowed.

"Orion, you've already met," Andromeda said, smiling at the god who sat nearest to the entrance. "Sirius, too, I hear. Everyone else, this is Tessa Baran. Tessa Baran, this is Callisto and Perseus."

Unlike Andromeda, Callisto's hair was a brilliant silver with strands that seemed to glow from within. Her skin was like ice with a blue tint to it, the color of a clear sky at the edge of the horizon. She flashed me her teeth, as elongated and sharp as the beasts she undoubtable controlled.

Perseus still wore his armor, but Sirius and Orion had discovered the fine clothing of the lords who had once controlled this pocket of land along the coast. They both wore elegant long-line doublets crafted from gold-dyed linen with full-sleeved shirts underneath—Sirius in black and Orion in blue. The sleeves were a bit too short and the doublets a bit too tight, as if they'd poured themselves into the material.

I gave the gods a tight smile and moved toward the table. Orion narrowed his gaze, shoving the nearest chair away from him as if that would stop me from getting too close. Fine with me. I hadn't planned on sitting near him. Out of all the gods, he made me the most uncomfortable, even more than Perseus with his battle attire and aura of fear.

As if to punctuate his annoyance, Orion ran his fingers through his pale hair and said, "Did you have to bring her here? This was supposed to be a nice family meal before our quest truly begins. Now we can't talk about anything important."

My ears pricked up. Quest?

"Relax," Callisto said with a tinkling laugh. "It isn't as if she can leave to tell anyone our plans."

Not yet, anyway.

"She is our enemy," Orion argued. "The one from the prophecy. Letting down our guard around her is the worst thing we could do."

Sirius eyed me from his spot at the far end of the table. He drummed his fingers against the oak, but his face betrayed none of his thoughts or emotions. "Orion is right. We should be careful what we say in front of the human."

"For now." Andromeda motioned to a chair. Frowning, I took it. I didn't particularly appreciate being spoken about as if I wasn't even inside the room, but to be honest, I'd expected much worse. Other than Orion, the gods seemed to tolerate my presence. It was a good start.

I took a seat, sandwiched between Callisto and Sirius. Andromeda moved to the other end of the table. She sat and folded her hands before her, then tapped a longer fingernail against her empty plate.

"Well," she said. "Why are we not eating?"

A look of disgust crossed Orion's face as he plucked a single carrot from a platter. Honey dripped down his fingers. "I did not miss this food."

Sirius leaned forward and scooped some meat and potatoes onto his plate. "It isn't so bad."

"You only feel that way because you're still healing from the sister's attack, and your body needs the sustenance." Perseus shifted toward me, his armor creaking. "Speaking of, is the little wolf in Dubnos?"

"You stay away from my sister," I snapped before I even knew what I was doing. Even now, I could not control my instinct to protect her.

"Relax," Andromeda said with a dark look at Perseus. "We don't want your sister. Just you."

"Because of the prophecy," I said.

"Yes, only you can destroy us."

I didn't ask the question burning on my tongue. If I could destroy her, why had she let me live? It would have been so easy for her to kill me. There must be something more she wanted from me, more that she wasn't saying. If I completed these trials, she would get it. And I had to make them wonder if I was considering joining their side.

"I'm curious," I said carefully. "From a scholarly standpoint only. Many fae have powers. Like Oberon, for example, when he was alive. What would happen if I'd tried to use his powers?"

Andromeda's laugh was low and harsh. "You want to know if you can channel another fae's power against us, since our vow cut you off from Kalen Denare. Unfortunately for you, you cannot. But even if you could, would your vow not prevent you from harming us?"

"Of course it would," I said quickly, "which is why this is nothing more than a *theoretical* conversation. I'm just wondering why I can't use another fae's power. Knowing that might actually help *you* more than anything, just in case there was someone else out there who could do what I can do."

Orion narrowed his eyes. "Fae power is useless against us. It's only potent when channeled through you."

"Me and other descendants. But not my sister," I said quickly. "She's never had that power. But there must be others out there who have an inkling of it in their blood."

The last thing I wanted was for the gods to capture someone else, believing them to be like me. This was a move in my game and nothing more. I needed to get them to trust me, to relax and lower their barriers.

"Someone else from your village?" Perseus asked. His tone suggested a frown, though he wore a helm, and I couldn't see his face.

I thought of all the innocents of Teine, who were sheltering in Endir now. Most of Kalen's warriors had left that city behind to fight in the battle at Dubnos. It was the last place I wanted to send the gods.

"No, I doubt that," I said, measuring my words. "I've always been able to feel the darkness—the, ah, *power*—of Andromeda's essence." I turned toward the God of Death with a tight smile. "When you were inside Oberon's gemstone necklace, I could feel you. And I've always felt that within myself, too, even though I didn't understand what it was at the time. No one else from my village feels like that. If there are others, they'll be scattered throughout the world."

"They'll be in Talaven," Andromeda said, nodding. "Or in one of the other human kingdoms, hidden away and never spoken about. That would be just the kind of thing Ovalis would have done in his scheming against me."

King Ovalis Hinde. Father had listed him at the top

of our family tree. His line had connected to Andromeda. He was how this entire thing had begun.

I had so many more questions, so many thoughts colliding in my mind. If I could lead Andromeda further down this path, perhaps I could get some more answers. With faux nonchalance, I took the platter of potatoes Callisto offered me and spooned a few onto my plate.

The doors swung wide. A tall, muscular fae prowled into the Great Hall. His pale blue horns glimmered beneath the candlelight as did his silver hair streaked with red.

I stiffened when his gaze swung my way. *Caedmon.*

"Ah, look who has finally arrived," Andromeda said with a delighted laugh. "Tessa, it's time for your second trial."

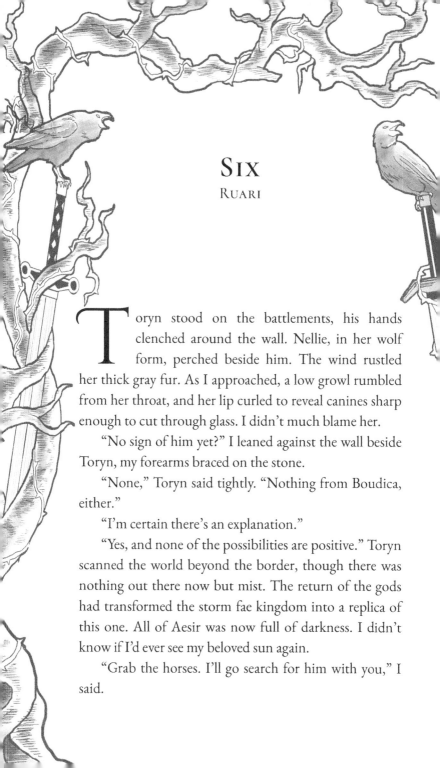

Six

Ruari

Toryn stood on the battlements, his hands clenched around the wall. Nellie, in her wolf form, perched beside him. The wind rustled her thick gray fur. As I approached, a low growl rumbled from her throat, and her lip curled to reveal canines sharp enough to cut through glass. I didn't much blame her.

"No sign of him yet?" I leaned against the wall beside Toryn, my forearms braced on the stone.

"None," Toryn said tightly. "Nothing from Boudica, either."

"I'm certain there's an explanation."

"Yes, and none of the possibilities are positive." Toryn scanned the world beyond the border, though there was nothing out there now but mist. The return of the gods had transformed the storm fae kingdom into a replica of this one. All of Aesir was now full of darkness. I didn't know if I'd ever see my beloved sun again.

"Grab the horses. I'll go search for him with you," I said.

Toryn slid his narrowed gaze my way. "*You* want to search for my king?"

My king, he'd said. I didn't miss the emphasis, and the meaning behind it. He didn't trust me. And again, I couldn't blame him, much like I couldn't blame Nellie for snarling at me. He likely assumed I'd only fought for Dubnos because of my vow to Kalen. Every time he looked at me, I saw the unspoken question in his eyes.

Why are you still here?

"I know we didn't get off to a good start—"

Toryn shoved off the wall and faced me. Deep lines bracketed his mouth. "You showed up in Albyria with a knife to Nellie's neck."

His voice shook when he spoke the girl's name. He shifted in front of her, blocking me from getting closer. Ah, that explained things, then. He had the feral protectiveness only a fae in love could have. I could only imagine how worried he must be that she was still in this strange wolfish form.

"Yes, well, I was never actually going to hurt her." I sighed when his eyes narrowed even further. "Listen, I just want to survive. And I want my family and my people to survive. So far, I've done nothing but trust the wrong people. But from where I'm standing, Kalen Denare is fighting on the right side. And I think we need him if we're going to win the inevitable battle against the gods."

"You're the one who told him Bellicent fled to Gailfean. How can we be sure you didn't send him into a trap? A trap that you want to lead us into as well?"

"That's...an excellent point, actually." I shrugged. "You can't be certain unless you send me out there alone to search for him, but I have a feeling you'll want to come along."

His entire body seemed to sigh as he closed his eyes. For a moment, he looked less like the newest leader of the storm fae and more like a man drowning beneath an avalanche of rubble. Nellie rose from her haunches and pressed her head against his leg. He dropped his hand and rested it on her fur, fingers sliding between the thick gray strands. He held on to her for a moment like that, then opened his eyes.

"All right. So be it. You and I, we'll search for Kalen together."

Nellie growled. I glanced at her, not entirely certain she wouldn't attack me.

Toryn smiled at the look on my face. "I believe she's trying to say that if you try *anything* while we're out there, she'll rip your throat out."

"I wouldn't expect anything less," I told her.

The Temple bell clanged. Toryn frowned and turned toward it. A breathless warrior rushed up the steps of the battlements. The paleness of his sweat-stained face turned my stomach.

"Your Grace," he said in a rush. "Dubnos is under attack."

"Already?" I asked sharply. We'd only just defeated the enemy army, killing dozens of the gods' monstrous creatures and many of the storm fae who had joined their side. They'd taken heavy losses. So had we, which was why we'd yet to send our army outside the safety of these walls. How had the enemy regrouped so quickly? How did they already have the numbers for another fight?

The only way they could be attacking now was if the gods themselves had come here.

Nausea churned my gut. We weren't ready to face them. Kalen Denare was not here. Neither was Tessa Baran and her glorious power. Dubnos did not stand a chance without either of them.

Toryn chewed on the scout's words for a moment, his thoughts no doubt matching mine. After a time, he asked, "How many gods have come?"

As if that would make a difference to our survival. They could mute our elite fae powers and our healing abilities. If only one arrived at our gates, we were done.

"None of the gods, Your Grace," the scout said. "It's Star Isles, based on their banners. They've brought an army of at least two hundred. Fae only. No beasts."

Toryn exhaled in relief. But it was only short-lived. The bell clanged again, and another scout rushed up the steps. Blood painted her face. "They've started up the mountain path now. I just barely got away. What do we do, Your Grace?"

A muscle worked in Toryn's jaw. "Get the civilians into the castle. All of them. Tell anyone who can wield a sword to meet us in the courtyard. We *must* find a way to save this city."

SEVEN

TESSA

My second trial had come far sooner than I'd expected. Mistakenly, I thought tomorrow would be the earliest we'd continue, if not longer. I stayed seated, my fork digging into my fisted palm. For my first trial, Andromeda had forced me to kill a human. Would she have me turn my power onto a fae now? But why Caedmon? He'd willingly served her, going as far as betraying us and leading her beasts into Dubnos.

In the end, that attack had failed, but we'd suffered for it. He'd helped weaken the gods' enemy. And to do it, Caedmon had turned his back on his people, on his family. Was death to be his reward?

Andromeda seemed to read my mind. "We have already tested your power over death. This evening's trial evaluates something my brethren might argue is far more essential. The power over life."

I looked from Andromeda to Caedmon, who smiled smugly. What was it he'd said to me in those parting moments? *I'm sure I'll see you soon enough.* He'd expected to see me in Malroch, specifically for this. In return for his allegiance, Andromeda had promised him something. The same thing she must have promised Bellicent, maybe even Oberon. Those who pledged themselves to her would gain eternal life.

And she wanted to see if I had enough strength within my blood to give that gift to Caedmon.

"I've barely used that side of the power," I said, turning back to Andromeda. "Give me a few days to practice."

"We don't have a few days to spare, I'm afraid." She snapped her fingers at Perseus. "Did you bring the stones as I commanded?"

My heart thumped painfully as I watched Perseus stand and pass a small leather pouch across the table. Andromeda eagerly took it and gazed inside at the contents. My mind continued to spin, trying to make sense of her words. If she only had a few days to spare, did that mean she planned to make a move against the mortal kingdoms soon? Val and Niamh were on those Talaven ships, heading this way. Had they been warned?

So many questions and so few answers. And I was running out of time to get them.

"Perfect." Andromeda pushed back her chair, the wooden legs shrieking against the stone. "Tessa, stand."

The defiant part of me, the part I would never truly shake, balked against her orders. This was how Oberon had always spoken to me. It was how his fae warriors had barked at the mortals of Teine every time they came down from their glittering city on the hill to force us to do their every bidding.

But I did not let my defiance control me now. I shoved away from the table and stood.

I felt the crimson eyes of the others on me, as heavy as an anvil. Callisto reclined and draped her arms across the back of the chair to watch. Orion was scowling, though that didn't surprise me. It was Sirius's glittering stare that unsettled me the most. He watched me unblinking, and a preternatural stillness transformed his body to glass. It felt as if he could see straight through me, right to where my heart beat madly beneath my bones.

Perseus removed his helm and dropped it on the table. The steel rattled like thunder. A fist of fear suddenly clutched me by the throat. I gasped, then hated myself for the reaction.

Andromeda's smile dimmed. Her focus shifted to the God of Fear. Her face paled, then a redness dusted her cheeks. Her earlier conversation with Sirius echoed in my mind. He'd become her go-between with Perseus. She was clearly surprised he'd removed his helm in her presence. What was this all about, then? Could there be a *rift* in the enemy's faction?

And if so, how could I use it to my advantage?

The God of Death averted her gaze and cleared her throat. She motioned at me. "Come, Tessa. You will need these stones to bestow the gift on Caedmon."

I walked around the table to her side, trying not to show my surprise. The gods needed gemstones to control some of their powers. I thought touch was the only limiting factor for some. But this could explain why they hadn't left for Talaven yet. Perhaps they didn't have enough gemstones for...whatever this quest was they kept talking about.

When I reached Andromeda, I held out my hand. She dropped two crimson gemstones into my palm. I'd never seen a gemstone this color before. Unless the storm fae had been hiding them from the rest of Aesir—and they might very well have been—these stones were not from this continent.

Their power pulsed against my skin, setting my teeth on edge. Shadows whorled through them. A tension pounded in my head. Whispers filled in my ears, though I couldn't understand their words.

"What is this? Where is it from?" I asked.

Andromeda smiled. "Successfully complete your trials, and I'll tell you."

I fisted my free hand, but was careful not to close my fingers around the stones. There was something *off* about this power, even if it held the gift of life. The darkness inside it, those shadows...

"Well, what are you waiting for?" Caedmon asked with an impatient huff.

I lifted my gaze and narrowed my eyes. "All right. I just needed to catch my breath. This power is...incredible."

The words were poison on my tongue. Caedmon did not deserve immortality, though perhaps I could find a wicked sense of satisfaction in knowing one day— hundreds of years from now—he would find himself unbearably lonely. Everyone he knew would be gone. His future would be forever marred by what he'd done.

"Very good," Andromeda said, pacing beside us. Something about the way she moved seemed powered by nervous energy. "Now here is what you must do. Take both stones, press them against Caedmon's skin, and force all your power into them."

"All my power?" I cocked an eyebrow. "Won't that kill him?"

"The stones will understand what you are asking of them."

As if to punctuate her statement, the stones pulsed in my still-open palm like a throbbing heartbeat. My stomach dipped. There was something very wrong here. Between the stones, Andromeda's anxious pacing, and the intensely curious eyes on every one of the gods' faces, I knew this was not just about immortality.

These stones did something else. And they weren't going to tell me what it was.

I bit the inside of my cheek. "What happens if I can't do this?"

"I wished you couldn't. Unfortunately, I know you can, so long as you're willing," Orion answered from the table. He smiled, showing his sharp teeth. "And I think Andromeda has made it clear the consequences of your inaction. Everyone in Dubnos will die. That includes your beloved Mist King."

At the sound of that name, I flinched and mashed my hand against Caedmon's bare forearm. The stones dug into my palm where they were embedded between us.

"All it takes is a little mention of Kalen Denare. You allow your soft side too much control. Such weakness," Callisto said with a laugh. "It's so mind-numbingly predictable. And it's why you human scum were always fated for failure, despite your temporary victory all those years ago. You humans won the battle, but we will win the war."

"You mistake my motivations as something soft," I said, seizing another chance to convince them they could trust me. "I do care for the people of Aesir. But the humans across the sea don't matter. Go after them for all I care."

She cocked her head. "You don't smell of lies."

"Enough," Andromeda snapped. "I am tiring of all this needless chatter. Why must everyone talk so much all the fucking time? Get on with the trial, or I will deem it a failure."

Orion chuckled. "Your time trapped in onyx has made you a bitch. Was it the celibacy? Couldn't stand not being pounded into submission by Ovalis's co—"

"Orion. I will take *your* power if you don't get out," Andromeda said with lethal calm. Then she whirled on her feet, pointed at the door, and shouted, "Get out!"

He held up his hands and laughed. "Your emotions betray you as always, dear sister. I suspected you care for this mortal scum. Seems I was right." He stood and looked at Perseus, whose lips were pressed into a tense line. "Coming with me, Pers?"

The God of Fear shook his head.

How I wished he would go. His aura of fear still dripped from every single shadow in this room.

"Fine." Orion glanced at the others, then shook his head. "Enjoy the show."

We all watched Orion take his time walking toward

the doors. My hand was still tight against Caedmon's arm. I didn't dare remove it, despite the shift in focus.

These monstrous beings were far less in tune than they'd first appeared. Perseus and Orion, they might be the answer. I didn't know how yet, but it was crack I wanted to explore. Perhaps if I beat at it hard enough, the crack would splinter, shattering everything.

Andromeda turned her attention back to me. "Do it now, Tessa. I will not wait a second longer."

Nodding, I closed my eyes and played the part of a willing participant. If anything, Orion's disrespect would act as the perfect contrast to my submission. *He'd* argued with her. I, on the other hand, was doing exactly what she wanted.

Perhaps this could take me one step closer to gaining her trust.

Releasing a breath, I focused my strange inner power on the gemstones. Until recently, my control over this power had been weak at best, but I'd learned how to search for it, to wrap my mind's hands around it, and tug it to the surface. It felt different this time, now that it was no longer linked with Kalen's magic.

Instead of his brutal, unyielding might, my power felt more like a shower of sparks lighting up every inch of my skin. It buzzed through me, burning the spot where my skin touched Caedmon's. This was life, not death, I realized. Like Andromeda had said, it somehow knew. And it was being channeled into Caedmon's body through the stones.

I couldn't help but wonder why we needed the stones

at all. Surely, all I needed was to touch his skin. That was
how it had worked with Fenella.

The gemstones suddenly vanished. Power exploded
between us. It slammed into my chest, throwing me
across the room. I fell hard, my knees and palms colliding
with the stone floor. Pain cracked through my bones, and
stars filled my vision.

I blinked away the spots. Halfway across the room,
Caedmon was in a heap on the floor like he'd been
thrown back as well. Strands of fire and shadow whipped
around him, surrounding his shuddering body like a ball
of writhing thread. The shadows screamed. Or maybe
Caedmon did. Never taking my eyes off him, I stood on
shaky legs.

"What's happening?" I asked Andromeda. Unlike
me, she'd drifted closer to the whorling mass of fire and
shadow. Her hands clasped her chest. Her lips were
mouthing words that were foreign to my ears. Callisto
had shoved back her chair. She watched Caedmon with
gleaming eyes. Perseus merely looked on impassively
while Sirius remained seated at the far end of the table,
eating another potato. He didn't seem to notice anything
was happening at all. Or if he did, he didn't care.

I remained where I was, but raised my voice. "What is
this? What did you make me do to him?"

Andromeda gave me a dismissive wave. "Return to
your quarters. Your trial is over."

My hands clenched.

Two guards appeared beside me. One took my elbow
while the other said, "You heard her. Your time here is
over."

My rage burned my chest. I didn't know what was happening, but I knew it wasn't the power of life. Andromeda had *used* me, and now she was locking me away without telling me what I'd done. I wanted to rip that fucking smile off her face.

But I didn't. Not yet. I let the guards lead me back to my gilded cage, and I started training my body for all it was worth. I started with the obvious. Kalen had taught me to fight, but my footwork needed some practice.

So I propped a pillow on top of the chest of drawers to use as a target, and I got to work.

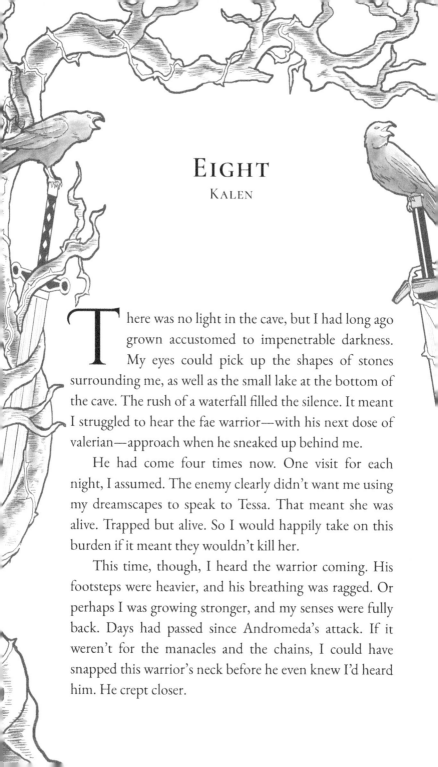

EIGHT
KALEN

There was no light in the cave, but I had long ago grown accustomed to impenetrable darkness. My eyes could pick up the shapes of stones surrounding me, as well as the small lake at the bottom of the cave. The rush of a waterfall filled the silence. It meant I struggled to hear the fae warrior—with his next dose of valerian—approach when he sneaked up behind me.

He had come four times now. One visit for each night, I assumed. The enemy clearly didn't want me using my dreamscapes to speak to Tessa. That meant she was alive. Trapped but alive. So I would happily take on this burden if it meant they wouldn't kill her.

This time, though, I heard the warrior coming. His footsteps were heavier, and his breathing was ragged. Or perhaps I was growing stronger, and my senses were fully back. Days had passed since Andromeda's attack. If it weren't for the manacles and the chains, I could have snapped this warrior's neck before he even knew I'd heard him. He crept closer.

"Hello again," I said, my voice scraping from my parched throat.

I heard the hitch in his breath and the scuff when his boots paused. "Stay quiet. I'm not to speak to you."

"Afraid I'll convince you to release me? Or are you worried I might take my mist and shove it down your throat?"

"You could try." The warrior moved in front of me. Like most of the enemy storm fae, there was an eerie glassiness to his eyes and a mark on his throat. Andromeda's poison had infected his mind, just as it has infected Oberon's—and my mother's.

My jaw clenched. I dare not think of Bellicent Denare. She had died a long time ago. The woman I'd faced here, who had trapped me and Tessa both, that wasn't my mother.

The woman Perseus had killed...it wasn't her. Not in any way that mattered.

Still, the thought of her death made my eyes burn.

I shook it off and focused on the onyx pillars scattered around me. When I'd awoken chained to a boulder, they were the first things I could see. They were blocking my power. It was the only reason this storm fae felt bold enough to face me.

"You'll regret this," I said when he stepped closer with the vial of valerian.

He gave me a skeptical look. "You're chained. I'm not."

"I don't mean me, though you'll also regret that. I mean siding with the gods. They want nothing good for you or anyone else in this world. You're being used."

"I know what you're doing. You're trying to get into my head, but—"

"And even if you don't worry about them, you should worry about someone else. Do you have any idea who you're up against? Her name is Tessa Baran, and she is the fiercest creature I've ever met."

"Tessa Baran is currently imprisoned by the gods," he said with a dry laugh. "So this 'fiercest creature' has become nothing better than a shadowfiend with all its teeth and claws cut out. Harmless."

Inwardly, I smiled. He'd walked straight into my trap.

I cocked my head. "Tessa is imprisoned? Doubtful."

He scoffed. "She is. In Malroch Castle, where the gods are preparing for their war against the human kingdoms."

Ah, there it was. The information I sorely needed. Now that I knew where they'd taken her, I would crawl from this grave and paint the castle with their blood.

The warrior must have seen the glint in my eye. He paled, then took a step away. "Fuck you. This is why they told me not to let you talk. You just tricked me into telling you where she is."

"And I thank you for the information." I curled back my lip. "Though I'm afraid it won't spare you when I break free from these chains."

He swallowed. "Threaten me all you want, but you're locked up and I'm not. Now, are you going to take this dose of valerian or are you going to make it hard? I'll happily knock you unconscious if you try anything."

"Go ahead and give it to me. Just know, I won't forget."

He lifted the vial to my lips, and I drank the poison willingly. Tonight, I would not see Tessa, but soon I would. These chains could not hold me much longer.

NINE
TESSA

The days passed slowly. I awoke every morning at dawn and donned my fighting leathers and cloak, even if I had no cause to wear them. I propped the pillow against the wall and took myself through a dance of punches and kicks until the leathers felt clammy against my sweat-soaked skin. Then I washed from the basin of water the maidservants brought every day. They caught on to my routine. For a while, I expected the gods to put a stop to it. But the days passed without a visit from any of them.

Sighing, I scratched another mark on the wall. I'd been confined to my room since my second trial, and this was the fifth morning I'd logged since then. That meant it was the eighth or ninth day I'd spent in this city.

I couldn't decide if that was a good thing. On the one hand, it had given me a chance to work on my strength and dexterity. And it meant I'd yet to begin my third trial. After the horror of the second one, I couldn't imagine what Andromeda would make me do next.

But on the other hand, I'd been cut off from learning anything about their plans or witnessing any more of the discord between them.

A pounding fist on the door knocked through my reverie. The door opened a moment later, and I expected the maidservant to bustle inside with her water basin and friendly smile. It was Sirius instead. He rushed past me, his eyes darting to every corner of the room as if he were hunting for a hidden enemy.

My heart jumped when he looked at me. He was the last god I'd expected to see. Sometimes, when I lay awake in bed, I couldn't stop myself from picturing the way he'd stared into my soul that day in Gailfean. It had felt as if he could have crushed me with his mind. All those haunted thoughts of the future of this world, I couldn't rid myself of them. If I didn't do something—and soon—it would come to pass.

He looked at my fighting leathers. "So it's true, then. You're spending all your free time training for a battle you'll never fight."

"Won't I be part of it?" I countered, keeping my voice steady and even. I couldn't let him see how much his unexpected visit had rattled me. "Isn't that why Andromeda chose these trials for me? She's making me into one of you."

He stared at me for a moment, then laughed. The sound was like knives on glass, and it echoed down the castle corridor. "Andromeda sees you as her little pet. She thinks she can strip you of your humanity, turn you into the child she never got to know. When she tires of this game, she'll discard you. She knows your heart is with the

Mist King. As long as he's alive, you'll never truly join us, no matter how much Andromeda's essence infects you."

I stiffened. "Is that some kind of threat?"

"Just an observation."

"Why are you here? To torment me?"

"Andromeda ordered me to bring you a message," he said, wincing. "Once you've bathed and dressed, you may enjoy two hours of freedom. She's been consumed by her work and didn't realize how many days had passed. You're due some fresh air."

My heartbeat quickened, though I tried to hide it. Andromeda could pretend she'd forgotten, but I didn't believe it. She knew about the marriage bond. She'd let me stew in my 'prison' until I was practically salivating for even a few minutes outside.

She was playing with me, and she'd just made her move.

"Freedom sounds wonderful," I said. "Will some guards come to escort me?"

Sirius narrowed his gaze at my cheerful reply. "No, the maidservants will leave the door unlocked after they bring you the water basin. You may go any time after you wash. You're free to wander where you will."

Anywhere but back to my mate.

He turned to go, then paused in the doorway. "You ought to know that if you try to escape right now, you will get caught."

"Why would I try to escape? This is my home now."

For a moment, a tense silence strained the air. Then he said, "Only one who has spent her entire life surrounded by fae would be so clever with her words. You say nothing that can be scented as a lie. But Andromeda is clever, too. She'll figure out your every truth."

Footsteps echoed in the corridor, and the maidservant scurried into view. Sirius tossed one last frown my way and vanished into the shadows.

After the maidservant left, I undressed and washed myself, mulling over Sirius's words. He seemed different now, so unlike the god I'd met in Gailfean. That day, he'd seemed larger than life. Now he seemed more human—or more fae. More *real*, rather than some otherworldly creature sent from the stars.

Was this their weakness? The longer they spent in this world—in Halen Mon—they grew more and more like *us*? Whatever the source of their power was, could it be dimmed?

If they remained here for a hundred years, what would happen to them?

Regardless of the answer, it scarcely mattered. Unless I found another weakness, none of us would be alive in a hundred years to fight them. This world would fully be theirs by then.

Sighing, I patted my skin dry and pulled on my leathers and my cloak. Then I padded over to the window, eager to chart my path to the docks. Unlike the last time I went outside, I wanted to spend my hours of freedom exploring the city. I wanted to see how many ships they had ready to sail across the Bantam Sea—and when they planned to leave.

Soldiers marched through the cobblestone streets between rows of white-washed buildings. The roar of their footsteps drowned out the caws of the seagulls overhead. I'd been watching them for days, and their numbers had multiplied. Andromeda must be calling upon every corner of the storm fae lands. She would find few soldiers from the Kingdoms of Shadow and Light. I could only hope she hadn't tried. Dubnos would need a brief respite from war.

As I turned away, something from beyond the city caught my attention. Heavy mist thickened the sky beyond the gates, but the sun over Malroch cut through the darkness enough to reveal the nearest field. It held at least a hundred beasts.

They stalked toward a wooden cage. My stomach twisted as I realized what was trapped inside it. A man curled against the bars. Fae or human, I couldn't tell. It didn't matter either way. Regardless of who he was, he didn't deserve to be fed to a flock of monstrous beasts.

My back twitched at the instinctual need to spread my wings and fly to this man, to take that cage and carry him far away from here. If I didn't do something, the beasts would destroy the cage and eat him alive.

I moved to jump out the window, but then a thought shuddered through my mind.

What were the fucking odds? After days, Andromeda had released me from my makeshift prison. Sirius had taunted me. He knew I'd see this. Light be damned, Andromeda had probably set this up to test my resolve.

I ground my teeth. I couldn't turn my back on this man. If there was a way to save him, I had to try.

But there isn't a way, my thoughts echoed back at me. *As soon as Andromeda sees you flying toward him, she and the other gods—because they are watching—will stop you.*

My hands shook as I latched my fingers around the window. I couldn't save him. There was nothing I could do, not unless I had *something* against the gods—anything. But I had nothing. No weapons, no information. Nothing but my power, which wouldn't work against them. My marriage bond nullified part of the vow, but not all of it, as far as I understood.

Andromeda had given me an impossible choice, knowing it would destroy me. I could fly to this man's aid and doom any chance I had of escaping, reuniting with Kalen, and helping the world fight against the gods. Or I could let him die.

It was him or everyone else. *Again.*

Another flash of movement caught my attention. I turned toward the gates. A gray horse charged toward the city, his mane blowing in the wind.

My chest tightened. Hope and fear tangled together in my gut.

Silver had found me.

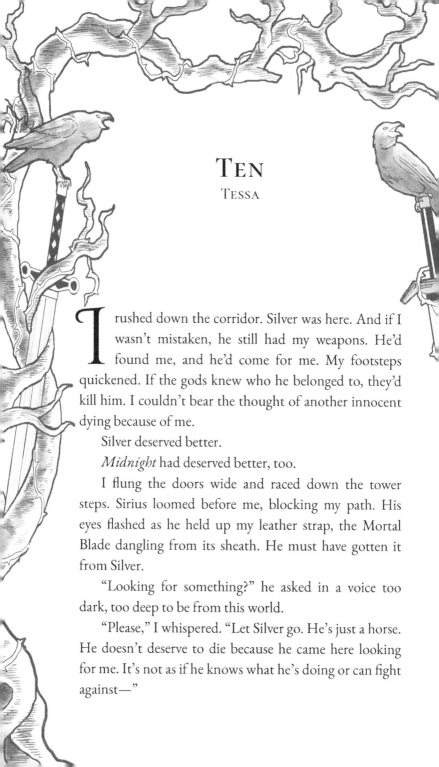

TEN
TESSA

I rushed down the corridor. Silver was here. And if I wasn't mistaken, he still had my weapons. He'd found me, and he'd come for me. My footsteps quickened. If the gods knew who he belonged to, they'd kill him. I couldn't bear the thought of another innocent dying because of me.

Silver deserved better.

Midnight had deserved better, too.

I flung the doors wide and raced down the tower steps. Sirius loomed before me, blocking my path. His eyes flashed as he held up my leather strap, the Mortal Blade dangling from its sheath. He must have gotten it from Silver.

"Looking for something?" he asked in a voice too dark, too deep to be from this world.

"Please," I whispered. "Let Silver go. He's just a horse. He doesn't deserve to die because he came here looking for me. It's not as if he knows what he's doing or can fight against—"

"Just a horse?" he asked with an arched brow.

"Y-yes," I stammered. "He was one of Oberon's horses, but now he belongs to no one. Just release him back into the fields. He'll find his way to shelter." Though, deep down, I wondered if that was really true. He'd come looking for me. If Sirius let him go, would Silver actually leave?

Sirius unsheathed the Mortal Blade and shoved the belt into my hands. He slid the dagger into his own belt, then folded his arms. "The one you call Silver is no mere horse. He's a joint eater, which means he *can* fight and he knows what he's doing. However, he cannot leave the mists without getting burned, so he can't come into the city. He is no threat to us. For now. I took your weapons and left him at the gates. He seems pretty agitated, I must admit. Strange that you have a joint eater who cares for you."

"A joint eater." That was impossible. When I'd first found him, he been with Oberon, which meant he would have had to belong to the Kingdom of Light, except...that wasn't necessarily true, was it? Oberon had been stuck in a cave for days before I'd found him—or rather, *he'd found me*. When he'd fled Albyria, he'd taken nothing with him. So where *had* Silver come from?

My lips parted.

He must have found him in the mists.

It explained so much. Silver had practically shoved me toward Albyria that day, when I'd been lost in my dark thoughts on the beach. If he hadn't interfered, I might have run from Aesir. If he hadn't encouraged me, I might have never again seen Kalen. Silver had even accompanied me on the long trek across Aesir, insisting to continue with me on the journey, even when the other horses had needed rest.

Midnight had been the same. I should have seen it.

"What's this?" Perseus strode toward us from the shadows, his steel armor clinking with every step. An intense fear swept through me, prickling my skin. He tucked his helm under one arm, nostrils flared as if he were scenting the air. His dark hair curled like strands of ink around his sharply pointed ears as a breeze suddenly swept across the courtyard. The cold bite of it scraped my skin.

"Perseus," Sirius said dryly. "I can't say I'm surprised to find you lurking around."

"Andromeda ordered me to keep an eye on that one." He inclined his head toward me. "Imagine my surprise when I spot her chatting with *you.*"

"Yes, me. What of it?"

"You're not to interfere."

"Interfere with the third trial, you mean," I said.

Perseus turned toward me, his dour expression shifting to something more akin to surprise. It had been a guess, but I could see I was right. This wasn't a sneaky test to determine my willingness to remain in Malroch. It was —like the two previous trials—designed to erode any lingering goodness inside me. Letting the caged man die meant destroying another piece of my soul.

She *was* trying to turn me into one of them.

"Does that mean you've made your choice?" Perseus asked. "Are you going to save the man in the cage, or are you going to let him die?"

"How is it a choice when I can't leave the city walls?"

"There are those who would attempt to save him, no matter how doomed their quest. I thought you would be one of them." His armor creaked as he lowered his helm over his face. "Come along, then. I'll take you to Andromeda."

"Wait," I quickly said. Perseus paused, but my words were meant for Sirius. "What did *you* think I would do?"

The God of Pestilence cocked his head. Clearly, he hadn't expected me to ask his opinion. "You are the Daughter of Death, but I must admit, I expected you to attempt to save him. Turns out you're more like Andromeda than I thought."

"Then you're mistaken," I said.

As I fell into step beside Perseus, the strange god in his creaking armor motioned at the looming stone building before us and said, "If you want to save him, you're heading in the wrong direction."

"Just take me to Andromeda."

His helm shifted, and I could have sworn it looked like he nodded. It was an eerily deferential act coming from an immortal being who could crush me beneath the weight of my worst fears. As we walked up the steps, I noticed that uneasy feeling I had around him, that cold, dark hiss against my skin, was gone. I took in his armor, his helm. Was that why he kept himself fully covered most of the time?

"You have a plan," he said, his voice slightly muffled by the helm.

I didn't deign to respond. Instead, I kept my ears as attuned to the sounds of the city as I could. So far, I had yet to hear the gurgling screams of a man being torn apart, piece by piece, and so I could only assume—and hope—that Andromeda was waiting to see what I would say when we reached her.

Thankfully, it didn't take long to find out. Perseus bypassed the Great Hall and led me to a study where Andromeda was flipping through several sheets of parchment that looked like maps. I couldn't see the details of them in the dim lighting. Located beside the interior stairwell, the room had no windows, only a few flickering candles. I couldn't help but think it would have worked well as a bedroom in Teine, if it weren't for the portraits of the gods hanging along the wall behind the desk.

But there was something about the frantic brush strokes that transformed the gods' faces into only a passing resemblance of what they were. It was as if the painter had been in a hurry. Somehow, the result made them look less like otherworldly creatures and more like regular fae one might encounter wandering the streets of Dubnos.

The most unnerving thing about the portraits was Andromeda's beaming smile. She actually looked happy.

"Well done, Tessa. You've passed your third trial," she said, almost dismissively. "You may visit the docks and enjoy the market. Will three hours be enough?"

"I want to discuss the man's life."

Her head jerked up. The hand clutching the maps dropped to the table. Now I could see a few details. On the top sheet of parchment, a handful of islands were clustered at the western edge of Aesir. *Star Isles*. What did she want with them?

"You want to *discuss* his life?" She wrinkled her nose in disdain. "You realize if you try to save him, you fail my trial."

"It just seems like such a waste."

"Not a waste. His blood and flesh will fuel Callisto's beasts. Do you dare deny them of that?"

Interesting.

"No, let them feast." I ignored the pounding in my head at my words, the wave of nausea that swept through me. What I was about to propose filled me with a horrifying revulsion I knew I'd not soon forget, but the alternative was...well, there wasn't one, as far as I could tell. "After they have their fill, I'll bring him back to life. I can tell him I did it against your will. He'd be forever indebted to me, which means he'll do anything I ask of him."

Perseus shifted beside me, rattling. With his face covered, it was impossible to read what his reaction meant.

Andromeda scoffed. "This trial was meant to determine how attached you are to the existence of these monstrous mortals, to see if your time spent here has helped loosen your misguided empathy for them. By bargaining for his life, you have failed."

"What's more important?" I countered. "These 'trials' you've designed for me or your quest for the mortal kingdoms? I thought it was the latter, but you've continued to focus on Aesir. Why?"

She motioned at the door. "Perseus, return her to her quarters and give the order to Callisto. Her beasts may feed."

Perseus's armored hand latched onto my arm, and he dragged me toward the study's open door.

"Wait," I called out, trying to think. "You're searching for something in Aesir, something you need before you launch your ships. That's why you're looking at maps, right? If you let me bring the man back to life, he'll spy for us. He can find whatever it is you're looking for."

Andromeda had returned her attention to the maps. She didn't acknowledge my words as Perseus dragged me out of her study. His steel-covered fingers dug into me. They were cold, harsh, and unyielding against my skin. I tried to pull out of his grip, but it was as unbreakable as manacles.

"Fuck," I muttered to myself, not bothering to hide my frustration.

"You would not have saved him either way," Perseus said. "Whatever choice you made, it would have been the wrong one. So do not blame yourself."

Torches passed by as we moved down the corridor. Their flickering flames cast an orange hue across the carpet, reminding me of Oberon, Albyria, and everything I'd been through this past year. And how I'd finally tried a different approach, but it wasn't working.

So I dropped the mask. "Why are you trying to make me feel better? You should be glad I failed."

"Glad," he said, as if testing out a word he'd never spoken before. "I am not certain that is how I would describe the emotion you assume I'm experiencing at this moment."

I peered up at him, frowning. "So then, how do you feel?"

"I do not feel emotion as you do. I simply am Perseus, the embodiment of fear and—"

"Perseus." Callisto stepped from the shadows.

Just like the God of Fear, she'd dressed for battle. Rather than the scraps of metal Perseus had collected, her clothes looked as if they'd been molded to her frame. The fighting leathers were dyed a deep crimson, and her elbows and shoulders were fortified by steel.

Perseus removed his helm. I winced as his powerful fear poured over me, drowning me, choking the air from my lungs. I had the sudden urge to run, but I knew I wouldn't get very far as long as he had a tight hold on me.

"Why aren't you out with your beasts?" Perseus asked as he shook out his hair, like he was trying to toss off the constraints of his helm. He seemed to mostly wear it in Andromeda's presence. Again, I couldn't help but wonder at the relationships between these five gods.

"I was, then I got bored with all the waiting." She turned her attention to me and smiled, though there was nothing soft in her expression. It was the kind of smile Oberon had always worn before he spoke his cruelties. "You've given up on your heroics, then? Can't say I'm surprised. You mortals are so easy to break."

"She didn't break," Perseus said. "Just like I said she wouldn't. Sirius, too."

Callisto frowned. "The wall's out there, and she's in here. I've been watching. She didn't even attempt a rescue."

"She thought she'd be clever and bargain with Andromeda. It didn't work."

Callisto looked far angrier about this than I would

have expected. Lines bracketing her mouth, she huffed out a breath, whirled on her feet, and vanished down the corridor without another word. As soon as she was out of sight, Perseus started dragging me toward my quarters again, his steel boots as loud as drums.

"She thinks you're a distraction, and that Andromeda should focus on our quest instead of you," Perseus, surprisingly, explained. "She's probably right. When one has a singular obsession, one will miss things that are happening right in front of them. Important things. Things that could change the course of everything."

"What are you talking about?" I shook my head, my frustration reaching a fever pitch. Very little about today made sense. Callisto was acting oddly. Perseus was acting oddly. Even Sirius was acting oddly. I bet if I encountered Orion, he'd be acting oddly, too. The only one behaving more or less like herself was Andromeda.

We reached the door to my quarters. There were no guards around, but Perseus would call for them after he'd locked me inside. He paused before opening the door, examining me with eyes so distant they might as well have been lost amongst the stars.

"I'm afraid there is little more I can explain in my current form," he finally said. I swore he almost sounded sad. "Just know, I am not *glad* about any of it. Our quest, I mean. It's difficult for me to explain when my words are...well, you will understand one day."

"*What* quest?"

My heart pounded as I waited for his answer. I knew this could be another trick. Another trap, another trial. Andromeda could be testing how I would react to a hint of...well, the only thing I could call it was *rebellion*. Perseus spoke as though he didn't want to be a part of Andromeda's quest to destroy humanity. But that couldn't be true, right? She just wanted to see if I would believe him, if I would offer to help him rebel.

But there was something in his eyes—a conviction I couldn't ignore. My gut told me it wasn't a test.

When I spoke, I could barely scrape out a whisper. "What are you trying to tell me? Speak it plainly, please."

"I cannot. My orders prevent me. But *he* can."

The God of Fear opened the door and pushed me forward. Inside, Sirius was waiting for me with the Mortal Blade clutched in his hand.

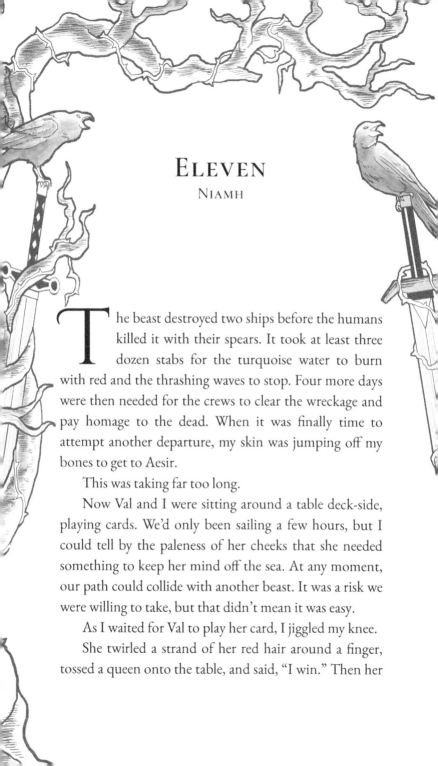

ELEVEN
NIAMH

The beast destroyed two ships before the humans killed it with their spears. It took at least three dozen stabs for the turquoise water to burn with red and the thrashing waves to stop. Four more days were then needed for the crews to clear the wreckage and pay homage to the dead. When it was finally time to attempt another departure, my skin was jumping off my bones to get to Aesir.

This was taking far too long.

Now Val and I were sitting around a table deck-side, playing cards. We'd only been sailing a few hours, but I could tell by the paleness of her cheeks that she needed something to keep her mind off the sea. At any moment, our path could collide with another beast. It was a risk we were willing to take, but that didn't mean it was easy.

As I waited for Val to play her card, I jiggled my knee.

She twirled a strand of her red hair around a finger, tossed a queen onto the table, and said, "I win." Then her gaze landed on my shaking thigh. "I'm not sure who needs the distraction more. You or me."

"You know, a king trumps a queen."

"You have a king?"

"No." I smiled, tossing down my cards. "Well played, Val. Go again?"

"Sure." She gathered the cards and started to shuffle them. "But only if you tell me why you're so on edge. Is it because of the...what *was* it, anyway? Octopi aren't anywhere near that big."

"Some monstrous creation of the gods, no doubt."

Val paused in her shuffling. The sea breeze rustled the loose hair around her shoulders, and the sun above brought out the pink flush of her cheeks. She'd never looked more beautiful, which was quite the accomplishment. Val looked beautiful all the time.

"And they're the reason you're so on edge?" Val asked.

"No, not particularly," I admitted. "I'm frustrated that it's taking so long to get back to Kal. I've spent almost every day of the last four hundred years by his side. Now he's up against the gods and their army of beasts. It's the biggest fight he's ever faced. I should be there."

"I know how you feel. Tessa and I have a thing we've said to each other for as long as I can remember. 'If you fall, I fall.' We stand by each other, no matter what. But I'm not standing beside her right now. I'm across an entire fucking sea."

I nodded. "You're loyal to her. It's a commendable trait, especially when you aren't bound to her by oath or blood. You chose her, and she chose you."

"And what about you and Kalen? I suppose he's your

king, so you didn't have much choice but to serve him."
Val dealt the cards, though she kept her eyes on me.

"No, I did choose Kal," I said, half-smiling at the
memory. "He gave me the option to leave after his mother
went missing. I was her Queen's Shadow, and he didn't
expect me to serve him when he took her place on the
throne. But I saw something in him, something different
from his mother. Where she was cunning and sharp, he
was—*is*—well...I can hardly call him soft. There's blood
on his hands, too, but he's—"

"Honorable?" asked Val.

"He tries. And in a world like this, trying matters."

"So you stayed."

"And so I stayed. Now that he's met Tessa, hopefully
I won't have to worry about becoming the next ruler of
the Kingdom of Shadow."

Val sat back in her chair and focused her attention on
her spread of cards, but then said, "I didn't know he'd
named you his heir."

"It's nothing to boast about. He only named me
because there were no better options."

Val smiled. "Something tells me that's not true."

"I'm a fighter, Val. A warrior with an ugly scar on her
face."

"There is nothing ugly about your scar." She put her
cards down, braced her forearms on the table, and leaned
forward with fire dancing in her eyes. "And you'd make a
damn good queen."

I sat back, caught off guard by the intensity in her
voice. She'd never been so blunt with me. I kind of liked
it. And so, of course, Alastair chose that moment to

return from his tour around the ship. We needed to have a good chat about the timing of his interruptions.

He nodded to the both of us. "Duncan wants to have a chat. He's waiting for us in his cabin."

"*Duncan?*" I asked with a laugh. "Since when are you on a first-name basis with the sandalled-footed, prophecy-whispering King of Talaven?"

"Well, he's not my king, is he? I'll call him whatever I damn well want." He shrugged. "You coming? He sounded kind of frantic."

"Wonderful, a frantic king. Just what we need." Sighing, I stood, leaving the cards forgotten on the table. Val joined us, and we headed down into the bowels of the ship, where the king's cabin was located at the end of a cramped corridor. Cramped for Alastair, anyway. His shoulders brushed the walls as we walked.

I raised my hand to knock, but the door swung wide before my knuckles made contact. The king motioned us inside in a distinctly frantic manner. His emerald robe was wrinkled, and his eyes were spiderwebbed with red. It looked like he hadn't slept in weeks, though I could have sworn he'd been fine only a few hours before.

"None of this should be happening," he said seconds after he'd slammed the door behind us. He paced across the wood panelled floor, from one end of his luxurious cabin to the next, passing a sleek oak desk, a table holding glass jars of various spirits, and a four-poster bed draped in silks. It was a far cry from my cabin two doors down, with its cots, scratchy wool sheets, and steel floors.

The king stopped beside the spirits, poured himself a

shot, and tossed it back. Smacking his lips together, he slammed down the glass.

"What *is* supposed to happen, then?" I asked carefully. Duncan Hinde needed to be treated with the utmost caution. He looked seconds away from losing his grip. If he'd ever had it.

"We were to leave on time without any casualties." His white-knuckled fists trembled by his sides. "No creatures were to be in the waters. Something's gone wrong. None of this is as it should be."

I exchanged an uneasy glance with Alastair. Ever my blunt companion, he twisted his earring and said, "Looks like you were wrong."

When the king looked at Alastair, his expression sent a shudder down my spine. He'd been nothing but strange since we'd first arrived in Talaven, but he'd carried a certain harmlessness about him, like he was nothing more than words and thoughts and visions. All his power came from that comet and the prophecies left behind by his ancestors. There was no violence in him, no fight.

But now he looked fucking mad.

"I did not see you three coming, either." He pointed at the collection of papers on his desk. There were several on top in perfect condition. The ink was bright and shining, as if it had been added to the page only recently. But there were others here with flaking edges and words so pale I couldn't read them from where I stood. These were his visions and the visions of those who had lived centuries before.

"You're trying to blame this madness on us?" Alastair chuckled, though there was a darkness in the sound.

These humans were our allies for now, but my old friend would never back down from a confrontation. In fact, he was probably itching for it. I was, too. But I wouldn't do anything that might put Val in danger. If we pushed too hard, the king might retaliate.

King Duncan Hinde sighed and closed his eyes. "I forgot how quick to anger you fae can be. Insulting you was not my intention."

"Then what was your intention?" I asked.

"I am merely pointing out," King Duncan Hinde said, "that things started shifting from their predetermined path after you three unexpectedly arrived in my kingdom. I can't help but wonder if you've set off a chain of events that cannot be undone. One that will lead to the very end of us."

"The end of us?" Val asked, alarmed. "But Tessa got her wings. They're tipped in sapphire, like you said they needed to be. Isn't that the most important thing?"

"Yes, yes." He fisted his hands against the table and stared down at the pile of visions.

I stepped toward his desk and reached for the top sheet. "What does it say happens next?"

He snatched the parchment away from me and clutched it to his chest. I narrowed my eyes.

"No." The king shook his head. "No, no, no. You cannot read these. Only I can. I just...I have one question for you." He blew out a breath. "Have any of you ever wielded an axe?"

Beside me, Val went still. I wanted to press my hand to her back, to hold her steady, to let her know I was here. But I fought the urge. Val had told me about the axe.

OF DUST AND STARS   87

She'd never wielded one herself, but her parents had tried to during a brief rebellion against Oberon. His soldiers had slaughtered them both in retaliation. It was not my place to speak about any of that to this secretive king.

"An axe?" Alastair cocked his head. "No, can't say I have. Got one I can use against the gods?"

"Hmm." The king's eyes slid my way.

"I tend to stick to arrows," I said.

"I haven't swung one, either," Val said. "Why are you asking us this?"

The king audibly sighed. Was that relief? "No matter. This must be nothing more than a small ripple. That can happen, especially if the visions weren't written down quickly enough. The details can begin to fade once you walk away from the comet. There's nothing more to it than that. Everything will proceed according to plan."

The king dismissed us.

When we returned to the deck and picked up our cards, Val leaned across the table and whispered, "Should I have told him about my parents' axe?"

I tapped my finger against the back of my cards. "He didn't ask if we *knew someone* who had wielded an axe. 'Cause I knew quite a few axe-wielders during our war with Oberon. He asked if *we* did. And you didn't."

"I don't think my mother and father got the chance to swing it, anyway." She sat back in her chair. "But why would Duncan Hinde be asking about an axe?"

I smiled. "We'll have to break into his cabin and find out."

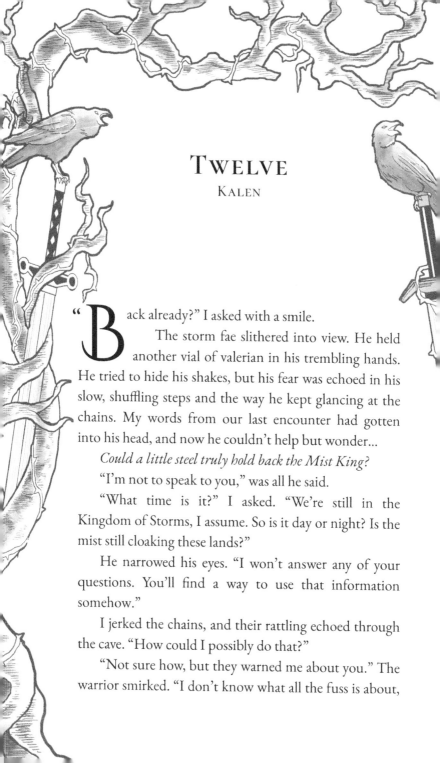

TWELVE
KALEN

"Back already?" I asked with a smile.

The storm fae slithered into view. He held another vial of valerian in his trembling hands. He tried to hide his shakes, but his fear was echoed in his slow, shuffling steps and the way he kept glancing at the chains. My words from our last encounter had gotten into his head, and now he couldn't help but wonder...

Could a little steel truly hold back the Mist King?

"I'm not to speak to you," was all he said.

"What time is it?" I asked. "We're still in the Kingdom of Storms, I assume. So is it day or night? Is the mist still cloaking these lands?"

He narrowed his eyes. "I won't answer any of your questions. You'll find a way to use that information somehow."

I jerked the chains, and their rattling echoed through the cave. "How could I possibly do that?"

"Not sure how, but they warned me about you." The warrior smirked. "I don't know what all the fuss is about, really. Look at the monstrous Mist King. You can't even stand on your own fucking feet."

With my eyes locked on the warrior's face, I wrapped my hands around the chains and wrenched them free from the manacles attached to the rocky ground. I stood, lungs heaving from the exertion. The onyx pillars blocked my elite shadow fae power, but they did not fully dampen my strength. It had taken every ounce of my concentration to pull it from the depths of me, to call upon the ferocity I'd always feared.

But no more. I would gladly let it loose upon my enemies. I was not the monster here.

I stepped out of the circle of onyx. My full power flooded back to me.

The storm fae gasped and stumbled back. He turned to run, but I grabbed his shoulder and hauled him back to me. He shook as I gripped his belt and snapped it in half, reaching for the key ring. With one hand still on his shoulder, I shoved the keys into his hands.

"Unlock the manacles."

He shook his head, his bottom lip trembling. "I can't. They'll kill me."

"Look into my eyes," I said evenly.

He blinked, but he did not turn away from my steady gaze. The fear in his expression deepened. I knew what he saw. I'd just spent the past few days trapped in a cave with no wife, no bedroll, and no food but the scraps he'd brought me just to keep me alive. My power burned within me now, and the sapphire of my eyes glowed brightly. The deep blue color spilled across the warrior's face, illuminating his terror.

"Yes, they might kill you," I finally said. "But if you don't unlock the manacles, so will I."

He swallowed. "Fuck."

"Every second that ticks by is another second you're keeping me from my wife."

"You can't go near her." He tried to jerk away from me, but my grip on his shoulder was too strong. "She vowed to stay away from you. Threaten me all you want, but that won't change anything. Only Andromeda can release her from the vow, and she would never do it."

"I don't think you understand. Nothing can stop me from getting to my wife. Now unlock the fucking chains."

"Even if you manage it, Tessa Baran won't be the same woman you knew before. The gods made her go through trials that stripped her of her humanity. She's like them now. Not like you. Bet she'll try to kill you if—"

"You've made your choice." My body powered by the enhanced strength running through my veins, I swung my chains around the warrior's neck and squeezed. He choked, dragging his nails across my arms. His legs flailed, his chest heaved. I grit my teeth and held on until the breath fled from his lungs. His convulsions stopped. I released him and let his body hit the stone.

My lifelong guilt and shame threatened to overcome me again. I hated killing. I hated death and blood and hate. But these people had stolen my mate from me. They threatened to doom this world. Fuck shame and fuck guilt. If there was ever a time to embrace who I was—who I always had been—it was now.

I was the Mist King.

I knelt, took the keys from the dead warrior, and unlocked the manacles. The steel hit the ground, ringing loudly in the silent cave. Trying to ignore what he'd said about Tessa's lost humanity, I rubbed my palms against my wrists and winced at the raw skin. No matter. It would heal soon enough.

I left the body where it was and took a tunnel leading toward a distant, hazy light. It took longer to reach the surface than I'd expected. An hour passed, maybe more. The incline steepened. Piles of jagged rock narrowed the path. I had to scale a rocky wall the last few meters before I finally broke through a hole in the ground.

Sweat dripped down my forehead as I blinked against the light. It took a moment for my vision to adjust. When it did, I spotted at least a dozen beasts circling me. Mist cloaked their bodies, even though the sun was shining nearby. Boudica rushed toward me and shrieked out a warning.

Before I could make sense of it, the beasts charged.

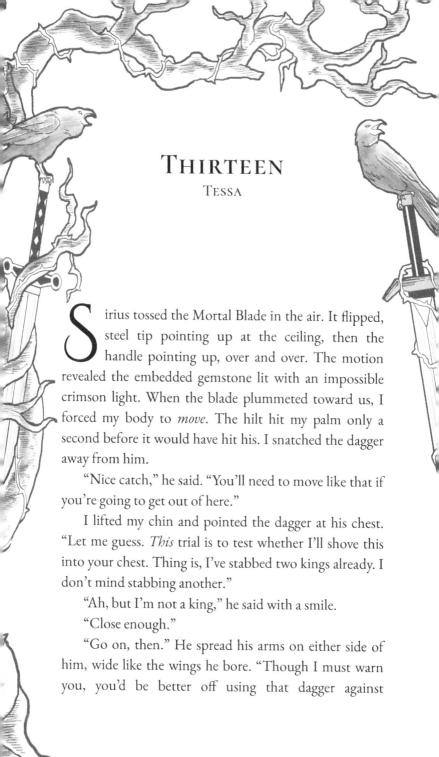

THIRTEEN

TESSA

Sirius tossed the Mortal Blade in the air. It flipped, steel tip pointing up at the ceiling, then the handle pointing up, over and over. The motion revealed the embedded gemstone lit with an impossible crimson light. When the blade plummeted toward us, I forced my body to *move*. The hilt hit my palm only a second before it would have hit his. I snatched the dagger away from him.

"Nice catch," he said. "You'll need to move like that if you're going to get out of here."

I lifted my chin and pointed the dagger at his chest. "Let me guess. *This* trial is to test whether I'll shove this into your chest. Thing is, I've stabbed two kings already. I don't mind stabbing another."

"Ah, but I'm not a king," he said with a smile.

"Close enough."

"Go on, then." He spread his arms on either side of him, wide like the wings he bore. "Though I must warn you, you'd be better off using that dagger against someone else. As soon as you leave this room, whether by door or by window, you'll be spotted. One of the other Lamiae will come after you. You'll need a powerful weapon if you hope to best them."

Lamiae? Was that what they called themselves when they weren't parading around as gods?

I narrowed my eyes, trying to guess his angle here. "Andromeda really wants to find out if I'll go for that fucking wall, doesn't she? If she's so afraid of what will happen if I do, why doesn't she just lock me up?" I flicked my eyes toward the manacles hanging by the bed. "She has the gear for it."

"This has nothing to do with Andromeda. I want to help you escape."

Hissing, I pressed the tip of the dagger against his tightly fitting doublet. What would happen if this blade pierced his skin? It was a weapon designed to kill fae, so long as it had the correct gemstone powering the hilt. Could it harm a god? And if it could, for how long? Would it be permanent?

"Why should I believe you?" I finally asked.

He took the dagger between his thumb and forefinger. He shifted the tip to the edge of his throat, though he held it just far enough away to keep it from making contact with his skin. "Because I let you overhear me tell Andromeda about your bond with Kalen Denare. I thought you might be more cautious if you knew she'd found out. I also let your 'horse' go free. I have brought you the Mortal Blade. And I am letting you decide if you want to stab me with it. If that isn't enough for you to believe me, then nothing will be."

I shuddered, my hand shaking where I held the dagger. It would be so easy to lean forward and let the blade slice into his throat. He was one of the gods. He threatened the future of this world. He and the others wanted nothing but destruction. And yet, I spoke around the pit of anger in my throat and said, "Why?"

A fist pounded on the door. Perseus. "Hurry."

"All you need to know," Sirius said quietly, "is that we are only monstrous because of how we were made. Your sister nearly killed me. As I healed myself from her attack, I found a part of myself I'd thought was lost." He lifted his chin. "And now I'd rather see the world healed than doom it all to plague."

"And Perseus?" I asked, nodding toward the door.

"He has his own reasons."

I stared at him for a long moment, shocked by his words. "If you expect me to believe all this, then explain to me why you haven't tried to stop Andromeda. You're still following her orders. Her aim is *certainly* not to heal."

"Ah, but it *is* her aim. She's just doing it in her own way," he said sadly. "Either way, I cannot lift my hand against her. I made a vow, much like you did, a very long time ago. I must follow her every command, and she has commanded me to never harm her."

"I thought vows didn't work on gods—or Lamiae. That's what you called yourself earlier, right?"

"I was not always a Lamiae."

I stumbled back, dropping the blade to my side. "But if you weren't always a god, then—"

A loud bang interrupted.

"Sirius!" Perseus shouted through the door. "It is time!"

My heart dropped into my stomach. Sirius shifted sideways, motioning toward the window. His body seemed to vibrate—with fear or excitement, I couldn't tell. But I knew if Andromeda walked through that door, and if he was here and I was gone...she'd suspect he'd helped me.

I took two steps toward the window. "What will she do to you?"

"Nothing I can't handle, though I might not be the same if we ever meet again. She doesn't have me on a tight leash right now. She will after this," he said with a smile that did not reach his eyes. "I'll hold her off as long as I can. Leave the city—you *can* leave, just as I'm sure you suspected. Find your mate. Oh, and keep these gemstones safe. They're what she's been looking for."

His eyes flicked to the Mortal Blade, then passed me another stone that matched the first. They both looked like the ones I'd used on Caedmon, brimming with an energy that made my bones ache.

More questions filled my mind, but there was no time to ask them. I took a steadying breath, spread my wings, and leapt out the open window. Wind blasted my face as I soared down the side of the tower, then pushed off the stone to spin over the bleached roofs toward the city wall in the distance.

Several cries of alarms followed close behind. Guards in the castle courtyard had spotted my escape. They'd head straight to the gods to warn them. I cast a quick glance over my shoulder at the rapidly vanishing castle. Sirius stood in the window, watching me with a smile.

I shook my head and turned my attention back to my escape. Nothing he'd said made sense, and yet I could not shake the feeling that none of it was a lie, a trick, or a game. And even if it was, the time for waiting was gone. I had to leave this place while I had the chance.

Soaring toward the gates, I spotted the field of shadowfiends pacing in the whisper-thin mists. Would they attempt to give chase once I flew past them? I pushed higher into the sky. I'd have to avoid catching their attention, lest risk leading them to Dubnos.

A body slammed into me.

My breath exploded from my lungs as my wings twisted beneath me. I fell, the wind snatching at my hair and face. The world was a tunnel of feathers and fear. A flash of crimson shot by my head. One of the gods had reached me.

Gritting my teeth, I tried to angle myself to the left and spread my wings. Callisto hurtled into me once more. I spotted her cruel face and twisted expression only a second before she hit me. Pain lanced through my stomach. I curled in on myself, trying to find my breath.

The ground rose to meet me. My body hit the street hard.

Dirt misted around me as I coughed around the pain, wearily blinking the stars from my eyes. Everything hurt. My bones felt as if they'd been ground into dust, and my ears rang from the impact. But...but I was alive. I shouldn't have survived that.

Callisto landed lightly before me and raised her hands

by her sides. Her crimson eyes flashed with rage as she stalked toward me. "You finally tried to flee."

I coughed and pushed up from the ground. The ringing still filled my head, but I wouldn't let her see weakness. I pulled the blade from my leather strap and bent my knees into a defensive stance Kalen had taught me. I'd been practicing in my quarters for days.

She looked at the blade, then scoffed. "You think you can wield a dagger against me? I am a god."

"So am I." I smiled around my fear.

Shaking her head with a laugh, she started moving closer. "The little scrap of power you inherited from Andromeda is nothing. It is so watered down by centuries of mortals that it's laughable she wanted you to join us. She should have killed you the moment she set eyes on you. All it would take is a flick of my wrist to crush you into dust."

"It sounds like you're stalling," I said. "Afraid to test your theory?"

Callisto laughed, but didn't move toward me. "I almost feel sorry for you. Andromeda would have gifted you with immortality if you'd only followed her commands. But you are a mortal, a *human*. I shouldn't be surprised you'd choose destruction and betrayal over eternal life with us."

I'd only meant it as a jab before, but I was beginning to think I'd been right. Callisto kept talking instead of fighting. She *was* stalling.

I moved toward her with my dagger raised. Her eyes darted to the weapon before she whistled. From the shadows of a nearby abandoned building, two shadowfiends crept into the street. My heart sprang into action, and inwardly I recoiled. I'd faced these beasts half a dozen times now, but it never got any easier, especially now that I remembered everything that had happened to me when I was young.

That and the fact I desperately needed a sword.

Callisto had one strapped to her back, but she'd yet to arm herself with it. It seemed she wanted her beasts to do her dirty work for her.

"Don't want to fight me yourself?" I asked, edging even closer. The beasts were behind her, moving slowly. I still had time to reach her before they rushed me. I needed to get my hands on that sword.

As if reading my thoughts, Callisto reached behind her and drew her weapon from its scabbard. The steel was long and gleaming, the setting sun glinting along the blade. Symbols decorated the length of it—the same symbols I'd seen on the rocks at the Ivory Cliff Falls. That seemed important, but I didn't have time to think it through. Callisto suddenly launched toward me.

She moved with lethal speed and grace, like she was going through the motions of a familiar dance. I was almost too slow to see the aim of it. She swung the blade at my head. I dropped as fast as I could and flattened myself against the ground.

I rolled to the left and sprung back to my feet. Callisto was already moving toward me. With a wicked smile, she lifted her sword above her and brought it down. The sharp edge was coming straight for my head.

I didn't have time to move, time to think.

Instinctively, I lifted the small Mortal Blade above me

and held on tight, pressing my palm against the flat end.
Her sword collided with my dagger. The blow was like an
earthquake, vibrating my entire body. My teeth knocked
together; stars stormed my vision. My arms ached as I
desperately tried to hold off the strength and weight of
Callisto's sword.

But I held it. I held the damn thing and then *shoved*
with all my might.

Callisto stumbled back, her eyes wide with shock.

"How?" she whispered.

I rolled back my shoulders and smiled. "Because while
you may think of me as an insect beneath the heel of your
boot, I am strong. All of us humans are strong. And we
will stop you."

Truthfully, I didn't think what I'd done was down to
only me. There was magic in the Mortal Blade. It had
helped me. I'd done my part in it, of course, but I wasn't
alone. And while I'd hated help in the past, now I was
glad for it.

Callisto's face went hard as she seemed to recollect
herself. "We all know you can leave Malroch. Your bond
with Kalen Denare overrides the vow you made with
Andromeda. But there is a part of the vow that still holds.
You cannot use your power against us." Her eyes flicked
to the blade. She'd guessed, too. "But that's not *your*
power, is it? So without your little toy, you are nothing."

"Try to take it from me, then," I said, bracing myself
for her next attack.

"Gladly." She tossed a glance over her shoulder and
whistled twice. The shadowfiends leapt into action. Their
paws pounded the dirt. I bit the insides of my cheeks and

took a few steps back, glancing around the silent street. Curtains fluttered in nearby windows, but that was the only sign of life.

The street was silent and empty. I couldn't spot anything that might be useful as a makeshift weapon. No one in the nearby homes would come to my aid, nor did I hope they would. To help me would be to sign their own death warrants.

There was only one way I could win against the beasts.

As they thundered toward me, I sheathed my dagger and held out my hands like twin spears. Callisto shouted in rage. I kept my focus on the shadowfiends' yellow eyes, their sharp, glinting fangs, and the matted fur that clung to their powerful forms.

I would not let them take me.

The shadowfiend on my left reached me only a breath before the first. As it widened its terrifying maw, I ducked low to avoid the fangs that raced toward me. Then I slammed my hand against its flank.

I grabbed a handful of its oily fur.

"Death," I whispered.

Burning, intoxicating power rushed from the depths of me. It flung outward, launching me into the air. I flew backward. My backside slammed against the ground, knocking the breath from my lungs. I blinked. And breathed. Then I blinked and breathed again until the stars abandoned my vision.

The shadowfiend was dead. Its body was curled oddly against the ground, limbs twitching like a fallen scorpion. Ashes flaked off its fur as my power consumed its flesh. Soon it would be nothing but a pile of black sand.

But the other shadowfiend was stalking toward me now. It was slower, more deliberate, its yellow eyes pinned on where I'd fallen.

"You can't do that. You vowed not to use your power against us!" Callisto shouted. "Take it back. Take it back!"

Slowly, I stood, careful to keep my gaze locked on the second shadowfiend. "I vowed not to use my power against Andromeda or any of the gods. That includes you, Callisto. But that doesn't include any of your beasts."

Steel sang. Callisto must have armed herself again. But I didn't dare look. The shadowfiend was only a few steps away now. If I loosened my focus for even a breath, it would attack.

"You will die for this, you piece of human filth," Callisto said.

Saliva dripped from the shadowfiend's fangs, big droplets that hissed when they hit the dirt. Its eyes roamed the length of me, as if sizing me up. Curious, almost.

No more waiting.

Clenching my teeth, I launched toward it with my hands splayed. My fingers made contact as it tried to flinch back. But the beast was too slow. My power slammed into the creature, burning like liquid fire in my veins. The shadowfiend shuddered before collapsing onto the ground.

Callisto rushed toward me with her sword raised. I drew the Mortal Blade. The god reached me only a second later and swung her sword at my head. I ducked and stabbed at the small gap between her leather tunic and trousers. The Mortal Blade sank into her stomach.

Callisto gasped.

She shuddered and fell. I pulled the dagger from her stomach and scrabbled back, horror and relief a tangled mess inside my gut. A guttural scream ripped from Callisto's open mouth. Her gaze locked on my face. Ribbons of red streaked through the whites of her eyes until the crimson was all that was left.

The moments shuddered by, my heartbeat loud in my ears. At long last, she stilled. Ash flecked off her body.

I looked at the dagger, at the weapon that had been with me for so long. The gemstone in its center was still intact, but that shouldn't be possible. Any time I'd ever used the blade before, the power of the weapon ate up the gemstone like some kind of hungry shark, desperate for its next meal.

I didn't understand it, but it hardly mattered right now. If Orion and Andromeda weren't on their way to stop me, they would be soon. Just as I turned to go, I noticed two crimson gemstones sitting in the pile of Callisto's ash. Before I could talk myself out of it, I grabbed them and added them to my pouch.

After stashing the dagger in my belt, I ran for the gates. Windows opened as I rushed past. Several shouts followed, encouraging me onward. The sound of their voices kept the speed in my limbs, though I hated leaving them behind.

"I will come back for you," I whispered, knowing they wouldn't believe me if they heard me. I was running

—fleeing from certain doom. I couldn't use my power against the gods. And I was only one person against a sea of storm fae who had chosen to side with the immortal enemy.

Why would anyone believe I'd return?

But I would.

I would find a way to defeat these gods, and I would free the people of Malroch.

I would free the world.

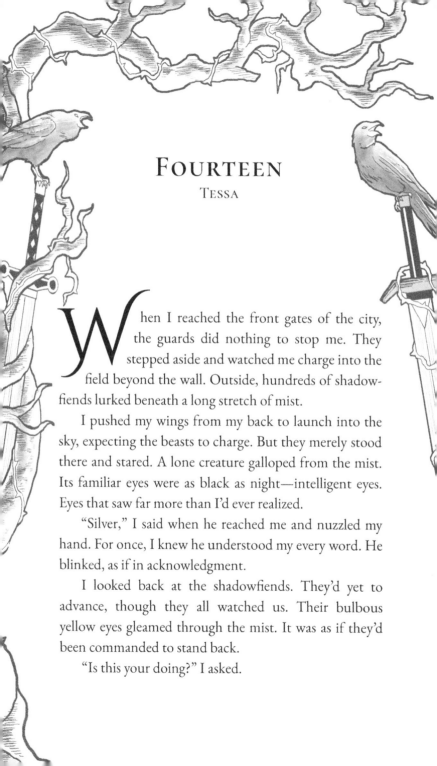

FOURTEEN
TESSA

When I reached the front gates of the city, the guards did nothing to stop me. They stepped aside and watched me charge into the field beyond the wall. Outside, hundreds of shadow-fiends lurked beneath a long stretch of mist.

I pushed my wings from my back to launch into the sky, expecting the beasts to charge. But they merely stood there and stared. A lone creature galloped from the mist. Its familiar eyes were as black as night—intelligent eyes. Eyes that saw far more than I'd ever realized.

"Silver," I said when he reached me and nuzzled my hand. For once, I knew he understood my every word. He blinked, as if in acknowledgment.

I looked back at the shadowfiends. They'd yet to advance, though they all watched us. Their bulbous yellow eyes gleamed through the mist. It was as if they'd been commanded to stand back.

"Is this your doing?" I asked.

He whinnied and shook his head, lightly stomping the dirt.

"No?" I frowned. "Then how?"

I wished he'd speak to me, the way Midnight had. But he'd been in his joint eater form that day—his true form. Perhaps that was the only way he could communicate with me.

Silver pressed his wet snout against my arm, then nickered. I blinked and stepped back.

"*Me?* I'm doing this? But how?"

He huffed and shifted to the side to show me his back. I frowned. Either he didn't know the answer or he didn't know how to tell me—*if* he wanted to tell me.

A part of me wanted to demand answers, but I couldn't waste any more time. The gods likely expected the shadowfiends to stop me when I left the city. As soon as they realized the beasts were docile now—a fact I'd never thought possible—they'd find another way to capture me. I could not spend another day trapped inside that castle. I needed to find Kalen.

Grabbing Silver's reins, I launched onto his back. He charged forward, cutting a path through the gathered beasts. Wind gusted the thickening mist into my face, drowning the world in shadows. I breathed it in, finding a strange comfort in the sudden darkness. I'd only spent a few days back in the light, but I'd missed this. The scent of it, the cool breath of it against my skin. The mists felt like Kalen somehow.

Kalen, who must believe I was lost to him.

I leaned forward, urging Silver onward. "To Dubnos."

The mists vanished not long after I left the field of shadowfiends. The sunset streaked the sky behind me. Hours passed, and night came. When I finally reached Dubnos, the first scent to hit me was rot. The city gates hung open. The wood was bent and broken, like someone had taken a battering ram to the fortifications.

Dread sliced down my spine. I dismounted and approached slowly, listening and searching for any sign of an enemy. Or even a friend. But the silence was as thick as the mists that had once plagued this city. There was no sign of them here, either.

My heart clenched as I shoved the wood aside and strode into the empty streets. Well, *empty* wasn't quite right. Tables and chairs and stores of food were scattered everywhere in broken, smashed piles. Flies buzzed around the brown flesh of apples and moldy heels of bread.

Dubnos had been ransacked.

"Nellie," I whispered around the sudden lump in my throat. As eager as I was to see Kalen, it was my sister who propelled my feet toward the castle. I ran until my breath was ragged and my shins ached from my thundering steps.

The castle gates were open, too. No guards manned the battlements, not that I'd expected anything else. There'd clearly been some kind of attack here, though I couldn't help but notice—with a hefty measure of relief

—there were no bodies anywhere. None alive, but none dead, either. And there was no blood that I could see. If there'd been a fight here, there would be evidence of it.

I walked through the battered doors of the Great Hall, where the storm fae from Gailfean had been taking refuge. All the pallets and packs were gone. The buffet table was empty. Shoes and trousers had once hung from the makeshift washing line that stretched between the overhead timber beams. The line was still there, but the clothes were missing.

It was as if everyone had packed up and moved on.

I staggered forward from relief, trying to piece this puzzle together. If no one was here, they must have gotten out before the attack. But where would they have gone? And who had ransacked this place? The gods? No, it couldn't be. The gods had been lurking around Malroch for days.

But more importantly, would Kalen have abandoned Dubnos like this? It didn't make sense based on everything I knew about him. He would protect his city until his dying breath. If the gods weren't the ones who had invaded, he could have used his power against the enemy. He wouldn't have run.

I rushed to the meeting room and flung open the door. This part of the city had been left untouched, as if the invaders had realized no one was left. They hadn't bothered to investigate the castle's innards.

The room was empty, just like everywhere else, but there was a raven feather perched on the desk right above a drawer. Eagerly, I pulled the drawer open. Inside was a single sheet of parchment, curled at the edges.

Kalen,

Star Isles came for us. We were going to fight, but there were too many of them. We evacuated to Endir. I did not want to leave without you, but we had no other choice. Please communicate by stone when you receive this.

Toryn

(Tessa, if you're reading this, know that Nellie is still in wolf form, but she is safe.)

I crumpled the parchment in my fist, my heart thundering. Star Isles had attacked. It was a city that had held allegiance to the Kingdom of Shadow until the creation of the Great Rift, based on what Kalen had explained to me. Many of his people had left to join the Isles when they'd decided they didn't want to bow to the Mist King. He'd let them go and allowed their independence, so long as they never raised their swords against him. They never had. Until now.

Nellie had gotten out safely. So had the others. But Kalen...if this note could be trusted, he'd never returned from Gailfean. Ash coated my tongue. If he'd never returned, where in the name of light was he?

I understood at once. He was still in Gailfean. He'd never escaped. I'd heard Sirius say he was alive, but what if he'd been lying? He'd helped me, but that didn't mean I could fully trust him, especially if he was compelled to do whatever Andromeda ordered.

I had to find Kalen. My head throbbing, I retraced my steps through the castle. My feet pounded stone, pain lancing my shins with every collision. Silver was waiting for me in the courtyard, and he twisted to the side as I approached.

"Gailfean," I said through belabored breaths. He took off and galloped toward the gates.

We went down the treacherous mountain path, back toward the border between the kingdoms. I'd only just escaped the storm fae lands. I knew it was dangerous for me to cross the border again. But it didn't matter, not when Kalen could be stuck in the ruins with his mother. Or worse. He would never willingly stay there. He would have fought to escape.

He would have tried to reach me, even if he thought it was impossible.

A pit of despair yawned wide as we approached Gailfean. The thought of reuniting with Kalen had been my fuel these past few days. When all had seemed lost, picturing his face had gotten me through it.

If the gods had killed him, I didn't know how I could find the strength to go on, much less fight back.

The distance city was nothing but a smudge of darkness in the night. The fiery braziers that hung along the walls no longer emitted light, so it was difficult to judge the distance. I tugged on Silver's reins to slow him down as we grew closer. My heart was as loud as his hoofbeats. When we reached the back gates, I leapt to the ground and told him to stay put.

He snorted and stomped, wildly shaking his mane in agitation.

I frowned. "If you want to come into the city with me, you need to change into your other form. It's not safe for you in there as you are."

Silver blinked at me and shook his head. He flicked his mane and turned away, clearly irritated by my decision.

"You're like Nellie, aren't you?" I asked. "You can't change."

The horse huffed.

"I'm sorry." I walked over to him and ran my hand along his snout, wishing there was something I could do to fix this. Based on his agitation, he didn't want to be stuck like this. And I could understand why. When Midnight had changed into his joint eater form, he'd been far more powerful. He'd taken out fae warriors like they were nothing more than insects. The shadowfiends wouldn't have stood a chance against him.

If he hadn't fallen into the chasm.

I sighed. It still hurt to think of him dying like that, just so he could give me a chance to kill Oberon. In the end, I'd done it, but I had failed him that day.

"I'll find a way to fix it." Silver didn't meet my eyes, so I ducked to the side so he could see the determination in my expression. "I swear it, Silver. One day soon, you'll be able to change into any form you can dream of." I gave him a sad smile. "But in the meantime, I need you to stay here and wait."

My words seemed to encourage him, for now. He stood aside and let me walk through the crumbling city gates. I took my time picking through the rubble. Without the fires to light the way, it was difficult to find the mountainous pile where Kalen and I had confronted his mother.

But soon, I reached the base of it. I quietly moved up

the hill, rocks crunching beneath my boots. My heart thumped painfully, and my jaw tightened with every step. When I crept over the ridge, I braced myself to face Bellicent or a slew of angry shadowfiends. But the top of the rubble pile was eerily silent and empty. Even the onyx pillars were gone.

The only thing to mark Kalen's presence was the dried crimson stain where he'd fallen on Andromeda's sword.

I walked over to it and knelt. My fingers traced the outline of his blood, following the path. Dark red ribbons stretched to where I'd been held behind the pillars, though none of it got that far. It was as if his lifeforce had tried to reach for me in his dying moments. And now he was gone.

Anger pulsed in my veins.

"Where the fuck is he?" I whispered into the darkness.

I half-expected an answer. Bellicent would emerge from the mist, flanked by Andromeda and Orion. They'd tell me they'd killed Kalen, destroyed the traitorous Perseus and Sirius, and now they'd come for me.

But the only answer was the wind whistling through the rubble. I glanced up at the sky, trying to read the shape of the clouds. I swore it felt like rain was in the air. If a storm hit now...I had nowhere to take refuge. No matter. I wasn't done here yet.

I continued onward, exploring the ruins for any sign of Kalen. There was nothing much to find. Life had abandoned this place. And for whatever reason, it seemed Bellicent had abandoned it as well.

Perhaps she'd decided this dead city wasn't worth the effort it would take to rebuild it. Had she taken Kalen with her? She must have.

A distant roar echoed in the distance. I tensed and swung toward the sound. It echoed again, somewhere beyond the city. My breath fled from my lungs as if the sound called to it, pulling it from the depths of me. A rush of emotion welled in my chest, filling my eyes with tears.

He was here. He was alive. And nothing, not even a vow with a god, could keep me from him.

I shuddered. The relief nearly buckled my knees.

"Kalen!" I raced across the rubble.

A roar rent the night again, though this time, it sounded nothing like the man I loved. This roar was wild and animalistic. It was a sound I knew far too well.

I'd found my husband, but the shadowfiends had found him first.

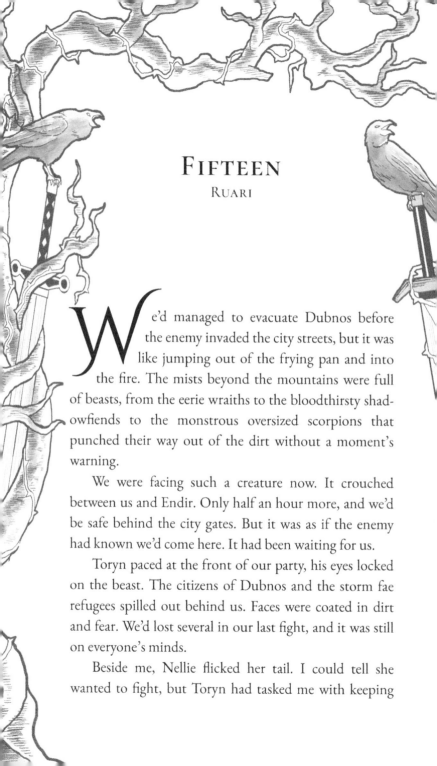

FIFTEEN
RUARI

W e'd managed to evacuate Dubnos before the enemy invaded the city streets, but it was like jumping out of the frying pan and into the fire. The mists beyond the mountains were full of beasts, from the eerie wraiths to the bloodthirsty shadowfiends to the monstrous oversized scorpions that punched their way out of the dirt without a moment's warning.

We were facing such a creature now. It crouched between us and Endir. Only half an hour more, and we'd be safe behind the city gates. But it was as if the enemy had known we'd come here. It had been waiting for us.

Toryn paced at the front of our party, his eyes locked on the beast. The citizens of Dubnos and the storm fae refugees spilled out behind us. Faces were coated in dirt and fear. We'd lost several in our last fight, and it was still on everyone's minds.

Beside me, Nellie flicked her tail. I could tell she wanted to fight, but Toryn had tasked me with keeping her safe. He seemed to think the fact she hated me meant she was more likely to take my warnings seriously. It was strange logic, though I could kind of see his point. If even *I* warned her back, then the threat was real.

"Don't pounce on that creature," I told her. "It's ten times larger than you. You'll be dead before you can even draw blood."

She growled at me.

"Toryn won't be happy if you bite off my head," I said.

Roisin scowled from where she stood on my other side. The captain of the guard looked even more eager for a fight than Nellie did. "I'm tired of running. Let's kill the damn thing and get it over with."

Her voice carried toward Toryn, who stopped his pacing. Without taking his eyes off the beast, he backtracked and joined us on the front lines. "Why hasn't it tried to fight us yet?"

"I would guess because there are hundreds of us and only one of it," I said wryly. "Doomed odds, if you ask me."

"And yet it would still take out dozens of our fighters if we engaged with it," Toryn countered. "I've seen it in action. It's quick."

"So let's launch some arrows from here." I shrugged. "If I were to guess, it's been ordered to stop anyone from travelling to and from Endir. As long as we don't try to go past it, it won't do anything. Probably."

Toryn sighed. "I don't want to sacrifice a single life to this beast. If we agitate it, it could rush our civilians."

"Then let me at it," I said.

Roisin turned toward me, her dark brow rising.
"You?"

"Your shock wounds me." I pressed a hand to my
heart. "My father might have been an evil bastard, but he
did make certain his sons and daughters knew how to
fight. I can take out the beast."

Toryn eyed me. "What's your angle here, Ruari?"

"Haven't I proven myself enough? Or will you always
hold my father's actions against me?"

"It isn't that. It's—"

Shouts peppered the air, nearly drowning out the
deep-throated growl of a shadowfiend. *Fuck.* More beasts
had come. We'd soon be surrounded. But as I turned
toward the sound, my stomach dropped. It wasn't a shadowfiend at all. A bundle of soft gray fur hurtled toward
the scorpion, claws outstretched.

It was Nellie.

Toryn let out a strangled cry. Nellie launched onto
the beast's leg. It was so large compared to her diminutive
size that she could barely reach the top half of its leg.

The scorpion screamed and tried to shake her off.
Nellie clung tight, then scampered up to its back. She
loosed a roar so loud I nearly stumbled back. Then she
sank her teeth into the scorpion's back, finding flesh
hidden between its protective plates.

Blood sprayed. The scorpion's high-pitched scream
sent the surrounding warriors to their knees.

An unexpected wave of pride washed over me. I'd
watched Nellie since she was a small child. I'd seen her
grow and blossom into the woman she was now. But
she'd never lost the fear all Teine mortals wore like an

anchor around their necks, constantly dragging them into the dirt.

Just the way my father had wanted it.

Nellie had always looked haunted. She'd always kept her eyes averted, focused on the ground. She'd been so afraid.

"Look at her now," I murmured.

The beast swung up its claw, reaching for its back. It grabbed Nellie and flung her off. A cry ripped from her throat as she soared through the air.

The world seemed to stop.

Nellie slammed into the ground, the thunk so loud it was like a thunderclap.

Warriors sprang into action. They rushed the beast, even without a command. Toryn ran forward, joining the fray. He went to Nellie while the warriors swarmed the beast. Just as he pressed his fingers to her neck, the scorpion closed its pincers around Toryn's arm and tossed him into the mist.

"Fuck," I muttered.

I ran toward her, dodging arrows and spears. When I reached her, I fell to my knees. Her eyes were wide, vacant. Gone were the fangs, the fur, and the claws. In their place was the brunette girl she'd always been in Teine. I dropped my sword to the ground and pulled off my jacket, then draped it over her body.

"I swore I'd protect you, that I'd make up for what I did that day in Albyria. I'm so sorry," I murmured.

"Ruari, watch out!" Roisin screamed from behind me.

In the chaos, I'd taken my eyes off the fight. I lifted

my gaze, bracing myself for death and blood, for the scor-pion to have its eyes trained on me. But it was flat on the ground, surrounded by dozens of fighters. They'd dispatched of it. So then what—

Claws raked through my back. And the last thing I saw were fangs drenched in blood.

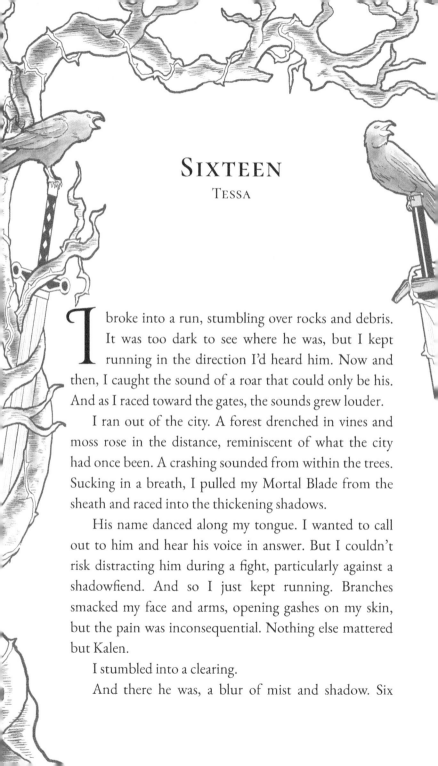

Sixteen
Tessa

I broke into a run, stumbling over rocks and debris. It was too dark to see where he was, but I kept running in the direction I'd heard him. Now and then, I caught the sound of a roar that could only be his. And as I raced toward the gates, the sounds grew louder.

I ran out of the city. A forest drenched in vines and moss rose in the distance, reminiscent of what the city had once been. A crashing sounded from within the trees. Sucking in a breath, I pulled my Mortal Blade from the sheath and raced into the thickening shadows.

His name danced along my tongue. I wanted to call out to him and hear his voice in answer. But I couldn't risk distracting him during a fight, particularly against a shadowfiend. And so I just kept running. Branches smacked my face and arms, opening gashes on my skin, but the pain was inconsequential. Nothing else mattered but Kalen.

I stumbled into a clearing.

And there he was, a blur of mist and shadow. Six

shadowfiends had him surrounded. Blood drenched from
his face. His or theirs, I couldn't tell. They were heaving,
their oily fur dripping sweat onto the ground. A few of
them heard my footsteps and jerked toward me, but I
barely noticed it.

All I saw was him.

He lifted his gaze. Those sapphire eyes cut through
the heart of me. I nearly stumbled from the weight of the
sudden connection, the indescribable snap that echoed
between us. He sucked in a breath so sharp that it echoed
through the clearing, bouncing off the trees.

"Tessa," he ground out, as if my name was almost too
painful for him to bear. His entire body shuddered, and a
feral glint lit his luminous eyes. But then a shutter
slammed down over them, and the skin around his jaw
tightened. "Get out of here. They'll kill you."

I lifted both my chin and the Mortal Blade in unison.
"Whose blood is that? Yours?"

His gaze hardened even more. "I'll heal."

"So will I."

Two of the beasts rushed toward me. The others
converged on my mate. I shouted a cry of alarm, far more
worried about Kalen than myself. Yes, he was the brutal
Mist King with powers beyond imagination. But he
would never use them with me so close by, not even
knowing he couldn't harm me. He would never risk
trying, just in case something had unexpectedly changed
during our time apart.

The shadowfiends reached me. Sucking in a breath, I
dipped low and darted sideways. Their claws raked
through the air where I'd just stood. I gritted my teeth

and slammed the Mortal Blade into the right one's flank. A feral shriek blasted my ears as blood gushed from its stomach. The beast tipped sideways and hit the ground.

The other was already coming for me. Out of the corner of my eye, I tried to see how Kalen was faring, but he and his enemies were nothing more than a blur of mist.

The shadowfiend lunged at me. I threw up my blade, aiming for its jaw. But I was too slow. I barely grazed the beast's skin, and it closed its teeth around my arm. Pain like fire rippled across my skin, and I howled, unable to hold it back. Wetness coated my hands as my blood poured.

Tears pierced my eyes as I tried to wrench myself free. The beast clung on tighter, then jerked me sideways and tossed me into the air. I was flung across the clearing. My back slammed into a tree. My head hit the bark. Stars filled my vision. I groaned, trying to think through the blinding pain.

I glanced down. Through the flickering stars, I could see my arm was a mangled mess. Blood covered my leathers, staining them a bright, angry red. I breathed around the pain, steadying myself, knowing that if I did not fight through this, I would die here in the dirt. I needed to heal.

The shadowfiend thundered toward me. My blood painted its fangs. Blearily, I stood and called upon the darkness inside me. That wicked power flared to life, lighting me up like an infinite inferno. I focused the power on my arm, on every inch of me that hurt.

Within seconds, the pain vanished.

A low growl rumbled from the beast's throat, as if it could sense my wounds were gone. Wounds it had inflicted, wounds it thought had given it the edge.

"I am the Daughter of Death," I hissed, and angled the Mortal Blade toward its throat. "Did you truly think you could best me?"

The beast froze. It scanned my face, then fell back, letting out a howl more sorrowful than a dying man's cry. And then, before I understood what was happening, it took off through the trees. The other shadowfiends—there were only two left alive—quickly followed.

For a moment, all I could do was stare after them, trying to understand why they'd ceased their attack. I'd have liked to think it was me who'd scared them off, but they'd been on the offensive only seconds before.

I glanced around, trying to spot any signs of danger.

The mists in the center of the clearing swept aside. Kalen knelt, one knee on the ground, looming over the two beasts he'd slain. He swiped the blood from his face and met my eyes. I swallowed, taking a step toward him. My vision went dark in the corners. All I could hear was the pounding of my heart.

Kalen stood and sheathed his sword. He strode toward me. His body carried all the power and might of the Mist King, the cruel, destructive fae he'd tried so hard not to be. But I could see it in his eyes now. He had become that and more. He'd embraced it.

And I had never loved him more than I did in that moment.

He opened his arms, still moving toward me with purposeful steps. "Come here, love."

I ran toward him, desperate to feel his touch. The space between us quickly vanished. Our bodies collided. He wrapped his arms around me, and my feet left the ground. My cheeks were wet from my tears as he pulled me close, as one of my hands slipped into his silken midnight hair and the other palmed his powerful, rugged neck. Emotion surged within me, so hot and thick it clogged my throat, making it impossible to speak.

All I could do was stare into his eyes, relishing every spot where his body pressed against mine. I traced the line of his jaw. "You don't look surprised to see me."

"Because I'm not," he said, his voice rumbling against my chest. "I never doubted you for a moment. You are my mate, and they could never keep you from me."

My chest warmed. "Because we made a marriage bond."

"No," he said firmly. "Because you're *you*, Tessa Baran. Brilliant and fierce and determined. They could never hold you down, not now that you understand what you're capable of. I knew you'd come back to me because of that, not because of any vow or bond. You were always going to find me, and I was always going to find you."

"Kalen," I whispered. The tears were coming quickly now. "I was afraid I'd never see you again. I thought they might have killed you."

"I would have crawled from my grave if they had. Nothing was going to stop me from reaching you, not even death."

I leaned in and kissed him. His mouth was hot and hungry against mine, his lips full of a need I felt deep within my soul. I tightened my arms around his neck and hung on, unable to let go of him, unable to put even a breath of distance between us. I needed him to *consume me* until I could no longer tell where I ended and he began.

But a vicious howl cut through the moment. Kalen pulled back, and all the light in his eyes vanished like a candle blown out. His jaw tightened as he glanced around the silent clearing.

"We have a lot to catch up on, but we can't do it here. The beasts might have gone for reinforcements."

I wasn't entirely certain that was true, not after what I'd seen from the shadowfiends outside of Malroch. But the gods might think to look for us here. Andromeda would expect me to search Gailfean for Kalen, and the scent of our blood would be fresh on the air, even though we'd both healed.

"You want us to run?" I asked.

He lowered me to the ground and took my chin in his hand, tilting back my head. "I know what you're thinking. We'll never win against the gods if all we do is run. But we also won't win unless we have a plan. Fighting them here, like this, it won't work."

I blew out a breath. "You're right."

Another shriek echoed through the night, and Silver came charging into the clearing. He looked agitated again and nudged me, telling me we needed to go. I mounted him first, then Kalen climbed on behind me.

"To Dubnos," he murmured.

"No." I sighed, hating what I had to tell him next. "To Endir."

SEVENTEEN
FIADH MacCAIN

THOUSANDS OF YEARS AGO

Orla sat cross-legged beside the fire, roasting a rabbit she must have caught while I was investigating the remains of the star. She looked up and smiled as I walked into our camp. Her skin crinkled around her eyes. As fae, we didn't age the same as humans did, but Orla's eye crinkles had been with her since we'd been nothing but wee things tumbling through wheat fields taller than us. Until that bastard lord had come into our lives.

My heart clenched painfully. It had been a long time since I'd seen her smile like that.

"Fiadh?" Her smile vanished. "You look frightened. Is everything all right?"

I cleared my throat and tried to smooth away the tension on my face. The gemstones throbbed in my pocket, thumping in time with the beat of my heart. It almost felt as if they were reaching inside me, searching for something they wanted. Searching for a way to consume me whole.

I should have left them where I'd found them. They were dark things, come from the dark skies above. Deep down, I knew that messing around with them would lead to nothing good. And yet...I couldn't free myself from the hope one of them had given me. It said it would help Orla. She'd never have to worry about returning to Aesir. No one would ever find her.

For that, I would gladly give my soul.

"I'm fine. Just got a tad too close to being discovered by the king," I said, trying to sound more lighthearted than I felt.

Alarm flashed across her face. "King Ovalis Hinde? You ventured that close to Moonstone?"

"The comet went closer than it seemed from a distance." I moved near the fire and sat a few feet away, wincing at the blast of heat. Sweat dampened the back of my neck from the return walk, and I never had been one to love the heat. The cooling shores of Star Isles had always been my home. I would have happily stayed there for the rest of my life, if fate had dealt us a different hand.

Orla frowned, an expression I'd grown much more accustomed to seeing on her face. "I warned you not to go near it."

"That you did."

She sighed and moved back to the fire, turning the rabbit. "Well, did you find anything?"

Do not tell her about me, the voice whispered in the back of my mind. *It is not yet time. You must help yourself before you can help anyone else.*

I frowned. *You didn't mention this before.*

The king was coming. Time was of the essence. Tell your sister you found nothing, and tonight, we will do what must be done to save you both.

I did not like lying to my sister. In fact, I couldn't remember a time I had, even when I knew she'd rather believe a falsehood than face the truth. And she had always done the same with me. It was just how things worked between us. It was how our bond stayed so strong, even when the world had tried to pull us apart.

How can I be certain this isn't some kind of trick? I asked the gemstone.

Faith is a tricky thing, the voice replied. *I have no proof to offer you. Either you believe I am your god with the power to save you, or you do not. If you have faith in me, you will be greatly rewarded. If not, you will continue to exist as you do now. You must decide if the risk is worth it.*

I pursed my lips. I didn't much like that answer. I'd always been the practical one. While my sister loved to daydream about the natural energies of the world, I'd never believed the Druids had any true power. They said they did, but they never demonstrated them.

"Our powers are not for show," they liked to recite.

Orla leaned closer, her brow pinched. "What's going on, Fiadh? You're starting to scare me."

I blinked, then shook my head. I'd sat here in silence, talking to a voice in my head, for far too long. "Everything is fine. I just...well, I was worried the king might follow me and discover you here."

Her face softened. "He wouldn't know who I am, Fiadh. I doubt Star Isles has sent word to Talaven to keep an eye out for me. Why would they think we'd travel here?"

"Because it makes the most sense. If we stayed in Aesir, someone *would* have tracked us down. They know we're too clever for that. So where else would they think we'd go?"

"Perhaps." She shrugged. "But when has Talaven ever done anything to assist Aesir? Never, that's when. Don't you remember those rumors? I don't think peace between the realms is as solid as they want everyone to believe." She leaned forward and took my hand. Her skin was hot from the fire, blazing like the color of her crimson hair. "We're safe here, all right?"

I nodded. Safe, as long as I did what the gemstone asked. Then we'd either be safe or we'd be dead.

T stared wide-eyed into the darkness, the heat from the dead embers at my back. The fire was nothing but ash now, thanks to my insistence we douse the flames. As much as Orla wanted a warming fire to get us through the night, I wouldn't risk it, not when the Talaven king might be out there somewhere. I would not tempt fate by having a beacon lit all night.

When Orla's snores finally reached my ears, I pushed up from the ground and stalked into a nearby copse of trees. Then I pulled the gemstone from my pocket and frowned at it. The thing had stopped speaking, but I knew it had been listening all day.

"Well?" I asked it. "You said we'd do the thing tonight."

You are an impatient one. That could be interesting.

Unease skittered down my spine. "Keep talking like that, and I'll bury you here. No one would ever find you."

She laughed, louder now than she had before. *I would soon be found. I have not been here long, but I can already tell the people of this world are easily drawn to power.*

"I'm starting to think you're not a god at all. You're the opposite. The anti-god, for lack of a better name."

You have such a mortal perception of things. Black and white, right and wrong. Power—true power—is far more complex than that. There is a 'dark side' to me, yes, but there is also what you would call light. I am good. In my own way.

I ground my teeth. "So you lied to me. You're not a god."

"To this world, I am. You will be, too."

I gasped and stumbled back, clawing at my throat. This time, the voice from the gemstone had not echoed inside my own mind. It had *spoken through me*, using my mouth, my tongue, my lips. I tried to scream, but no sound escaped. Laughter echoed in my mind, a swelling sound that drowned out my own thoughts.

Darkness flooded my vision. I could see nothing—nothing but a brilliant night sky full of a million shining stars. The stars called for me, beckoning me into the void.

And so I went into the aether.

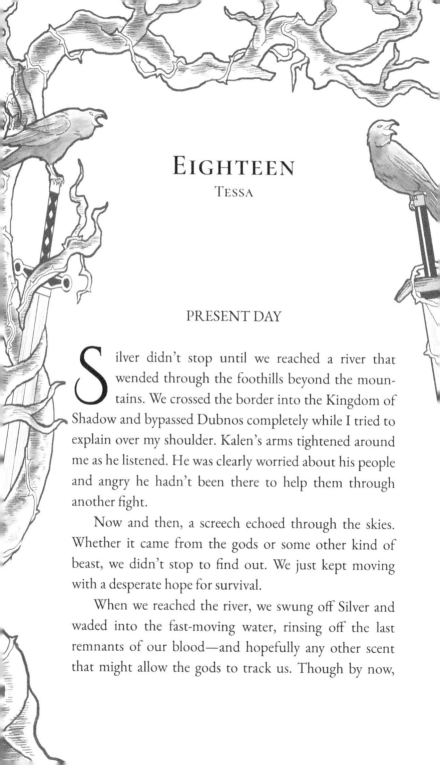

EIGHTEEN
TESSA

PRESENT DAY

Silver didn't stop until we reached a river that wended through the foothills beyond the mountains. We crossed the border into the Kingdom of Shadow and bypassed Dubnos completely while I tried to explain over my shoulder. Kalen's arms tightened around me as he listened. He was clearly worried about his people and angry he hadn't been there to help them through another fight.

Now and then, a screech echoed through the skies. Whether it came from the gods or some other kind of beast, we didn't stop to find out. We just kept moving with a desperate hope for survival.

When we reached the river, we swung off Silver and waded into the fast-moving water, rinsing off the last remnants of our blood—and hopefully any other scent that might allow the gods to track us. Though by now, they likely knew the residents of Dubnos had gone to Endir. They'd soon realize we'd followed.

Silver clopped along the rocky shore and entered the water, standing fast at the edge of the rushing stream. I swam toward him to splash water along his legs and flank, washing the dirt and grime from his coat.

"Tessa," Kalen murmured from behind me. I hadn't heard him approach, but the sudden sound of his voice didn't startle me like it once would have. If anything, it unknotted some of the tension in my shoulders.

"We need to clean Silver off as well. He's been near Malroch, and they'll know his scent."

"Just breathe, love. Your hands are shaking," he said quietly.

I glanced at where I'd rested my hands against Silver's back. Kalen was right. I hadn't noticed them shaking, hadn't noticed my entire body was trembling like a leaf. Closing my eyes, I tried to call upon my courage to chase away my fear, but I could find no trace of terror. Not as I'd known it before. Just...exhaustion.

Kalen wrapped his arms around me, tugging me close to his chest. He rested his chin on top of my head, then simply breathed. The motion of his chest against me soothed the frayed edges around my heart. I wasn't truly scared, not in the normal sense. But I felt stripped raw, like someone had taken a rough brush to my skin and rubbed it so hard it brought upon a wicked, angry rash.

"I don't know why I'm shaking," I whispered, leaning into him.

"You have the post-battle shakes," he replied, his voice rumbling against me. "It happens sometimes in war.

You've been operating with a heightened sense of danger. It's kept you moving, kept you surviving. But now that you feel safe, the true depths of what you've been through are hitting you." Carefully, he loosened his grip on me and turned me to face him. His eyes scanned my face, soft, concerned. "I think it's time you tell me what happened in Malroch. Did they hurt you? Tell me if they even so much as looked at you wrong. I will kill them for it."

A bubble of laughter popped from my throat. "You're going to have a lot of death on your hands, then. Everyone inside that castle looked at me wrong."

"Hmm." He narrowed his eyes. "And did they do anything worse?"

I sighed, then nodded. As much as I wanted to leave Andromeda's trials in the past, I needed to tell Kalen about them. Not just to get them off my chest, but so he could understand more of what we were facing. There were things I still didn't understand. Hopefully, he had answers I hadn't yet found.

And so I told him everything. I left nothing out. Not the death Andromeda had forced me to inflict. Not the strange ceremony she'd made me perform on Fenella's cousin. And certainly not the part where two gods had helped me escape. His expression grew darker with every word I said, though I noticed he didn't seem particularly surprised. Until I got to the part about the Mortal Blade.

He held out his hand, his head cocked. "Let me see the gemstone."

I handed it to him gladly. He held the dagger up before him and angled it to the side, trying to catch the pale light of the moon. There was no mist here to block it.

"This is odd," he said. "It's not the usual gemstone."

"No, and it didn't shatter when I stabbed Callisto with it."

His head snapped up. "You stabbed Callisto? When? Why didn't you mention that before?"

I frowned at his tone. "There's been a lot to tell, and I hadn't gotten to that part yet. Besides, I wanted to see the look on your face. Surprised?"

The tension fell away. He laughed, an easy, full-bodied laugh. "Not in the fucking least. What did it do to her? I'm guessing it stunned her long enough for you to escape."

"Well," I said slowly, "that's where you *actually* might be surprised. She, ah, turned to dust."

"She did what?"

"She turned to dust. As far as I can tell, this blade actually killed her."

Kalen frowned, then he held the gemstone before his eyes again. It was a long moment before he finally spoke. "This gemstone, it's like the ones Andromeda had you use on Caedmon?"

"Very similar, though the coloring is slightly different. What do you think it is?"

"I don't know," he murmured, "but I have a feeling the gods are going to want it back."

Dread tiptoed down my spine. "Then we can't go to Endir. We'd lead the gods to our friends."

"I'm not sure we have another choice." He sheathed the dagger in the hilt attached to my waist, then brushed a wayward strand of hair behind my ear. My breath caught at his touch, at the heated look in his eyes. I leaned toward him. He pulled me closer, his hand splayed across my backside. With the other hand, he cupped my cheek and scoured my soul with his eyes.

I smiled up at him. "I know what you're thinking. Here?"

"Here, there, anywhere. On the highest mountain peak or in the deepest, darkest chasm, I would want you."

I clutched his leathers and tugged him toward me. Our lips collided in a hunger-fuelled frenzy. I did not want to take things slow. Not this time. I needed him inside me. I wanted to scream his name until it was the only word I knew.

"Kalen," I murmured against his lips, drinking in the scent of leather and steel.

He lifted me into his arms as his tongue dipped between my lips, tasting me. His groan rumbled through me, sparking the hair on the back of my neck. Desire tightened my core, and I arched against him. His hard length pressed into me, even through our leathers.

Kalen pulled back. With a delicious smile curving his lips, he picked at my leathers. "We're bathing fully dressed. I think it's time we remedy that, don't you think?"

Even now, I blushed furiously. "You first."

"Gladly."

After I unwound myself from his arms, he pulled off his shirt, tossing it onto the shore. I palmed his chest to feel the familiar thud of his heart, relishing his slick skin. He unbuckled his belt and threw it toward his shirt. His trousers were the last to go, but not before he tugged off the leather vest I wore over my tunic.

Heat curled through me when he carefully lifted the shirt over my head, leaving me in my undergarments. The cool water lapped at my breasts, peaking my nipples. My fingers danced across the ridges of his abs. Mist whorled between us.

He cupped my cheek and dropped his forehead against mine. "Never leave me again."

My heart pounded. I wrapped my fingers around his and clung on tight. "I only did it to save you. Andromeda was going to let you die."

"My world will never make sense if you're not in it."

"I love you," I whispered. "My husband. My mate."

The word seemed to spark something within him, something he'd been holding back until now. With a growl, he pulled me back into his arms. I dug my fingernails into his skin and whimpered when his tongue dove between my lips. And when his cock throbbed against my core, I nearly shattered.

I'd wanted him before, but it was nothing compared to now.

"Fuck me," I whispered against his mouth.

He pulled back and nipped my ear. "Be a good girl, and I will."

My body slipped against his chest as I shuddered. Pleasing him felt like a higher calling I'd never known. I slid my free hand into the water and wrapped my hand around his cock. It was rock hard. A delicious smile curved his lips.

He rocked against me, his eyes locked on mine. I

brushed my thumb against his tip and drove my hand downward, aching to feel his hardness buried inside me. A low groan rumbled in his throat. I could feel it in my chest. With desire pulsing between my legs, I dragged my hand up once more.

"Fuck." He shuddered, hefting me into his arms and wading toward the shore. His lips skimmed mine as the water sloshed around us. "I can't wait to make you come."

NINETEEN

KALEN

I finally had my hands on Tessa's delicious body again. It had only been a week or two, but it felt like years. Decades, even. Her thighs felt so soft against me, and my length throbbed in her hand. When we reached the shore of the river, I lowered her to the grass. At the sight of her naked body beneath me, I hardened even more. She still wore a tight undergarment that accentuated her breasts, and the hardness of her nipples strained against the material.

I palmed the ground beside her head. "I want to bury my cock inside you, but I'm going to taste you first."

She shivered at my words, gazing up at me with a love that took my breath away.

I tugged her undergarments over her head. Her breasts were even more perfect than I'd remembered, and her nipples begged for my tongue. I took her flesh in my mouth and sucked hard. She writhed beneath me, her entire body trembling from my touch.

And I couldn't help but wonder just how wet she'd become.

I pulled back and gazed down at her, dragging my thumb across her swollen nipple. When she spread her legs for me, I growled in approval and knelt between her thighs, my knees digging into the soft ground. Her core glistened only inches from my face. The scent of her laced through my mist that was fogging the surrounding air.

I could lap up every last drop. And I would.

I dragged my tongue across her core. She shuddered and squeezed her thighs tight around my neck. With a wicked smile, I pressed her thighs back open and continued to lick. She arched her back and dug her fingers into my hair, moaning so loud it was all I could hear.

"Kalen," she gasped between heavy breaths. "Please fuck me. I want to feel you inside me."

I tasted her again, driving her near to the edge. Then I slid back up the length of her body. And as I pressed my cock against her wetness, a part of me wondered how the hell I'd gotten so damn lucky. This was my wife. My mate. The enemy had tried to rip us apart, but no one could stand in the way of us.

She'd come into my life when I'd needed her the most. And I was going to do whatever it took to make sure I didn't lose her again.

"Are you ready for me?" I murmured into her ear. My length pressed against her thigh.

"More than ever," she whispered back.

I slid inside her. My body became flames. She was tight and hot. It took all my self-control not to let loose my feral fae side and pound into her with all the strength I had.

But I would take it slow. Tessa was a descendent of the gods, but she was still a mortal. I couldn't bear the thought of hurting her.

I rocked against her, slowly opening her up. Her back arched as her mouth dropped open, her eyes rolling back in her head. Her thighs widened, and she whimpered. Fuck, I loved that sound. With a grunt, I captured her wrists and trapped them on the ground.

Her breath caught, and I could see the pulse in her neck quicken. Desire roared through me. I needed to go deeper.

I pulled out and flipped her over. Palming her backside, I thrust deep inside her. Whimpering again, she lifted her arse higher. *Fuck, fuck, fuck.* My pace quickened, and she dug her fingernails into the dirt. Her whole body trembled as I took her, her gorgeous backside bouncing with each and every thrust. I could feel her tightening around me.

"I think," she breathed, "I'm going to come."

"Not until I say so, love."

I wanted everything. Every single part of her. I wanted to taste her as she exploded and feel her trembling against my mouth.

Even though I throbbed with need, I pulled out again and lowered my back to the ground, flipping her so her lips touched my cock. My mouth found her core, and I slid my tongue inside her. She tasted so fucking sweet.

She cried out, bucking against my mouth.

"That's it," I said between licks. "Don't stop until you come."

She wrapped her hand around my length while she writhed against me. Her wetness spread across my lips, and her screams rang in my ears. As she reached her climax, she took me deep in her mouth. Pure pleasure exploded through my body, pouring my seed onto her lips. Growling in satisfaction, I licked up every last drop of her delicious pleasure. I could stay down here for hours, exploring every inch of her until she was fully spent.

A splash sounded nearby.

Tessa rolled off me, her eyes wide. I pressed my finger to my lips and listened, the feral instinct to protect my mate rising inside me. I never felt it more than when I had her naked body in my hands.

I slowly stood, scanning the river. But I saw no movement in the darkness. Perhaps it had only been a fish, frightened by all the noise. I smirked at the thought. I'd given my mate so much pleasure we'd scared off all the animals. How many men could say that?

But then a deep, dark dread crept toward me from the river. Something felt wrong. I cocked my head, breathing in the familiar scent of night. A spice of some sort cut through it. That hadn't been a fucking fish. Someone else was here.

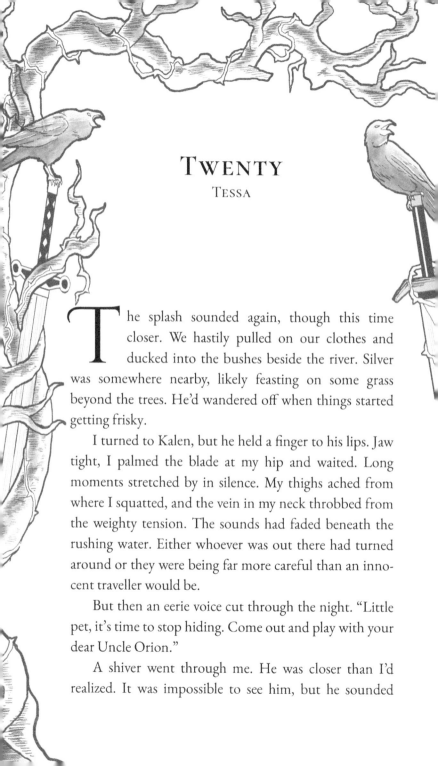

TWENTY
TESSA

T he splash sounded again, though this time
closer. We hastily pulled on our clothes and
ducked into the bushes beside the river. Silver
was somewhere nearby, likely feasting on some grass
beyond the trees. He'd wandered off when things started
getting frisky.

I turned to Kalen, but he held a finger to his lips. Jaw
tight, I palmed the blade at my hip and waited. Long
moments stretched by in silence. My thighs ached from
where I squatted, and the vein in my neck throbbed from
the weighty tension. The sounds had faded beneath the
rushing water. Either whoever was out there had turned
around or they were being far more careful than an innocent traveller would be.

But then an eerie voice cut through the night. "Little
pet, it's time to stop hiding. Come out and play with your
dear Uncle Orion."

A shiver went through me. He was closer than I'd
realized. It was impossible to see him, but he sounded

only a few steps away. And yet, if he was calling out, he didn't know exactly where we were, either.

I looked up at Kalen. His jaw was tight, his gaze was hard, his brow was furrowed in rage. I'd told him everything that had happened in Malroch. He knew how Orion had taunted me, how he'd wielded his anger like a sword. He might not have physically harmed me—yet—but he'd done enough in Kalen's eyes. Any threat against his mate was a threat against himself.

Shaking my head, I palmed his arm, hoping he could read my expression. He couldn't give in to the overwhelming pull of our bond and leap into a fight against an enemy who was immune to his power. Because he was right. If we fought the gods like this, we'd never win. We needed a plan first. An army. We needed answers on how we could stop them for good.

But...I glanced down at the Mortal Blade. The gemstone glowed faintly. It was throbbing like a heartbeat, like it was trying to answer Orion's call. My stomach dipped. It was a light in the darkness, giving away our position. And I hadn't noticed the glow until now.

Fuck.

I wrapped the edge of my cloak around the gemstone, but it was too late. Orion's boots hit the ground in front us, his wings gusting powerful fists of air. The bushes bent back to reveal our location, though the gemstone had already given us away.

Kalen punched the tip of his sword into the dirt and pushed to his feet. With a snarl, he levelled his weapon at the god now before us. But Orion only had eyes for me.

His pale hair danced across his forehead as he stalked toward me. His powerful body was clad in steel plates, much like the ones Perseus seemed to favor. His movements were smooth yet precise, like he was made of the wind itself.

"Give me Callisto back." He curled back his lips, snarling like the predator he was.

"I can't do that," I said, finding my voice. "She's dead."

He stared at me. My heart thundered, and for a moment, I wondered if I'd said too much. Did he think I'd taken her alive rather than killing her with my blade? And now that he knew the truth, his rage would be unquenchable.

So when he tipped back his head and laughed, I started.

Kalen put an arm in front of me like a protective barrier. When he spoke, his voice was barely a whisper. "When I say run, run. Will you listen to me for once?"

I nodded.

He took a step back, and his arm put pressure on my stomach. I followed with a step of my own.

Orion's laughter died. "Did you truly believe it would be that easy to kill us? We are *immortal gods*. Give her back to me, Tessa. Pandora, too."

I fought the urge to glance at Kalen. Who in the name of light was Pandora?

"I haven't laid a finger on anyone named Pandora," I countered. "I don't even know who that is."

He strode toward me, his eyes narrowing. "That's because you're too small of a creature, too focused on your own tiny life on your own tiny pocket of rotten land. Even when you hold the truth, you cannot see it."

My hand tightened on the hilt of my dagger. I was starting to understand now, even if it made little sense. The gemstones I'd taken from Callisto's ashes...somehow, they were her. And the one inside the Mortal Blade was whoever this Pandora was—another one of the gods, perhaps. Were the gemstones working as a prison that could hold the essence of them, like the onyx gemstone had been for Andromeda? Were these two gods *trapped*?

Had I done it without even realizing?

It felt too easy.

"Wait," Kalen suddenly said, shielding his eyes as he gazed into the distance. "What's that?"

Orion took the bait. He glanced over his shoulder, his hands fisting as if tensing for a fight. Kalen grabbed my hand and mouthed, *Run!*

We leapt from the bushes and ran through the trees. It only gave us seconds before Orion followed. His heavy footsteps pounded the ground behind us. My legs ached, and my lungs burned. I held tight to Kalen's hand and ran with every ounce of speed I could conjure. I was just barely fast enough to keep up.

We dashed beyond the tree line and into the expanse of open field. The gently rolling hills vanished into the darkness, though I knew from our previous travels they went on for miles and miles. If we carried on, these fields would lead us to Itchen and then Endir. But we would never get there, not with Orion hot on our trail.

"We'll have to fight him," I puffed out between breaths. "And we have the blade."

"I don't want you that close to him," Kalen said, casting a quick glance over his shoulder at the enemy. "He's not like Callisto, who merely controls the beasts. He's Famine, love. If he touches you, he could starve you to death."

"There's one of him and two of us. It's the best odds we'll ever have."

I released his hand and stopped, whirling to face Orion. He was only a few steps behind us. If we hadn't stopped, it would have only taken him seconds to catch up to our pace. Bending my knees, I lifted my hands and braced for impact.

But he slowed to a stop and raised his brow, clearly caught off guard by my sudden willingness to fight him. "You'll hand over my sisters?"

"No. If you want them, you'll have to take them from me."

A slow smile curled his lips. "Gladly."

He stalked through a small pocket of mist Kalen had left behind us—I'd noticed the skies were strangely clear again. I fisted my hands and breathed it in, filling my body with the power I felt zinging through Kalen's veins. If anything, we would find out once and for all if my vow to Andromeda stopped me from using Kalen's power against the gods. And if it didn't—if my marriage bond to Kalen could void *everything* I'd promised— then, well, we had much better odds than we ever could have hoped.

The power burned through me, singeing my veins. It filled my head with a strange song. It sounded like the call of something wild and unfettered. I lifted my hands and spread my fingers wide, palms held toward Orion and his rapidly approaching form.

He didn't slow when he saw what I was doing.

Clenching my jaw, I loosed the power.

It sizzled on my hands, then that force knocked me back. I landed in a crouch several steps behind Kalen. Orion just laughed as he continued to advance on us both.

"Fuck," I muttered.

"Your marriage bond only negates the part of the vow that kept you from your mate," Orion said. "I thought you were clever enough to realize that. You have no way to kill us. No way to stop us. No way to protect these pathetic, wicked mortals from what needs to be done. Give me back my sisters and get out of our way."

"And what will I get from you if I give them back? A swift death? You'll drag me back to Malroch? Or will you send your Star Isles army after everyone I know and love?"

He slowed. "How's this? You'll get none of those things. Give me the gemstones, and I'll leave you to rot here in the fae lands with your mate. And if Andromeda asks, I'll tell her I couldn't find you. As for your loved ones, we don't care about Aesir. They can live."

My heartbeat thundered in my ears. "That sounds too good to be true."

"I don't care about you, Tessa Baran. You've just proven your vow with Andromeda holds strong, so you can't use your power against us. Give me the gemstones, and I'll leave you be."

"And what will you do with them?" I had to ask.

"Bring Callisto back and what else? Bring whoever Pandora is here, too? What happened to Caedmon?"

"We will smite the humans, just like we always planned." With a scowl, he moved toward me, but Kalen edged in, blocking the god's path to me.

"Stay away from her," Kalen said in a low growl.

"Or you'll what, Mist King?" Orion asked, snarling. "You'll mist me? You'll stab me with your pathetic Halen Mon sword?"

Kalen stood his ground as the god advanced on him. And then my mate pushed me to the side, moving me out of range of their weapons. Fear jumped in my veins. I opened my mouth to warn him back, but Kalen had already lifted his arms to blast the god with his own power.

"It won't work, Kalen!" I screamed, though my fear held back my voice. The words scraped through my throat and came out as nothing more than a hoarse gasp.

Kalen's power exploded out of him. But like with me, it didn't make contact with the god. The power threw Kalen back, and he vanished into the darkness.

The god turned his crimson eyes on me. "Now that he's out of the way, I will ask you one more time. Hand me the fucking gemstones, Tessa Baran. I won't hesitate to rip your head off your body if you refuse, and your mate is no longer here to protect you."

"I don't need anyone's protection but my own," I said, my lips curling back to expose my teeth. "And no matter what you promise me, I will not give you these gemstones. Not if it means bringing more gods into this world."

I shoved my wings from my back. They punched through the slits of my leather armor, and I pushed off the ground. Flinging myself into the dark sky, I cut a path toward the lakes near Itchen. As long as I could stay far enough ahead of Orion, he wouldn't be able to see me. I'd drop the gemstones into the lake once I'd lost him, then I'd double back to where I'd left Kalen.

Orion would be angry when he realized I'd dumped the jewels, but judging by his desperation to get them back, I had a hunch he'd choose to hunt them down rather than fight me. He'd never find them, and it would give us enough time to get away.

The thunderous sound of wings rushed by me. My heart jumped as Orion dove into my path. I tried to change course, but he was brutally fast. As I twisted to the side, he grabbed my arm. I kicked his chest, my boot colliding into his armor. The contact jolted me, knocking my teeth together.

"Tessa!" Kalen's furious roar rose from the ground. I shuddered against the instinct to return to him. I'd sworn to stay by his side, and he was calling for me.

Orion tightened his fingers around my wrist and jerked me toward him. He hissed into my face. "Give me the fucking jewels or I will rip your mate's head off his body."

Something stirred in my gut. It was like a poisonous snake uncoiling after a long, blissful slumber, and now some fool of a bastard was repeatedly kicking its nest. It rattled its tail and looked into the face of the enemy while venom dripped from its brutal fangs.

I'd been ready to run. But I was done backing down.

I grabbed Orion's arm and tugged him even closer, so close I could smell the wine on his tongue. "You shouldn't have threatened my mate."

With my free hand, I slid the Mortal Blade through the gap in his steel plate. Fear flashed in his eyes, but he caught my arm before I could shove the dagger into his gut.

"So this is how you fucking did it. I should have known it was that blade. It always is."

Before I could wonder at what he meant, he made a grab for the weapon. His hand clutched my wrist, and his fingers tightened like a vise. Pain flared as he bore down as hard as he could. A bone snapped, and a wrenching pain rippled down the length of my arm.

I howled and broke free of Orion's grip. He reached for the blade again. I drove my wings down hard and slammed my boot into his gut. It knocked him back, his body curving like a crescent moon in the dark sky.

From below us, a deep rumble shook the ground. The sound grew like an avalanche of tumbling rocks, like a stampede of horses bearing down on us. As Orion struggled to recover from my blow, I risked a glance down.

Kalen rose in a brutal storm of wind and mist. The ground below him cracked, spiderwebbing as it shook from where he focused his power. Awestruck, I watched as he climbed higher in the air. He was using his power to lift himself into the clouds, where Orion and I duelled. I'd never seen anything like it before.

He might not be able to launch it at Orion, but he could use it like this, focused on the ground. Unless Orion muted it, which he could.

Kalen's sapphire eyes latched onto my face as the wind whipped his hair. Pure fury tightened his jaw. Rocks and dirt jumped against the ground as another crack widened from the force of his power. But he was too focused on me to notice. With a wicked glint in his eye, he pulled the sword from his back.

I was so distracted by the impossible beauty of him that I didn't sense Orion's approach. He grabbed my wrist and squeezed the broken bone.

Furious fire flared through my hand and arm, and my vision filled with darkness.

"Take your hands off my wife," Kalen said in a voice that commanded all the hair on my arms to rise. They obeyed.

Orion responded by tightening his grip on my wrist. The pain took my breath away and nearly blinded me.

Kalen roared and swung his sword. The steel hissed as it cut through cloud and mist. Blade hit skin, and just like before, the weapon didn't wound the god. It bounced off him, barely leaving a mark.

Orion released me. He wrapped both hands around Kalen's sword. Soothing relief echoed through my aching hand, but it was short-lived. Orion gripped Kalen's sword and *shoved* with a kind of strength I'd never seen before. The hilt slammed into Kalen's chest, throwing him backward.

He fell through the mist.

I cried out and reached for his vanishing hand, but Orion jerked me back.

I growled and spit into the god's face, no longer caring what he tried to do to me next. I'd had enough.

Orion just laughed as my spittle dripped into his glowing crimson eye. "Fight as hard as you want, little pet. You and your lover king will never best me. I am a force of nature itself. *You* are nothing but an insect." He shoved Kalen's sword into my hands and smiled. "How about a deal, eh? I know you like those. Try to harm me with that sword. If I win, you hand me those gemstones."

My first instinct was to tell him to go fuck himself, but... "And what do I get if I win?"

He scoffed, then rolled his eyes. "You can say you're the only mortal who has ever harmed me."

"That's not good enough," I replied carefully. "You said it yourself. You're immortal, so this sword can't kill you. You'll heal if I manage to wound you. Quickly, judging by what I've seen from you and the other gods. So, what exactly do I get by risking the gemstones in this little game of yours? Do I get to keep them if I win?"

"No," he said quickly.

"Ah." I backed up, my wings pounding the air. "Then I'm afraid we *don't* have a deal."

He snarled. "I will kill you if I have to."

Smiling, I lifted the sword, arms aching from the weight of it. But Kalen had trained me in this. He'd helped me build the strength I needed for this fight. "Go ahead, then. Try."

I sounded a lot more confident than I felt, and my mind was partially elsewhere. Kalen had fallen far. I knew he was fae, and he could survive impossible things. But still, I worried.

Orion flicked his eyes toward the Mortal Blade, then toward my hands, before finally settling them on my face.

There was something in the furrow in his brow that tipped me off. He was actually worried I might stab him with the Mortal Blade. Because even though Callisto was still alive, she was nothing more than an essence trapped in a gemstone. The same would likely happen to Orion if I could stab him with it, too.

Eventually, he said, "Fine. I won't let you keep the gemstones, but I can agree to something else. You're heading to Endir, yes? If you win, you can have an hour's head start before I come for you."

"I thought you wanted nothing to do with Endir. You said you'd leave my loved ones alone."

"You'll have the gemstones. So yes, I will attack Endir even if you win our little game. See, you've already won a prize. The truth."

My heart pounded.

"A *day's* head start." I watched him carefully for a reaction. He started to object, but I interrupted him before he could. "I thought this sword couldn't hurt you. Why shouldn't you agree to day's head start if it's impossible for me to win?"

His brow slammed down. "Vow you won't cheat and use that bloody Mortal Blade instead of the sword."

I tapped the sword, considering my reply.

"Ah, see." His lips curled back in a sneer. "You and the other mortals of this wretched world have no honor. You plan to—"

"I vow I won't use the Mortal Blade against you in *this fight* and this fight alone. After our day's head start, this fight will end. And then I'm free to use it against you."

"Very well." He held out a hand. "Your vow is accepted."

I took his hand and shook it. His skin was like ice, so cold it burned. He dug his fingers into mine, and a flare of pain raced through my wrist from where he'd shattered the bone. It felt like I was being stabbed by a million needles. I winced and jerked away.

With a chuckle, he spread his arms. "The deal is done. Have at it, little pet."

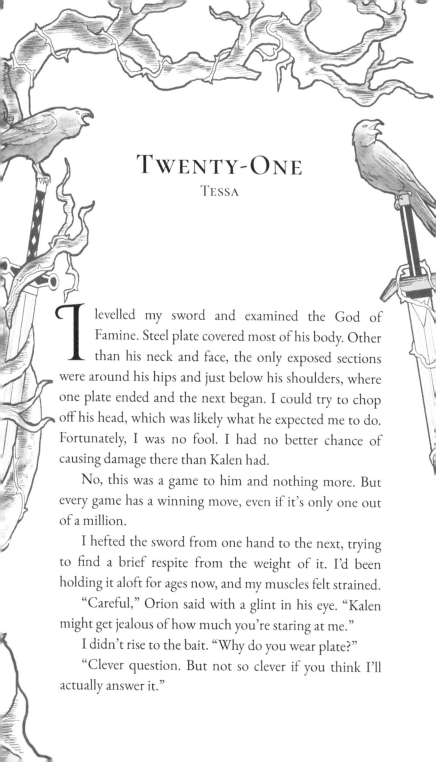

TWENTY-ONE
TESSA

I levelled my sword and examined the God of Famine. Steel plate covered most of his body. Other than his neck and face, the only exposed sections were around his hips and just below his shoulders, where one plate ended and the next began. I could try to chop off his head, which was likely what he expected me to do. Fortunately, I was no fool. I had no better chance of causing damage there than Kalen had.

No, this was a game to him and nothing more. But every game has a winning move, even if it's only one out of a million.

I hefted the sword from one hand to the next, trying to find a brief respite from the weight of it. I'd been holding it aloft for ages now, and my muscles felt strained.

"Careful," Orion said with a glint in his eye. "Kalen might get jealous of how much you're staring at me."

I didn't rise to the bait. "Why do you wear plate?"

"Clever question. But not so clever if you think I'll actually answer it."

"Something can harm you other than my dagger. And you must think we have it, or you wouldn't be dressed for war."

"Hmm, could be." He gave me a beastly smile. "Unfortunately for you, you've just revealed you have no idea what it is. Now get on with it, pet. You're stalling for time, and I'm weary of speaking mortal words."

But I knew the answer. *Nellie.*

She'd harmed Sirius, even if it had only been temporary. And it had *changed* something in him, something fundamental. An idea started to take shape in my mind. It wouldn't help me now, but it just might be the salvation we'd been hoping for.

Destruction wasn't the answer. Killing them was impossible, anyway. Even if I trapped them in these odd gemstones, I'd only be punting the problem forward several centuries, just like King Ovalis Hinde had. Trapping the gods would save *us*. But they would find a way back again, eventually.

So maybe there was another way...

For now, I needed to escape Orion. Shoving the sword into his neck wouldn't work. Fortunately, there was something else we hadn't yet tried. The only other exposed part of him was his wings.

I raised the sword over my head. Orion watched in amusement.

Bracing myself, I brought the blade down hard. The steel cut through flesh and bone, spraying black feathers. They filled the air like ash and shadows. Orion screamed and jerked away from me. Black blood sprayed my leathers.

I watched as the god tumbled, head over feet. He scarcely caught himself before he fell, one broken wing barely beating. His head whipped toward me, and his eyes were full of fury.

He spit, "Fuck you, Tessa Baran. You get your one day's head start, but then I'm coming for you. We're *all* coming for you."

And then he was gone.

Kalen was pacing when I found him, his body wound as tight as a ball of string. When I gently landed before him and tucked my wings into my back, he crushed me against his chest. He breathed long and hard, like he'd been stuck underwater all this time.

"I tried to reach you again, but he was muting my powers," he said roughly. "I've been going out of my fucking mind!"

"I'm all right, Kalen," I said into his chest, relaxing at the familiar scent of mist and leather and steel. "But we need to move. Now."

He pulled back and searched my eyes. "What happened? Where is he?"

I held up Kalen's sword. The blade was dripping with Orion's black blood. "He said if I could hurt him with this sword, he'd give us a day's head start to Endir." I shrugged. "Turns out his wings aren't as impervious to blades as the rest of him."

"I see." A muscle in his jaw ticked. "I don't want to run, though, love. I want to rip his head off."

"We can do that later," I said, quickly tossing a glance over my shoulder for any sign of Orion. I knew that if Kalen saw him now, wounded as he was, he'd go after him. "But I have an idea that can only work if we go to Endir now. I think I know how we can win."

It took another couple of days to reach Endir. The mists had cleared, and we could see the blood that painted the dirt outside the gated city. I stepped over a broken arrow, my throat tight. All I could think about was my mother. She'd died out here because of her long-held fear of the Mist King. It had taken me a long time to stop blaming myself for what had happened to her. She never would have been here if not for me. If I'd taken more time to convince her that Kalen was on our side...

But no. I couldn't go back there. I couldn't live in the past and keep beating myself up for my bad choices. The only way to become a better me was to accept it and move forward. I couldn't fix the past, but I could make a difference for my future.

For everyone's future, I hoped.

"I know what you're thinking," Kalen said. I could feel the weight of his gaze as I moved carefully across the bloodied ground. "You're wondering if this bloodshed is from that night we lost your mother. It's not. It's too fresh for that."

I tensed. "Then there was a recent battle here. How many died? Can you tell?"

"A few. But even the loss of one life is too many. I should have been here."

"Could it have been...?" A lump lodged in my throat. I didn't want to voice the thought aloud for fear the universe would hear me and make it true.

"Yes. It was likely those who fled here from Dubnos." Kalen knelt and placed two fingers against the blood. It was still fresh enough to paint his skin. He brought his stained fingers to his nose and sniffed. His lip curled. "A beast. That's what this blood is from." He glanced around. "There are a few other places where the blood's a different color. Lighter than this."

I followed his gaze and noted he was right. The splatter he knelt beside was much darker, like the shadow of blood. The other smaller patches were bright red. So the Dubnos lot must have run into a beast on their way to Endir. Judging by the blood, they'd killed it, but the beast had taken a few fae or humans with it when it died.

"We need to get to Endir." I turned back toward the city and moved quickly, my worry for Nellie, Toryn, and the others like a gust of brutal wind against my back.

But when we eventually reached the bolted gates, the guards called to us in jovial tones.

"Oi! Glad to see you two are here!" A tall, armored woman with flowing yellow hair leaned out a window and grinned. "Everybody's been making bets on when you'd get here. And *if* you'd get here."

Kalen surprised me by grinning right back. Sometimes, with all his brooding and scowling, I forgot he had a mischievous side when around his constant friends. Sometimes it was easy to forget he even had friends. Kalen Denare was larger than life. A king of kings, it often felt like.

But around his companions, he was just a fae man who would do anything for his kingdom.

"Judging by your smile, I'm guessing you bet we'd return right about now, alive and well," he called back to the guard.

"I always bet on you, Kal." She shifted to me and nodded, still smiling. "It's good to see you well, too. Your Highness."

Surprised, I cleared my throat. I didn't know how to respond in a situation like this. Back in Albyria, I'd been instructed to stay silent when addressed and keep my eyes trained on a spot above the subject's head. But those were Oberon's rules, and I'd never been meant to *truly* rule. None of the mortal brides had been. I didn't know what real queens did.

But I also hadn't realized anyone knew about our marriage. No one except...

"I see Fenella has been spreading the word," Kalen said. "I'd been waiting to make the formal announcement first."

"Ah, she just wanted to give us some good news is all. Plus, it made the humans happy. You know how it's been tense around here. The news calmed the whole thing down, 'cause we've got a real alliance now." She ran her fingers through her hair, then brought back her smile. "Anyway, I'll let you both in. I can tell it's been a long journey. And I'm sure you'd like to see your sister, Your Highness."

"Yes, about my sister..." I said, hoping to ask the guard how Nellie was. But she'd already started rolling up the heavy gate, and my words were drowned beneath the rumble and creaking of the wood. Once she'd raised it enough for us to duck through, I followed Kalen into the streets of Endir.

We wound our way toward the castle, across the bridges and past the markets—now shut for the night. Everything was silent and still. I noticed several homes were occupied that hadn't been before. Washing lines were draped between buildings, and mist-resistant greenery crowded window boxes.

"These are the homes I suggested we share with the humans from Teine," Kalen said, nodding toward a house that had two pairs of boots sitting on the front porch, bottoms coated in dried mud. "I'm glad to see some of them decided to take up that offer."

"Things are actually better here."

"Seems so." Kalen Denare smiled. And when he smiled, so did I. "Gaven has really pulled through."

"Yes, but if it weren't for you—"

"Kal!" A voice called from further down the street. "Tessa!"

I looked up. Fenella stood at the crest of the hill, waving at us from the path leading into the castle court-yard. She practically beamed, which was a little discon-certing. Fenella was supposed to twirl her daggers and threaten people, not look like she'd just tasted water after a year spent wandering the desert.

She jogged toward us. Kalen picked up his pace. I followed just behind and watched as they embraced, thumping each other on the backs with enough force to knock a hole in a stone wall. When Fenella pulled back, I swore there was a tear in her eye. Just the one, though. No more than that.

Then she looked at me and lowered her head, as if in a partial bow. "Your Highness."

"Oh, come on," I said.

She lifted her gaze and grinned. "I told everyone you're our queen now, so you best get used to it."

"I think I liked it better when you were threatening to gut me."

"Don't worry. I have plenty of threats to throw around, just not toward you anymore. Is it time for us to murder those gods yet?" She patted the twin daggers at her hips. "I have two blades. One for each of Andromeda's eyeballs."

I couldn't help but laugh. "There's the Fenella we know and love."

"I take it everyone made it here safely?" Kalen asked as he took Fenella's elbow and started leading her across the castle courtyard. I fell into step beside them, sobering as we waited for an answer.

Fenella frowned. "We lost a few warriors in a fight against one of those scorpion beasts. No civilians, neither storm nor shadow fae, were harmed. "

Hazy moonlight cut a path through the darkness, past ancient statues built by Druids of the natural elements they served. Our boots clicked against the stone, almost drowned out by the sounds of the city. Endir had become a safe haven for so many these past months. Light fae, shadow fae, humans, and storm fae were all crammed inside these ancient walls. It was probably the best place in all of Aesir. Or it would be, if the gods couldn't fly. As it was, walls would do nothing to keep them from invading.

"Where's Nellie?" I finally asked. I knew if she was hurt, Fenella would have led with that, but I needed to hear the confirmation. I needed to know my sister was all right.

Fenella smiled strangely. "She's in the Great Hall with a few others who haven't yet retired to their chambers for the night. I'll take you to her."

I breathed a sigh of relief. When we passed through the doors that led inside the castle proper, the torchlight chased away the dark. Fenella led the way, though I knew the path by now. We swung a left when we came to the grand staircase, and I let the siren call of laughter, cheers, and clinking glasses grab me by the throat and lead me there. I had not been gone long, but it felt like years since I'd heard true joy like that. My heart leapt in response.

But that was nothing compared to the moment I crossed the threshold of the Great Hall and saw my sister —in human form—sitting at the table with a smile so bright it nearly blinded me. Surrounded by Toryn, Gaven, Ruari, and Roisin, as well as tankards and empty plates and playing cards scattered everywhere, she looked at home. Like part of a family.

She glanced my way, then her mouth dropped

opened. Jumping to her feet, she exclaimed, "Tessa? Oh, thank the light!"

I grinned and crossed the room in two quick strides, widening my arms as she leapt toward me. She crashed into my chest. With a laugh, I stumbled back, but I did not let go. My sister was here. She was back. The gods could tear me apart, piece by piece, but I would be okay as long as I had her.

She took a long, low sniff against my shoulder, then pulled back, wrinkling her nose. "You smell odd. Like rot or something. How long has it been since you washed these clothes?"

Fenella cackled as she walked up beside us and slung an arm around Nellie's shoulder. "Nellie might be my new favorite Baran now."

But Nellie did not smile. Her eyes latched on mine. Understanding flickered across her expression, flattening her thin lips. "You don't come with good news, do you? What's happened out there? Where *were* you?"

I sighed and glanced over my shoulder at Kalen. "That is a very long story. Have any fion to help it go down?"

TWENTY-TWO

TESSA

I sat on the wooden bench, sandwiched between Nellie and Ruari—it seemed those two got along now—while Kalen took the spot at the head of a table. Fenella tried to insist I take the other end, where an elaborately carved chair sat empty, its seat softened by a plush silk pillow so deep a crimson it reminded me of dried blood. But while I was married to Kalen, I did not yet feel comfortable proclaiming myself his queen. I knew so little about the shadow fae kingdom. I had no experience ruling. And there'd been no ceremony, no formal announcement. Kalen's wife I proudly was. Just not his queen.

Kalen and I filled the others in on what we'd both been through. It was a difficult story to tell. I choked up a few times. First when recalling the moment Kalen's blood had spread toward me in Gailfean, and I was unable to do anything but watch the pain on his face. And then again when I had to admit I'd killed a human in Andromeda's trials. No one seemed to judge me, though I felt something strange—like uneasiness—pass through the bond. But when I examined Kalen's face, he didn't look concerned.

"So you were trapped in a cave for days," Toryn said to Kalen before turning to me. "And you were trapped in Malroch, forced to dance for the gods."

"I wouldn't exactly call it dancing," I said quietly. "That would suggest some kind of enjoyment on my part."

Nellie rubbed the knots on my shoulders. It was difficult not to turn and stare. I could scarcely believe she was herself again.

"There is one thing I haven't told anyone yet," Kalen eventually said. He heaved a sigh, closing his eyes. "Before Perseus knocked me unconscious, he murdered Bellicent Denare."

"What?" Shocked, all I could do was stare at him. Why hadn't he mentioned it before now?

"But I thought Bellicent was Andromeda's anchor," Toryn said with a frown. "That's what Niamh told us she discovered from Talaven. She's the one who had to die for us to be able to banish the gods. Have we misunderstood?"

I wet my lips, thinking. "I don't think he told Andromeda he killed Bellicent. Perseus helped me escape."

"Sirius *and* Perseus," Fenella said, twirling her dagger. "So two of the gods are working against the others. Interesting. Very interesting. This could get fun."

"So what does this mean?" Nellie asked.

"It means the anchor is dead. We can rid this world of

Andromeda," Toryn said. "We just need to figure out how."

Fenella tipped back her tankard and slammed it onto the table. The sound reverberated through the mostly empty hall. Unlike in Dubnos, Gaven had been able to find enough space for the refugees elsewhere. The barracks were packed now, but it was better than everyone camping out on the Great Hall's cold stone floor.

"I know we're all trying to be sensitive to feelings since this whole thing obviously sucked." She twirled one of the miniature daggers on her necklace. "But I'm going to ask what we're all wondering. What did you find out when they were tormenting you, Tessa? How can we destroy the gods? If there's no anchor protecting Andromeda, we need to kill these fucking monsters now."

I smiled, pulled the Mortal Blade from my hip, and dumped it onto the table between a slice of cake and a half-empty tankard of ale. The gemstone glimmered ominously beneath the candelabra overhead, the deep color swirling from crimson to black to crimson again.

Toryn plucked the dagger from the table and examined the gemstone.

"Careful," Fenella said, scooting away from him. "One scratch and you're ash."

"I'm not mortal," he reminded her. "It won't work in my hands. What is this gemstone, Tessa? I've never seen one like it before."

"I think it holds a god," I said.

He dropped it. It hit the table hard, the sharp tip

punching the wood. The steel sang where it remained upright, vibrating, singing, whispering doom throughout the hall. I gritted my teeth and winced.

Gaven sat forward. He'd been mostly silent so far, but his keen eyes took in the dagger with the same ferocity I often saw in Kalen. "You're right. Can't you feel it? That's definitely a god."

"Which one?" Fenella asked eagerly. "How did you trap it? Why did you put it in the Mortal Blade? Does it do the same thing Oberon's gemstones did?"

"I don't know. I think it's one we've never met. I didn't trap it or put it in the blade. Sirius did. And yes, it does the same thing."

"Sirius did?" Gaven asked, cocking a brow. "I think we need to hear the rest of your story."

And so I explained as best I could. I told them about Callisto. There was a lot of shouting at that point. They were exuberant now, determined this was the answer to winning it all. Until I explained the gods could just come back, like they always did.

"I think their beings, their essences, are in these stones. Somehow, they can be drawn out and put into fae bodies. It's like what Oberon did with Bellicent." I looked around the room. "We need something more permanent. Something that will change the nature of the gods, so they're more like Sirius. He doesn't want to destroy us. If we can make the others see things the way he does, we won't have to risk our lives fighting them. No one will have to die. And we won't have to worry about them coming back if we merely trap them again. People have already tried that. It doesn't work forever."

Ruari caught my eye, understanding where I was going with this. I'd explained to them what Sirius had said, that Nellie's attack was the reason he'd softened. It was as if the forced healing of his body had healed the darker side of him.

"You want Nellie to attack them all?" he asked, narrowing his eyes. "You're saying we shouldn't risk our lives to fight them, but you're willing to let her do it instead? Your own fucking si—"

"Ruari," Nellie said quietly. "Stop."

"No," he breathed. "I swore to protect you. If that means protecting you against your sister's machinations, then so be it."

I caught Kalen's gaze across the table, expecting him to step in, but that uneasiness in the bond was back. "You would risk Nellie?"

I sighed and tried to answer, but Nellie cut in.

"Ruari, I appreciate what you've done to protect me. Truly. But this is my decision, not yours. And if I'm the one who can stop this, I'll happily do it."

Toryn watched from his seat directly across from Nellie. His face was impassive, but his jaw faintly twitched. His fingers tightened against the table. But then he sighed and folded his arms, doing his best to appear unbothered. I wasn't certain if my sister noticed these two men hanging on her every word. Nothing in her expression seemed to indicate she did.

I cleared my throat. "I appreciate your dedication, Nellie." I turned to Ruari. "And I appreciate what you've done for my sister." Then I addressed everyone else, including Kalen, with his strange expression of suspicion.

"But no, I don't want to risk my sister. We have Callisto's essence in a gemstone. The beasts I encountered after trapping her acted strangely docile around me. Some attacked me when I found Kalen, but then they ran off. I think we might be able to use her essence to control the beasts. We can turn them against the gods. Their claws and fangs will do the same thing to them that Nellie's did."

A deafening silence blanketed the hall. Everyone at the table stared at me. I suddenly wished I could take it all back. It was a monstrous idea. I never should have suggested it. Using the gods' power had doomed Oberon. The last thing I wanted was for one of us—or all of us—to end up like him.

Fenella cracked first. "What a ridiculously terrible idea. I love it."

I blinked. "You do?"

"Well...*love* might be the wrong word. But I definitely think you're on to something, and it might be the only way to save the world. Though, I'll admit, I'm disappointed we can't just kill them all."

"If there was a way to do that," I said, "I'd agree. But they're indestructible. I truly believe there's no way to wipe them from existence."

"So that's what we must do," Ruari said tiredly, though a smile played across his face. He was clearly relieved he wouldn't have to battle with me to keep Nellie safe.

But I looked at Kalen. His opinion mattered most. He massaged his jaw, his gaze locked on the far wall. He shook his head, and my stomach dropped.

"Andromeda's power corrupted my mother. It led to her death, Oberon's death, Morgan's death, and countless others. I would not sacrifice any of you to that kind of power, just so we could win. It is the worst fate I can imagine, and I cannot believe we're even considering this."

"In every war, there is loss, Kal," Fenella argued. "No matter what plan we conjure, someone will die. It is inevitable."

He thumped his fist on the table. Dishes rattled. Fenella arched her brow at him, but took it all in stride. The Mist Guard knew their king better than he knew himself and had likely braced themselves for this reaction.

"I don't accept it. We need a better plan."

After taking a long, slow sip of his ale, Gaven said, "Tessa could do it without risking her soul. She's had Andromeda's power running through her veins her entire life, and she's doing just fine."

Kalen flinched. "No."

It wasn't a bad idea. Gaven was right. I'd been able to resist her so far. Perhaps I could resist Callisto, too.

As if reading my mind, Kalen pinned his torturous gaze on me. "No. I won't lose you like that. I'm not afraid to admit to everyone here that it would destroy me. I would become a shell of the man you see now."

I loosed a breath, thorny vines slithering around my heart and scraping me right where it hurt. When I'd made the marriage bond with Kalen, I hadn't truly understood what it meant for him if I died. But I knew now. If he lost me, he'd lose himself, too. Fenella often wore a wicked smile, but the ghost of her pain lingered in her eyes. She'd never fully healed from losing her husband.

"Gaven is right, though," I tried to explain. "I can feel the darkness of Andromeda's power inside of me. I always have. But I also know how to withstand it now. I've fought against it. Being here with everyone in this room, being in Endir now, it's proof of that. She did everything in her power to bring me over to her side and rip away my humanity. But I rejected it as surely as I say to you now that I can do it. This could be how we win."

Ruari reached out and squeezed my hand, nodding. "My father ordered me to watch you for most of your life. I've seen the battle you've faced, and I've seen you fight back. If anyone could do this, it's you. I truly believe that."

I looked at him, surprised. He'd never mentioned that before. "He had you *watch* me?"

"Well, yes, and..." He winced, then pulled back his hand. "He knew about your power, of course. I watched Nellie, too. I suppose I feel a bit responsible for you both."

That explained a lot.

Kalen shoved up from the table and walked away. His shoulders were tight as he strode the length of the Great Hall, his back facing us. I started to follow, but Fenella shook her head in warning.

Toryn sighed. "Give him a moment. He's grieving for his mother, even if she was no longer herself in the end. To him, it likely feels as if he's losing her all over again, and the first time he lost her..."

"He started a war," I finished for him.

"And now he's worried he'll lose you, too," Gaven supplied in a quiet voice. "To the same thing, in fact. The manipulation and corruption of the gods."

Ruari suddenly coughed. I turned to him with a frown. Fae never coughed, though he was part human. His face had gone ghostly pale. Even his horns looked ashen compared to their usual midnight black. He rubbed his chest, shaking his head. His lips were quivering like he was seconds away from a sob.

"Are you all right?" I asked, leaning toward him.

He scooted further down the bench, away from me. "My stomach aches."

"Your *stomach*?" Toryn grabbed Ruari's tankard and frowned into the depths of it. Then he sniffed. "You've had the same ale as the rest of us, yes?" He looked around the table. "Anyone else in pain?"

Gaven shook his head. "Fine here."

"You think someone tried to poison us?" Fenella took the tankard and smelled the contents. "Nothing seems off. And wouldn't we all feel the effects by now?"

"He's part human. Perhaps that's why it's hit him first." Nellie climbed from the table and approached Ruari, but he held up his hands in warning.

"Stay back. We don't know what's wrong with me." His voice was shaky and rough, barely above a hoarse whisper.

She frowned. "Could it be from the beast who attacked you? Perhaps your wound hasn't fully healed yet. We should get someone to take a look at you and—"

Shouts erupted from the corridor. I straightened, my breath catching as several armored fae rushed into the

Great Hall. The one leading the charge was the guard who'd welcomed us at the gate. Her yellow hair was plastered to her damp forehead, and deep lines bracketed her mouth.

She looked around the room until she spotted Kalen near the far wall. Her shoulders relaxed, though the fear in her eyes remained. "Kal, we've got company. The gods are here."

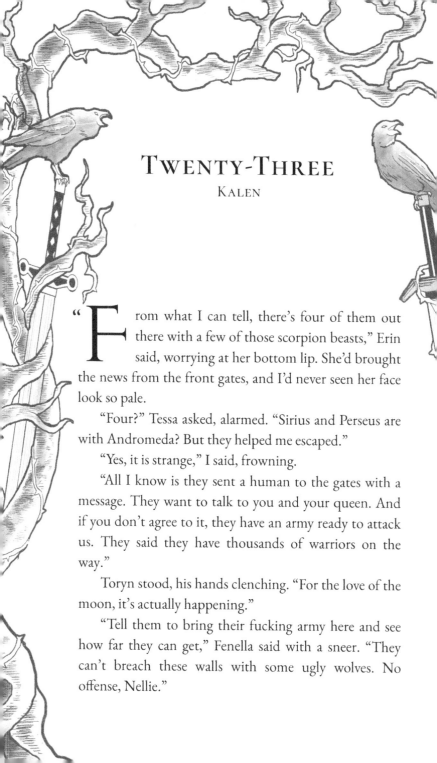

TWENTY-THREE
KALEN

"From what I can tell, there's four of them out there with a few of those scorpion beasts," Erin said, worrying at her bottom lip. She'd brought the news from the front gates, and I'd never seen her face look so pale.

"Four?" Tessa asked, alarmed. "Sirius and Perseus are with Andromeda? But they helped me escaped."

"Yes, it is strange," I said, frowning.

"All I know is they sent a human to the gates with a message. They want to talk to you and your queen. And if you don't agree to it, they have an army ready to attack us. They said they have thousands of warriors on the way."

Toryn stood, his hands clenching. "For the love of the moon, it's actually happening."

"Tell them to bring their fucking army here and see how far they can get," Fenella said with a sneer. "They can't breach these walls with some ugly wolves. No offense, Nellie."

"No, but the gods have wings. A wall will never stop them," Tessa pointed out.

I nodded, though I didn't meet her gaze. I wanted to. Fuck, I wanted to. But she's suggested doing the very thing I'd always fought against. Everything in me was against everything she'd said. I couldn't even believe she'd suggested it.

It was the very thing that had taken *everything* from me.

And I couldn't stop thinking about what my storm fae captor had told me in that cave. The gods had planned to strip away Tessa's humanity. They wanted to change her into someone more like them. Had they actually done it? She'd admitted to killing an innocent human. And now she was suggesting we use a god's power. A power that would corrupt us all. Not to mention Sirius and Perseus were now on the offensive. If they'd helped Tessa escape, why would they be here? What if she hadn't escaped the gods, after all? What if they'd *let her go*?

I couldn't bear to think it.

I cleared my throat and forced away those thoughts. "We'll ride out to meet them. Get the horses ready."

"Kal, no." Fenella shoved back her chair. "That's not what I meant. You can't go out there. They'll kill you both."

Tessa shook her head. "No, they won't. Not unless I take the gemstones with us. They're our bargaining power."

The gates cranked open, and a whistling wind rushed in from the depths of the night. The mists were back now. Strands of darkness swirled around us, like fingers of our worst nightmares dragging us toward our enemies. Out of the corner of my eye, I saw Tessa straighten on her horse. She faced the danger ahead with brave determination. She wouldn't back down from this. It was one of the many things I loved about her.

That courageousness, that unyielding side of her, clashed with her sudden interest in using the gods' power for our own gain. The Tessa I'd met all those months ago, the one who had been fleeing in the mist, she never would have wanted that. I could scent Tessa's lies before, but what if I no longer could? What if my worries were right? What if they'd changed her, then let her go?

I shook my head. I couldn't let my thoughts stray in that direction. Not now. Not when we were moments away from facing the gods.

I urged my horse onward. Sand dusted my legs as he took off at a gallop. Silver kept pace, falling into a rhythm beside me. According to the messenger, the gods were only a few hundred meters east. They were holding torches to act as beacons to draw us near.

"Kalen, you've barely said a word to me," Tessa called out over the thundering hoofbeats.

"Now is not the time for talking. We draw near to the gods. Prepare yourself."

Tessa might not need to prepare herself. If this was some kind of trap, I would have to act quickly to get out of it alive. My power was clearly dangerous to these creatures, even if they could mute it. They'd gone to great lengths to minimize how it could be used against them. They'd even trapped me in a cave, hoping to neutralize me that way.

What if they'd decided just to kill me?

"If this is about what we were talking about earlier—" Tessa tried.

"Torchlight ahead." I pointed at the hazy orange light spilling toward us. From here, I could make out four darker shapes outlined by the mist. They each stood with wings flared behind them. Not a single beast was in sight, but that didn't mean they weren't near.

"Stop!" a woman's voice commanded as we slowed. "Approach the rest of the way on foot, or you forfeit any chance of negotiation."

I frowned.

"My fault, I think," Tessa said quietly. "They must have learned what Silver is."

I didn't like it, but I did as they asked. Before moving away, I patted my horse on the snout and whispered in his ear, "Stay close. Be ready to run if I command it."

The horse whinnied and stomped his hooves. He wasn't a joint eater, like Tessa's beast was, but he understood me all the same. Most elite shadow fae were able to communicate with animals. I tipped back my head. Boudica soared overhead, keeping watch with her keen eyes. If all went wrong this night, she would fly straight to Toryn and show him everything that had happened here.

"You ready?" Tessa whispered as she pressed down the front of her fighting leathers. She wore a sword at her back, though the sheath at her hip was eerily bare. I'd gotten so accustomed to seeing the Mortal Blade there.

"Just stay close to me," I replied, praying to the moon that I was wrong about my suspicions. But even if I wasn't, she was my mate. I'd still lay down my life to protect her. "If I say run, run."

She nodded.

Together, we walked into the circle of light, where three monstrous gods stood shoulder-to-shoulder. All wore plated amor with slits on the backs for their wings, making it impossible to tell much about them. All I could see were their crimson eyes, glowing through their helms. Andromeda stood in front, clad in black leathers that were painted with golden ancient symbols. She hissed when she saw us, flashing her elongated canines.

Beside me, Tessa stiffened. I pressed a hand against her back by instinct.

"Hello, daughter," Andromeda said, pinning her narrowed gaze on Tessa. "How lovely it is to see you again, though I question your company. Kalen Denare is no good for you."

"Better company than you," Tessa replied without even a hint of fear in her voice.

Andromeda laughed. "I'm not sure I can agree with that. He's weak. And he's going to lose. You are on the wrong side."

"He hasn't forced me to kill anyone. That alone makes him ten thousand times better than any of you."

Orion stood on the far left with Perseus and Sirius beside him. The two who'd helped Tessa escape averted their gazes. But Orion looked right at her and growled, "You say that and yet you murdered one of my sisters."

"I thought you said I didn't kill her."

"Came close enough for me to want to rip your head off," he snapped back.

"How's your wing?" she asked sweetly.

"Fully healed. A pitiful thing like you could never do any lasting damage."

"Enough," Andromeda snapped at Orion, clearly irritated. "We have not come here to bicker." She turned to Tessa. "Give us the gemstones, and we agree to fall back to Malroch. As I told you before, we have no wish to see the end of the fae people. We do not need to battle you to achieve our mission."

"You sent the warriors of Star Isles against Dubnos," I said. "Is that not battle? Is that not war?"

Andromeda waved her hand dismissively. "That was not our doing. The people of Star Isles took it upon themselves to attack you, hoping it would gain our favor."

"And didn't it?" I asked.

"Well, it certainly proved their loyalty to us, and for that, I am grateful. It's more than I can say for you and your people, Kalen Denare."

I laughed bitterly. "Why would I be loyal to the creatures who have taken everything from me?"

"Gods, not creatures," Orion snapped.

"You are no gods," I said, smiling at the way he

flinched against my words. "You're locusts called Lamiae and nothing more."

Andromeda's face screwed up in rage. She took a step toward me, reaching for the sword at her back, but then she stopped. After a moment, she burst out into laughter. "You have no idea just how ridiculous that sounds."

"We don't have the gemstones," Tessa suddenly said. "They're hidden away, and no, they're not in Endir. Killing everyone inside the city will do nothing but paint more blood on your hands. Oh, and by the way." She quickly flicked her eyes toward Perseus before dealing Andromeda a keen, wicked smile. "Bellicent Denare is dead. And without an anchor, you're fucked when we banish you from this world again. Checkmate, Andromeda."

I smiled. *That's my wife.*

Andromeda moved in a flash. One moment, she was a few feet away. The next, she had Tessa's leathers gripped in her hands, and she was lifting my mate from the ground. I grabbed the hilt of my sword. Steel hissed against my neck as Orion got there first. He looked into my eyes with his blade pressed against my throat and said, "Careful."

I swallowed, and the sharp edge cut my skin. A trickle of blood danced down my neck.

Andromeda spat into Tessa's face. My vision went black, and rage burned the back of my throat.

"Get your fucking hands off my mate," I growled.

"Here is the deal, *daughter*," Andromeda whispered into Tessa's face. "We want our brethren back. Give them to us by dawn, or we will attack this city. I don't care if the gemstones are inside Endir or not. We will kill every living soul you're trying to protect. You can consider it your punishment for murdering my beloved Bellicent."

She released her hold on the leathers. Tessa thumped to the ground, and her knees buckled beneath her. I flinched and tried to reach out for her, but Orion's blade kept me pinned in place.

Tessa brushed herself off and stood. She threw back her shoulders. "You're inside the Kingdom of Shadow now, Andromeda. Dawn will never come."

"You best believe it will." Her smile was animalistic. "Look to the east in five hours' time. I think you'll find that the gods control more than you think."

Andromeda took several steps back to join the silent Sirius and Perseus. Mist engulfed her form. "Five hours, Tessa Baran. Meet us here with the gemstones, or your people will meet our swords. And we will bring death, fear, pestilence, and famine upon you."

Orion laughed. "Famine is already there, of course."

"What?" I cut my eyes toward him.

He lowered his sword and sketched an exaggerated bow. "I'm surprised you aren't the one she infected, to be honest. Does she not touch you the way you yearn to be touched? Or does she save that touch for another? Either way, I infected her with famine. As Andromeda's daughter, she's immune to it and can only spread it to one person, but..." He grinned wickedly. "If she touched anyone recently, she passed it on to them."

But who...?

Tessa gasped. "Ruari."

"Fuck," I muttered, rushing toward my waiting horse.

If Ruari was infected with famine, it was only a matter of time before he spread it to the rest of the city. I'd been too distracted, too focused on Tessa's sudden change of heart about the gods' powers. I should have seen it. I should have known.

We hadn't faced a single battle yet, but Endir was doomed.

TWENTY-FOUR
NIAMH

"Wait, he's doing it now?" Val ran a comb through her burnished red hair and sighed. She dropped the comb onto her cot and stood, her stomach growling. "It's time for dinner in the mess hall."

"You know what Alastair is like." I shrugged and leaned against the doorframe. Val's gaze swept down the length of me, back up, then down again. She blushed.

"You look very intimidating when you stand like that," said Val.

"The last thing I want is to intimidate you."

She stepped a little closer, smiling. "It's not a bad thing. In fact, I—"

Heavy footsteps thundered down the corridor in a unique canter that could only belong to one person in the whole fucking world.

"Now?" I whirled toward him, no longer caring about hiding my feelings. I'd been holding them back for so long, they were spilling out of my eyeballs. And Val was looking at me like she might see it, too, and she wasn't running away from it.

"It worked," Alastair said as he slid into Val's cramped cabin. He closed the door quietly but firmly behind him. "Old Duncan is leaving his nest."

I waited a moment, calming my irritation. This was important.

"How long do you think we have?" I asked.

Alastair spun the ring in his left ear and went silent, thinking. Sometimes I wanted to snatch that damn thing out of his fingers. "It was only a small fire, so...it'll take ten minutes or so for him to deal with it. Then it'll probably take him ten more to shout at the poor deckhands."

"Fire?" Val gaped at him, her pale cheeks reddening to the color of her hair. "You didn't say anything about a fire."

"Well, you asked me to lure him out of his room. On a ship, fire's the best way to do that," he said with a shrug. Then he laughed. "I waited to see the look on his face when he ran out of his cabin. Think I nearly gave the old man a heart attack."

Val squinted at him. "You have a strange sense of humor."

"That's because I have a good sense of bullshit. And that king is full of it." He threw open the door and dragged Val with him, motioning for me to follow. "Come on. I know you're dying to see what he's been scribbling."

Val just sighed. Like me, she'd learned it was best to go along with Alastair's whims. When he got an idea into his head, he was fairly relentless. If we didn't go with him, he'd go by himself. And besides, he was right. I *was* dying to know what was in those papers.

When we reached his cabin door, we found it was locked. Not a problem. Alastair used his dagger to pick the thing with ease. We all hurried inside and closed the door. Immediately, I wrinkled my nose. The pungent scent of fish clung to the air.

Alastair pointed at the king's desk. It was hidden beneath piles of parchment, but a stack of plates sat on the edge of one side, where remnants of his last meal sat collecting flies. It looked like it had been there for a while based on the mold splotches.

"Suddenly, dinner in the mess hall no longer seems so appealing," Val said, looking a little green.

"We should still go there once we're done. Duncan's less likely to suspect us if we can make it seem like we were there the whole time." I moved to his desk and lifted a piece of ancient parchment. It rattled like old bones.

"You two look around." Val swallowed. "I'll stand outside as a lookout."

"Sounds good, Val," I said.

She hurried back outside and closed the door behind her. I turned my attention to the paper, squinting at the strange words.

"What's it say?" Alastair asked, coming to stand behind me.

"It says you have the worst fucking timing in the world."

Alastair's chest rumbled with deep-throated laughter. "I knew you'd cave. You kiss her yet?"

"No," I said, throwing him a look over my shoulder.

"I might have, if you hadn't thundered into the middle of a conversation. Again."

"Kind of couldn't be avoided. There was the fire and the old king to deal with, remember?" He snatched the parchment from my hands. "If you're not going to read it, give it here."

"Has anyone ever told you that you're like an annoying little brother who—"

"Niamh." Alastair's smile dropped, and he suddenly looked far more serious than I'd ever seen him. Gone was the joking tone, the glint of laughter in his eye. He looked stone cold, as if a bucket of blood had been dumped over his head. Though he'd probably still laugh in that situation.

"What is it? What's it say?"

"This doesn't make any sense."

"*What* doesn't make any sense?"

"Here. You look at it." He shoved it back into my hands, then he moved over to the desk to grab another piece of parchment.

Frowning, I looked down at the words, written in an inky scrawl that had faded so much it was difficult to read.

Beasts of all shapes and sizes will claw from the depths of the earth. The Aesirian lakes, rivers, and seas will turn red with blood. But there shall be no beasts in or near Talaven. The mortal kingdoms will remain safe.

"This is a bit odd." I glanced back up at Alastair. He'd

moved behind the desk and was rifling through all the papers.

"Stating the obvious, eh?" He slid a paper across the desk. I quickly read it.

When the end comes, stars glisten, gleaming brightly. A lone blade curves through the waterfall of terror. An axe rises from the dust to deal the death. Crimson flashes teal. A song wails. Ancient forces answer. Doom drips freely upon me as ravens fly.

"Well, this one is certainly something." I added it to the stack nearest me, shivering.

"Another one." This time, Alastair read it out loud. He said, "The warriors of Talaven should answer the call for aid." Alastair paused and glanced up. "You will incur no losses until you reach the shores of Aesir."

I winced. "That didn't exactly happen."

"Two different people wrote these." He fanned the crinkling pages. "Maybe more than two. The cadence of the words is different."

"It's more than that." I pointed at the first paper and then the one he'd read. "These two are clear and to the point. The one about the doom dripping freely sounds more like a dream. Or a nightmare."

"What do you think it means?"

"I think it means something's fucked. The king said we'd be on the right path if Tessa spread her wings. Talaven rejoiced when she did. And yet, there are beasts in these waters, Talaven has lost people already, and the king is panicking. We've gone off course."

Alastair sank into the chair. "That's what I thought you'd say. So what do we do about it?"

"We get back to Kal, and we fight." I sounded a lot more emphatic than I felt. Inside, I was wavering against the reality of this. We'd come all this way. If these visions were right, it had all been for nothing. "How do we win? I don't know. Maybe we don't."

"Very optimistic of you," he drawled, twirling his earring.

"See anything to indicate I'm wrong?"

"No." He waved the pages. "But there are a lot of visions here. Maybe we shouldn't jump to conclusions. Maybe we should keep reading."

I sighed. I didn't think it was going to make a lick of difference, but we probably wouldn't get another chance to look at these. "Might as well. Hand some over."

The door cracked open, and Val poked her head inside. "I heard shouting. I don't know if they're coming this way, but it might be a good idea to get out of here." Her gaze shifted to the parchment I held. "Find anything?"

With the door open, I could now hear the shouting. They did seem closer than was comfortable. I carefully placed the pages back on the desk where I thought we'd found them. "Come on. We should head to the mess hall and—"

The floor bucked. The sudden movement tossed me sideways. I skidded across the wooden floor toward Val. Alastair jumped to his feet to follow. A steel beam crashed down from the ceiling, landing between us. Chunks of wood and sheets of paper sprayed the air.

"Niamh!" Val shouted and grabbed my arm, tugging me away from the debris. I shook her loose and ran toward the beam. My heart shot up to my throat.

"Alastair!" I tried to shout his name, but it came out a croak. Fear had stolen my voice away. Still, I tried, desperate to reach him. "Alastair, can you hear me? Alastair!"

The ship groaned. A shudder went through the floor. Val stumbled into me. I grabbed her around the waist and held her close.

"What's happening?" she whispered.

"Something's hit the ship."

Together, we edged closer to the beam. Val held me steady as I peered beneath the wood. I hadn't seen or heard Alastair since the thing had fallen. He could be stuck beneath it, unconscious. I was strong, but I didn't think I'd be able to move it if he was. Eyes burning with unshed tears, I braced myself to call upon every ounce of my strength.

His face popped in front of me, grinning. "You sound worried about me. Careful. I might start to think you don't find me as annoying as you say you do."

"Fucking fuck, Alastair." I snarled at him, and he snarled right back. But then he tried to move the beam so he could reach us, and my irritation died. It didn't budge.

"You're stuck," I said.

"Technically...the beam is stuck. I just happen to be on the wrong side of it."

"Can't you lift it?" Val asked.

Alastair shrugged and wrapped his beefy arms around the beam. A moment later, he was sweating and groaning and making all sorts of noises that should be reserved for the bedroom. Breathing heavily, he stopped and sagged against the wood.

"No, you're not allowed to give up," I snapped. "Grab the beam again. We can move it together."

He looked at me through the crack, and I could tell by his expression he'd accepted defeat. But without argument, he wound his arms around the wood and waited for me to do the same. Heart pounding, I nodded.

"Ready? One, two, three, heave!" I shouted.

I pulled with all my might, straining to lift the beam. The damn thing didn't so much as creak from our efforts.

I let go and stepped back, frowning. "Let's try again."

"It's not happening, Niamh." Alastair shook his head. "It's too heavy, even for us."

"I'll go find some more strong people," Val said, then hurried out the door.

The ship shuddered.

That was when I noticed my feet were wet.

I looked down. Salt water coated the entire floor like a thin layer of paint.

"We're sinking," I said.

"Stating the obvious again, my old friend," Alastair said with a wink.

Sighing, I turned and leaned against the beam, settling my head on the wood. I felt Alastair do the same on the other side. A few strands of his glossy dark hair sprang through the crack and tickled my neck. It was so familiar, so him.

I exhaled heavily. "What are we going to do?"

"You and Val are going to escape to the deck and hope for the best. People have survived shipwrecks before."

"I'm not leaving you," I said with a scowl.

"You've got to. For Val. I doubt that girl has ever swum in a choppy sea before. She's got no hope of reaching the shore without your help."

"The humans have some smaller boats on board. They'll put her in one of those, and she'll be fine."

"I love you, too, Niamh," he murmured.

I swallowed around the lump in my throat. "Don't you get mushy on me now. If I'm going to face the end with you, you better damn well do it like you face everything else. Start grinning and cracking jokes and being so bloody annoying I could punch you in the face."

He chuckled, then fell silent. A moment later, he asked, "What if I remind you that you're Kalen's heir? Will that get you to leave?"

"I don't think heirs matter anymore." A few tears sliced my cheeks. "The ship will sink. The gods will win. No one will be alive to rule the Kingdom of Shadow because Aesir will be no more. The doom is here."

Alastair's booming laughter drowned out the ship's creaks and pops. "You sound like the parchment that had the nightmare written on it."

I pressed my lips together, then said, "I wonder if that's the prophecy King Duncan Hinde has been so desperately trying to stop from happening."

"Ah." He sighed. "Well, it's a shame he failed. This is a good life."

"A good life," I repeated.

I threaded my hand through the crack. Alastair

wrapped his fingers around mine in a soft but steady grip. We fell silent as we listened to our world falling apart around us. The shouts had grown louder now. Some of them were screams. Water crept higher, seeping into my trousers. The ship shuddered and popped. Every now and again, it lurched to the side before rocking back the other way.

For so long, I'd believed I was meant to die in the glory of battle. I would go down the way I lived, furious and determined and loyal to my kingdom. I would protect my people with my life. I would rage against any enemy who threatened us harm. My final breaths would be worth something.

They would *mean* something.

I never would have expected that dying in the belly of a ship would mean a moons-damned thing. But it did. It meant staying with my friend, the man who had become like a brother to me. No bard would ever sing a tune about my bravery. I wouldn't be commemorated as a statue, forever memorialized with an arrow in my hand.

I had no children, no heirs of my own.

I would be forgotten. But none of that mattered when Alastair needed me.

I smiled. "Hey, Alastair, you remember that time I fought Oberon on the battlefield?"

My old friend groaned and thunked his head against the wooden beam. "Oh no, not this again."

"You see, this scar on my face came from Oberon. I was an archer that day, fighting on the border between the Kingdom of Shadow and the Kingdom of Light, and—"

"You weren't in the thick of it yourself," Alastair finished for me.

I grinned. "You're supposed to let me tell the story."

"Only if you promise this will be the last time you force it upon me."

My heart throbbed. Swallowing, I nodded and tried to sound lighthearted. "I swear it."

Val rushed into the king's cabin, wielding an axe. The light from the gemstone lanterns glinted along the twin curving blades, cutting sharp shadows across the bucking floor. Val took one look at my face, pointed a finger, and frowned.

"No, you're not giving up. Move out of my way," she said with the kind of bravado only Val could possess at a time like this.

I slowly climbed to my feet. "Where did you find that?"

"I took it from the storeroom," she snapped. "You're not getting out of the damn way. We don't have much time. The ship is sinking!"

Dumbstruck, I shifted to the side, then thought better of it. "Let me do it. You don't know how to swing an—"

Val charged in and slammed the axe into the wood with enough force to crunch the beam. It shuddered inwardly, and splinters exploded toward us. I danced out of the way, watching in awe as Val swung the axe at the beam again. She kept going, over and over, until she'd made a big enough opening for Alastair.

He awkwardly twisted through the rubble, patted Val

on the shoulder, and gave me a look. "You better keep your promise now that we're not dying."

I barked out a laugh, delirious with relief. "We're not out of danger yet."

Val handed me the axe. She smiled. "Glad I finally got to swing one of those things."

We took off running down the dimly lit corridor toward the stairwell that would lead us to the deck. Water sloshed around our feet. It was up to my shins now, and up to Val's thighs. Remnants of a ship's life bobbed by: wine goblets, boots, buckets, and broken gemstone lanterns. We ducked our heads into each room we passed, just in case anyone else had gotten trapped. Thankfully, the rooms were all empty.

When we finally reached the stairwell, my entire body was soaked from the rising water. I motioned for the others to stop. "Listen. We don't know what we'll find up there. Blood might paint the deck. From pirates or gods or beasts, we don't know. But something has attacked this ship. Hold yourself steady."

Val swallowed and nodded. Alastair simply grinned. He'd been born for this.

We rushed up the stairs, leaving the watery depths behind. I flung open the door at the top. Chaos met my eyes.

Sailors screamed, running past. A tentacle, twice the size of me, searched for purchase. It squirmed its way across the deck with suckers the size of my head. I ground my teeth. So that was it, then. Another one of those beasts had found us.

I ran toward it with the axe raised. Val shouted at me, panic in her voice. But we had to stop this thing or—

The ship lurched sideways. My boots slid across the wet deck, and my body slammed into the edge. Pain exploded through my ribs.

I reached for purchase, but my fingers slipped.

The waves consumed me.

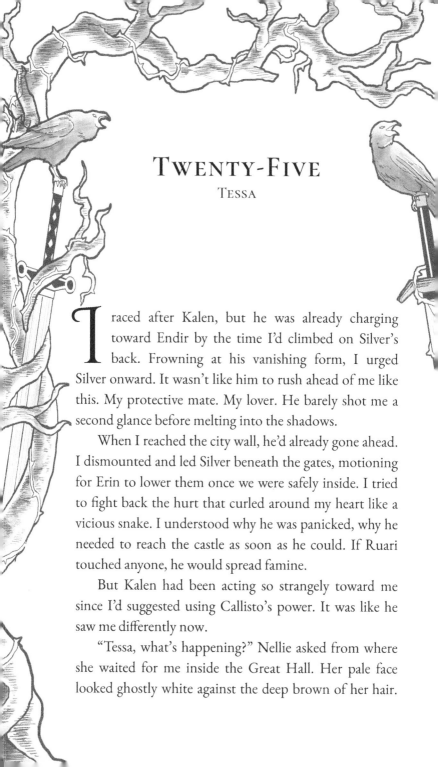

TWENTY-FIVE
TESSA

I raced after Kalen, but he was already charging toward Endir by the time I'd climbed on Silver's back. Frowning at his vanishing form, I urged Silver onward. It wasn't like him to rush ahead of me like this. My protective mate. My lover. He barely shot me a second glance before melting into the shadows.

When I reached the city wall, he'd already gone ahead. I dismounted and led Silver beneath the gates, motioning for Erin to lower them once we were safely inside. I tried to fight back the hurt that curled around my heart like a vicious snake. I understood why he was panicked, why he needed to reach the castle as soon as he could. If Ruari touched anyone, he would spread famine.

But Kalen had been acting so strangely toward me since I'd suggested using Callisto's power. It was like he saw me differently now.

"Tessa, what's happening?" Nellie asked from where she waited for me inside the Great Hall. Her pale face looked ghostly white against the deep brown of her hair.

"Kalen came back extremely agitated. He barked at every-one, demanding to know where Ruari went."

Alarm flashed through me. "Ruari's not here?"

"No, why? What's going on?"

"Where did he go?"

She shrugged. "He wasn't feeling well, remember? I sent him to Druid Balfor."

"Druid Balfor?" My stomach dropped. "Fuck. We need him."

I pushed past her, but she grabbed my arm. "You're scaring me, Tessa. Tell me what's going on. What happened out there with the gods?"

As quickly as I could, I filled her in. Her cheeks continued to pale as the reality of our situation sank in. "He has famine? But..."

"Did he touch anyone else before he went to Druid Balfor, Nellie?" I asked her. "Fenella and Toryn...they didn't...?"

"No, no." She shook her head, her bottom lip trembling. "I don't think so, anyway. I wasn't really paying attention to who he was touching!"

I grabbed her shoulders, grounding her. "Nellie, deep breaths."

Her gaze locked with mine. Tears rolled down her cheeks. "I hated him. I hated him so much. But he's tried so hard to make up for what he did. He protected me out there." She gestured vaguely at the outside world. "He almost died trying to save me. The scorpion attacked him, and he struggled to heal since he's not fully fae. I honestly thought he wouldn't survive it. But now he won't survive this, will he?"

"I don't know, Nellie. I think the truth is that there *is* a cure, but only Orion can give it."

"Then we have to *make* him give it," she hissed fiercely.

My heart ached for her. "I wish we could."

"Do something, Tessa." She tightened her grip on my arm. "If you don't, I will. I'll change back into that wolf, and I'll fight him. You said it yourself. My claws and fangs can hurt the gods. What good am I if I don't use that power to stop Orion, to save someone who, who..."

"Do you love him?" I asked quietly.

"What?" The rage vanished from her face. "No, no. Of course not. I love someone else. But I do care for him now. In a different way. He's a friend. And friends become family. They are with us through everything."

"Come, then." I hooked my arm through hers and led her through the doors. "Before you charge after the gods, let's see if Druid Balfor knows of a way to heal Ruari. He's ancient and full of knowledge. He might have the answers that no one else does."

"It's not like you to be so optimistic," she said, but she shuffled into step beside me, and I could see the hope in her eyes.

Deep down, I did not believe my words. There was no way to escape the curse of death, not without Andromeda's touch—or my touch. Orion's affliction would be no different. Ruari would not survive this. What was worse, he could not stay here. The entire city would fall.

D ruid Balfor's sparsely decorated room was on the top floor of one of the towers. The circular space held a small cot, a stool, a trunk, and nothing more. Not even a carpet softened the grim space. The wooden trunk was open, revealing an array of herbs and gemstones.

Kalen and Toryn were both in the room already, exchanging fierce whispers with the Druid. On the cot in the corner, Ruari curled in on himself. His eyes were closed, and he was sweating profusely. The pillow beneath him was drenched in it. His face had turned a mottled red, and now and again, he twitched.

Nellie gasped, her hand flying to her throat.

Toryn glanced over sharply. His eyes softened when he saw my sister's horror-stricken face. "Nellie, you shouldn't have to see this."

"We have to force Orion to fix this," she said, her voice trembling.

"Has he touched anyone?" I asked.

Toryn shook his head. "No, he was worried he'd caught something, and he didn't want to spread it to us. Now that we know what it is, I wonder if he suspected the truth."

Druid Balfor nodded sagely. "When he arrived at my door, he told me not to touch him. And then he said something about Talaven."

"Talaven?" I frowned. "What would Talaven have to do with this?"

"They once told me I would starve to death if I failed," Ruari said in a voice that crackled like fire. He laughed, then coughed. "I suppose this means I've failed."

"What are you talking about?" I moved closer to his bed.

He peered up at me with bloodshot eyes. "They instructed me not to tell you anything, that it would ruin it all. But if I failed, I suppose it doesn't matter now. You should know what's coming for you." Trembling, he held his hand out toward me.

My heart squeezed. I reached to take his hand, but Druid Balfor appeared by my side, pulling me back.

"He's delirious," the old Druid said. "Likely, he's hallucinating. He might not even realize who he's talking to right now, much less understand what he's saying."

"You don't think there's any truth to his words?" Kalen asked.

"How could there be?" Druid Balfor said. "He's rambling about Talaven and warnings of starvation. It's Orion's power doing this to him, I hate to say. And I do not know of a way to save him from it."

"I do," Nellie said, stepping inside the candlelit room. "I'll rake my claws across Orion's face. That will bring out the better side of him, right? Like it did with Sirius. Then we can bring him here. He'll be compelled to undo his famine. He can make it stop."

Druid Balfor sighed heavily. "I'm afraid it would be too late, even if you managed it, my dear. A god can undo what they have done, but they must do it quickly. Within minutes."

"He's right, Nellie," I said gently. "At least that's how it's always worked with death."

She shook her head and brushed the tears from her cheeks. "This isn't fair. It isn't right."

"No, but it is my fate," Ruari croaked out. "A fate that I deserve. I've failed us all."

Back in the Great Hall, the mood was somber. After Druid Balfor confirmed our worst fears— Ruari *would* pass famine on to anyone he touched—we returned to the table to determine our next course of action. Remnants of a happier time littered the table: half-empty tankards, playing cards, and puddles of dried candle-wax. Until Kalen and I had arrived, everyone had been celebrating. They'd been happy.

Kalen now stood at the head of the table, chair pushed back, shoulders squared. Somewhere along the way, he'd donned his crown of twisting branches, and waves of his power radiated down the table. He still barely glanced my way.

"The gods are demanding we return the gemstones. If we don't, they will ransack this city and kill everyone within it," he said, his booming voice echoing through the expansive room. "We have until dawn."

I could have heard a pin drop.

Toryn braced his forearms on the table and groaned.

Fenella clucked her tongue, tossed her booted feet on the table, and started polishing one of her daggers. Gaven merely sighed.

Nellie whispered to me, "You can't return the gemstones."

"They've backed us into a corner," Fenella said. "We have to choose between Aesir and the mortal kingdoms."

Toryn nodded. "If we don't return the gemstones, they'll destroy us. But if we do, they'll use them against the humans."

"They'll bring back Callisto and put her in another body," I said. "Pandora, too, whatever she is. It means there'll be seven of them instead of five."

"Do you think that's all of them? Or are there more?" Nellie worried at her bottom lip. "What if there are hundreds of gods? What if there's an entire army of them?"

"There are seven." Druid Balfor appeared in the doorway. Lines streaked out from his eyes like whiskers, and he shuffled forward as if his body bowed beneath the weight of exhaustion. "Death, War, Fear, Famine, Pestilence, Shadow, and Storms. And they can cause a significant amount of damage if they're all in play."

"Shadow and Storms?" Kalen asked with a frown. "Those are the names of two fae kingdoms. You can't tell me that's a coincidence."

Druid Balfor ignored him and looked at me. "You have in your possession Storms and War. The essences of them, at least."

"How do you know all this?" I asked.

"I have been alive a very long time." He rubbed his

face. "And we must be careful, lest we choose the wrong fork in the path."

"What are you saying?"

"You cannot return the gemstones to the gods. Do not trust them when they say they will leave Endir alone. They want to destroy every last human in this world. And they will return here once they destroy Talaven." His eyes land heavily on me. "The mortals of Teine are in grave danger. Which means, so are the rest of us."

A shiver of dread scraped down my spine. "The gods want to kill the humans here?"

"They wish to destroy all of humankind."

Gaven let out a low whistle. "Well then. I think there's only one thing we can do in this situation. We must evacuate the city before dawn."

"And how do you propose we do that?" Fenella asked, scowling. "You don't think the gods will be watching?"

"Luckily, I know a secret way out."

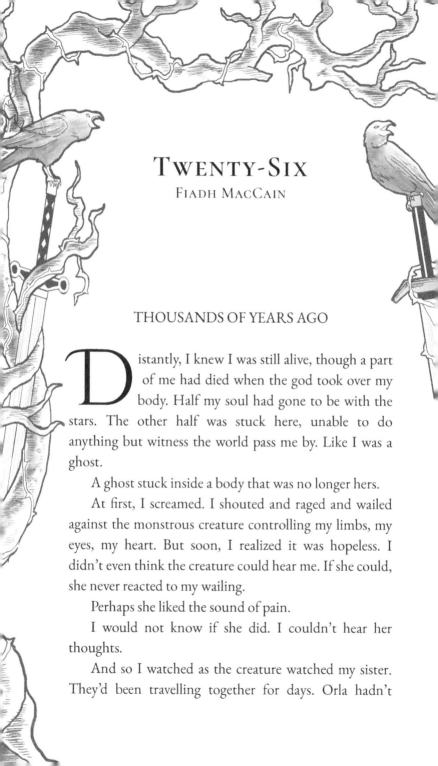

Twenty-Six
Fiadh MacCain

THOUSANDS OF YEARS AGO

Distantly, I knew I was still alive, though a part of me had died when the god took over my body. Half my soul had gone to be with the stars. The other half was stuck here, unable to do anything but witness the world pass me by. Like I was a ghost.

A ghost stuck inside a body that was no longer hers.

At first, I screamed. I shouted and raged and wailed against the monstrous creature controlling my limbs, my eyes, my heart. But soon, I realized it was hopeless. I didn't even think the creature could hear me. If she could, she never reacted to my wailing.

Perhaps she liked the sound of pain.

I would not know if she did. I couldn't hear her thoughts.

And so I watched as the creature watched my sister. They'd been travelling together for days. Orla hadn't seemed to notice I was any different, and the two of them had discussed nothing that might reveal it. Smart of the creature. She always steered the conversation toward other things when it was necessary.

So far, she had done nothing to harm anyone, let alone my sister. But I didn't like the way the creature was looking at Orla now, at her pale, sleeping face, and at the way a strand of her hair curled into her eyes like a crescent moon.

"I need your help," the creature whispered. "I cannot do this without you. I don't have the edge."

I knew she wasn't talking to me.

The creature pulled a glittering gemstone from her pocket and examined it beneath the light of the moon. It wasn't the one I'd been carrying, but another. Even in my strange, minuscule existence, I could feel fear. And it consumed me now.

"No," I said, pleading with the creature to hear me this time. "Please, leave her be."

But if the creature could hear me, she didn't care how much I pleaded or cried or begged. She flipped the gemstone in her hands, then placed it on the ground beside Orla's head. From her pocket came another stone, then another, until she'd spread thirteen of them across the parched grass.

"I could give life to some of you," she whispered as her fingers danced across the gemstones. "Bringing only the good into this world. We could help these people, give them peace and courage, abundance and health." Her fingers paused when they reached one slightly darker than the others, and her voice suddenly went hard. "But they do not deserve it."

I felt her heart pounding—my heart. She snatched the darker stone from the ground and pressed it against my sister's forehead.

"No," I moaned. "No, please."

But it was already too late. The gemstone vanished into Orla's skin. Whatever it was, it was part of Orla now.

The creature sometimes slept. It seemed to be the only thing she required, other than water and the occasional meal. I quickly gathered it was my body that caused her need for food and rest. She might be an immortal being from the clouds, but my body was fae. We lived longer than humans, but we were not immortal.

Still, I could feel a new strength in my bones. A fresh energy that buzzed like lightning. Colors were brighter. Sounds were sharper. From a mile away, I could spot a rabbit in the grass.

But when the creature slept, all I saw was a darkness so profound that I oftentimes forgot my own name. I forgot there was a world beyond the night.

She slept after touching Orla with the gemstone. I supposed the ritual had made her tired or that she was still growing accustomed to this new body she'd stolen. Either way, she slept and I screamed, and then I forgot again. When she opened her eyes sometime later—it only been hours, I knew, but it felt like decades—it all came flooding back.

The creature stood and stretched. Pink and orange streaked across the sky to signal the end of another day. For a moment, the creature watched the sunset. I could feel the awe in her. The grass whispered against her bare legs, and a light, summery breeze rustled her hair. Strands danced across her shoulders. The creature breathed in the fresh air. She savored it, tasted it.

It was as if she had not felt a breeze for a very long time. Understanding dawned.

"So, that's why you're doing it," I murmured, more to myself than to her. "You're desperate for a world and for a body to experience it. That is why you came here. That is why you changed me." A sadness stole through me at the thought of my sister. "And there are others just like you. Look at my sister. I want to see what you've done to her."

As if answering my command, the creature turned. It took me a moment to understand what she was seeing. A form huddled on the ground, right where my sister had slept. But Orla did not lie there now. In her place perched a creature unlike any I'd ever seen. It resembled a wolf in part, with its long snout, monstrous claws, and dark gray fur. But it was nearly three times the size of one, and there was a madness in its eyes. A rage so deep it made me stumble back—made *her* stumble back.

"Oh no," the creature whispered. "Andromeda, you idiot. What have you done?"

Andromeda was the creature's name. I wanted to scream at her. My hands were desperate to fight. But all I could do was watch as she crept closer to the wolf beast and place a trembling hand on its maw. The beast growled and showed its teeth. They were massive, monstrous things that could cut through flesh like it was nothing but air.

Andromeda sucked in a breath and stepped back. "I see. As you are only the darker side, there is nothing to keep you whole. You have corrupted the body and mind and have created this beast. I see, I see."

Andromeda started pacing while the wolf watched. I didn't understand what she meant. All I knew was my sister was stuck inside that beast's body. And she would see and feel *everything*. The pain and fear would be overwhelming, like it was for me. I could do nothing to comfort her. Nothing to avenge her.

Andromeda was no god. She was a monster.

"Well," Andromeda finally said. "We must try something else."

She knelt before the beast—*my sister*—once more and pulled the gemstone from her skin. Instantly, the beast collapsed, her body thumping hard against the ground. I cried out. What had she just done? Where was my sister now? Had she killed her?

Time passed slowly. Andromeda placed a blanket over my sister's body. The sun rose and set again while Andromeda waited motionless. At long last, as darkness consumed the sky, the beast stirred. Andromeda frowned and pulled back the blanket.

The beast blinked. I relaxed. She hadn't killed her. My sister was still alive in there—just trapped, like me.

Andromeda held up the gemstone. That dark

crimson light flickered faintly within it, just as it had before.

"Hmm," she said. "Very odd. The fae didn't transform back from this beast form, even though you're no longer in there. It seems the transformation is permanent when a fae is imbued with death and death alone. You always were so strong, weren't you?"

"What?" I asked, panicked. "Imbued with death? What does that mean? Have you killed my sister?"

Andromeda rubbed her thumb across the surface of the gemstone. "I had hoped to avoid this. I know you will overpower me. My light cannot fight against your rage." The creature loosed a heavy sigh. "Is there any alternative?"

A moment passed in silence. If the gemstone answered back, I could not hear it.

"Very well." Andromeda stood. "I will do this, but you *must* agree to coexist with me. Do not push me too far down. You know what must be done, and we will not succeed unless we work together. I'm the only one who can bring life."

None of this made any sense. Life and death and beasts from other worlds. Was this nothing more than a cruel dream? A nightmare? Or had something happened to steal my sanity? I tried to close my eyes against these visions, to block out the voices I clearly must have conjured. None of this was real. It couldn't be real.

But the nightmare persisted. Try as I might, I could not close my eyes.

Andromeda placed the cool stone against her forehead—*my* forehead. Power rumbled against my skin.

Horror and pain and rage crashed down on me. It felt like the weight of a thousand ships crushing my bones. My entire body shuddered. The rage slammed harder and harder against me, knocking me further into the deepest recesses of my mind. I struggled against it, desperately clinging on to the person I'd once been.

To Fiadh McCain, the girl who loved running barefoot in the grass. The girl who'd once dreamed of dancing on a stage in front of hundreds.

The girl who loved her sister fiercely.

But that girl was gone.

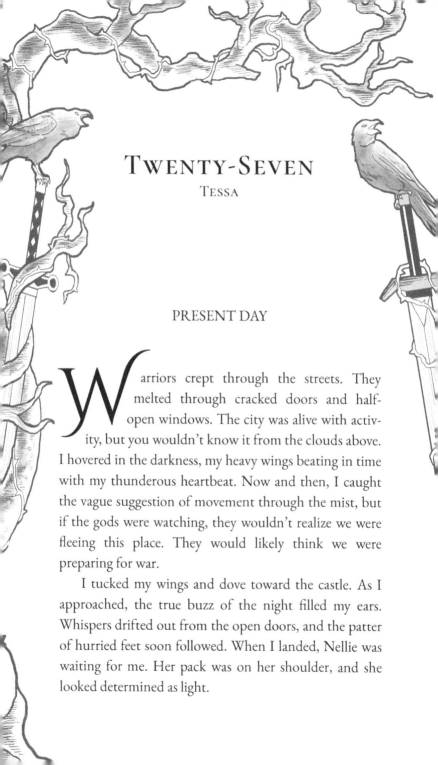

TWENTY-SEVEN
TESSA

PRESENT DAY

Warriors crept through the streets. They melted through cracked doors and half-open windows. The city was alive with activity, but you wouldn't know it from the clouds above. I hovered in the darkness, my heavy wings beating in time with my thunderous heartbeat. Now and then, I caught the vague suggestion of movement through the mist, but if the gods were watching, they wouldn't realize we were fleeing this place. They would likely think we were preparing for war.

I tucked my wings and dove toward the castle. As I approached, the true buzz of the night filled my ears. Whispers drifted out from the open doors, and the patter of hurried feet soon followed. When I landed, Nellie was waiting for me. Her pack was on her shoulder, and she looked determined as light.

"This is a good idea, yes? We're not making a mistake?" she asked.

"How about I answer that after dawn?"

She clutched my arm as I moved toward the door leading back inside the castle. "Are you sure we shouldn't be fighting them?"

"No," I answered honestly. "This city is full of innocent people, so of course we should do whatever it takes to keep them safe. If that means evacuating them, then so be it. But a part of me wants to order the warriors to stay behind. There might be enough of us to make a stand. I want to fight the gods, same as you."

"I would fight them with you."

"And I love you for it." With a sigh, I pulled my sister to my chest and hugged her fiercely. Whispering into her hair, I said, "I know this war is stealing everyone's focus, but don't think I've forgotten you, Nellie, and what you've been through. If you need to talk about it, I'm right here."

Her small arms clutched me tighter. "I know. But there's not much to say. I turned into a wolf, then I turned back."

I pulled back, searched her eyes. "Do you know why? Or how?"

"I think it's always been inside me, and leaving Teine made it come out. I couldn't control it at first, but when the scorpion knocked the wind out of me, it's like it knocked something loose. I can transform back into a wolf anytime I need to now."

"Well, let's hope it doesn't come to that."

"Why? It's just a part of me, Tessa." She smiled. "Just like death is a part of you."

I winced and looked away, but Nellie stepped in close and wagged her finger in my face. "No, you won't do that. If I'm going to accept my strange powers, you're going to accept yours. It's not a curse. It's just who we are."

"You're so much wiser than most, even the centuries-old fae," I said, unable to stop myself from smiling back. "And I'm proud to call you my sister."

"*I'm* the proud one." She pulled the Mortal Blade out from behind her back and placed it in my hands. "You're going to lead us to victory, Tessa. I've never been more certain of anything."

Surprised, I wound my hand around the hilt, the familiarity of the steel cold and refreshing against my palm. "I thought Gaven hid the gemstones somewhere outside of Endir."

"That would have taken too much time. Anyway, it was easier if you believed they were somewhere else, just in case the gods were able to scent your lies."

"Clever." I slid the blade into my sheath. I'd never removed it, despite no longer carrying the weapon. The weight against my hip grounded me. I'd grown so accustomed to it being there that I felt unsteady without it.

"I still have the other stones in my pocket. Do you want them back?"

Instinctively, I started to reach for the stones, but then thought better of it. "No, you keep them. If the gods come for me, it's best if I'm not carrying them all."

She nodded gravely. "I'll protect them with my life."

I opened my mouth to argue, but swallowed the words instead. I'd spent too long treating my little sister like she was nothing more than a fragile glass doll that could shatter from so much as a scratch. That was how I'd always seen her, and I understood why now. I'd wanted to be able to protect *someone*, since I'd never been able to protect myself from my father. And because my mind had shut down after everything he'd done, I'd forgotten that Nellie was quite capable of protecting her own damn self.

She was her own person, and I couldn't control her. I needed to loosen my grip on her. I needed to accept she might take risks I didn't want her to. And right now, she probably was the best person to be carrying those gemstones. She could damage the gods when no one else could, even me.

"Come on," I said. "Let's get our people into the tunnels. We only have a few hours until dawn."

In the depths of the earth, Endir's dungeons tunneled through the dirt. Gaven carried a torch at the head of the party, and the light illuminated empty cells stained with all manner of grime. Dust motes danced in the flickering beams, and just in front of me, Ruari coughed into his hand. I'd taken it upon myself to extract him from this place. His fate was sealed, but I would not leave him here to face the gods alone.

Nellie walked in front of him so that he was sandwiched between the only two people among us who were immune to his touch. Everyone else gave him a wide berth. Kalen had threatened to execute him if he touched a single other person. Ruari had gladly agreed to the deal.

Behind me, the humans and fae stretched out in a snaking line. The back of our party was rounded out by Toryn and Fenella. Kalen had chosen the middle of the group. He wanted to be amongst the people, to give them hope.

The hours crept by slowly. We left behind the dungeons for cramped tunnels. The fae had to duck to keep moving forward, though the low ceilings weren't a problem for me and Nellie. It was the spiders and bats that stole my breath and pushed my heart to beat faster. Now and then, dangling webs of vibrant green scratched my arms and face. Insects crawled into my hair. And it was all I could do to hold back my screams.

Ruari stumbled, boots scratching the dirt. But he laughed. He was surprisingly chipper for a man on the brink of death.

"What's so funny?" I asked him.

"This is how my mother escaped Endir. And it just seems fitting she chose this path as her salvation. She likely didn't even notice the bugs." He coughed, then laughed again. "Only Bellicent Denare would choose to slither among the grime."

"We are also slithering among the grime," I pointed out to him.

"Because we are doomed."

"You keep saying that. What makes you so certain?"

He was silent for a moment. "Because Talaven told me."

"You still haven't explained what that means."

"Druid Balfor told me to stop talking about it," he said quietly, twisting his head to gaze behind me, as if he were searching for the old man behind us. "Where is he, anyway?"

"With the other Druids, I'm guessing. I think they're near the back." I paused. "Which means he won't hear you if you tell me what you mean about Talaven."

He grumbled beneath his breath, then fell silent. I sighed. For whatever reason, he would not explain his mad mutterings. Perhaps Druid Balfor was right. Ruari was too far gone for his words to make sense.

Another hour passed by, and then another. Soon, dawn would transform the sky from mottle black to brilliant blue streaked with purple pink strands of light. It seemed impossible. The Kingdom of Shadow had not known dawn for centuries. But I didn't doubt the gods.

And when that pink filled the sky, Endir would fall.

Luckily, no one would be there when it did.

Ahead of me, Ruari slowed. I tried to crane my head around him to discover what was happening, but the walls were closing in around us too tightly for me to see anything but his head.

"Why have we stopped?" I asked.

"It looks like we've reached the exit," Nellie responded excitedly from her spot just ahead of Ruari. "I see light."

"Light?" I repeated, my heart dropping. "So dawn truly has arrived."

A part of me had hoped the gods were wrong, even though I'd expected this.

Movement began again. Ruari shuffled forward a few more steps. The walls expanded outward as the tunnel opened up somewhere ahead. His footsteps quickened, and so did mine. Soon, I was walking out into the fresh morning air. The sun shone brilliantly in the east, burning away the mist. Kalen stood in the clearing ahead, his head tipped back. Sunlight danced across his carved cheekbones, highlighting the cut of his jaw and the shadowy ink of his hair.

He looked up and caught me staring. My lips twitched as a smile threatened to fill my face. But then he turned away and stole the smile before it bloomed.

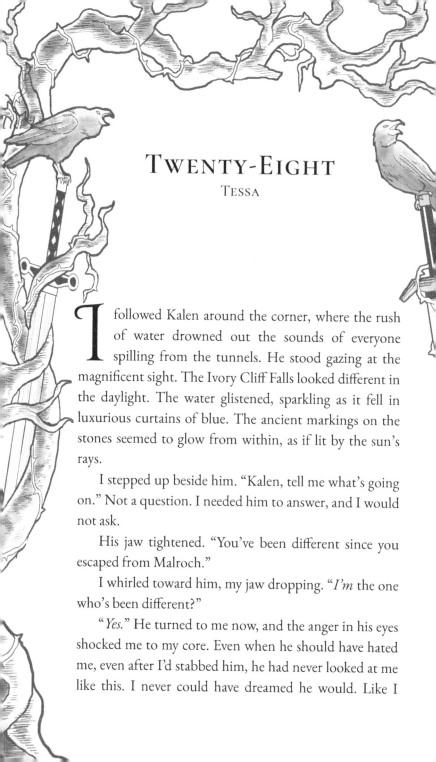

Twenty-Eight
Tessa

I followed Kalen around the corner, where the rush of water drowned out the sounds of everyone spilling from the tunnels. He stood gazing at the magnificent sight. The Ivory Cliff Falls looked different in the daylight. The water glistened, sparkling as it fell in luxurious curtains of blue. The ancient markings on the stones seemed to glow from within, as if lit by the sun's rays.

I stepped up beside him. "Kalen, tell me what's going on." Not a question. I needed him to answer, and I would not ask.

His jaw tightened. "You've been different since you escaped from Malroch."

I whirled toward him, my jaw dropping. "*I'm* the one who's been different?"

"*Yes.*" He turned to me now, and the anger in his eyes shocked me to my core. Even when he should have hated me, even after I'd stabbed him, he had never looked at me like this. I never could have dreamed he would. Like I truly was his enemy. "Tessa Baran would never suggest using a god's power. Whatever happened in that city, it changed you. Just like it changed my mother. They stripped you of your humanity just like they said they would."

Realization crashed over me. Tears filled my eyes. I reached out for his hand, but he shook his head.

"I don't believe it's you in there," he said, nearly choking out the words. "Not anymore. Look at what's happened to Ruari. You gave him famine. Tell me that doesn't seem like a design of the gods, like you haven't been working with them to tear Aesir apart."

I swallowed. He was wrong, of course, but I could see how it looked. I might have wondered the same in his shoes. But it still hurt. Light, it hurt. I trusted him more than I even trusted myself.

"Kalen, it's me. I'm more me than I ever have been. All that darkness I've fought so hard against all my life... this is the first time I've ever felt like I can *actually* control it." I ducked in close, forcing him to look into my eyes. "Look at me. Tell me you can't see the truth of me."

A pained expression crossed his face as he met my gaze. "I'm not the best judge of character. I never suspected my mother. All these years passed, and I never knew."

"If you're not a good judge of character, then neither am I." Finally, he let me take his hand. His palm was rough against mine as I threaded my fingers through his. "*We are the same*. Don't you remember? My father, everything he did...I refused to believe he was anything short of heroic. I so badly wanted to believe the best of him that I tossed a blanket over my memories and pretended they didn't exist."

He took a moment to reply. "And now?"

I blew out a breath. "And now I've moved on. With *your help*. I thought you felt the same."

"It's not that—"

I tightened my grip on his hand. "I am yours, you are mine. We made a vow, Kalen. One that supersedes all others. If I wasn't *me*, don't you think you'd be able to tell? Don't you think you would be able to *feel* the change in me through our bond? I can feel you here." I tapped my heart. "I can feel your power and your anger and your love. Can't you feel the same from me?"

He dropped his forehead against mine. Heat stormed through me. His nostrils flared as he scented me, tasting me as only he could—by reaching for the thread between us and touching the very soul of me. I leaned into him and let him pry, let the fingers of his mind dance over mine. I could feel him brushing up against my heart. I could feel his pulse quicken to match the rhythm of mine.

He was so close. Too close, if he were anyone else. If he tugged the right thread, he could unravel me. But I met his gaze and did not pull back.

His brow furrowed, and his hands slipped into my hair. His fingers tightened around my strands as he gripped me there. Finally, he spoke, his voice rough. "Why would you suggest it, love? Didn't you understand what it would mean?"

"It doesn't *mean* anything," I whispered. "You can feel me. Every part of me. I am who I say I am, and they have not changed me. Not the way you mean. What they *have* changed is my understanding of who and what they are. And I know we can use the beasts to fight them. Or at least, I can. For better or worse, I'm one of them, and the sooner we both accept that, the sooner we can save this world from ruin. Isn't that what you always wanted me to do? Accept who I am and the power I wield?"

His eyes scraped through me. "If I lost you, love, my body would buckle from the weight of my grief. And I would rip every star from the sky just to find the one that was you."

I shuddered, nearly overcome with the need to feel every part of him. "That won't happen, Kalen. I will vow it, if that's what it takes. Because I know I'm strong enough to resist their darkness."

At long last, a wicked smile curved his lips. My heart beat faster. For that smile, I would have given anything. "I love your strength. It makes me wish we were alone."

It was only then I noticed several others were wandering around the rocks, watching the sunrise over the Ivory Cliff Falls. I wondered what we looked like to them, leaning against each other and fiercely whispering words I hoped no one else could hear.

"Oh yeah?" I cocked an eyebrow, blocking out the audience. "And what, in very specific words, would you do if we were?"

"Ah." Kalen suddenly pulled back as heavy footsteps drew closer. "Unfortunately, we'll have to wait until later to discuss all things I plan to do to you."

Toryn, Gaven, and Fenella walked over with Nellie and Druid Balfor just behind them. They were covered in cobwebs, and dust coated their black leathers. Fenella looked relieved to see us together. I wondered how much our momentary rift had been noticed by the others, despite my attempts to keep it under wraps. But she'd always seen far more than everyone else.

"That's the last of them. We got everyone out," Toryn said, thumbing the hilt of his sword. "Now where to?"

Gaven pointed to a small hole in the rocks just beside the falls. It was no taller than me. "That leads into the caves beneath the lake. We can cover it up with branches once we've all gone inside. The gods shouldn't find us in there, even if they investigate this area. It's not on the maps. I made certain of that."

"Another tunnel," Fenella said flatly. "Wonderful."

"So we go into the caves and then what?" I asked. "Where do we go from there?"

Gaven sighed. "Follow the tunnels to wherever they lead. Or wait out the gods. Eventually, they'll leave, right?"

I winced. "Something tells me it won't be as easy as that."

"It won't be," Druid Balfor said, frowning. "I do not think we should go into those caves."

"The only other option is to go into the open fields, where they will spot us," Gaven said. "But it's your call."

Everyone looked at me, even Kalen. The weight of the choice pressed down on me. If I made the wrong decision, people could die.

"Is there another way out of the caves if the gods find the entrance?" I asked.

"There is," Gaven said a little hesitatingly, "but I don't know where it leads."

"Well, we're about to find out, I'm afraid." I nodded to Toryn. "Get everyone together. We're going back underground."

L uckily, squeezing through the entrance of the cave was the worst part. Carved by nature itself, the tunnels were vast, open things, where cobwebs were nothing but a distant memory. The distant rush of the falls faded as we made our way down a long, sloping ramp pockmarked by ancient stalagmites. A few bats rushed by, their black bodies spinning ahead into the darkness.

Gaven continued to lead our party, sweeping the torch left and right to illuminate strange golden carvings embedded in the stone walls. I stepped off the path, motioning for him to pause for a moment while I examined them. They were ancient things, reminiscent of the symbols on the rocks outside, where the water poured through five circular stones. But there were more of them here.

I'd seen those same symbols a few times over the years, though only ever in storybooks. They were said to be from the ancient world, carved by the people who had lived in these lands before the fae and humans. Before Aesir and Talaven had even been a dream in someone's mind, before kingdoms and wars and all the rage that permeated these lands.

But I remembered I'd seen them on Andromeda's armor, too.

Druid Balfor started to shuffle past me, but I turned and touched his arm. "Do you know what these symbols mean?"

He averted his gaze. "Same thing the symbols on the stones outside mean, I assume."

"Ah." I tried not to be disappointed. It didn't matter in the grand scheme of things. "They're interesting, don't you think? It's like they've been painted in gold, but that can't be, right?"

"Truly, Tessa Baran, sometimes it is best not to look too closely at things you don't understand. Whatever they are, they're ancient. Much like the gods. And you know, better than anyone, the depths of their wickedness."

"You think these carvings have something to do with the gods?" I asked, confirming my suspicions. "How could that be, though? Don't these symbols come from a time before the gods came here the first time?"

"Yes, of course. The symbols are far older," he replied, steepling his hands beneath his chin. "My point is, these markings are just as ancient and unknowable as the gods. And it's best not to delve in to those kinds of things, yes? They are not the gods, but they could be just as dangerous. Understand now?"

I frowned. "Right. Of course. I should have known better than to ask. Carry on then, Druid Balfor. Thank you for your advice."

He nodded sagely, then hurried away. I watched him go, my frown deepening. Druid Balfor knew more than he was saying. The look on his face when I'd asked him about the carvings wasn't curiosity or surprise or uncertainty. It was fear.

Kalen came up behind me and observed the wall of carvings. "What were you talking to Balfor about?"

"I asked him about these. He seemed alarmed." I looked up at him. "Do you trust him?"

"I don't fully trust anyone but you and my Mist Guard. Why?"

"He's been acting strangely, don't you think?" I placed my palm against the rock and felt the rough edges of the markings. The ridges were deep, carved by something forceful. "He's made it clear he knows more than he's saying, but I'm not entirely certain that's a good thing. And then when I asked him about these, he lied and said he knew nothing about them."

"What makes you think it was a lie?" he asked.

"I...I don't know. I'm just certain it was."

"You may be right." He paused as a few fae shuffled by us. When they'd passed, he spoke in a quiet voice. "There are carvings like this in some caves near Dubnos. When we were mining there, he warned us to stay away from them."

"So he did lie to me. He knows what these are, and he doesn't want to tell us." I furrowed my brow. "But why?"

Kalen's expression grew hard. "We'll have to find out. In the meantime, memorize these as best you can. We need to keep moving, but the symbols might be important. Do you think you can remember them long enough to write them down once we reach somewhere with a pen and parchment?"

"I'll do my best," I said.

Kalen gazed down at me, brushing a wayward strand of hair behind my ear. My belly flipped. "I'm so sorry for fearing the worst had happened."

"It's all right. I understand why." I palmed his leathers, then clutched them tightly, holding on to him for all I was worth. Having him here with me was the only thing keeping my feet steady. "Do you think we're going to get through this?"

"I don't know. But even if it's hopeless, we have to try. For when darkness takes us all, at least we'll know we reached for the light."

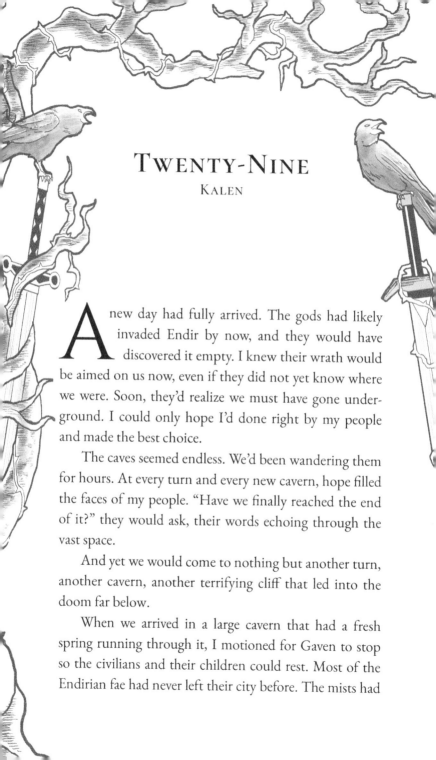

TWENTY-NINE
KALEN

A new day had fully arrived. The gods had likely invaded Endir by now, and they would have discovered it empty. I knew their wrath would be aimed on us now, even if they did not yet know where we were. Soon, they'd realize we must have gone underground. I could only hope I'd done right by my people and made the best choice.

The caves seemed endless. We'd been wandering them for hours. At every turn and every new cavern, hope filled the faces of my people. "Have we finally reached the end of it?" they would ask, their words echoing through the vast space.

And yet we would come to nothing but another turn, another cavern, another terrifying cliff that led into the doom far below.

When we arrived in a large cavern that had a fresh spring running through it, I motioned for Gaven to stop so the civilians and their children could rest. Most of the Endirian fae had never left their city before. The mists had kept them trapped behind their walls, so they were not accustomed to walking for miles. As they sat heavily on the stones and drank from the stream, I went to where Gaven was examining another wall of those golden carvings.

"We need a way out of here," I said to him. "Our people are hungry and cold."

"I know these tunnels no more than you, my king." Gaven sighed, weariness tightening the skin around his eyes. "I thought the carvings might lead us out. If people were once down here marking up the place, then surely there must be some kind of path."

I glanced around, searching for Druid Balfor. His familiar hunched figure was by the stream with the others. The bottom of his robe was filthy and he shuffled his steps, but there was a sharpness in his expression that unnerved me. He was playing at being tired, but he was as alert. More alert than Gaven. Fuck, he was more alert than me. It was as if the exertion was child's play.

"He's hiding something," I said.

"I've never trusted the Druids."

I turned my attention back to Gaven. The golden carvings almost seemed to glow, casting a bronze hue across his dark brown skin. "Why not?"

He thought for a moment before speaking. I'd always liked that about him. "They say they want to live a peaceful life worshipping the forces of nature, that they don't want to be involved in politics and war. And yet, where is Druid Balfor every time we need to discuss politics and war? Right in your war room. He always has an opinion."

"Hmm."

I thought back to my recent battle against the storm fae. I'd called for him to ask if we had any valerian, and he'd said no. Later, he'd admitted he'd lied. At the time, I'd thought little of it. I'd been annoyed, yes, but I'd assumed Balfor hated war. That assumption was quickly proving to be wrong.

A fae quickly crossed the floor, heading toward us from the tunnel we'd just exited. Shorter than most fae and as pale as an albino rat, he wore a black cloak and padded boots to soften his footsteps. I recognized him as one of my scouts. He was an expert at stealth. I'd never seen him look so frightened.

"Cathal?" Fenella asked as he ran by her. Frowning, she followed him, grabbing Toryn's arm. Tessa spotted the commotion and fell into step beside them. The four of them quickly approached.

Cathal reached me, his breath ragged, his cheeks as red as blood. He bowed. "My liege, I have a report."

"Go on, then," I said grimly.

"The gods found the entrance to these tunnels. They've followed us, my liege."

"Fuck," Fenella barked. Her voice echoed, spreading through the hushed cavern. Almost instantly, frightened murmurs spread through the crowd. She winced.

I ignored her and focused on the scout. "All of them?"

"I saw four," he said, his voice trembling. "There was one in front of the other three. A woman with red hair. She was ordering two of the others about like they were her servants. Then the fourth, he was in the back. Tall with white hair."

I nodded. "And did they see you?"

"I don't think so, my liege. No one ever sees me."

"Good work, Cathal." I firmly gripped his shoulder. "I'm going to ask you to do something now. Something extremely important to the survival of these people. But it's risky, and you might get trapped in the caves for a long time. You can say no if you don't—"

Cathal bowed lower so that the strands of his wispy hair hung into his face. "I will do it."

"All right. Good lad." I looked around at the people crowded in the cavern, fae and human alike. Children perched on rocks, where they were palming water from the stream to drink. Men and women huddled together to warm themselves from the cold. And every one of them watched us, even if they couldn't hear our words. They knew something was happening, and they were trusting us to lead them to safety.

I looked back at Cathal, hating myself for this. It should be me, not him. But I was the king, and I had to lead my people out of here. "I want you to create a diversion. Draw the gods down other tunnels, away from us. It might give us long enough to get everyone out of here safely."

Cathal's reddened cheeks paled. His hands began to tremble. But he nodded. "I will do it, my liege."

I gripped his shoulder tighter. "If we win this war, you will rise in the ranks and hold land. Itchen needs a lord."

Cathal glanced up, his eyes widening. "You would give me Itchen?"

"A city like Itchen should only go to the bravest among us. To me, that's you."

"Wait," Tessa cut in. She looked at Cathal with compassion in her eyes. I knew what she was thinking. Cathal would never hold the title of lord because he wouldn't survive this. If he led the gods away from us, no matter how good he was at stealth, they would eventually find him and cut him down. "Cathal, you've done us proud, and you should be rewarded for what you've done already. But I should be the one to draw the gods away from here."

"Tessa," I said, my jaw clenching. "You cannot—"

"They want the gemstones, and they'll assume I have them," she said quickly, tapping the dagger at her hip. "I'm the one they're after. I should be the one to lead them away from here."

"Well, if we're all throwing our hats into the fucking ring," Fenella said, brandishing her twin daggers, "I might as well volunteer my own damn self. I've got no one counting on me any longer. I should do it."

Toryn closed his eyes and sighed. "Fenella, you can't keep trying to throw your life away just because—"

"Because what?" she hissed. "Because everyone I know and love has been taken from this light-forsaken world?"

He pressed his lips together. "I wouldn't put it that way, no."

"It's a lie, anyway," Gaven said with a wink. "She loves *us*, even if she doesn't want to admit it."

A weak cough cut through the argument, followed by a rough laugh. We all turned toward Ruari, who had curled against a rock nearby. Nellie tried to dab his forehead with a wet rag, but he swatted her away. His face was screwed up in pain, but he kept laughing. After a moment, he sobered and wagged a finger at us all.

"I can't believe I have to spend my last moments in this wild and fucked up world listening to you lot. Put me out of my misery. I'll go."

"Ruari, no," Nellie said.

"It's the only solution." Ignoring Tessa's sister, he crawled onto his hands and knees, then slowly teetered to his feet. Red rimmed his eyes. His lips were white and cracked. He looked thinner somehow as he hunched over, like his body was caving in on itself. Ruari did not have much time left.

Tessa gently said, "You can hardly walk, Ruari. They'll catch up to you. And you won't be able to fight."

"I'm going to die anyway," he croaked. "At least this way I can go out doing something good."

Tears filled Nellie's eyes. Clenching her jaw, she turned away, tossing the wet rag onto the ground. She knew, just like the rest of us, that this truly was our best option. Ruari could lead the gods away from the civilians, and no one would die. No one but Ruari, whose fate was already sealed.

It didn't mean I liked it. In fact, I fucking hated it. All of us did.

"It's your decision, Ruari," I finally said. I wished I could reach out and clasp his shoulder. We'd never had time to talk about what I knew was on both our minds. In a weird and twisted way, Ruari was my half-brother.

He met my gaze, coughing. "Glad I got to meet you, even if it was brief."

"You're a good man, Ruari," I said.

From behind me, Cathal exhaled in relief. His entire body shuddered, the full depths of his fear now finally on display. The lad would have done it without complaint, without question. He would have sacrificed himself for his people. That type of courage was rare, even amongst scouts. And for that, he would be rewarded.

And then he surprised me by saying, "While Ruari leads the gods away from here, I'll continue to scout. Then I'll report back to you once they follow him."

I nodded. "If that's the plan, we best get started." I turned to Gaven. "And find us a way out of here, eh? We have one opportunity to escape, and we cannot waste it."

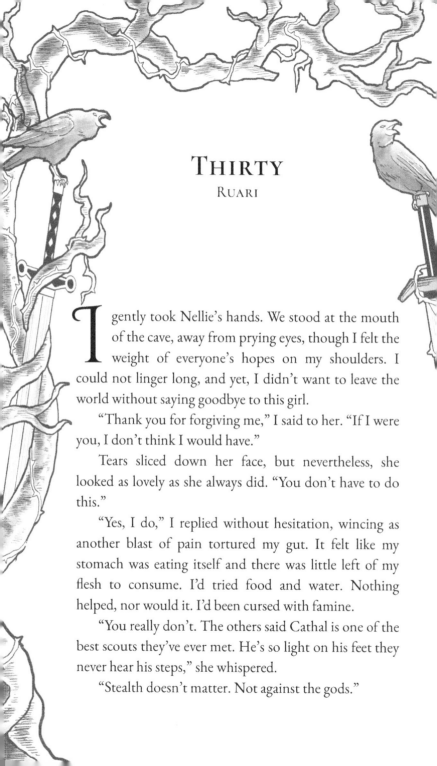

THIRTY
RUARI

I gently took Nellie's hands. We stood at the mouth
of the cave, away from prying eyes, though I felt the
weight of everyone's hopes on my shoulders. I
could not linger long, and yet, I didn't want to leave the
world without saying goodbye to this girl.

"Thank you for forgiving me," I said to her. "If I were
you, I don't think I would have."

Tears sliced down her face, but nevertheless, she
looked as lovely as she always did. "You don't have to do
this."

"Yes, I do," I replied without hesitation, wincing as
another blast of pain tortured my gut. It felt like my
stomach was eating itself and there was little left of my
flesh to consume. I'd tried food and water. Nothing
helped, nor would it. I'd been cursed with famine.

"You really don't. The others said Cathal is one of the
best scouts they've ever met. He's so light on his feet they
never hear his steps," she whispered.

"Stealth doesn't matter. Not against the gods."

She shook her head. "We can find a way to undo this."

"The only end to my story is death. I can feel it in my bones now, Nellie. No matter what anyone does, this is it for me. I'm fated to end this way." I looked at the floor, then met her deep brown eyes. "There is something I must tell you."

The mortals of Talaven had been clear. I was to never share the truth of my mission with anyone, not even my brothers and sisters. The fate of the world hung in the balance, they'd insisted. Any stumble off the path would end in ruin. But they'd also been clear about one specific thing: my death. They said it would only happen if I failed, if I did something different from the orders they'd given me.

So, I no longer saw any reason to keep the truth to myself.

I tugged Nellie closer and leaned in to whisper in her ear. "The mortals of Talaven have the power of foresight. They've been putting pieces into play across the centuries. They believe it's the only way to save the world from the gods. You and Tessa are part of it. But I've failed us all. We've gone off the correct path." I pulled back, hating the fear and confusion swirling in her eyes. There wasn't enough time to fully explain this to her. "But I made some preparations, just in case something went wrong. There is a cave in the mountains just outside of Albyria, near where you found my camp. You remember the location?"

She nodded, silent.

"Good." Another flash of pain cut through my gut. I

doubled over, but I wouldn't let a little hurt stop me from this. "I put some weapons there. Some gemstones and valerian. Even some food. It won't be enough for everyone, but it's a start. After you gather the supplies from my store, cross the bridge into Albyria. Burn the damn bridge down if you need to. And use everything in that cave to fight the gods."

"All right. I will." She swallowed. "But I don't understand all this. How can the humans see the future? What path were we on? Which one are we on *now*? Can we fix it? I need more than what you've told me."

"There's one more important thing." Pain wracked my skull. It took every ounce of self-control not to scream. "Look for the tiger-eyes. They hold a great power, one I think few know. A light fae can use it to form a shield. I saw it once. It works. Use them to protect yourselves."

"Tiger-eyes." Nellie nodded. "I'll look for those first."

Coughing, I sputtered blood into my hand. "I'm surprised you believe me. Druid Balfor has been spreading rumors I'm deranged and hallucinating."

"Tessa thinks he's hiding something. Is he?"

"The Druids know everything Talaven does," I replied. "He's likely trying to influence events based on what they've told him about the future."

Her eyes grew distant. "He thought coming into these caves was a bad idea. If he knows what path we should be on to win, we should have listened to his warning."

"Except Balfor didn't see me coming, did he?" I smiled through the pain. "This is how I will put us on the right path again. I will die fighting the gods, not by famine, like I was told. I will take the doom I've brought upon us, and I will turn it around."

She choked out a sob, then she wrapped her arms around me and gripped me tightly. Warmth flooded me, chasing away the aching cold and the hunger nearly driving me to madness. I held her close, and I wondered at the warmth I felt. This girl, this stranger I'd watched. Somehow, she'd become family.

I pulled back. "Take care of my brothers and sisters for me. And the Crones. They need someone to look after them."

"I will," she whispered.

"I won't say goodbye." And with that, I turned and hobbled into the darkness.

I didn't carry torchlight. The caves were cold, silent, and dark, and my shuffling footsteps were as loud as my father's angry roars. I could still hear them echoing in my head after all this time. I diverted my thoughts, choosing instead to focus on my brothers and sisters, on Nellie, and even on Kalen Denare. If I didn't succeed, they would die.

Wincing, I placed a gnarled hand against the wall and spat some more blood on the ground to add to my trail. Weariness rattled through me. Perhaps...perhaps I should just sit here for a time. I didn't know how long it had been since I'd departed from the cavern, but it...had been a while. Of course, everything felt like a long while underground. There was no sun to guide me.

I almost had to laugh at the irony of it all. For so long, I'd dreamt of the darkness. Unlike most light fae, I grew weary of the light. In Albyria, it had just been so...*persistent*. So unyielding. We used shutters to keep it out when we yearned for sleep, but it still found a way inside, like creeping vines slithering through every crack. If there was a way to breach a wall, it would.

And now I would get my wish. I'd die in a place so dark I couldn't even see my own hand.

Funny how these things go.

A breath of cold whispered across my face. Distant footsteps soon followed. Groaning, I pushed up onto unsteady feet.

"That would be it, then," I muttered out loud. No sense in trying to stay quiet. Hopefully my voice would slither down the tunnels and into the ears of the gods. I wanted them to find me.

Come here, you bastards.

I patted down my leathers, feeling the lump near my chest. Grinning, I crept further down the tunnel, feeling my way along. I probably should have brought a torch, but Nellie had insisted otherwise. She wanted to make it difficult for the gods to find me. Deep down, I knew she hoped I'd survive.

But I had taken a little something from the castle when no one had been looking. I hadn't thought I'd get to use it...until the Mist Guard started bickering about who was better suited to serving themselves up as a sacrifice. Their honor was almost sickening. If only they could see me now...

Hands slipping across the rocks, I found a cluster of stones off to the side I could hide behind. Anyone who went past with a torch might not spot me here, but I'd be close enough to deal my damage when they did. And so, I hunkered down and waited.

Moments throbbed by. My pain intensified with every beat of my heart. Breathing felt hard, like my lungs were wrapped in taut rope. I gnawed on the inside of my cheek as the hunger rocked through me. I knew if I could see, everything would be bouncing around, shimmering and waving as dizziness claimed me.

But I didn't need to fucking see. I just needed to hear them.

"They can't be far," came a voice. Female, harsh, angry, commanding. That would be Andromeda then, the God of Death. I shivered, despite the bravery I'd been carrying with me through the tunnels. Despite my hatred of them, I did fear them.

I feared her.

"There's more blood," a man said. He sounded more polished, more refined. That likely made him just as dangerous as Andromeda, if not more-so. Orion, then. It had to be. The other two had helped Tessa escape. According to scout reports, Perseus and Sirius were with them, but were being ordered around.

The man continued, "Shouldn't there be more signs of them by now? There's several thousand in their party. Men, women, and children. We should hear their voices, see their mess."

"There is mess," another said in a tired voice. "Blood."

"That's not enough, Sirius," Orion replied. "I think we've followed the wrong tracks."

"We could split up," Sirius answered. "Perseus and I can continue down this tunnel and—"

"I smell something," Andromeda said, cutting through the argument. "Something rotten, like eggs. I want to see what it is."

That would be me, I was guessing. Lovely to know I'd die stinking of rotten eggs. But if it meant the gods would come closer, I would gladly embrace the stench.

Their footsteps drew near. At long last, I pulled the gemstones from my pocket. They were my father's, the few that were left in this world. I'd found them in Balfor's trunk. They buzzed beneath my fingers, frantic with energy. When I'd been but a boy, Oberon had taught me how to fight. He had worn me down in the dirt so I would understand what it was like to wallow in the mud on a battle-field. There were no wooden swords during our practice. He came at me with true blades, slicing my skin.

He'd thought if he fought me hard enough, it would somehow force me to find the elite power he'd believed lay dormant inside of me. But even though I was very much my father's son, the fire had never come to me. My fingers had never danced with flames, not once in my life. I was the eldest, but I was also the weakest. According to my father, at least.

And so he taught me a hack.

It would not kill them, but it would sure as light slow them down.

The gods grew closer. With all the strength left within me, I crushed the gemstones in my fists, shattering them. Fire curled through my fingers, burning my skin. I ground my teeth and held on tight, forcing myself to wait for the perfect moment.

"Look, there's a glow!" Orion shouted. "Someone's there!"

Andromeda's face appeared over the boulder. I smiled and released the fire.

Flames consumed us all. I revelled in it, even as my flesh melted off my bones.

THIRTY-ONE
TESSA

Distant howls echoed toward us. They were distinctly human or fae. Cathal scurried into the cave and reported that the gods had taken the bait. They'd followed Ruari down the tunnels.

"And now they've found him," Nellie said flatly.

"Yes, but it sounds like he's put up a fight," I said, though I knew my words would do little to ease her pain. I turned to Gaven, who had just returned from exploring two separate tunnels that forked from this path. Sweat beaded his brow, despite the cool wind that whistled through the caverns. "Any luck?"

"One tunnel has markings. The other doesn't. Which way do you suggest we go?"

Druid Balfor shuffled up behind us. Nellie had told me what Ruari had said about him. It was hard to know exactly how much was true and how much was fabricated by a fractured mind. I was tempted to believe the former. Could I hinge the fate of all these innocents on a hunch?

"Balfor," Kalen said with ease, giving nothing away. "What do you think?"

"Well, Gaven made a point earlier that I'm inclined to agree with. If there are markings here, people were, too. And where there were people, there should be an exit."

"You didn't want to come down here in the first place. And you warned me to ignore these markings," I pointed out.

"You're right. But none of that matters now. We're here, and the gods will be upon us soon if we don't find an exit." His voice was grave. "We cannot turn around and go back, so we can only plow forward. Choose the tunnel with the markings."

"Will you tell us what they mean?" I asked.

He gave me a dark look. "You have questioned me once. Do not question me again."

"Balfor," Kalen warned. "You are a Druid and officially outside of the court, but you will show my wife respect."

Druid Balfor stood a little taller, and his face tightened to reflect the fury roaring in his eyes. But then he looked at me and blinked, as if catching himself. "Yes, of course. I did not mean to upset you. I may be a Druid, but I am not above stress. This situation is quite intense."

Kalen frowned but moved on. Turning to Toryn, he said, "Prepare our people to leave this cavern immediately. Tell them time is of the essence."

The sky was a deep, endless blue free of mist. We walked from the mouth of the cave and into a valley filled with dead grass and baked white sand. I breathed in the fresh air, nearly sagging to my knees from relief. Druid Balfor had been right. We'd made it out of the tunnels before the gods had found us.

The lands beyond Endir looked different in the clear moonlight. Death and decay surrounded us. The sporadic rainfall and lack of sun had parched the fields that had once been lush with verdant grass. The dirt had once been rich enough to grow vegetables by the thousands. A part of me still yearned for the soft kiss of mist, though that part of me was duller now that I saw the destruction it had caused. I stepped forward as fae and humans spilled from the cave. Dead grass crunched beneath my boots. Wind snatched flecks of it, and it danced away like ash.

We had to keep moving. The gods would know we'd tricked them by now, and they'd be on the hunt. These fields were no safer for us than the caverns were. And so we carried on toward Albyria.

We reached the chasm almost a day later. Kalen now stood at the edge of the Bridge to Death, his cloak flapping around his legs. Boudica perched on his shoulder and cawed into his ear. His face transformed, lines bracketing his mouth. He motioned me closer.

"Boudica just returned from scouting. The gods are on their way with an army of beasts. They'll be here by nightfall."

"So it's happening. Here and now. We don't have time to rest from the journey or brace ourselves for what's to come," I said, watching the humans and fae trek wearily past us toward the burnt out husk of a city on the hill. Once, Albyria would have made for a fine fortress during a war. Its defensive structures were not as impressive as those in Dubnos, but they would have held strong for a time.

But the fires had damaged more than just Oberon's golden shine. There were holes in the defensive wall. The battlements were still cluttered with charred debris. Weapons were limited, and arrows were nothing but ash.

Albyria was no better than Endir. If anything, it was far worse.

We could keep running, but there was nowhere to go. The mountains blocked our path, not that there was anything on the other side. Just a great expanse of sea and no ships to carry us across it.

As if reading my mind, Kalen took my hand and pressed it to his heart. "We will face this together."

"How, Kalen?"

"I don't know." He turned to gaze at the distant city on the hill. "But we will take our final stand in the lands of our old enemy."

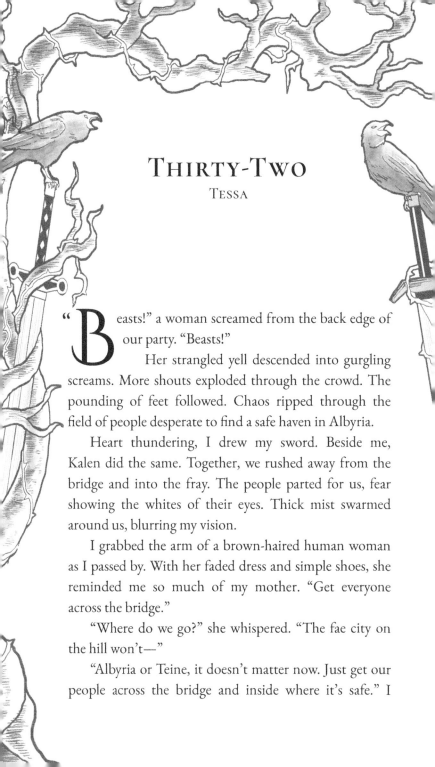

THIRTY-TWO
TESSA

"Beasts!" a woman screamed from the back edge of our party. "Beasts!"

Her strangled yell descended into gurgling screams. More shouts exploded through the crowd. The pounding of feet followed. Chaos ripped through the field of people desperate to find a safe haven in Albyria.

Heart thundering, I drew my sword. Beside me, Kalen did the same. Together, we rushed away from the bridge and into the fray. The people parted for us, fear showing the whites of their eyes. Thick mist swarmed around us, blurring my vision.

I grabbed the arm of a brown-haired human woman as I passed by. With her faded dress and simple shoes, she reminded me so much of my mother. "Get everyone across the bridge."

"Where do we go?" she whispered. "The fae city on the hill won't—"

"Albyria or Teine, it doesn't matter now. Just get our people across the bridge and inside where it's safe." I glanced up as Kalen roared ahead, swinging his sword at the first beast he reached. The humans and fae scattered, screaming and running toward us. From behind them, at least a hundred shadowfiends launched into the air, their claws outstretched and already soaked in blood.

My heart jumped into my throat. The woman beside me shuddered.

I exhaled. "There are so many."

"We will not survive this day," she murmured.

Her arm slid from my grip as her knees buckled. She sat hard on the ground, palming the dirt. Dead grass speared the gaps in her fingers. Pressing her forehead to the ground, she breathed in, as if she were memorizing the scent of it, as if she were taking her last moment to find peace where she could.

"Get up." My voice cracked. "You need to take everyone to safety."

"There is no safety in this world." She curved forward, her gray dress rippling in the wind. It was as if she'd become one with the earth. Perhaps that was the point. Because soon, she would.

Kalen's roars filled the air. Nearby, more steel sang from Toryn, Fenella, Roisin, and other warriors. But it wasn't enough. No matter how well Kalen could fight, he could not kill a hundred of these things. Not when they were amongst his people, not when the gods were likely close enough to block him from using his power.

I cast a desperate glance around, searching the mists for someone else to lead the civilians across the bridge. Those who weren't scattering were kneeling on the ground with tears streaking down their faces. Dozens of humans who I recognized from my village. They'd been through so much these past few months, and now they were giving up. They didn't want to fight for survival any longer.

Motion near the bridge snagged my attention. I could barely see my sister as she motioned people across with one hand while holding the other against her chest. She sensed my attention and found me in the chaos. With a grim nod, she lifted her fisted hand in the air.

"Callisto's gemstones," I murmured.

She read my lips. She always could. And then she arched her brow in question.

My heart pulsed a frantic beat. I glanced back at Kalen, now surrounded by four or five shadowfiends. It was impossible to tell how many there were with how quickly he danced between them. He'd kill all these, but there were dozens more. They'd rip hundreds of fae and humans to shreds.

These beasts would decimate us.

Kalen had insisted we'd find an answer—that there would be another way for us to win. And he was right. There was a way. At least for this battle.

Loosing a breath, I resigned myself to the decision I knew I had to make. I turned back to Nellie and nodded. *Use the damn thing.*

Determination flashed in my sister's eyes. She brought her fist up to her lips, cracked open her fingers, and whispered. Instantly, the howling, thundering horror stopped. All around us, the beasts went still. They blinked and sat back on their haunches, as if waiting for their next order. Sobs and whimpers still echoed through our group, but they quieted after a time. Then the patter of hurried footsteps rose quickly in their place as everyone rushed toward the bridge.

I nodded at Nellie. She nodded right back, then slipped the stones into her pocket.

Bracing myself, I turned to Kalen. He stood drenched in blood in the middle of the battlefield. Twenty dead shadowfiends surrounded him. His eyes flashed as he met my gaze, then he strode to the nearest passive beast and chopped off its head.

He grabbed the beast's fur and lifted the head into the air, waving it so all the warriors could see. "This is our enemy. Kill them all."

"No," I called out to him.

Kalen's sapphire gaze slid my way. He arched his brow. "Explain your objection."

Gone was the warmth in his voice. I'd done exactly what he'd feared. And now I was taking a stand against him in front of his own warriors. I wanted to swallow down my words, but I couldn't. Not when the answer was so clear to me.

And so I said, "These beasts can harm the gods, and we have the power to control them. If we don't use that power, they'll attack *us*, just as they've done now. We need to take them into our army and turn them back on the gods. It's the only thing that makes sense."

Murmurs went through the gathered fae fighters.

Toryn, clearing the blood off his spear, looked between me and Kalen. "We don't need to make this decision now. First, we must get everyone to safety. The beasts can remain here in the meantime."

Fenella sidled up to my side. Her face was splattered with blood, but she wasn't wounded as far as I could tell. She must have taken out several beasts herself. "The gods are coming. They'll have more creatures with them. Let's at least order the ones here to guard the bridge and kill anyone who comes near it."

Kalen worked a muscle in his jaw. He wouldn't much like having this conversation so publicly, in front of the warriors looking to him for orders. For a long moment, all he did was stare at the bridge as if imagining what might happen when the enemy arrived with its greater forces.

"Fine," he finally said with a snap to his tone. "Order the beasts to guard the bridge, but nothing more. And then we're going to rid ourselves of these fucking gemstones, so the temptation to use it is gone."

The gemstones seemed to *perch* on the table, like some kind of animal ready to spring into action at a moment's notice. Kalen hadn't spoken a word to me since we'd crossed the bridge. I helped make sure all the humans found places to rest, either in Teine or in Albyria's castle halls. Most buildings and rooms weren't habitable yet, thanks to Oberon's fires, but the light fae had rebuilt more than I'd expected. There was room for everyone. It was just cramped.

"Where is Ruari?" asked Mykon, a fae man with horns creeping through his hair. One of his brothers, then. "Is he not joining us?"

"Ruari didn't make it. He got wounded. Then he used his final moments to help us escape," Nellie said quietly. She hadn't wanted to release her grip on the gemstones. Kalen had taken her reluctance to mean it was infecting her with its darkness, but I was fairly certain she and I were on the same page. Destroying them or hiding them wasn't the answer. Not until the other gods were defeated.

I hated being at odds with Kalen about this again. It felt like a part of my soul was twisted up like tattered ribbons. We'd talked through it back at the Ivory Cliff Falls, but now I understood we'd only punted the issue down the road. We'd wrapped our problem in gauze, but the wound was still there.

Pain flashed across the light fae's face. "I see."

"I'm sorry," I said. "He was very brave."

Mykon clenched his jaw and looked away. He was the only one of the Albyrian light fae contingent to join us in Oberon's old quarters. His rooms were one of the few that had remained intact during the fires. All his furniture and luxurious silks surrounded us like the ghosts of the past. It felt like we were standing in his crypt.

"So, the gemstones." Fenella folded her arms.

"The gemstones," Toryn repeated.

Kalen looked at me. "We need to destroy them so they don't infect anyone."

"I don't think that's a good idea," Nellie answered for me. "It's just like Tessa said. We have a tool we can use in the war. *Weapons*. It would be a mistake not to use them."

"I'll also remind everyone we're low on actual

weapons. Like swords and daggers and things," Fenella said.

Low on daggers. That gave me an idea, not for the army but for the humans of Teine. It was only a small thing, but perhaps I could find a way to give them a bit of comfort during the looming battle.

Kalen looked at Mykon. "Remind everyone what happened to your father. Who was he in the end? What became of him?"

Mykon opened his mouth, but Fenella cut him off. "We don't need to hear it. We all know what he was like. But Oberon used that damn power for centuries. Four in fact, if I'm doing my math right. I doubt using that thing for one measly battle is going to turn us all into Oberon the Second."

"This war might linger on for decades." Kalen paced at the head of the table. "And I would daresay it didn't take centuries for Oberon to become a monster. It happened much more quickly than that. Isn't that right, Tessa? You saw the visions of his life. How long did it take for the God of Death to infect him with her darkness?"

I pursed my lips. Fuck, he was right. "This is different."

"Is it?" His eyes sparked with that fire of his, then he swept them down the length of me to where the Mortal Blade hung at my hip. "I'll agree you have the ability to withstand it, but what about everyone else? What about the civilians out there who could be drawn toward these powers?"

"I have an idea," Nellie said, perking up.

We all turned toward her in unison. There was a grim

set to her lips and a spark in her eyes. Head high, dark hair thrown back over her shoulders, she looked like a force to be reckoned with. Pride swelled in my chest. That was my little sister.

"I think we should do what Ruari suggested. Take the tiger-eyes and form a barrier around Albyria and Teine. Just like old times."

Toryn nodded. "We're already on it. Kalen and I sent a score of warriors to collect what they could from that store of his. We told them to prioritize the food, the gemstones, and the weapons."

"Good. So here's what we're going to do." Nellie plucked one of the gemstone from the table and flipped it in her hands. "We're going to set a trap for the gods. They said they want these back, so let's dangle them like bait. When they come for us, we'll use the beasts *just this once* to attack them. Just once won't do us any harm. Their claws and fangs will wound the gods long enough for Tessa to stab each of them with the Mortal Blade. It won't kill them, of course, but it will trap them. Then we can hide the stones away in Oberon's vault and make sure no one ever opens it." She took a deep breath before continuing. Silence rang through Oberon's room. "While we're fighting, all the innocent civilians can be safely ensconced behind the tiger-eye barrier. And if something goes wrong, Tessa and I can set off a signal for you to lower the barrier. We'll run across the bridge—or Tessa will fly us across—and then you'll put the barrier down again. Simple."

Fenella barked out a laugh.

Toryn frowned. "You and Tessa?"

"I know what you're going to say. Someone else should do it, right?"

"No. I was going to say you shouldn't go by yourselves. You two up against four gods and a horde of beasts? That's a terrible idea, Nellie. You'll..." His voice cracked.

"If you go with us, the trap won't work," I said quietly, putting voice to my sister's thoughts. "The gods need to think we're alone or they might hold back."

"They've had no problem attacking us so far," Kalen said, his eyebrows furrowed.

"But we don't want them to attack. We want to lure them in and make them think we're coming over to their side. That way we can get close enough to actually 'kill' them," Nellie argued. "If we go out with a team of warriors, they'll think it's fighting time. And we don't want that. We want them to believe Tessa and I have seen the light, that we want to return the gemstones."

"Good luck getting these fae men to agree to that," Fenella muttered.

Roisin slung her hands into her pockets, then leaned back on her heels. "We're forgetting about Niamh and the human kingdoms in all of this. Shouldn't they be on their way? They can help us fight."

"We don't have time to wait for them," I countered.

"We have plenty of time if we put up that barrier and hunker down behind it," Roisin said. "All we have to do is bide our time. It's been weeks now since the humans left Talaven. They'll arrive on Aesir's shores any day now."

"Hmm, yes, but what can the humans possibly do

that we can't?" Fenella asked, thumping a finger against the table.

"We were hoping they had answers on how to win this," Toryn said.

"Hoping for answers is not a good battle strategy." Fenella looked at Kalen. "I think we should do the Baran sisters' plan. If it works, this will all be over in a matter of hours."

"And if it doesn't, they could both die."

"I would never let anything happen to my sister," I said fiercely.

Kalen looked at me then—*really* looked at me—but I couldn't read his expression. He seemed furious and weary and defeated and strong all at the same time. Backlit by Oberon's gaudy wealth, the mist seeping from his skin made him seem like a phantom shadow who had stepped from the depths of a different world. But through the bond, I felt him soften.

"I trust you, Tessa," he finally said. "If you insist on setting this trap, you best go get yourselves prepared."

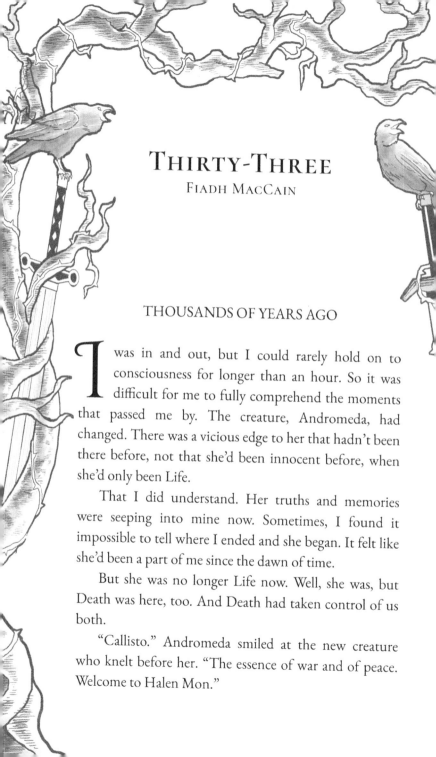

THIRTY-THREE
FIADH MACCAIN

THOUSANDS OF YEARS AGO

I was in and out, but I could rarely hold on to consciousness for longer than an hour. So it was difficult for me to fully comprehend the moments that passed me by. The creature, Andromeda, had changed. There was a vicious edge to her that hadn't been there before, not that she'd been innocent before, when she'd only been Life.

That I did understand. Her truths and memories were seeping into mine now. Sometimes, I found it impossible to tell where I ended and she began. It felt like she'd been a part of me since the dawn of time.

But she was no longer Life now. Well, she was, but Death was here, too. And Death had taken control of us both.

"Callisto." Andromeda smiled at the new creature who knelt before her. "The essence of war and of peace. Welcome to Halen Mon."

"Andromeda," the new creature murmured. Andromeda had chosen a tall, lanky fae with silver hair. She was female with bright eyes, though the brightness was quickly fading to crimson. This was the first she'd found a body for. She was hunting for others, but she was picky with the fae. They had to be powerful and strong. They needed to be fully grown, but still young and in their prime.

"Rise, Callisto. I have a job for you." Andromeda cleared her throat. Her one mistake she'd yet to fix. The wolf beasts had somehow multiplied. They were raging across the lands, feasting on human blood and flesh. It turned out they could not survive without it. Fires followed wherever they went. "You are the essence of war, and I need you to find a way to control the beasts. They are wild and ruinous. We can't have that. Control them, and then use them as your army when the time comes."

Callisto bowed. "Of course. So long as you will allow me to release my war across these lands."

"When the time is right," Andromeda said, frowning. The Life side of her was not in control, but she tempered Death's worst instincts. She had a plan, and it would only work if they kept their heads. "We are not here to cause utter destruction. In fact, we want the opposite of that. Do not forget your Peace."

"You made me this way," Callisto said, narrowing her eyes. "You made it so War has a greater edge, greater control."

"Peace alone would not allow us to do what needs to be done."

My sight wavered in and out, and things went dark once more. Now that I'd fully lost myself, the panic had subsided. I was curious more than anything else. What were these creatures up to? It had something to do with humankind and war, but the details were still hazy.

A long time passed with nothing but floating darkness. When I finally clawed my way back, there were four of them now besides the leader—besides me. Orion, Callisto, Perseus, and Sirius. I didn't need her to say their names aloud for me to know them. They echoed through my mind like distant shouts.

They sat around a gleaming oak table inside a Great Hall. Fae banners hung along the wall. They were familiar to me, drenched in shades of orange, crimson, and gold. A one-eyed dragon threaded across them. This place I knew. I'd been here before. It was the home of the King of Aesir, Aodhan Grenat.

What were they doing here? Why was the king sitting proudly at the head of the table, smiling and laughing while his great red beard danced?

"You make a strong case for your war against the humans," King Aodhan said with a booming voice, "but why should I join my army with your slew of murderous beasts? It would be like taking my own knife and stabbing myself in the back with it."

Andromeda watched the king like a hawk. She was

not smiling or laughing. "The humans are your enemies. They will eventually destroy you."

The king's smile dropped. Leaning forward, he hooked her gaze with his. His ruddy face reddened. "You are not from this world, so you do not know us and our people. We are stronger than humans. Faster. Lighter on our feet. When we're gashed with swords, we heal. They do not. To suggest they can tear us down is to insult me and my kingdom. For that, I should have you hanged."

Perseus reached for his sword. Orion shoved back his chair and gripped the sides of the table until the wood creaked. But the king remained sitting, staring into Andromeda's eyes.

"And now you threaten me in my own home," he said evenly.

"Please forgive my brethren. They are new to their bodies and have not yet learned to manage the ridiculous emotional highs your kind possess," she said icily. Indeed, Andromeda rarely felt much at all. Except for rage. Rage against this king. Rage against the humans. Rage against her own self, at *Life*, for holding her reins. She wanted to break free of her bridle and loose her full might upon the world.

The king folded his beefy arms and leaned back in his high-backed chair, the arms carved to look like dragons. "If you want me to ally with you, you'll have to control your *brethren*."

"Perseus, Orion, sit."

The creatures sat.

The king squinted at them. "Not bad. Now, can you

do that on the battlefield? Can you do that when you're not around to watch their every move?"

"They've made vows to me," she said crisply. "I control what they do and don't do."

"Hmm. And the humans? What do I get out of it? I presume their kingdoms will be yours and not mine."

Andromeda smiled. She'd been waiting for him to ask this very question. With a dramatic flair, she dropped four of the gemstones on the table. They clattered across the rough surface, their effervescent light splashing color onto the king's ruddy face. He leaned forward, squinting.

Uh oh. I did not like this.

"This some new kind of gemstone?" he asked, picking it up and turning it so the light of the candelabra illuminated the crimson. "Where'd you get it?"

"It's where we came from. It's what we are. Within those gemstones, you will find the power over Shadows and Storms. It is a great sacrifice for us to gift you with these, but we will do so for your loyalty."

I noticed she did not mention Light and Tranquility to him. The positive aspects of the creatures were not as impressive as the negative. Why would a brutal fae king wish for light?

The king looked up. There was a greedy look in his eye. "I can have these powers once we win our war against the humans?"

"Say you'll join us," said Andromeda, "and you can have them now."

Deep down, I felt the flicker of pain. Andromeda was giving two of her brethren away, and it hurt her. I hadn't thought it was possible for her to feel that kind of loss.

But she had accepted that it was the only way for her to get what she wanted.

The end of humanity.

"Deal." The king swept up the gemstones. They clinked together in his hand. Andromeda shifted on her feet, and I could feel her unease, but she remained silent. The king looked at her and smiled. "But if we are going to do this, you and I, you should speak with King Ovalis Hinde, the ruler of the humans."

"What? Why?" Andromeda had not expected that.

"You do not know Ovalis," the king said. "Go meet him. See his city. Get close to him and listen to his heartbeat when you mention war. And I will fight him if you still believe he means to destroy us."

Andromeda clucked her tongue. "This was not part of the deal. The power of the gemstones should be enough."

"This is my attempt at preventing needless bloodshed." He took a long pull of his ale, then slammed his tankard on the table. "Or are you monstrous enough to deny us of that?"

Perseus growled. I could see it in his eyes, the desperation to loose his fear upon this man. But if he did, the king would never ally with Andromeda, so he tempered his base instincts as best he could.

Andromeda sighed. "Very well. I will meet with him, but I must warn you. It will not change my mind. The humans need to die. Including Ovalis Hinde."

"We'll see," he said, smiling.

Darkness crept into my vision, but I was too focused on the glint in the fae king's eyes. A glint Andromeda had missed. How had she not seen it? This man was not her ally, nor did he mean her well. This was some kind of trap.

Good, I thought, just before the haze took me. *I hope he stabs her in the heart.*

Thirty-Four
Tessa

PRESENT DAY

"Kalen seems frustrated," Nellie said.

She'd waited until the glittering city was nothing but a smudge of gold against the moonlit night before she'd brought it up, but I could tell she'd been thinking about it since we'd left. We wended through the gathered beasts on the other side of the Bridge to Death, silent and careful even though we knew we controlled them with the stones. There was no sense in tempting fate.

It was quiet out here in the darkness. The mists still hung around the gathered beasts, but it was clear up ahead. We could see for miles, especially with the torches we carried across the once-verdant fields. Answering torches flickered on the distant horizon. The fae army of the gods was coming, but they were still at least a full day's walk from us.

"Kalen thinks we're making a mistake by using the

gemstones. And he's frustrated that we have different views about it. We've been through a lot, he and I, but this is the first time we've disagreed on something as mundane as a battle strategy."

Nellie laughed. "Only *you* would see a battle strategy as something mundane. This is probably the most thrilling thing I've done my entire life."

"Spending time with Toryn isn't thrilling?" I asked with a small smile.

"Don't you start." She frowned. "What I don't understand is why Kalen is letting us go through with it if he thinks it's a terrible idea."

"Because Kalen Denare sees me as his equal, and he will not tell me what to do. That said, Boudica is likely watching us."

Nellie tipped back her head to search the skies. "I don't see her."

"That doesn't mean she's not there. Either way, Kalen's not far, either. He and the others are waiting in the chasm. If we run into any trouble at all, they'll come running."

"What? No one told me that. What if the gods sense them and realize this is a trap?"

"Kalen is made of mist and shadow. He knows how to remain hidden."

Nellie gripped my arm and hissed. "Good. Because they're coming."

I followed her gaze. Dark forms moved toward us, borne on wings. I dropped the torch and tossed sand over the flames to douse the light.

It only took a few moments for them to reach us.

Andromeda thundered to the ground. Sand sprayed from the powerful beat of her wings, and wind whorled around my body like a storm. The others shortly joined her. Perseus and Sirius took up the rear while Orion landed beside Andromeda. My two 'allies' wouldn't meet my gaze. She'd changed them, like Sirius had warned.

"I must admit," Andromeda said by way of greeting, "I'm surprised to find two little Barans wandering around unaccompanied." She sniffed. "Where's the fae filth?"

"Kalen and I had a disagreement. We left," I said. Technically, not a lie.

"*You left?*" Andromeda laughed, turning toward Orion. "Orion guessed you would, but I didn't believe it."

I looked between the two of them, then tried to catch the attention of Perseus and Sirius. But they kept their gazes rooted to the ground. "You thought we'd use the gemstones and change our minds about joining you. Why?"

"It was designed to be your final trial. Once you used the stones for your own gain, you would realize you were better off with us. No human or fae can withstand the call of them." Andromeda smiled at my surprise. "Though I will admit, it hasn't exactly gone according to plan. I wanted you to use the gemstones in Malroch and avoid all this...mess. I didn't anticipate your escape." She shot a sharp glance at Sirius.

I withdrew the Mortal Blade from my sheath and turned it sideways so that the gemstone flashed its crimson light upon their faces. "So when I got my hands on this, it was your doing?"

Andromeda pointed at the blade. "That is my sister, Pandora, who has always been loyal to me. I would never let her out of my sight unless I had a good reason."

Sirius shifted on his feet. Andromeda merely smiled, but didn't acknowledge his discomfort. I was certain she would make him pay for what he'd done, if she hadn't already.

She held out her hand. "Now give her stones back to me. Callisto's, too. I know you want to. Why else would you have left your lover, your army, and your people?"

"You're right. I don't want these gemstones." I started to give the blade to her, but stepped back instead. "I just... I have a few questions. Indulge me in my curiosity."

Andromeda frowned. "I do not have time for this. Give me the gemstones, Tessa Baran. Don't make me kill your sister to make a point."

"Ah, ah," Nellie said, withdrawing Callisto's gemstones from the front of her fighting leathers. She glanced back over her shoulder at the beasts gathered by the bridge.

Orion's gaze snapped to my sister. Instinctively, I shifted my body in front of hers.

"Questions first," Nellie said, her voice as calm as pond water. I felt her tighten her grip on the gemstones. She was quietly ordering the beasts to inch closer, stealthily, so the gods wouldn't notice.

"You get two questions," Andromeda said. "If you try a third, I'll slice open your sister's neck."

I narrowed my eyes. "Do not threaten my sister."

"Do not threaten me and mine," she countered.

I looked at the others. They stood resolutely beside

her. She kept calling them her brethren, and yet they had little in common. "You speak of them as if they're your siblings, but they look nothing like you. How are you related?"

A slow smile spread across her face. "You ask to learn the secrets of the universe even as you seek to destroy it."

"You're the secret of the universe?" Nellie asked. She sounded as confused as I felt.

"No, little pet. We *are* the universe. We are the powers that bring life where there was none. We are the wind through the trees, the hope for better days, and the rage that burns in all men's hearts. We are everything you feel and hear and see around you. And my brethren and I are related the only way we can be. Dirt and grass exist in tandem, yes? Storms give rain, watering crops to provide abundance. Abundance leads to war over territories. After war comes peace. Threading through it all are the two forces you mortals can never escape. Life and death. Death and life. The end of everything, and the beginning."

That was more information than I thought we'd get. And it was a lot to process. But I couldn't focus on that right now. I was only doing this to stall for time while our beasts drew nearer.

"Second question. You said you purposely let me have the Mortal Blade, so I would be tempted to use the gemstones. Did you intend for me to kill Callisto with it?" I asked.

Orion scoffed. "As I told you before, you didn't *kill* her."

"That wasn't the question I asked."

Andromeda pursed her lips as if she didn't want to answer the question, which was all the confirmation I needed. Me killing Callisto hadn't been part of their plan. A rush of satisfaction went through me.

"I didn't think you would stab her, no," Andromeda finally said. "We put the power of storms into your hands. I thought you would use that instead of the blade."

As if to punctuate her thoughts, a breeze rolled in from behind us. Her gaze dropped to where my hand curled around the Mortal Blade. I brushed my thumb across the gemstone, stroking it to life. Overhead, thunder cracked the skies. A rich, intoxicating power buzzed against my skin and crackled through the rest of my body. There was a darkness in it, a pulse that felt as familiar as my own two hands. But beneath the surface of that darkness, there was the beating pulse of a storm. The wind and rain called to me, urging me to unleash the powerful, thunderous intensity of it onto the world. I ground my teeth to hold it down.

"Clever," she said, smiling. "I'm pleased to see you're finally willing to use the storms, though I must say it took you far longer than I expected. At least you can finally feel it now, can't you? The power of it? The great darkness you cannot resist? How great you could truly be if you only drew upon the full strength of it. Show this world what you could do to it. Bring it to its knees."

My thumb stilled. "I will never be what you want me to be, Andromeda."

"You already are." Her smiled widened as she took a step toward me, her cloak rippling behind her from the gusts I'd conjured from the jewel. "There is a darkness inside of you, Tessa Baran. There always has been. You can tell yourself you're better than Oberon, than Bellicent, than any other fae or human who has touched our power. But you have always struggled with it. It has always controlled you."

I flipped the dagger in my hand, then pointed it at her chest, though she was still several meters away from me. "Oberon was weak and in pain, and you took advantage of his suffering. Bellicent was *dead*. And what's more, they weren't me. You think I'm weak. I am not. You think I will bend to your pressure. I will not. I have had your hatred and your rage inside me all my life, and I have not succumbed to it. You will not strip me of my humanity, no matter what you do to me. *You cannot break me.*"

Andromeda's smile never dimmed. "You speak so highly of yourself, but you've already shown weakness against my influence on your mind, your heart, your soul. All this rage you carry with you—*my rage*—has controlled you far more than you're willing to admit. You recklessly attacked Oberon in his own hall. You stabbed the Mist King when you thought you might love him. And now you've fled the safety of your army and your lover to make some kind of point. You could have fought bravely against us, and yet you have not. You want to believe you're better than Oberon, but you're just as weak. It's the humanity in you. None of you can help yourselves, not even the fae."

My heart thundered against my ribs. Her words scratched the scars around my heart. I'd fought hard to forgive myself for the things I'd done, but the reminders rubbed those scars raw. I had done all those things. I had felt the darkness, then. And I'd given into it.

But I was no longer that girl, and I would not let Andromeda's words unravel the woman I'd fought so hard to become.

"Your derision for humanity will be your undoing. We're stronger than you think we are, and you cannot destroy us." I took another step closer. My dagger was only a few inches away from her chest now. "I will never join you. This is *my* world. And if you refuse to leave it, we'll trap you for eternity in your fucking gemstones."

A strange urge came across me. I pursed my lips and let out a low, mournful whistle. It was a song my mother had sung to me when I was young. The wind snatched the sound from my lips and scattered it across the ruined fields. Andromeda and the other gods stared at me as if entranced. I knew the words as surely as I knew my own heartbeat, though it had been years since I'd last heard them.

The darkness cries for the light
  And comes undone beneath the sky
  An old wind blows
  With ancient woes
  But light will never die

"How do you know that song?" Andromeda asked when I fell silent.

But before I could answer, Nellie whispered, "Now!"

The beasts sprang to life from behind us and charged.

THIRTY-FIVE
TESSA

Andromeda's attention shifted off me for one beautiful second. I lunged toward her with the Mortal Blade. She threw up her hand and caught my arm when the tip brushed the front of her shoulder. Hissing, she shoved me back.

"You attempt to wound me with the power of my own brethren?" Her eyes sparked with fury. "You're right. You are no daughter of mine, and you will pay for your mistake."

Nellie grabbed my other arm and yanked me away from Andromeda. Together, we tumbled out of the way as the beasts rushed past. I hit the ground, my knee cracking from the impact. Gritting my teeth, I rolled. My cloak got tangled up in my legs.

Dirt sprayed into my face when a pair of hands jerked me to a stop. One of the gods lifted me from the ground and tossed me sideways. This time, I landed in a crouch, though the impact jarred my skull. I blinked at the chaos, trying to make sense of it, trying to understand who I faced now.

The beasts had reached the gods, mist swirling around them all. They were attacking in a furious frenzy. Andromeda and Orion fought side by side, their majestic swords cutting down the beasts faster than they could swipe their claws. Nellie was backing away, watching with horror as a group of wraiths lurched toward her. Tattered cloaks hugged their frail forms. Poisonous sand dripped to the ground in their wake.

Perseus stood just before me, his face screwed up in pain. Steel plates covered the rest of his body, but he'd removed his helm. It sat by his feet, along with the tip of his great sword.

"Fight against her," I said to him. "Help me help the beasts. They can stun her long enough for me to use the Mortal Blade."

He shuddered against my words, and a single tear leaked from his eye. "I cannot, Tessa Baran. My vow prevents me from going against her orders. She is forcing me to do this."

"You helped me escape," I pleaded with him. "That means you can do *something*, Perseus."

"She didn't know we were trying to work against her then, and her orders for us were less specific. She has made it clear now. We cannot allow Nellie to control the beasts. I am so sorry, Tessa Baran, and it's difficult for me to say even that. This is not how I wanted your fight against Death to end."

Us. Nellie.

My heart lurched into my throat. Where was Sirius?

I whirled toward Nellie. Perseus grabbed my shoulder and anchored me in place. Sirius was hovering over Nellie's head. I cried out as he grabbed her. Pumping his powerful wings, he hauled my sister from the ground. She screamed and kicked out her legs, trying to wrench herself free. I yanked away from Perseus so hard I had to stumble forward to catch myself.

And then I was off. My wings exploded from my back, nearly getting caught up in my cloak. I ran toward Nellie and shoved myself into the air, my eyes trained on their vanishing forms. Because of Perseus, Sirius had a head start, but he was not fuelled by love and desperation. I wouldn't let him take her from me.

I ground my teeth as I hurtled toward them, faster than I'd ever flown before. Wind gusted against me as my anger grew. The skies cracked with thunder. Lightning pierced the skies, illuminating Nellie and Sirius locked in a strange embrace. She was fighting him, I realized, when another bout of lightning flashed across them. Her hands had transformed into claws, and he was holding her back as she tried to slice his face.

"That's it, Nellie," I whispered as I pounded my wings faster.

Rain slashed against my face. The cold droplets stung my skin, drenching me instantly. I blinked through the sudden haze, and I almost lost sight of them. But no, there they were.

I'd almost reached them. Two more minutes, and I'd have Sirius's head in my hands. I didn't care what he'd done to help me, or how hopeless he was against Andromeda's whims. I would not let him harm my sister.

Sirius shoved his hand into Nellie's pocket while holding back her claw. He ripped out the gemstones, then shoved his boot into her chest.

The world shuddered to a stop. Rain misted. The thunderous boom slowed. Nellie screamed as her body tumbled away from Sirius. She arched toward him, arms outstretched. My own hands reached out instinctively, though I was too far away to catch her.

And then time sped up. Nellie fell.

I screamed and dove after her, tucking my wings close to my body. My sister tumbled over and over on herself. Her brunette hair whipped her face, and her cloak wrapped around her legs, holding them together like a cocoon. Suddenly, her body went slack. She stopped fighting, though she pointed one finger at the sky. At the stars.

A sob choked me. I squeezed my fists against the pain and tried to force my body to move faster. Nellie had given up. She saw death coming for her, so she was embracing the stars.

"No!" I shouted at her, not knowing if she could hear my voice through the storm. "You can't give up, Nellie, you have to fight!"

But fight what? my mind shouted back at me. There was no enemy here with us now. There were no beasts to defeat. It was just the wind and the rain and the ground rapidly rising to greet her in its deathly embrace. I choked, tears spilling from my eyes.

I'd thought I'd lost her once. It had nearly killed me. I couldn't go through it again. She deserved more from life than this, and the world would not be the same without the brightness of her smile and the kindness in her eyes. Another sob shook me.

Nellie was only seconds from hitting the ground. I strained to reach her, but I wasn't moving fast enough. I couldn't do this. I needed help.

A feral scream ripped from my throat. "Kalen!"

My shout echoed like thunder. Nellie looked up and met my gaze. A thousand beautiful memories passed between us. I could picture her running through the village on her bare feet. I could smell the apples on her breath and the lake water in her hair. I could feel her arms wrapping around me when I hid in the woods and cried. And I could feel her whispering into my ear, "Fly away from here, like the ravens."

I sucked in a breath, and the rain nearly choked me. "Fly, Nellie! Fly like the ravens!"

Her eyes widened. The ground quickly approached. My sister curled in on herself, transforming her body into a ball, and then—

Wings exploded from her back. Blood sprayed the air. She screamed from the roaring pain, but she forced the wings to spread. They jerked hard against her back. She careened wildly, arms and legs flailing, a spiral of panic and feathers and kicking limbs.

She caught herself before she hit the ground. I spun toward her with my arms open wide. Shaking, she reached up for me, but then her face went white.

"Tessa, watch out!" she screamed.

I twisted mid-air as the gods descended around me. Andromeda, Orion, and Perseus formed a circle while

Sirius swept in below me. I looked up toward the sky, and my stomach dropped.

Caedmon grinned down at me, his black wings a whorl of shadows, his horns glinting from the light of the moon. "Hello, Tessa Baran. Thank you for the vessel."

Andromeda grabbed me and trapped me against her chest. My wings melted into my skin, abandoning me. The god curled an arm around my throat to hold me in place. Her lips moved against my ear as she dragged a fingernail across my cheek.

"Death," she whispered.

I squirmed against her, hatred burning through my veins. "Your power doesn't work against me."

"It doesn't? How surprising!" The mocking tone in her voice scattered shivers across my skin. "I suppose that means I'll have to try something else, then. First, we'll be taking this."

Caedmon dropped in front of me, though I supposed he was no longer Caedmon now. He was the essence of Shadow made flesh. He grabbed my fingers and twisted sharply. Bones cracked, and pain lanced through my hands. I ground my teeth to keep from crying out. I wouldn't give them the satisfaction.

My fingers betrayed me, loosening their grip on my dagger. The Mortal Blade fell into Caedmon's waiting palm. His eyes flashed as he brought the gemstone up before him. "At last."

Then he popped the gemstone free and tossed the blade into the storm.

"Thank you, Pollux." Andromeda tightened her grip on me. "It seems we have everything we need now. It's a shame, little pet. I would have liked it if you'd joined me, but I can't allow you to live if you refuse my call. I know who you are." Her fingernail dug into my neck, and I felt my slick blood trail down my skin. "Daughter of Stars."

She dragged her nail across my throat. Pain exploded in its wake. I gasped for air, but it eluded me. A wetness coated my skin, soaking the front of me. My vision grew dark almost instantly, and my body spasmed. Dimly, I understood I was dying, though my mind struggled to hold on to more than just the pain.

Nellie's distant screams were the last things I heard before I could not hear or see or feel anything at all.

Thirty-Six
Niamh

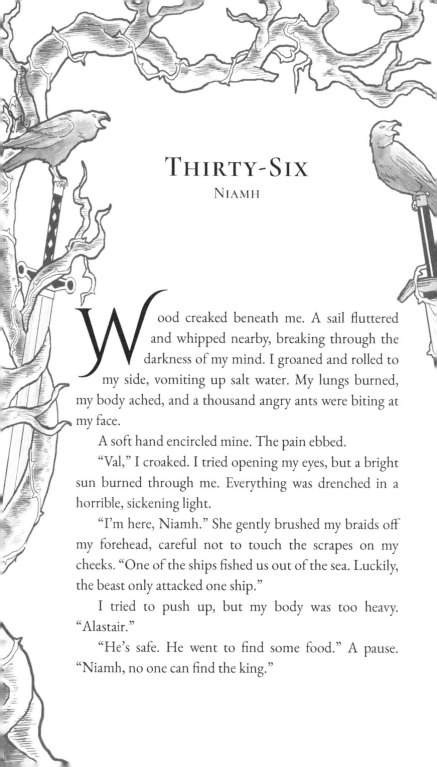

Wood creaked beneath me. A sail fluttered and whipped nearby, breaking through the darkness of my mind. I groaned and rolled to my side, vomiting up salt water. My lungs burned, my body ached, and a thousand angry ants were biting at my face.

A soft hand encircled mine. The pain ebbed.

"Val," I croaked. I tried opening my eyes, but a bright sun burned through me. Everything was drenched in a horrible, sickening light.

"I'm here, Niamh." She gently brushed my braids off my forehead, careful not to touch the scrapes on my cheeks. "One of the ships fished us out of the sea. Luckily, the beast only attacked one ship."

I tried to push up, but my body was too heavy. "Alastair."

"He's safe. He went to find some food." A pause. "Niamh, no one can find the king."

A splitting headache cracked my skull as I forced my eyes open. Val's face wavered in and out of view. She looked relieved, but worried. "How long have they been searching the sea for survivors?"

"Hours," she said quietly. "No one knows quite what to do. Some are saying we should give up and move on. The longer we wait around, the more likely we are to endure another attack. But others can't bear the thought of leaving their king in the sea. What if he's still alive and just floating along somewhere...? And then there's another problem. Half the fleet has turned around to head back to Talaven. They've abandoned us here."

"Someone needs to take charge." I sat up, and my head spun.

Val clutched my shoulder to keep me steady. "Not you. You need to rest."

"No, not me," I agreed. "The humans will never answer to a fae, especially not one who got their king into this mess to begin with. Where's his heir?"

"Gone. Also missing."

"The captain of his guard."

"Missing."

I blew out a breath. "Let me guess, his second in command is also missing."

"Exactly," Val said. "That's why no one knows what to do."

"For fuck's sake." On wobbly legs, I forced myself to stand. Dozens of other soaked men and women huddled around the deck of the ship. "We need to find a lord or a lady. Or one of the king's distant relatives. It doesn't matter how little authority they have normally. We just need someone willing to take control and make the call."

"And what call is that?"

"The king and his carefully laid plans are gone. We cannot linger. We cannot turn back. We will find someone who will order these ships to sail straight for Aesir. Fuck anyone who tries to stop us."

It turned out there were a few lords and ladies on board. Alastair herded them into the bridge, where the captain of the ship watched with one skeptical brow raised. He'd informed us that no lord worth his salt would agree with leaving the king behind. And so I informed him that the king was likely dead. That hadn't gone down very well.

A lady named Vera with short golden hair stood at the front of their noble party. She wore breeches the color of sand and a pale blue blouse that curtained her small frame. But despite her petite stature, she had a commanding sense about her. I wouldn't have chosen her as a leader by picking her out of a crowd, but now that we stood face-to-face, I knew she was the right one for the job.

"I understand you're our guests," Lady Vera started, but I quickly cut her off.

"Not guests. Ambassadors from Aesir. We journeyed to Talaven to make an offer of an alliance to your kingdom, which your late king accepted."

"You speak of him as if he's dead. Can you produce a body?"

Alastair snorted. Gritting my teeth, I elbowed him in the side. I'd asked him to stay in the mess hall while I took care of the situation. But he'd conjured one of his shit-eating grins and had decided it would be more entertaining to watch me bicker with human lords.

"There are many bodies in the sea, but we can't collect them without risking another attack from that beast," I argued.

She lifted her thin, dainty nose. "Then you cannot be certain he's dead."

"We can't stay here," I said, my voice growing hard. "I know you were safe on this ship during the attack, so you don't understand the gravity of the situation. But I was there." I motioned to Val, to Alastair. "They were there. And they can tell you we're lucky to have survived. The beast tore a hole in the ship and then dragged it into the depths of the sea. The only things left are a few floating planks of wood. Dozens drowned. Hundreds, even. If the beast attacks again, *you're all going to die*. As a lady, I understand you don't want to fight, but—"

"Do not lecture me." She snapped her fingers, and a couple of warriors strode in from the hallway outside the bridge. They handed her a very impressive-looking sword. I arched my brow as she crossed one ankle over the other and leaned against the weapon, like it was an oversized cane. Quirking a smile at the look on my face, she said. "Don't always judge a lady by her title. Some of us like to don pretty clothes *and* fight."

"Apologies," I said. "I meant no offense. I merely wanted to ensure you understand the gravity of the situation."

"I understand the gravity. I have spent many hours with the king, listening to him ramble on and on and on about the visions. It became quite the focal point of my life for a long while. He seemed certain I would need to know about it one day."

"Ah." I smiled in relief. "Then surely you must see why we should move on. Aesir needs us to fight for them."

"Us?" she asked sharply.

"Well, yes, I am on this ship with you."

"The thing is, Niamh..." She paused, cocking her head. "Is it all right if I call you Niamh? Or do you like to go by the King's Shadow?"

"I don't care what you fucking call me, as long as you get this ship moving to Aesir."

Alastair chuckled. Once again, I elbowed him in the side. Vera didn't strike me as a woman who liked to be laughed at.

"Very well," Vera said, ignoring me. "I like the name Niamh. It's very unique, at least for us in Talaven. I don't think I'd ever heard it before you arrived on our doorstep. And I would have remembered it, seeing how beautiful I think it sounds. Do you see where I'm going with this?"

I sighed. I knew. Because the king had made it more than clear. "None of the visions showed me coming to Talaven."

"The visions have shown none of this." She waved

aggressively at the windows overlooking the bow of the ship. "Monstrous beasts have attacked our ships *multiple times*. Many of our soldiers have died. We've lost our king. And now a fae, who we never saw coming, walks into our bridge and tries to take command."

"I am not trying to take command," I told her. "All I want is—"

"To sail to Aesir, where a realm of monstrous gods and terrifying beasts wish to destroy every last human in this world?" Vera's lips thinned. "Unfortunately, that is not what *I* want. We will continue the search for our king. And when we find him, we will turn our ships around and go home."

Alastair shoved past me. He erased the distance between us and Vera. His towering form dwarfed hers, but she stared up at him with a set jaw and fiery eyes. Then she eased her weight off the sword, lifted it, and pressed the blade to his neck.

I moved toward them, but Alastair held out an arm, holding me back.

To Vera, he said, "Well, aren't you a feisty little thing?"

"I am neither little nor a thing, thank you," she spat back.

He chuckled, and it sounded almost like a deep-throated purr. I rolled my eyes. If we made it out of the bridge in one piece, he was probably going to ask Vera to join him in a cabin. And I'd have to make myself scarce for a while. I didn't fancy listening to the noises that man made when he fucked someone.

"Everyone needs to calm down. We're all on the same side," he said. "And all we want is to help our people."

Her furrowed brow softened, but she did not lower her sword. "Leave the bridge. Don't return or try to influence our decisions moving forward."

He held up his hands. "If you insist, though surely there must be something I can do to—"

A deafening boom sounded outside. Vera paled and lowered her sword. Alastair turned toward me, his gaze locking with mine. My pounding heartbeat returned.

I didn't want to think the worst, that the beast had already started another assault on us. But what else could it be?

"Keep your sword at the ready," I told Vera.

Her voice shook when she replied. "As if this tiny weapon will mean anything against a beast that size."

"You could chop off one of its tentacles, at least." I moved toward the door and braced myself for the blood-soaked carnage we'd find on the deck.

When I pushed outside, all was strangely still. No sailors rushed by screaming. No blood painted the wooden planks. The only signs we hadn't conjured the sound were the sailors clustered on the bow of the ship, gazing toward the distant dark sky.

Somewhere far ahead, a wicked storm churned the blue into a shadowy black.

Vera stepped up beside me, her eyes locked on the horizon. "Oh."

"You think that sound was from the storm?"

"Yes," she said tightly. Suddenly, she spun on her heels and went back inside.

Alastair furrowed his brow as he watched her leave the deck. "Hmm."

I followed her, but not before casting one last look at the storm. There was something strange about it. We'd been sailing toward Sunport, which was south of the Kingdom of Storms. But the churning sky looked even further south than where we were aiming. It looked like it could even be as far as Albyria.

But Albyria never got storms like this. Unless it was god-made.

Clenching my jaw, I followed Vera back into the bridge. She stood over an old, wrinkled map, charting a course to Albyria.

"What's going on? I thought you were dead set on staying here until you found your king."

"The storm changes things," she said flatly.

"I don't suppose you're going to tell me why."

She shoved away from the map, pacing the length of the bridge. The captain and the other lords and ladies had left after the sound, and Alastair and Val were still standing on the deck watching the storm.

"If it's sensitive information, I'll vow to keep it to myself." I motioned to the empty bridge. "It's just us in here."

She stopped, looked at me, then sighed. "I am in a tricky position. The king made it clear that certain details cannot be shared. There are some things I can say, though."

Just as I suspected, this storm was part of the king's bloody visions. That could only mean we were back on the right path, at least partially. I knew I should be glad for it, but all I felt was dread.

I followed her back over to the map, where she pointed at the coastal city we'd been sailing toward. "What I can tell you is that Sunport will be surrounded by beasts now. We can no longer go there."

"So we're sailing to Albyria instead." I nodded. "Fine with me. That's where the storm is."

"Yes, the storm." She cleared her throat. I narrowed my eyes. Mostly, that smelled like the truth, but there was something a little off about it, like it was fresh meat left out in the sun for too long.

"You certainly changed your tune quickly."

"I was only doing what I thought the king would want me to do. You have to understand he left instructions in place to ensure our survival. I thought everything had gone wrong."

"But the storm appeared," I said, testing her to see if she'd spill a half-lie again.

She cut her eyes my way. "It's not the storm that's tipped me off. The king warned me of a booming sound and a dark sky. It would begin in Aesir and echo through the world. It is a signal that things have turned in a certain direction."

"Are you going to tell me that direction?"

"All I can say is there's a fight ahead of us."

Interesting. That bit was fully the truth. "And did your king see his own death?"

"No," she said vehemently. "That's why we're still searching for him. In any case, we have to move on now, as much as I hate it. He was clear we should sail to Aesir immediately if I heard that sound. If we don't, your kingdom will fall, and so will ours." Her neck bobbed as she swallowed hard. "This is it, Niamh. What our king and his ancestors have spent their entire lives preparing for. This is when we win or we die."

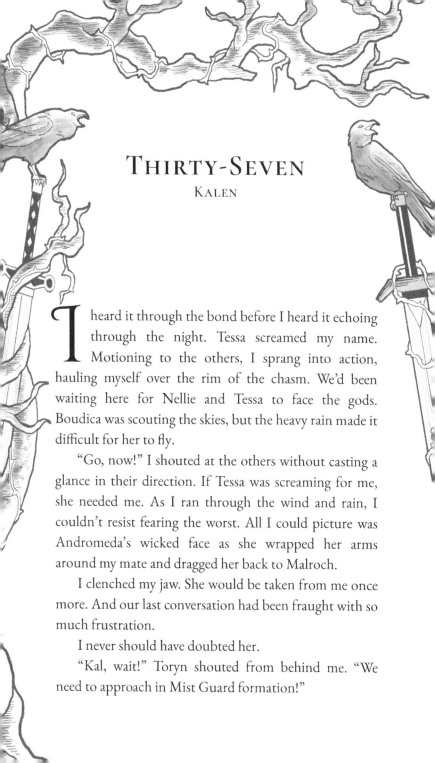

THIRTY-SEVEN
KALEN

I heard it through the bond before I heard it echoing through the night. Tessa screamed my name. Motioning to the others, I sprang into action, hauling myself over the rim of the chasm. We'd been waiting here for Nellie and Tessa to face the gods. Boudica was scouting the skies, but the heavy rain made it difficult for her to fly.

"Go, now!" I shouted at the others without casting a glance in their direction. If Tessa was screaming for me, she needed me. As I ran through the wind and rain, I couldn't resist fearing the worst. All I could picture was Andromeda's wicked face as she wrapped her arms around my mate and dragged her back to Malroch.

I clenched my jaw. She would be taken from me once more. And our last conversation had been fraught with so much frustration.

I never should have doubted her.

"Kal, wait!" Toryn shouted from behind me. "We need to approach in Mist Guard formation!"

But I ignored him and just kept running. We didn't have Niamh or Alastair, and their absence was like an aching wound in our Mist Guard. We would be no better off in formation, not without them by our sides.

Tessa's scream still echoed in my mind. She needed me now. We didn't have time to waste.

Sounds of fighting rose before us. Beasts roared, then whimpered in pain. Rain sprayed into my eyes. It was almost impossible to see what was happening up ahead. Now and then, steel blades caught the glint of the lightning, but whoever was fighting was nothing more than a moving shadow.

"Tessa!" I shouted. My voice got snatched away by the wind.

This was no normal storm. It never rained like this in the Kingdom of Shadow. Fear gripped me. I kept running.

A *boom* shook the world. The ground beneath me cracked, knocking me off my feet. My body slammed into the dirt. Roaring filled the air, and screams rose in answer. The world shook and rattled and quaked. I climbed to my knees, stunned from the sudden impact.

Several beasts ran past me, scattering in every direction. I barely paid them any attention.

Through the rain, I saw two figures. A girl, whose brown hair was plastered to her rain-soaked face, hunched over another. My heart fractured as the wind gusted, blowing the rain off course and providing me with a better view.

Blood painted the ground around her head. Her eyes

stared up at the stars, unseeing. I stumbled forward, choking from the pain. This couldn't be happening.

"Kalen!" Toryn ran up behind me and grabbed my shoulder. "What's—oh."

"Oh fuck," Fenella moaned.

"I see," was all Gaven said.

Nellie looked up and saw me there. The pain in her eyes reflected the horrible ache sawing at my chest. Something was ripping me apart. Something was cutting through my skin and bones and flesh until I was nothing but bloody remains. Nothing but a pile of guts and broken bones left scattered on the ground.

"This is my fault," she whispered. "All of this was my idea."

I stumbled toward Tessa. A low rumbling sound escaped my throat when I saw the full depths of what they'd done to her. A deep crimson gash cut across her throat.

Nellie stared up at me. Her hands were painted with her sister's blood, as if she'd tried to stop the bleeding. "Why isn't she healing? She has powers. She's part god. She's healed before. Someone tell her to heal herself."

I tried to answer, but I couldn't find my voice. I could only fall to my knees.

Gaven walked past me and put a comforting hand on Nellie's shoulder. "She was gone too quickly. She wouldn't have had time to heal. Even fae cannot heal from a wound like this."

Fenella squeezed my hand. Her eyes, usually hard and edged like the steel of her daggers, were soft. She was crying. "Kal, you should look away. Gaven, Toryn, and I can take care of this."

"No," I managed to grind out. "She is my mate. She is my wife."

"Kal," Toryn tried.

"No!" My shout exploded out of me, and the ground beneath us shook again. The crack nearby yawned wider.

Fenella snapped her fingers in my face, though her eyes remained soft. "Kal, I know you're hurting. We all are. But you need to get a grip on your power. Or you're going to get us all killed."

"Move out of my way."

I climbed to my feet. Fenella sighed and shifted to the side. Pain lanced through me with every step I took toward my mate. Sobs shook Nellie's body, and the sound of her cries nearly broke whatever was left of me. There was so much blood. A flash of rage cut through the pain. These monsters had done this to her.

"Help me remove her cloak. I'm going to wrap it around her neck," I found myself saying, though it didn't feel real or sound real. It was like I was trapped inside a tunnel, where no one could ever reach me.

"Kal," Toryn said quietly. He had walked with me, though I hadn't noticed until now. "Wrapping up her neck isn't going to do anything. She's gone."

I whirled toward him, anger punching through me, making the veins in my neck throb. "Help me wrap her neck in my cloak."

My cloak. The chasm in the ground shook wider. She was wearing it now. It was hers, not mine. It always would be.

"All right, Kal. Come on." Toryn knelt on the ground beside Nellie and gently gathered her in his arms. She sobbed into his chest. He murmured comforting words into her ear. I fought the urge to tell him to stop, that it was pointless, that nothing could comfort her at a time like this. The sisters were inseparable. Their bond was so strong it could be sung about in epics. Tessa had nearly killed me from the pain Nellie's supposed death had caused her. Nellie would never be the same after this.

I would never be the same after this.

My mate. My wife.

They had taken her from me.

I roared and pounded my fists on the ground. The dirt sprayed into my face as another rumble shook beneath me. I shuddered, relishing the full force of my power and the small measure of relief I felt in loosing it upon this fucking world.

"Kalen Denare," Fenella said from behind me.

"Don't you start, Fenella."

"No, I *will* start, and you *will* listen to me. I've been where you are, remember? I lost my husband so long ago that one might wonder if he's nothing more than a vague, hazy memory to me, right? But we were bonded, just like you were. I know the pain. I know the rage. I understand you feel like your entire body is breaking apart, and it will never be whole again." She slumped to the ground beside me and took my hand in hers. "And you're right. You won't be. But you have to control your pain anyway. Tessa would never want you to break the world in your grief for her. She would want you to find these fucking gods and murder the shit out of them."

I lifted my gaze to hers. She pressed her lips together and nodded vigorously. "That's right. We're going to *destroy them*, Kalen. For Tessa."

"We can't do it without her." My voice cracked.

Nellie sagged. "The gods took the gemstones. I saw the Mortal Blade over there, but it's useless against them now. I don't see how we can fight them. Unless you... unless you use *me*." Her voice hardened. "And you should. This is all my fault. I never should have suggested we do this. I'm the reason my sister is dead."

"Oh, Nellie." Toryn pulled her against his chest. "None of this is your fault, and we won't sacrifice you like that."

"We'll find another way," Fenella replied. "Niamh and Alastair should return to Aesir soon with the human army. They'll—"

"Stop," I said, scraping the word from my throat. "Just stop. I do not care about the gods and the humans and what we do next. I want to take care of my mate. Help me wrap her neck or leave me be."

Toryn nodded and gently helped Nellie stand, holding her close when her knees buckled. Gaven remained nearby, watching, while Boudica spun overhead. Her mournful cries echoed through the night. Fenella helped me remove the cloak. My hands shook as I undid the clasp. I didn't want to shift her body too much. Blood still leaked from the wound, and I needed to keep it there inside her where it belonged.

I didn't want her to lose any more of herself.

When we finally pulled the cloak from beneath her, I ripped the fabric into strips. Silent, Fenella lifted Tessa's head while I wrapped the fabric around the cut. Blood instantly soaked it, but it stopped the trails from dripping onto the ground.

When I was done, I sat back on my heels, scarcely understanding what I was seeing. This wasn't real. It couldn't be real. I did not want to exist in this world without her.

"Come on," Fenella said gently. "Carry her home, Kal."

Her *home*. That tiny village called Teine, where she'd experienced so much fear and pain. And yet she loved that village and everyone in it. She'd fought to save not only herself but them. They'd been part of her bargain with me, that vow. I'd been meant to find them a safe haven far from the mist, and yet I'd failed her on that.

I'd failed her now.

I should have told her I loved her before she and Nellie had set off to save the world.

"She will be remembered." I gently slid my arms under her body and lifted her, careful to keep her head against my chest. I carried her through the darkness as the rain returned. Nellie and my Mist Guard surrounded me. Together, we walked to the bridge in silence. There was nothing left to say.

Only goodbye.

THIRTY-EIGHT
KALEN

I took her to the little house with the faded blue paint. Oberon's destructive fires hadn't touched this place, though several of the nearby homes hadn't been as lucky. A broom sat on the front porch, leaning against the door. The brown bristles were coated in dust. Nellie took one look at the broom and sobbed.

"Where would you like me to take her?" I asked, though the voice hardly felt like mine. Rain still crashed down on us, but I'd stopped feeling it. I'd stopped feeling much of anything at all.

"Should we bury her? Does your village have a cemetery?" Fenella asked Nellie.

"Not in the rain," Nellie said with a gasp. "Not in the mud. We should let her rest in her bed until it stops. It should be...it should be light outside when we bury her. She should be able to see the sun one last time. There's a book in her room. She was reading it before we left Teine. She hasn't reached the end of the story yet."

"Of course," Toryn murmured, brushing the wet hair out of Nellie's eyes.

We trudged up the small steps leading into Tessa's childhood home. I didn't want to open the door and go inside. It held too many memories, and none of them belonged to me. The house would reek of them. She and her family had not packed up their things and moved away. They'd left in a hurry, and there would be evidence of their life here at every turn.

I slowed when my boot hit the top step. A lump stuck in my throat.

Nellie glanced over her shoulder at me. Compassion shone through her tears. "It's all right. She wants you to come inside so you can see this place. It's a part of her. It's a part of both of us."

Her words rang hollow in my ears, just like the sound of the rain. But I nodded and followed her into the dark house. I couldn't say no to Nellie Baran right now.

She moved over to a kitchen table and lit a gemstone lantern. Light spilled through the dust-coated room. There was a rocking chair beside the only window. It faced a small sofa and cluster of armchairs. Paintings decorated the walls. A drab carpet stretched across the stone floor, leading toward a set of rickety stairs.

There wasn't much to the home at all, but a hollow ache formed around my eyes. I could picture her here, sitting in that rocking chair. I could see her laughing and running toward the stairs.

She would have had that wild look in her eye, that defiance.

I cleared my throat, blinking rapidly.

"Our rooms are upstairs." Nellie started up them. The wood creaked beneath our boots.

When we came to the top landing, Nellie led us past two other doors and went to the room at the end of the hallway. Tessa's room. I took a deep breath and stepped inside.

It was cramped. A tiny cot sat in the corner, hidden beneath a pile of wrinkled blankets. A book sat open on the bedside table, spine pointing up at the ceiling. Unlike downstairs, decorations were sparse. There was only one thing on the walls. With black paint, she'd drawn a raven on the wall.

Nellie saw me looking. Tears leaked from her eyes as she leaned over the bed and traced the lines of the bird. "There's a thing we always say to each other. 'Fly away from here, like the ravens.' She has always dreamed of an escape."

Nellie kept speaking of Tessa like she was still here. I wasn't going to correct her.

Clearing my throat, I gently laid my wife's body on the bed. My arms got stuck beneath her. Or I couldn't find the strength to move them. I couldn't tell the difference. Fenella gently wrapped her hand around my arm and tugged me back.

My hands slid out from under Tessa. The weight of her vanished. I felt like a piece of me had fallen off my body.

For a moment, no one said anything. We just stood there, staring at the floor. Nellie sank onto the bed, perching on the edge of the mattress. She'd stopped crying now, and her eyes were distant, haunted.

Distantly, I understood that she was feeling a lot like me.

From the doorway, Gaven cleared his throat. "We should have a chat downstairs. There are some things we need to decide moving forward, and we should talk about what exactly happened out there. I know this is a terrible time, but our people are depending on us to save them."

I gave a noncommittal nod, but I couldn't stop watching Nellie. She carefully moved Tessa's braid to the side and tried to dry her face with the blanket. Her fingers fluttered here and there, gently brushing her cheeks and forehead. After a moment, her shoulders hunched, and she sighed.

"Nellie," Toryn said. "Would you be able to join us downstairs and tell us what happened?"

She blinked up at him. "I don't know if I can talk about it."

"Of course. Just a few details would help, though. You can stop at any time."

"If you promise not to let go of my hand," she whispered.

He cupped her cheek, knelt beside her, and started speaking to her quietly.

I backed out of the door and went down the stairs. Gaven and Fenella followed. When we hit the ground floor, they quickly brushed a cloth across the table and chairs to clear the dust. They each took a seat, but I remained standing. A moment later, Toryn and Nellie joined us.

Nellie's eyes were rimmed with red as she paced from one side of the room to another. She took a moment to speak. Finally, she said, "Andromeda wanted Tessa to use the gemstones. So that the power would infect her, like you warned us about. When Tessa told her she'd never become like them, no matter what Andromeda did to her, she—" Nellie coughed.

We waited for her to take a moment. Then she said, "I ordered the beasts to attack the gods. But it wasn't enough. Sirius tried to take me."

"Sirius?" Gaven looked surprised. "I thought he helped Tessa escape."

"He told me he was sorry, but that he couldn't go against Andromeda's orders. He'd made a vow."

Fenella nodded. "How did you get away from him?"

"He took the gemstones, then dropped me. Tessa saw. She tried to catch me, but..." A strange expression crossed Nellie's face. She stopped pacing. "I...Tessa shouted at me to fly. So I tried. And I suddenly had wings. Like Tessa..."

Nellie gasped. She whirled on her feet and ran up the stairs. The thud of her steps was loud.

Toryn jumped to his feet. "Nellie?"

My entire body shuddered in realization. I took a step after her, not daring to hope.

"Kal, what's going on?" Fenella asked.

"If Nellie can conjure wings, she has the same powers Tessa does." Now that I'd spoken the words out loud, I couldn't move fast enough. I threw myself toward the stairs, and my boots thundered against the wood.

I ran into the bedroom at the end of the hallway. Nellie was beside Tessa again, curving over her. She palmed both of Tessa's cheeks. Nellie was quivering. She could barely hold her hands in place. Gently, I leaned over her and took her hands in mine to steady her. Breathing out, she nodded.

"Kal, Nellie," Toryn said from the door. "It's too late for this. Even if you're right, Tessa can't come back. Not into her own body. And I know you would never want to put her in someone else's. We all know Oberon's story. We understand how Tessa's powers work. To bring someone back into their own body, it has to be done quickly. *You know this.*"

"Let them try it," Fenella said.

"It's only going to cause them more pain when it doesn't work," he argued.

"It will work," I said through clenched teeth. "Go on, Nellie. You can bring your sister back. I know you can."

Nellie pulled in a breath, then closed her eyes. She sat in silence for a long while. Her hands trembled. And then her skin flared with heat. Gasping, she jerked forward. I could feel something building within her, something that felt achingly familiar. It was power born from dark and twisted things. The power of the gods.

I felt that darkness slither through her veins. I felt it light her up, like a star in the darkest part of the night.

"Life," Nellie breathed.

That power surged out of her, rushing into Tessa. Nellie cried out from the force of it. And still I held on, steadying her, knowing how brutal this power must feel when she'd never so much as laid a finger on it before now.

When the moment passed, and her shakes subsided, I released her hands. Tessa still hadn't moved.

Nellie shook her head, crying. "It didn't work."

Grinding my jaw, I started to turn away.

Tessa's body suddenly arched. Her body bucked on the bed. She sucked in a deep, gasping breath of air, and everything within me cracked.

I fell to my knees, taking her hand in mine. My finger found her pulse. Her heart was beating. It was weak, but it was beating. I couldn't breathe. I couldn't think. The surge of emotion made me nearly blind to everything but my mate.

Her eyes were still closed, but her lips had parted. She was breathing.

My mate, my wife.

She's breathing.

Tessa was alive.

She's alive.

If anyone else reacted, I didn't notice. I clung to her hand and watched her face, waiting for the moment she'd open her eyes.

Nellie leaned forward and whispered, "Tessa, can you hear me?"

No answer, no reaction. There wasn't even a flicker of acknowledgement.

There was movement beside me. I looked up at Toryn. His expression was full of concern. "Perhaps she needs time to heal."

But I heard the doubt in his voice, and his earlier words echoed in my mind. Nellie had gifted Tessa with life, but it had been hours since she'd taken her final breath. I'd known Toryn had been speaking the truth before, but I'd wanted to ignore it. The reason Oberon had used Andromeda's power the way he had was because he'd waited too long to bring Bellicent back. Her body and her soul had no longer been intertwined. She had needed a living vessel to survive.

Tessa's body was alive, but...what if she wasn't in there?

"No," I moaned, dropping my head onto my fisted hands. "No, please. She has to be here. She has to be."

Nellie looked at me through blurry, red-streaked eyes. She looked like she was about to pass out. "I don't understand. The body shouldn't come alive by itself. I don't think it can."

"We don't know everything about your power," Gaven said softly. "But...I will hold out hope Tessa is in there and she just needs time to heal."

Roughly, I stood. "I need a bed. If she's in there, I'll be able to find her in her dreams."

"Use mine," Nellie said, staggering to her feet. That flicker of hope had returned, but the power she'd conjured had taken a lot out of her.

She led me to the room next door, where an identical cot sat beneath a tangle of birds in flight. Nellie had attached ribbons to the ceiling. Each string held a raven.

I lowered myself to the bed, lying in the shadow of the wings, and closed my eyes. And then I went to that familiar place again, where mist and shadow danced with the stars, where I knew I'd always find my love.

It was her favorite place to dream.

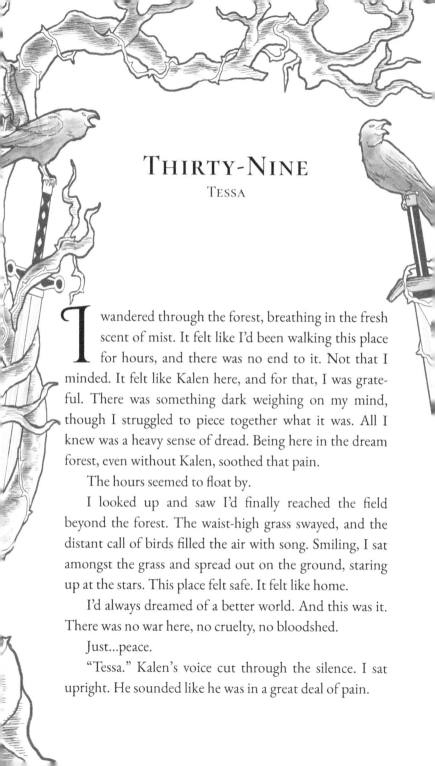

THIRTY-NINE
TESSA

I wandered through the forest, breathing in the fresh scent of mist. It felt like I'd been walking this place for hours, and there was no end to it. Not that I minded. It felt like Kalen here, and for that, I was grateful. There was something dark weighing on my mind, though I struggled to piece together what it was. All I knew was a heavy sense of dread. Being here in the dream forest, even without Kalen, soothed that pain.

The hours seemed to float by.

I looked up and saw I'd finally reached the field beyond the forest. The waist-high grass swayed, and the distant call of birds filled the air with song. Smiling, I sat amongst the grass and spread out on the ground, staring up at the stars. This place felt safe. It felt like home.

I'd always dreamed of a better world. And this was it. There was no war here, no cruelty, no bloodshed.

Just...peace.

"Tessa." Kalen's voice cut through the silence. I sat upright. He sounded like he was in a great deal of pain.

I looked around, trying to find him. A flash of shadow caught my eye. There he was, clad in his black leathers and writhing with mist. He strode through the grass, heading in the direction of the forest. His back was more tense than I'd ever seen it. As he walked, he pumped his hands by his side. They were shaking.

Something was wrong.

I climbed to my feet. "Kalen?"

He stopped. Then he heaved out a breath. Slowly, he took one step, then another, turning toward me as if he was too afraid to see my face. I started trembling myself, not understanding. What was going on? Why did he seem on edge? Had we lost someone? Had the...had the gods won?

He finally faced me. His sapphire gaze raked across me, and he shuddered. "You're here. My love, come to me."

The desperation in his voice drove me forward. He stumbled toward me, his face screwed up in horrible pain. I ran, picking up my pace. When I reached him, his body slammed into mine. He gripped me against him, his mouth against my hair. His body shook like thunder. He loosed choking breaths, and the power of him whorled and crashed against me. Shadow and mist surrounded us in a furious storm.

When he pulled back, he palmed my cheek, my hair, my shoulder. He looked at me like he hadn't seen me in years. "You're all right. You're here. My love, you're here."

"What's going on, Kalen?" I asked, my voice cracking.

"You..." He shook his head. "Andromeda tried to kill you."

At the sound of her name, it all came flooding back. The storm, the fight, the nail across my neck. The pain and darkness that had consumed me until there was nothing left but this.

I shuddered. "Is Nellie all right? Did Andromeda take—"

"Nellie is fine," he said roughly. "It was...it was you, Tessa. You're the one she hurt. You were gone from us, but Nellie managed to bring you back. I thought I'd lost you."

I swallowed. "You're saying I'm dead?"

"You *were* dead. Nellie brought you back."

I needed to sit, but there was nowhere to go but the ground. Instead, I reached for Kalen. He wrapped his arms around me, and I found what comfort I could in the feel of him, firm and steady and strong. My vision swam as the realization thundered around me.

I died.

My life had ended. Oblivion would have taken me, but...

"How?" I whispered. "Nellie doesn't have the power of Andromeda."

"It turns out she does. She just needed to be motivated enough to find it."

"Is she all right?" I asked again.

"Tessa, love." Kalen pulled back to gaze down at me with a fondness that rattled my soul. "You keep asking about your sister when you need to focus on yourself. Nellie is alive. We're all fine. But we need you. You have to find a way to bring yourself back."

"What?" I didn't understand. "You said she healed me."

"She healed you enough to get you breathing, but you're not waking up. I need you to come back to yourself. I need you to open your eyes."

I looked around at the dream, understanding now why it felt as if I'd been walking in it forever. My mind was lost here. And when I thought about walking away from it, a deep-seated pain lanced through my heart. It was all just too much. I had fought so hard, and I had died because of it. The world had taken absolutely everything from me.

Everything but this man I loved. The sister I loved. And the friends who had become my family.

Tears streaked down my cheeks. The idea of going back to that realm of pain made me shake. I wanted this better world.

"I need you, love." He roughly cupped my cheek. "I would destroy every star in the sky just to look into your eyes one last time."

"You're looking into them right now."

"Our dreams have always felt real, but they're nothing more than a figment of our imaginations. You—the *real* you—belongs in the world with me. You are my wife, my mate, my love. My soul is not complete without you."

I closed my eyes and leaned against him. If I asked to stay here, I knew he would walk out of my dreams and leave me in peace. It would kill him to do it, but he would. And I would spend the rest of my days wandering the mists, the fields, and the trees. I wouldn't have to fight anymore.

The gods had won. We'd failed to defeat them. Now, they would unleash their rage upon the world.

But I would never leave him, especially to face the end of everything on his own. I'd made a promise.

I pressed my hand against his thundering heart. "Open your eyes. I'm coming back."

T blinked. Everything was hazy and dark. A small hand gripped mine as gasps filled the air.

"Oh, Tessa," my sister sobbed. She pressed her lips against my cheek, and her wet tears rained on my skin. "Thank the light."

My neck felt like it was on fire. Wheezing, I lifted my free hand to my throat and felt a wet cloth. Another flash of pain tore through me. I flinched.

"It's all right, love," Kalen said softly from somewhere nearby.

"Tessa, I'm so sorry. This was all my fault," Nellie whispered, dropping her head onto my chest. I stroked her hair, though I didn't have the strength to answer.

"Shh," was all I could manage.

She held me like that for a long time. It could have been hours or days for all I knew. But eventually, she pulled back and said, "I love you. You have no idea how happy I am you're here."

I squeezed her hand.

"Come on, Nellie," Toryn said gently. "You need to

lie down. This has taken a lot out of you." A pause.
"You've done so well."

I squinted against the pounding in my head to watch
my sister stumble out of the room. Kalen stood beside
me. I reached for him. When he took my offered hand, I
closed my eyes. His calloused palm brushed against mine
as he settled on the bed beside me.

"I've got you," he murmured.

And then I slept again.

The next time I woke, I no longer felt as if I'd
been carved into pieces, which was a start. My
neck still throbbed, and I had the worst
headache of my life, but opening my eyes didn't hurt
anymore. Kalen was still here. I didn't think he'd left my
side, but he was gazing at a spot beside the bed and hadn't
noticed me wake. He'd seen the raven drawing, then.

I took a moment to look at him, to memorize each
curve of his face. I traced the line of his lips with my
mind, and I committed the pointed tips of his ears to
memory. No matter what happened next, no matter what
horrors we faced, I hoped I could carry him with me to
the next life, even if he was nothing more than a painting
in my mind.

I wanted to draw him in the stars.

Sensing my attention on him, he looked down. He
smiled, though his eyes still looked haunted. "Feeling
better?"

"A bit," I said.

"You can speak." He sat up a little straighter. "Should we...can I...?"

"Look at my wound?" I asked him, tenderly touching the edge of the cloth someone had wrapped around my neck. I guessed that someone had been him.

"I don't want to rush you, but it would be good for us to know if the cut has fully healed."

Cut. Such a simple little word for what it was. Andromeda had sliced my neck open. I'd lost so much blood so fast that it had killed me almost instantly. There were no more games, no more trials and tests. She'd ripped away my life without hesitation.

Kalen frowned at the look on my face. "It's all right. It can wait."

I gripped his hand. "No. We need to know, so you can get back to being king."

He sighed and raked his fingers through his hair. "That can wait."

"No, it can't. Your people—and mine—need someone to lead them through whatever comes next. Andromeda insisted she didn't care about the fae. Destroying them is not her main goal. The humans are. Talaven is. But there are humans here, too. And when she and the others have finished with Talaven, they'll turn their sights on the humans here. They'll come back."

Kalen didn't need to tell me the gods had vanished after Andromeda had killed me. I could feel it in my gut. They'd gotten what they came here for, and now they'd moved on. They had all their gemstones. Their greatest threat was gone. Nothing could stand in their way now. They would take their fight to Talaven.

"Tessa," Kalen said with a sigh. "You need to focus on healing, not everyone else."

"Just help me check my throat. That's all I'm asking."

He nodded. With gentle fingers, he carefully unwound the bandage from my neck. As he pulled it away, I saw silver crescent moons embroidered on the blood-drenched fabric. It was then I realized I was still in my fighting leathers, but the cloak was gone.

"Your cloak," I whispered, staring at the ruined material.

"It was all we had to staunch the bleeding, although it was too late for that. I'm afraid the cloak is ruined. I'll find someone to make you another."

It pained me, saying goodbye to that cloak. To some, it might seem like any other garment, a way to keep me warm or hidden amongst the shadows if I didn't want to be seen. And it had done both of those things. But it was so much more than that, too. That cloak had been the first thing Kalen had ever given me. I'd carried it with me from the beginning. And now it was gone.

"Does this hurt?" He paused, noting the pain in my eyes.

"No, I just...well, I very much liked that cloak. It felt like you."

Half-smiling, he pulled the rest of the fabric away from my skin. When he saw my wound, he sighed, sagging against the chair in relief. "It's practically healed. You still have a scar, but the wound has closed completely."

I carefully touched my neck. Pain hissed through me, though it was nothing compared to before.

Kalen frowned. "Would you like me to wrap it back up again?"

"What I would really like is a bath, some dry clothes, and a moment in bed with my husband." I winked at him.

"Tessa," he said.

"I'm fine."

"I don't want to hurt you."

"You won't." I reached up and wrapped my hand around the front of his leathers, tugging him toward me. "Want me to heal? Take me to bed. I need you to make me forget what happened."

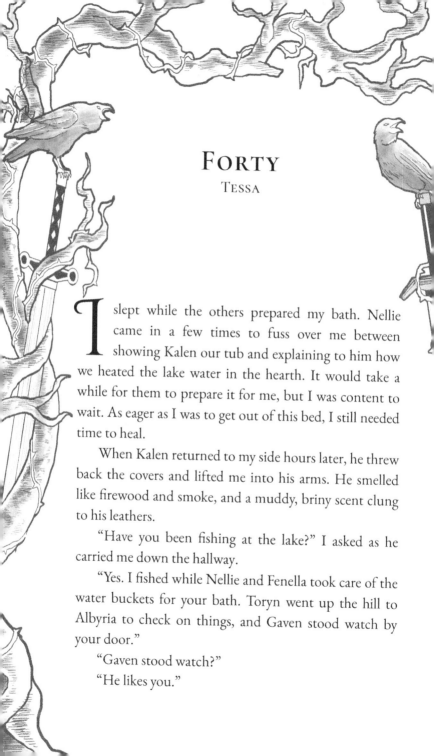

FORTY

TESSA

I slept while the others prepared my bath. Nellie came in a few times to fuss over me between showing Kalen our tub and explaining to him how we heated the lake water in the hearth. It would take a while for them to prepare it for me, but I was content to wait. As eager as I was to get out of this bed, I still needed time to heal.

When Kalen returned to my side hours later, he threw back the covers and lifted me into his arms. He smelled like firewood and smoke, and a muddy, briny scent clung to his leathers.

"Have you been fishing at the lake?" I asked as he carried me down the hallway.

"Yes. I fished while Nellie and Fenella took care of the water buckets for your bath. Toryn went up the hill to Albyria to check on things, and Gaven stood watch by your door."

"Gaven stood watch?"

"He likes you."

"He does? That's not the impression I got from him."

"Nellie told us what you said to Andromeda." A ghost of a smile crossed his lips. "That won him over."

"What I said to Andromeda got me killed," I pointed out.

"Don't regret showing your strength of heart. It took courage and conviction. It showed that you will never turn into one of them. And I am so sorry I ever feared you would."

"Oh, Kalen." Sighing, I reached up and traced the line of his strong jaw. "You don't need to apologize. I would have feared the same thing, too. You lost your mother to their madness. You went to war against their puppet of a king. Of course you were going to fear I'd lose myself to that power just like they did."

"I'm your mate. It's inexcusable."

We reached the door to the bathing chambers, though calling it a 'chamber' would be overstating it by a mile. It was a closet only big enough to hold a small bronze tub. A gemstone lantern lit the space, revealing the cobwebs drenching every corner. After I pulled off my clothes and climbed into the tub, Kalen squeezed inside and shut the door. The soothing water lapped against my tired, aching body. I sighed and relaxed into it.

"This is smaller than I expected," he said. His body did take up almost all the space, him being as tall and broad as he was.

"We're lucky to even have a bath. Most of the homes in Teine don't. Want to join me?"

He chuckled. "I can't fit in there with you."

I looked at him, then looked at the bath. My knees were pulled up to my chest as it was.

Smiling, I said, "I have a better use for you, then. Find a job for the others so—"

"Already taken care of," he said gruffly. "They're doing the rounds to check on all the humans who have returned to their homes here in Teine. Then they're heading into Albyria to help Toryn. We're to join them when you feel up to it."

My chest warmed at the implication. But then I laughed. "You could have kept the door open."

"Oh." He smiled. "Instincts took over. You're my mate. I can't handle the thought of anyone else seeing you naked."

I blushed and extracted the soap from the shelf beside the tub. "No one's going to see me but you. You can relax."

He nodded, but nothing about his posture said relaxed. My 'death' had brought something out of him. Kalen had always been protective of me, even when we'd been at odds. But there was a ferocity to him now. He looked ready to rip apart anyone who so much as looked at me.

I used my rag to shoo him out the door. "I'll be done in a few minutes."

He finally relented and left the bathing chambers, though he kept the door open. I could hear him moving down the hallway, his boots thudding heavily on the creaking floor. As I washed away the sweat and blood, a rustling sound drifted toward me. It was soon followed by creaks and thuds. What in the name of light was he doing out there?

After I washed, I eased back and soaked in the cooling water for a few extra moments. My muscles unwound, and my breath steadied. The sounds from down the hallway soon quieted, and a luxurious, peaceful silence cocooned me. I dipped my head below the water after unbraiding my hair, and the last remnants of the battle with Andromeda released their grip on my skin.

I knew I would never be the same. The trauma from that day would dog my steps for the rest of my life. I would never forget the pain from when she'd dragged her nail across my skin. Echoes of it flared across my neck even now. But I had survived. I was still here, even if her power had been the thing to bring me back.

She'd tried to rid herself of me, but I would not go down that easily.

I was not done fighting.

After towelling off, I padded down the hallway, leaving wet footprints in my wake. I poked my head into my bedroom, half-expecting to find it empty. But Kalen was sitting on the bed surrounded by a pile of my hand-carved daggers.

He gave me an amused smile. "I know I shouldn't be surprised to find a stash of weapons in your closet when searching for some clean blankets, but here we are." He motioned at the whittled blades. "How long did it take you to make these? Were they all meant for King Oberon?"

I nibbled on my bottom lip, a little embarrassed. "I did imagine him on the receiving end, yes."

"You should decorate the wall with them."

"Actually, I was going to hand these out to the other Teine residents," I said, moving over to the bed. "I thought of it before, when we still had the gemstones and thought the gods would attack at any moment. I realize these things wouldn't do much in a real fight, but at least it's better than nothing. Thought it might give them a little comfort, a little hope. They've been through a lot."

"It isn't a bad idea. Hope is a powerful thing." He patted his lap, a feral glint in his eye. "Come sit on me, love. Without the towel."

I dropped it, sauntered toward him, and slid onto his lap.

My whole body came alive as he dove his tongue into my mouth. Whimpering, I closed my eyes and pressed my body against his, feeling the hard planes of his chest. His cock dug into my thigh as he ground against me. Within moments, his trousers were soaked with my need for him. He'd have to find a replacement. But I found I couldn't care. Not right now.

All I cared about was him. His hands, his lips, his cock. I wanted every single part of him to be touching me, stroking me, taking me so hard that I forgot about the looming war and all the death we'd soon face.

So that I forgot about my death, too.

His teeth nipped my neck when he pulled back. My nipples tightened, and the ache between my thighs intensified. With a possessive growl, he tasted my breast, teasing and sucking and taunting me with each exquisite stroke. Shuddering beneath his touch, I dropped back my head and moaned.

Gently, he shifted me off his lap and stood.

"Don't you dare move," he said before lifting his shirt over his head, and quickly followed it with his trousers. Even though I'd seen him so many times by now, I couldn't help but stare. His entire body was corded with pure muscle that rippled as he moved. Mist stormed off his glistening skin.

He tenderly pushed me back onto the soft mattress, his lips trailing across my skin, his fingers digging into my hips. My whole body shivered in anticipation as he stroked my core with his cock. Then he gently pushed inside me. His hard length almost filled every inch of me.

"That okay, love?" he asked, clearly still concerned about how little time I'd had to heal. Leaning down, he brushed soft kisses against my cheek and forehead. I nodded, trembling. He was being so gentle, so kind. But I did not want to stop now. I was still tired, yes, but I was coming alive beneath his touch.

Slowly, he pushed deeper inside until his cock hit the back of me.

He pulled back, then thrust harder. My muscles tightened around him as my pleasure began to build. Arching my back, I opened my legs wider, wanting him deeper—wanting to block out everything in the world but him.

His thumb brushed my cheek, and his eyes cut through me, chasing away all the pain and fear. What had happened to me no longer mattered now. Against all odds, I was still here. I was alive and in the arms of my mate.

Not even death could rip me away from him.

"I love you," I whispered, tears spilling down my face.

His thumb brushed away the tears. "I love you so much I cannot breathe when you're not around."

He thrust harder, deeper. But it wasn't enough. I wanted more.

"Take me as hard as you can," I whispered. "I need you to not be gentle with me. Make me feel alive."

He slowed. "Are you certain?"

"Yes."

Kalen's eyes sparked. He pulled out and flipped me over, my knees digging into the bed. He slid his hands into my hair and pushed the side of my face onto the bed. The tip of him brushed my core. A feral groan spilled from his lips as he cupped my thighs, and a thrill went through me. He thrust inside me once more, this time so much harder. Moaning, I lifted my backside higher so he could get the angle just right.

And he did. His pace quickened. He thrust harder and deeper. My pleasure built, my heartbeat loud in my ears. I clutched the blanket, clinging to it as we rocked so hard the bed creaked. He was taking me as his; he was *claiming me*.

Fuck the gods. Fuck the prophecies and visions and impending doom that threatened to tear us apart.

He was mine, and I would never let go of him.

He gripped my waist and shuddered. My desire built to a roaring crescendo. And as we came together, our cries of pleasure filled the empty house. He kept himself inside me as he leaned forward to wrap his arms around me. His breath tickled my ear, and his finger grazed my nipple. Despite myself, it tightened again at his touch. Desire still roared inside me, insatiable. For Kalen. For my husband. For my mate.

And so I flipped over and pulled him toward me. This night might be the last we ever shared like this. I wanted to make the most of it.

FORTY-ONE
TESSA

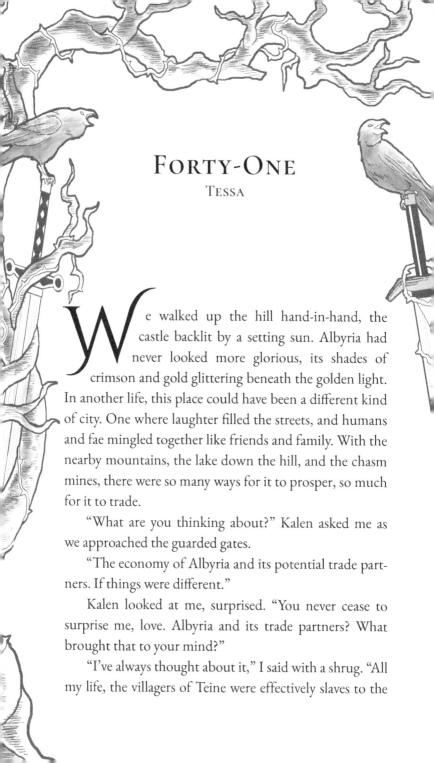

We walked up the hill hand-in-hand, the castle backlit by a setting sun. Albyria had never looked more glorious, its shades of crimson and gold glittering beneath the golden light. In another life, this place could have been a different kind of city. One where laughter filled the streets, and humans and fae mingled together like friends and family. With the nearby mountains, the lake down the hill, and the chasm mines, there were so many ways for it to prosper, so much for it to trade.

"What are you thinking about?" Kalen asked me as we approached the guarded gates.

"The economy of Albyria and its potential trade partners. If things were different."

Kalen looked at me, surprised. "You never cease to surprise me, love. Albyria and its trade partners? What brought that to your mind?"

"I've always thought about it," I said with a shrug. "All my life, the villagers of Teine were effectively slaves to the fae. We produced everything for them, helped keep things running. Oberon didn't want to rely on trade with any other kingdoms." I sighed. "I couldn't help but conjure up ways things could be different. Better. So I've spent a lot of hours thinking about Albyria's economy and its trade. For example, we've always done well with apples here."

"Hmm. You have a mind for politics."

I frowned. "Not politics. Just...the happiness of everyone."

"And the happiness of everyone is tied in to how well their rulers lead. It all matters. The laws. The freedoms. The punishments we order criminals to endure. If we rule with anger and fear, like Oberon did, the people suffer. And if we rule with kindness and generosity, prosperity has its time to shine."

I smiled up at him. "You're the one with the mind for politics. I've never heard anyone speak so poetically about what it means to be a king."

"I would happily never sit on a throne again," he said quietly.

"Really? I know you feel the burden of it sometimes, but—"

Shouts punched through the calm moment. Kalen palmed the hilt of his sword as we approached the gates, where the guards were facing *in*, toward the city, rather than out.

"What's happening?" Kalen barked.

One of the guards turned and said, "The Crones got out of the tower. They're putting on quite the show."

Kalen and I exchanged a glance before moving

quickly toward the disturbance. When we reached the castle square, we found all three of the living Crones dancing on bare, dirtied feet and waving crimson banners over their heads. Their eyes were brighter than the last time we'd seen them, and they were singing an oddly familiar song.

> *The darkness cries for the light*
>> *And comes undone beneath the sky*
>> *An old wind blows*
>> *With ancient woes*
>> *But light will never die*

When they stopped, one of them kept screeching, "Ancient woes, ancient woes, ancient woes!"

Fenella appeared beside us with both daggers in her hands. "Glad to see you're healed, Tessa. You arrived just in time for the madness."

"How long has this been going on?" Kalen asked.

"About an hour. The heirs went to visit the Crones just before it happened, but they swear up and down they didn't do anything." She jerked her head toward where a cluster of horn-tipped fae with human ears watched the dance routine. Horror was etched into the lines of their faces. Those would be more of Oberon's offspring, then. I recognized a few of them, like Mykon, but most I'd never met. Ruari had always been the one to deal with me.

"I didn't think they were physically capable of leaving. Something in Oberon's magic trapped them there."

"Oberon's dead," Fenella said. "The magic would have died with him."

"But Ruari said they were still trapped there after Oberon's death," I countered. "He was certain of it."

"Bet you Oberon fixed it that way somehow, just in case he met an unexpected end. He must have bound them to Ruari's life, too."

"Is that even possible?" I asked.

She shrugged. "Oberon was a tricky bastard. I'm sure he could have figured something out."

The wailing song restarted, effectively ceasing all hope of conversation. I watched as the Crones spun in wide circles. Their cheeks were gaunt, and their hair was ragged, but they were full of so much life. One of them caught sight of me and stopped.

Her eyes widened, and she shuffled closer. With a long, quivering finger, she pointed at me. "The Daughter of Stars."

I flinched. "No, you're mistaken."

"The Daughter of Stars," she insisted. The others began to slow as they noticed her attention on me. "You are the one from the prophecy."

I shifted on my feet and exchanged an uneasy glance with Kalen. "What prophecy?"

"The prophecy of the stars! The savior of the fae!" another Crone exclaimed before dancing away on frantic feet.

Fenella edged up beside me. "Seems the Crones think you're some kind of savior. Good thing we brought you back to life, eh?"

I shot her a look. "They don't know what they're

talking about. Until now, I didn't even think they could speak. What Oberon did to them...well, I don't understand how they're doing any of this. They were only shells the last time I saw them."

"A piece of them must be left in there," she said. "The human girls, I mean. The ones who were sacrificed to give Oberon his, erm..." She winced, glancing at Kalen. "Bellicent."

Frowning, I watched the Crones. Nothing in that vision they'd shown me, and nothing in Oberon's own confessions, had made it seem like the souls of those human girls could have survived becoming a vessel for someone else. But they'd still been cognizant enough to show me that vision. They'd reached out and touched my arm. Their eyes had been distant, but not *gone*.

An idea burned bright in my mind.

I touched Fenella's arm. "We need to gather everyone and have a meeting."

K alen, Toryn, Fenella, and Nellie were gathered in the remains of Oberon's Great Hall to discuss our next steps. Gaven had stayed outside to keep an eye on the Crones—someone had to watch them. They'd gathered around an oak table that had survived the blaze. Someone had made a start on cleaning up the place, and while the hall didn't glimmer and shine as it had before, most of the ash and rubble had been removed.

The one-eyed dragon banners were gone, replaced by simple teal tapestries edged in silver. The charred stone floor was hidden beneath a matching carpet, and several gemstone lanterns hung from the ceiling, twinkling with light. I walked inside after listening to the chants of the old Crones one more time. I thought I might make sense of it. I was wrong.

Nellie jumped from her chair when she saw me, then rushed around the table with a bundle of black cloth in her hands. She didn't embrace me when she reached me. I could tell she still worried I might fall apart. "You're on your feet."

"I'm on my feet." I smiled.

"I am so sorry, Tessa. I shouldn't have..."

"Nellie, don't." I grasped her arm. "It's not your fault. All right? I'm here, and I'm alive, *because of you*."

She nodded, then shoved the cloth into my hands. "I knew you were upset about the cloak, so I washed the strips and sewed them back together. It's not the prettiest thing, but I thought you'd like it anyway."

My lips tipped up in the corners. I unfolded the cloth, and the fabric rippled toward the floor. It was Kalen's cloak, with its silver crescent moons, with its stains of blood and mud that persisted despite being cleaned. Rough, jagged lines of silver thread now decorated the length of it, but I couldn't have cared less. It wore its remnants of battle and pain, and it was still here. Nellie had put it back together for me.

"Thank you, Nellie." I hugged her tightly, pressing my lips against her hair. "You have no idea how much this means to me."

After draping the cloak around my shoulders, I joined the others at the table.

Fenella leaned back in her chair and kicked her mud-encrusted boots onto the table. She pulled out a dagger and used it to pick at her nails. "Let me guess, *Daughter of Stars*. You called for a meeting because you want to chase down the gods."

"Don't call me that," I said.

"Why not? There's a prophecy about you. Probably an important one if those Crones out there woke up just so they could shout about it."

I pressed my lips together. Truth was, I *had* heard that name before. From the sky itself. At the time, I thought perhaps I'd been imagining the voice. I'd been flying for the first time in my life, and I'd been exhilarated from the thrill of it. Beasts had been hunting me. Kalen had been in danger. And so my mind had conjured this impossible thing.

Or so I'd thought.

Could the voice have been real? If so, what did it even mean, and how had I heard it that day? Surely the stars themselves couldn't speak to me. How could they speak to anyone at all?

"Anyway, that's not why I wanted to have a meeting," I said instead of acknowledging the prophecy. "Fenella, you said something out there that got me thinking."

She grinned. "Thinking is always a dangerous pasttime."

Toryn laced his hands behind his head, rubbing his fingers across the buzzed hair he'd cut again since we'd arrived in the Kingdom of Light. Nellie sat beside him, looking at him fondly. I bit back a smile.

"It got me thinking as well," he said. "You put one of the gods into Caedmon." He gave Fenella an apologetic look. "I'm sorry. I know it must be hard."

"It's fine. Caedmon made his choice," she said tightly.

"Yes, it seems pretty clear that the god was in the gemstone, and whatever I did passed the god into Caedmon's body. He became a vessel for him. Or her."

Kalen arched a brow. "I see where you're going with this. A vessel, like the Crones?"

"That's right. We'd already figured out they can put their essences into fae bodies, but what if it's exactly the same thing Bellicent was doing?" I asked. "And if the Crones still have aspects of themselves in there..."

Fenella let out a low whistle. "That would mean Caedmon could still be in there, at least remnants of him."

"All of them could have remnants," I said firmly.

"I don't see how that helps the human kingdoms," Nellie said after a moment. "Even if you're right and Caedmon and other fae are still alive inside them, how could we possibly use that to stop the gods from destroying Talaven and every other human in this world?"

I leaned back in my chair. "Well, that I don't know."

For a long while, we all sat there. The reality of our situation remained unchanged, despite our newfound understanding. There was only one thing that could stop the gods, and we'd had that power in our hands. Now we'd lost it. We no longer had control over the beasts, who could harm them with their claws and fangs. We did have Nellie, but one girl wasn't enough, no matter how strong she was. And without a god's gemstone powering the Mortal Blade, that was useless, too.

"So." Fenella tapped the tip of her dagger against the table. "Is it time for us to prepare for the inevitable end?"

"*No*," I said firmly. "The world needs us. We have to fight for them."

"And how do you propose we do that?"

I looked at Kalen, hoping he had the answers. But his gaze had gone hard, and his eyes held no spark. If he'd ever held on to hope for survival, he'd released his grip on it now. If only we could use his power against them. If only we could use mine.

Frustration tore through me. Andromeda had been so clever when she'd forced me to make that vow. She'd destroyed any hope we had of fighting against her. Physical weapons were useless against the gods. Fae powers were useless when the gods muted them. Humans had nothing. And yet I could not give up hope.

Kalen cleared his throat. "I've sent Boudica to warn Niamh and Alastair of what's coming. Hopefully, they'll get the humans back to Talaven, where they can shore up strength in their castles. It might give them more time."

"That's all we can hope for," Toryn said gravely. "Just a little more time. A few more weeks or months in this world with those we love." He looked at Nellie.

Tears burned my eyes. "Talaven has no hope if we don't do *something*. Even if they hide inside their fortresses, the gods will take them, and it won't be pleasant. They have the power of fear and famine, pestilence and beasts. They will wreak havoc on the humans." I stood, knocking back my chair. "We can't just give up like this. Val is with them. Niamh and Alastair, too. We have to do something."

The flutter of wings rushed toward us from the corridor. Boudica soared inside and came to perch on Kalen's shoulder. She rubbed her beak against his cheek, then cawed. Kalen's face tightened. She'd brought him news. I leaned forward, worried the gods had already begun their war with Talaven.

"Well, it seems we were wrong." Kalen scanned the length of the table until his gaze landed firmly on me. "The gods aren't going to Talaven first. Their army is camping in the fields a few miles away from here. It looks as if they intend to sack Albyria first. They're coming for us."

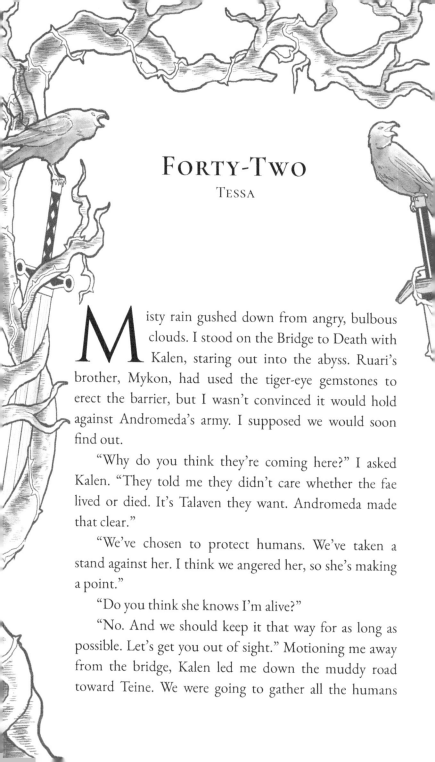

FORTY-TWO

TESSA

Misty rain gushed down from angry, bulbous clouds. I stood on the Bridge to Death with Kalen, staring out into the abyss. Ruari's brother, Mykon, had used the tiger-eye gemstones to erect the barrier, but I wasn't convinced it would hold against Andromeda's army. I supposed we would soon find out.

"Why do you think they're coming here?" I asked Kalen. "They told me they didn't care whether the fae lived or died. It's Talaven they want. Andromeda made that clear."

"We've chosen to protect humans. We've taken a stand against her. I think we angered her, so she's making a point."

"Do you think she knows I'm alive?"

"No. And we should keep it that way for as long as possible. Let's get you out of sight." Motioning me away from the bridge, Kalen led me down the muddy road toward Teine. We were going to gather all the humans who had only just returned to their homes, and take them into the city. It would be safer for them behind the walls if the gods broke through the barrier. Teine had fortifications. All the homes were built from flammable wood. As broken as Albyria was, it was the better place to wait out the storms.

"It looks like I'll be handing out those wooden daggers after all," I joked, though the words rang hollow in my ears. The last thing I wanted was to watch my people die with nothing but a sliver of wood to protect them. They were pale imitations of proper weapons and nothing more.

Kalen threaded his fingers through mine, understanding my fears better than anyone. It was his people and mine who were in danger. I might not be the Queen of Teine, but I still felt responsible for them. The Elders were dead. They had no leader now. No one but me.

The rain had turned the dirt-packed roads of Teine into muddy rivers. We went door to door and explained that war was coming. I expected some resistance, but none came. At every house, we were greeted with trembling hands and wide eyes. But they gathered their things and their families and followed us up the hill, where the civilian fae had hunkered down. Warriors marched through the streets and climbed the battlement stairs. Archers had spent the day collecting wood and whittling arrows.

I led the humans to the top few floors of the tower. They would hunker down in Oberon's quarters, as well as the ones I used to call mine. Fenella had removed all the stuffed animal heads at my request. All that was left was the familiar four-posted bed, the barred windows, and the scent of lavender that still lingered even now. It felt strange standing inside this place. Looking around, it didn't seem quite so grand anymore. If anything, it felt small, especially with a few dozen humans crammed inside it.

I passed out the daggers. It seemed like a poor gesture, but I had little else.

Before I turned to go, Ellen, a girl I'd grown up with, grabbed my arm. "Wait, Tessa."

I met her gaze. She pushed her midnight hair behind her ear, revealing mud-streaked cheeks. She'd once been so bold. But now she looked scared and alone, and I did not blame her at all.

"I..." She dropped her voice to a whisper, and her hand tightened on my arm. "What's going to happen to us?" Her eyes were pleading with me, begging for me to say that everything would be fine.

She didn't want the truth. She didn't want to know the odds were stacked against us. If the gods broke through the tiger-eye barrier, no amount of weapons or ferocity would stand a chance against them. We would fight for all we were worth, but unless something miraculous happened, we were doomed.

But she did not want to hear that.

I placed my hand over hers and held tight. "You will be safe in the tower. That's why I brought you here. We're going to close the shutters and block out the light, and the enemy won't know anyone is in here."

"And the enemies are the gods?" she said, her voice

cracking. "The creatures who want to enslave humanity so they can feast on our flesh and blood?"

I nodded, but Andromeda's words echoed in my mind.

This is the problem with lore, Tessa Baran. The years erode the truth, leaving nothing behind but a smudged portrait of the real history. We will not feast.

Andromeda had insisted, time and time again, that she and the other gods didn't consume human flesh. She'd made it clear the idea disgusted her. And yet, what did she want from the humans if that wasn't it? If I'd proven myself to her, she'd planned to tell me. But I never had.

"Are they after *us*? Is that why they're coming?" Ellen asked.

"I think it doesn't matter what they want or why. They are our enemy, and we will do our damndest to stop them."

I started to let go, but Ellen clutched me tighter.

"Thank you," she whispered. "I know things weren't great between us before Oberon chose you, and I wasn't kind to you. I've heard what he did to you and your family. We've all heard."

A murmur went through the crowd, and I realized we had an audience. A cluster of villagers had surrounded us. All were nodding their heads or gazing at me in pity. No, not pity, I realized. Understanding and something else. Hope.

They had yet to give up hope.

"You don't need to apologize or feel guilty about what happened to me." I raised my voice, turning so I could address the crowd. "All of you, you're my family. I grew up with half of you, and I looked up to the rest. Together, we survived the cruelty of the fae. That's what us Teine mortals do. We survive. And now we're going to survive this."

"I heard you're the answer to a prophecy," Milly whispered from her perch beside the window.

"I heard that, too," Pria added. "You're the Daughter of Stars."

Another girl asked, "Does that mean you can save us?"

I glanced around the crowd, noticing many of the villagers here were the other women my age. We'd all been offered up to Oberon as his next mortal bride. They'd followed me into this room while Kalen sorted out housing for the others. They must have hoped I had answers. I wished I did.

"I'm going to do my fucking best, all right? I'll do whatever it takes," I said, meeting every single gaze in the room. They nodded back, and some loosed sighs of relief. But I hated that I had nothing more comforting to offer them. "Now, we're going to close the shutters, we're going to douse all the lights, and you're going to remain silent. Don't open that door, and don't call out. Not until you hear my voice. Got it?"

Milly jumped to her feet and pulled the shutters closed. Pria moved to the gemstones and flicked them off. I paused at the door and held my fingers to my lips. Then I locked the girls inside. We hadn't been close since the Festival of Light, but I'd always considered them a part of my family. I always would.

I hoped this wasn't the last time I ever saw them.

Toryn met Kalen and me in the corridor. He looked weary, like he hadn't slept in days. A golden crown now weighed down his head. Like Kalen, ruling was a burden for him.

"The storm fae are safely ensconced on a lower floor. There weren't a lot of clean rooms, so some are huddling together on blankets in the hallway. I told them they should get some sleep, but I don't think anyone will be dreaming tonight." Toryn sighed with his entire body. "They just went through this in Dubnos not that long ago. I wish they could have a break from all this bloodshed."

"Everyone here could use some relief. Has Boudica returned from scouting ahead?" I asked Kalen.

He nodded. "A few moments ago. The gods have packed up their war camp, and they're on the march. They're heading this way, just like we thought."

"How many?" asked Toryn.

"They lead an army of a thousand beasts. But the fae contingent is our greatest worry. They've combined the warriors from Star Isles with the storm fae led by Toryn's brother. Together, they have at least three thousand fighters. Some of them will have elite powers, but it's impossible to know how many."

Toryn blanched. "Three thousand fae and a thousand beasts?"

"And seven gods, I'm guessing."

"That's what it looks like." Kalen frowned. "In addition to the five we know, and Caedmon, there is one other."

"Pandora, the God of Storms. Seven gods, three thousand fae, a thousand beasts." Toryn ran a hand down his face. "And we have, what? Five hundred warriors at most? And all our elite powers are useless when the gods can merely mute them."

"We have several thousand civilians, but they don't know how to fight," Kalen said.

"Don't forget the barrier," I pointed out. "And me."

The two fae kings turned toward me. They both looked skeptical.

"The Daughter of Stars," I said with a shrug. "It must mean something."

Toryn shook his head. "No offense to you, Tessa, but I wouldn't put much stock in what the Crones say. Their minds are muddled by what Oberon did to them."

"They were talking about a prophecy, and I think we all know that a prophecy is very much real," I argued. "Bellicent believed in it so strongly that she forced Kalen into a vow that was intended to kill her. She knew what she would become, and she tried to put a stop to it."

Kalen clenched his jaw and turned away.

I softly touched his arm. "I'm sorry to bring it up, but we can't ignore it forever. She made you vow to kill whoever brought back the gods. Because as long as they lived, we would never be able to rid the world of them. Isn't that what she said?"

"Yes. And now she's dead, but the gods are still here. So clearly she was wrong."

"Except the human king told Niamh the same thing. Bellicent became an anchor for Andromeda."

Toryn cocked his head, clearly thinking. "What are you trying to say?"

"I'm not certain," I said honestly. "The pieces of the puzzle are scattered around us, and the edges don't line up yet. All I know is this: there's a prophecy. It foretold of a time when the gods would return. Bellicent knew she would be the one to bring them back, and we couldn't rid the world of them again unless she died. And there's another part to the prophecy." I looked at Kalen. "Val's clippings, remember? It mentioned both of us and our bond. Mates, blessed by the stars."

"Daughter of Stars," Toryn murmured.

"The prophecy is real, and there's something I must do. I just don't know what it is." I looked at the door to my old quarters, where the humans were hiding. They were counting on me to survive. "But I intend to find out."

Forty-Three
Fiadh MacCain

THOUSANDS OF YEARS AGO

Andromeda was in bed with the human king. I did not know how long she'd been there, but there was a familiarity in the way she curled against him and splayed her fingers across the ridges of his broad chest. His fingers found her hair and danced between the strands. Peace, that was what she felt.

Andromeda felt peace.

"How long will you stay with me, my love?" Ovalis asked. She smiled and propped herself up on her elbow so that she could look at him. I could see now why he'd gotten into her bed, if not her heart. His brown eyes were hazy with lust, and a smile curved his full lips. With his broad jaw, carved cheekbones, and sweeping brown hair, he looked like he'd walked out of a painting. A dashing hero from a romance tale, the kind of man only found in books.

"As long as you live," Andromeda said softly. There

was a hint of pain. She knew he was a mortal man, destined for mortal years. She could gift him with life if he died, but she could not stop him from growing old. She'd tried. His life would be but a blip in her eternity, and yet she could not walk away from him, away from this. When Andromeda had taken a fae form, she hadn't anticipated what it would feel like to fall in love.

She was intoxicated by it.

He brushed his thumb across her bottom lip, and she quivered expectantly.

I flinched back. Now that I saw where she was and how little clothing they wore, I had a fairly good idea of where this was going. As much as I liked being aware, I had no desire to bear witness to Andromeda's sexual adventures. Especially as she was *in my body*.

Disgust roiled through me.

Thankfully, the haze seemed to hear me, and all went dark once more.

"What do you mean, the fae have rejected the gemstones?" Andromeda paced the stone floor, her fingers jammed into her hair.

She was somewhere else now, somewhere I didn't recognize. The scent of salt water filled the air, reminding me of home. She whirled toward the gathered creatures.

Perseus stood in front. There were angry lines across his handsome face.

He stepped closer to her. "The fae took the gemstones to the four corners of their continent and buried them. You should see what it's done to their lands. The power has seeped into it. Shadows and mist rage across one region. Light and fire across another. And one is plagued by vicious storms. They've tried to unbury the stones to undo what they did, but they cannot find them."

"And the fourth stone?" Andromeda asked.

"There is a place with tranquility, small though it is. The Ivory Cliff Falls." Perseus shook his head. "But that doesn't matter. What matters is they rejected the gift we gave them. They will not ally with us against the human kingdoms like they said they would."

Andromeda shifted on her feet. She wasn't so certain she wanted to wage war any longer. Death was no longer in control. Her love for Ovalis had brought Life back to the surface, and Life did not much like the idea of blood on her hands. In fact, it was why she'd wanted Death there in the first place. Life knew she'd never be able to make the hard decisions herself.

She was too soft for war.

Perseus eyed her. "You've changed your mind. After everything we've done for you, you would turn on us like this?"

Callisto folded her arms. On either side of her squatted two magnificent beasts. They'd been bathed and brushed until their coats shined, though their eyes were still as red as blood, reminding me they were the furthest things from pets a creature could be. "This is about Ovalis, isn't it? And your twisted offspring?"

Offspring? A ringing filled my ears.

Andromeda turned away.

Offspring?

"You brought us here for one reason and one reason only." Orion stalked toward her, fury shaking his arms. "We are to *stop* the humans. Not fuck them. That is why you gave our darker natures greater control. It is why the Famine in me is stronger than Abundance, why Perseus's Fear controls Courage. And why Sirius cares little for Healing. And now you're turning your back on what you made us to be."

I could barely listen to them, too locked on that single word. *Offspring.* Andromeda had a child. In *my* body. Pain ripped through me. That child should have been mine.

"Perhaps I was wrong to make you this way," Andromeda said, her voice cracking. She turned back to the others, and I could feel the tears in her eyes, though they'd yet to fall. Gods did not cry.

"Wrong?" Callisto looked at her, aghast. "We've all seen what will happen if we do nothing to stop them. And our gentler natures cannot do what needs to be done."

"What that man has done to you is only evidence we're right," Perseus said. "The Andromeda I know and love would never fall prey to this. That Andromeda wanted to protect the world, not some human king who cares *nothing* for her. Do you not know he has another in his bed as we speak?"

Andromeda narrowed her gaze. "That is a lie. And if you don't stop speaking to me this way, I'll force you to stop. In fact, I'll do it now. Perseus, I order you to say nothing you know will offend me."

Perseus blinked. He ground his teeth and looked away.

"Stop this. Ovalis is the one who is lying to you," Callisto spat. "And if you refuse to believe us after everything we've done for you, make him vow it. See what he says when our power ties his tongue."

When the haze cleared once more, it was only hours later. A day at most. Andromeda's reckless emotions had loosened her grip on me, making it easier for me to watch. What I saw worried me. King Ovalis Hinde was in his bed. He was mounted by three naked women moaning his name.

Andromeda's rage shook through me. She stormed into the room, ripping tapestries off the wall and knocking flower vases to the stone floor, where the glass shattered. Much like her heart.

The king calmly climbed from his bed, naked. His cock was slick from another woman's wetness. He held up his hands, then whispered for the women to leave quickly. They rushed by, fearfully glancing at Andromeda.

"This is not what it looks like," he said once they were gone.

"No?" She snapped the word. "One was on your face, the other was on your cock. I don't know what the third was doing, but it hardly matters. You're sleeping with other women after promising me the world."

"It is just sex, my love."

"I am not your love," she hissed.

Ovalis cocked his head, taking her in as if she were a stranger, not the woman he'd been sleeping with for the past few years. Not the mother of his son. "You've never spoken to me this way before."

"I just caught you with another woman writhing on your mouth." She threw up her hands. "How do you expect me to speak when I discover you've been lying to me all this time?"

"I have not been lying any more than you have," he said coolly.

She stormed toward him, grabbed his clothes from the floor, and tossed them in his face. "Get dressed."

"I'm comfortable as I am, thank you."

Andromeda did not like that answer. She grabbed his shoulder, and her long nails pierced his skin. Blood dribbled out, but the king did not even flinch. "You will vow to tell me the truth."

"I will not," he said darkly. He turned and pulled a dagger from a drawer. It was a small thing, and a gemstone sat in the center of the plain hilt. Ovalis tried to stab her with it, but she easily knocked it from his hand.

Shaking her head, she laughed. It was a hollow, aching sound that sent chills through whatever was left of me.

There was no Life in that sound. Death had returned to the surface. "You humans. Liars. Murderers. Vicious thieves and destroyers. You will tell me the truth, and I will know when you do not."

Power ripped from the core of me—from the horrifying depths of *her*—and crashed into the king. His face twisted from the force of it, from the realization of what Andromeda had done. She couldn't make him tell the truth. She couldn't force him into a vow if he would not speak the words. But in her rage and in her pain, she'd manage to conjure something else. A curse on all the humans.

Any lie they ever told, gods and fae could tell.

It was the last moment I saw before the very end of things.

The darkness faded to light. We stood on a snowy mountaintop surrounded by humans and fae. Their spears were raised, the painted ends coated in red, and pointed at Andromeda's face. Fear churned in their eyes. Fear and hate.

"What is this?" Andromeda hissed.

The fae king stepped through the crowd. His long orange hair hung to his waist, where an axe hung from his belt. A pale orange gemstone flickered in the hilt. Andromeda's attention snagged on it.

"You have come to our world to bring destruction

upon us all," King Aodhan said. "We cannot allow you to remain here."

She laughed, though there was a nervous edge to it. "And you think *you* can rid this world of me that easily? I am a god."

"You are a Lamiae. A force of nature and nothing more. You do not belong here, not in the way you are," he said quietly.

I perked up a bit at this, despite the heaviness of the moment. I'd never thought of it this way, but his words rang with truth. This creature was not a *god*. She was not some magnificent being with power over the world. She was just...an essence. A force of nature. She was not meant to be trapped in fae form.

Wind whipped Andromeda's crimson hair, biting her skin. She barely felt the cold. "I see you have discovered the truth of me and my brethren."

"Not me. The humans. They touched the remains of your star and read your visions. It gave them the truth of you. It showed them the horror you will wrought upon us all. And that is why I am here. I intend to stop you."

Andromeda was silent for a long moment. Tension ricocheted across the mountaintop like volleys of arrows, aimed at the heart. The creature, the essence, had touched the remains herself and seen what this world would become. And yet she had not seen the fae king's trap.

She had not anticipated Ovalis's betrayal, either.

The visions had blind spots. There were forks in paths, ways for the future to wend toward a far different fate. All it took was one wrong breath. And Andromeda had not returned to the comet's remains to search for those possibilities.

Ovalis had distracted her from it.

Suddenly, she laughed. The booming sound raced across the mountains. The ice and snow grumbled, waking from their slumber. Chunks of rocks tumbled into the ravines far below. And still, the fae king kept a steady eye on Andromeda, as if he knew something she did not.

Another trap, I realized.

"You have no idea what you're saying and just how ironic it is," she said.

The king motioned to something behind her— behind us—but Andromeda didn't turn. She continued, her words fuelled by the anger rising inside her. "Have you seen the visions yourself? Have you touched the comet's remains with your own hands?"

"Not necessary," the king replied. Something thunked behind us, pulsing. It felt like onyx.

"The humans are lying to you," she hissed. "Just as Ovalis lied to me. Where are the Talaven rulers? Ask them the truth. They won't be able to lie to you now, not without you knowing."

"I already heard what happened to Ovalis. You murdered him."

A pause. "It may seem that way, but—"

"You deny it?" He motioned again. This time, a human woman carried a bag forward. Aodhan took the burlap sack, turned it over, and dumped Ovalis's head on the ground. Gasps and shocked cries peppered the air. Andromeda swallowed thickly. "Well? Are you saying you didn't do this? If so, we have another enemy out there. One who needs to be cut down."

She pressed her lips together. "This is my doing. But not for the reasons you believe. He has betrayed me, just as you have. I know you buried the gemstones. I know what it's done to Aesir. You took my gift, and you rebuked it."

"Your *gift* has destroyed my kingdom," he said, his voice dripping with disgust.

Andromeda lifted her chin. "Very well. I can see our alliance is null and void. Just know you have made a grave mistake. If you try to kill me, you will fail. And I will treat you with the same contempt as you've treated me. The only difference is, you will not survive it. Those loyal to you will not survive it. And then the humans you are desperately trying to save will meet their end." She shook her head and laughed. "I tried to save the fae. Look at how you have rewarded me."

A heavy silence descended. The fae king stared at Andromeda for a good long while, measuring her words. The flicker of worry in his eyes spelled his thoughts. He did not trust her, but rejecting her meant risking the lives of his people. The humans had told him one thing. The gods were telling him another. And now the fate of the world sat in his hands. This one wrong choice could crush it.

He exhaled. "You came to me for an alliance and asked me to wage war against a man. Then you bedded that man, professed your love for him, and bore his child. You called off the war, vowed you wanted peace. And then you chopped off his head. I cannot trust you."

"That is fair," Andromeda said. "You see what is in front of you, and it's clear I cannot change your mind. Do your worst to me, then, fae. I am sorry for what will come of you."

The fae king pulled a glittering gemstone from his pocket. Dread pumped through Andromeda's veins. She knew that stone, that color. It was from the stars. Faster than the blink of an eye, he popped the orange stone from his axe and replaced it with the sapphire.

He swung the axe at the ground. It cracked through dirt and stone.

Andromeda screamed.

Power erupted all around us, shuddering through the earth. Ice and snow fell into the ravine in a thunderous applause. The world was glad to be rid of this god.

I held on as best I could, but it was too much. The darkness crowded my vision. Deep black swallowed me whole. But even though I could not see, I could feel the truth of what happened to her—to me. Whatever the humans and fae had done, it had worked.

This body—*my* body—was thrown to the stars. Andromeda did not come with me, somehow. The fae had taken their axe to her essence, and they kept her trapped in two separate onyx gemstones. For thousands of years I knew peace. I floated through the aether, my soul healing from all I'd lost.

At long last, I was just me, and I became one of the stars. Sometimes, I even whispered to those below, though I did not think they ever heard me.

Not until Tessa Baran came along. My daughter. Or at least the closest thing I'd ever had to one, a descendent of the child Andromeda had birthed through me all those centuries before. I watched her as she grew, hating how she suffered, wishing I could reach out a hand to help. But when she began to conquer her powers, I started to hope.

And then Bellicent Denare called me back. I was Andromeda's vessel. She demanded my return. A comet swept by me, ripping me from the stars. It dragged me down. Down and down to the world I thought I'd escaped.

To my daughter.

And so Andromeda's possession of me began once more.

But my time in the stars had strengthened me. I stayed aware, never falling into darkness. I cheered on my daughter when she fought, and I mourned when she died. And then I decided I was not yet done with this world. There was one thing I had to do.

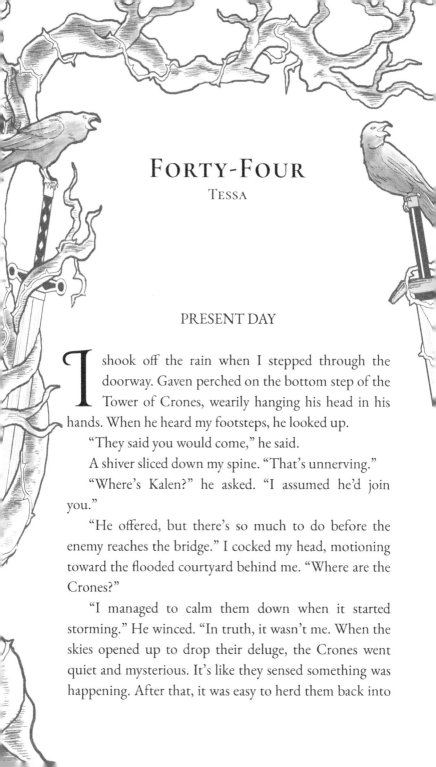

FORTY-FOUR
TESSA

PRESENT DAY

I shook off the rain when I stepped through the doorway. Gaven perched on the bottom step of the Tower of Crones, wearily hanging his head in his hands. When he heard my footsteps, he looked up.

"They said you would come," he said.

A shiver sliced down my spine. "That's unnerving."

"Where's Kalen?" he asked. "I assumed he'd join you."

"He offered, but there's so much to do before the enemy reaches the bridge." I cocked my head, motioning toward the flooded courtyard behind me. "Where are the Crones?"

"I managed to calm them down when it started storming." He winced. "In truth, it wasn't me. When the skies opened up to drop their deluge, the Crones went quiet and mysterious. It's like they sensed something was happening. After that, it was easy to herd them back into

JENNA WOLFHART

their tower room. I was going to come join the rest of you, but then the Crones told me you were coming. I thought I'd wait and see if they were right."

"I think there's more going inside their minds than anyone ever realized. Including Oberon, I'd bet."

"Is that why you came to see them?" he asked.

"There's a prophecy. Until now, all we've had is bits and pieces of it. Something tells me they know the full thing." I indicated toward the stairwell. "Want to join me?"

He climbed to his feet. "Oh, absolutely. This might be one of the most exciting moments of my life."

I couldn't help but laugh as I started up the stairs. He fell into step beside me.

"I assumed you'd had a lot of exciting moments, being part of the Mist Guard," I said.

"At times," he said with a shrug. "But even though I'm a decent fighter, it's not my true calling. I enjoy espionage. I enjoy mystery. And I very much enjoy *information*." He rubbed his palms together. "If we're about to find out the secrets of some ancient prophecy that could quite literally save the world? There's nothing better than this, Tessa Baran."

My booted footsteps echoed down the stairwell. "I hope I don't disappoint you." And as we continued to climb, I couldn't help but ask, "Why did you join Kalen, anyway? I know, like Fenella, you're a light fae, and you lived in Endir until he..."

"He attacked us?" Gaven chuckled. "Yes, the dreaded 'Mist King' invaded Endir during his war against Oberon. Thing is, I hated Oberon. I spied for him for a time, and so I saw what he was like behind closed doors. Didn't care much for how he treated his servants."

"Really?" I asked, surprised. "I heard he was fairly decent before the whole Andromeda thing."

"Decent? To whom? Bellicent Denare? Certainly. He was in love with her." Torchlight illuminated the ponderous expression on his face as we climbed. "I wouldn't say he was a terrible king, per se. Just that he was a typical king. And typical kings are never *kind*. They care more for themselves and their riches than anyone else. Unless your name is Kalen Denare."

"So you followed Kalen because he doesn't care for riches," I said with a smile. "Not the most exciting reason, I have to admit."

"True." Gaven shrugged. "I'm not like Toryn or Alastair, who feel they owe him their lives. I merely want to support someone who's trying to do the right thing for his people. Ah, here we are." Excitedly, he stopped outside the door as we crested the final steps.

I reached for the handle, but the door swung inward on its own. Hinges creaked ominously. I cast him a nervous glance and stepped inside. A wintry wind swept across me, freezing my bones. The Crones all huddled together on a single bed. Their heads were ducked together, and they were whispering furiously amongst themselves.

I cleared my throat, recalling the names that had been imprinted on my mind since I was old enough to hear them. "Elise? Layla? Mala?"

The Crones stilled and twisted toward me. Their eyes

were sunken and hollow once more. Milky white consumed their pupils.

I swallowed, then whispered to Gaven. "Is this what they looked like when they told you I was coming?"

"No." He shifted on his feet. The excited expression was gone. "No, this is new."

Suddenly, they sprang to their feet and started chanting.

The darkness cries for the light
  And comes undone beneath the sky
  An old wind blows
  With ancient woes
  But light will never die

I took a step back as they came for me, their arms outstretched. Heartbeat thundering, I glanced at the door. Maybe it had been a mistake to come here. These women were confused, that was all. Bellicent had always believed in a prophecy, and her ideas must have infected these women. And now, that was all they had. Hazy memories they didn't quite understand.

"Daughter of Stars," one whispered.

"Daughter of Dust," another said.

They came to a stop before me, and the third one said, "Of Gods and Men. Your light will never die!"

"Wait," I cried out as their hands crashed down on me. They gripped me tightly, jerking me toward them. I tried to wrench away, but they were far stronger than they looked, as if an impossible power had suddenly fuelled their bones.

They dragged me under, and a blinding light filled my head.

A woman stood in front of me, her form backlit by a hazy white. She had long, ebony hair and eyes as bright as torchlight. She clasped her hands in front of her flowing sapphire gown and examined me as if I were nothing more than a passing curiosity. I looked around. The hazy white stretched on for miles.

"Hello." She cocked her head. "What is your name?"

I thought about keeping that information to myself. She was a strange, glowing woman brought to me by three other strange women who were clearly half-mad. But there was something calming about her presence.

"Tessa Baran. And you are?"

She smiled. "I thought so. Nice to meet you, Tessa. I'm Bellicent Denare."

I started.

Her keen eyes caught the reaction. "Ah, yes. You've met me at my worst. Fear not, I am not exactly the same woman you've been dealing with. I'm the version of myself from before all that."

"I don't understand," I said.

She laughed. "Of course you wouldn't. So much has been hidden from you." Coming closer, she gestured at the expanse of brilliant light that surrounded us. "I left a piece of myself behind in the Crones so that I might converse with you one day. I had hoped it wouldn't be needed, but here you are, just as I suspected."

"Ah, so that's why they were able to speak earlier. It's *you*, not some leftover piece of themselves." I had to admit I was a little disappointed. If the Crones still lived, even just barely, so did Andromeda's vessel. And perhaps that could have helped us. No matter. Bellicent knew about the prophecy. I could get the information from her, hopefully quickly enough to make a plan before the gods reached the bridge.

Bellicent cocked her head. The move was so strangely familiar. I'd met her before, just in different forms. "No, they're still here. Well, a small piece of them, that is. Very clever of you to have figured that out."

"I suppose. What's this about, Bellicent? Why have you brought me to this place?"

She took another step closer. The sickly scent of lavender drifted toward me, and I couldn't help but take a step back. It reminded me too much of Oberon.

"Well, you see," she said, her tone sharpening," if you are here, then something has gone terribly wrong. Is that true?"

"A lot of things have gone wrong. You'll have to be more specific."

"You stood on a knife's edge, and your choice affected the survival of everyone. Which choice did you make?"

What choice could she be speaking about? Andromeda had offered me the opportunity to join her and the other gods. And I had turned her down as emphatically as I knew how. And if I hadn't? What then?

I searched her eyes, trying to make sense of her words. "Is this about the prophecy?"

A slow smile curled her full lips. "Oh, yes. I'm glad you know about the prophecy. So tell me, what did you choose?"

"I chose to tell Andromeda I'd never join her side. Is that what you wanted to hear? I'll become the Daughter of Stars and do whatever it takes to destroy her." I released a frustrated breath. This was taking too long. "Now that I've answered your question, can you answer mine? Do you know the words of the full prophecy? What am I to do? How do I destroy the Lamiae, the gods?"

Bellicent's smile died. "Where did you hear that name?"

"What name? The Lamiae?"

"No. Where did you hear about the Daughter of Stars?"

I furrowed my brow. Was she joking? "I heard it from you, from the Crones."

She hissed. A bell tolled in warning in the back of my mind. Bellicent had insisted she was from another time, from before she'd become a slave to Andromeda's every whim. But something did not seem right.

"Is there anything you can tell me?" Taking another step back, I wondered how far I could go before I hit resistance. "If not, I really should return to the real world. War is coming, and Kalen needs my help."

"Kalen," she snapped, whipping her head toward me. Her pupils had expanded, swallowing her bright irises until they were a circle of pure black. "Do not speak his name to me, mortal."

Hmm. That was not a good sign.

I raised my voice. "Gaven, can you get me out of here?"

I didn't know if he could hear me, but calling for him was my only option. There was no clear exit to this place. I tried to wake up, but nothing happened. Heart pounding, I could only watch as the fury transformed Bellicent's face into a portrait of deep lines and furrows that made her look like the Crones she'd sucked dry.

"No one can get you out of here," she said, stalking toward me. "If you know your name, you must die, Tessa Baran."

I braced myself. Bellicent attacked. She leapt at me with outstretched hands, her fingers morphing into claws. With a hiss, she swung at my face. I ducked low with only a breath to spare.

She growled and launched at me. Her body slammed into mine, knocking me off my feet. We hit the invisible ground. Breath flew from my lungs, and I grabbed her arms as she tried to rake her claws across my throat.

I shoved her off me and rolled to the side.

She leapt onto my back and sank her fangs into my neck. Pain exploded in my throat, a fearful reminder of what Andromeda had done to me.

"Gaven!" I shouted. "Help me, please!"

The light suddenly snapped away. A hazy room full of flickering shadows roared in around me. The weight of Bellicent was still on my back, and my neck felt wet. But stone was beneath my hands instead of the pale white nothing. I was back, but so was she. She dug her teeth into my neck again.

Gaven roared. The weight of her suddenly vanished. Before I could turn, I heard the sickening crunch of steel against bone. Blood sprayed the floor around my hands.

When I rolled over, Gaven held a Crone's head by the hair. Her body was a ruined mess by his feet. My stomach turned. I swallowed down the nausea and climbed to my feet. Every inch of me felt like it was on fire, and my lungs could barely find enough breath to keep me from collapsing to my knees.

It was then I noticed the other two bodies. They were in a similar state.

Gaven dropped the head. "Are you all right?"

"You killed them," was all I could say, feeling the weight of the world on my shoulders.

"They were trying to kill *you*, so yes."

I sighed and closed my eyes. "It wasn't their fault."

"Fault or not, I wasn't going to let them kill you." At the sound of rustling clothing, I reopened my eyes. To my surprise, Gaven had knelt before me. He bowed his head and placed his sword at my feet. "You are my queen."

I placed my shaking hand on his shoulder. "Thank you, Gaven."

After a moment, he stood and examined the wound on my neck with gentle fingers. "What happened?"

I explained to him what Bellicent had said and done. When I was finished, he looked as uneasy as I felt.

"What does it all mean?" he asked.

"I wish I knew."

Outside, the war horn wailed. Gaven and I both

turned toward it. His lips settled into a hard line, and I knew my expression mirrored his. That sound meant the gods had been spotted from the bridge. They were close now, which meant the battle would soon begin. And I had no answers. No plan to save us. No greater power to offer.

Nothing but a determination to fight for a better world until the end.

FORTY-FIVE
KALEN

There was nothing else like the sound of marching soldiers. Their uniformed steps formed a song of war, a promise of death and blood and fields of broken flesh. Many of the warriors who surrounded me at the edge of the chasm had heard this sound before. They'd been with me through it all, from the battles against Oberon to the skirmishes on the wall back in Dubnos.

But they'd never heard it quite like this. Neither had I.

The deafening march was only the start of it. The footsteps were punctuated by the roaring of beasts and the booming thunder in the skies. The rain had become a deluge, flooding the plain at the bottom of the hill, as well as the village of Teine nearby. Our boots were thick with mud, despite being on the rocky edge of the chasm. Soon, the water would reach us, too.

I was glad we'd taken the humans to the tower. They would have been forced out of their homes regardless.

Fenella stood beside me, cloaked in sapphire. A powerful broadsword was strapped to her back, and a quiver of arrows sat by her feet. She'd attached her two daggers to her thighs. Many other warriors had done the same. If the enemy breached our barrier, we would rain arrows on their heads. I'd hoped to flame the arrows before each volley, but the heavy rains made that impossible.

Tessa appeared beside me, returning from her visit to the Crones. She wore her brown leather fighting leathers and my mended cloak to hide her face from the gods. She'd braided her hair, though strands had already come loose from the wind and rain battering us all. Her eyes looked haunted, and her hands were a little shaky. Gaven was with her, and he gave me a solemn nod. I frowned. Something had gone wrong up there.

"What happened?" I asked her.

"The Crones attacked me. Gaven had to kill them."

"What?" That made little sense. Despite their strange actions earlier, they'd never been anything but harmless. Strange, yes. But hardly a threat.

The symphony of war grew louder, drawing my attention away. Through the rain and swirling mist, the enemy was a stretch of shadow, backlit by the occasional flash of lightning. It was difficult to make out their formation, but it was clear we were far outnumbered, particularly against the unit I'd brought with me to the bridge.

We were three score. They were thousands.

Fenella leaned across me and reached for Tessa's hand. My wife held tight to my friend and gave her a nod.

Fenella said, "I am glad to be fighting beside you, my queen."

Tessa smiled. "You really don't need to call me that, Fenella."

"I know. But now seems the right time, don't you think? These might be the last moments we share, and I want you to understand that you've become as dear to me as Kalen is."

I could have sworn there was a tear in Fenella's eye.

"Then call me friend, call me family." Tessa stepped around me and embraced Fenella. "And I'm honored to fight by *your* side. You're one of the best damned people I've ever met."

"All right," Gaven said, clearing his throat. He looked a bit emotional as well. "Let's stop acting like we're all going to die today, eh? We're going to beat these bastards. And we even get to do it in a rain-battle."

Fenella laughed and moved back to her post beside me. "Only you would find pleasure in rain like this. You sure you weren't born a storm fae?"

"I actually find this quite miserable, but look at the beasts next time the lightning flashes," he said, pointing at the shadowy expanse across the chasm. "They're much heavier than we are, and they're going to struggle in all this mud."

I stood up a little straighter, watching closely when the lightning briefly illuminated the enemy army. The beasts were near to the bridge, but they were moving slowly. Their legs and powerful claws were trapped in a thick layer of mud.

"You're right," I murmured.

"Of course I'm right. You didn't ask me to join your Mist Guard for my fighting skills." He tapped his forehead.

I continued to watch the beasts at every flash of lightning. Now that the army was only a few hundred meters from the edge of the chasm, I could see their formation more clearly. The gods had vanished from the front lines. Not surprising. They were likely flying through the clouds to gain a better view of our numbers.

Thankfully, they wouldn't be able to pierce the barrier, and we held no gemstone lanterns to illuminate ourselves. They would see very little of us, just as we could see very little of them.

Heavy footsteps sloshed through the mud from behind us. I turned, alarmed. No one else was due to join us at the bridge. But Toryn came toward us through the pounding rain, leading a horse. Nellie was with him, too. Both were decked in fighting leathers. Toryn was armed with his spear while Nellie carried a familiar-looking axe. As they drew closer, I recognized the weapon as the one Val had found in Teine, hidden in the local pub.

When Toryn reached us, he quickly said, "Before you say anything—"

"You and Nellie were to help Mykon lead the warriors on the city's battlements," I said. "It was an order."

Toryn smiled. "I suppose I've spent too much time around Niamh."

I barked out a laugh. Toryn came in for a hug, and we pounded each other on the backs. When he pulled away, I said to him, "I'm glad you came, even if you did defy my orders."

"Silver?" Tessa reached out and rubbed her horse's snout. "Why's he here?"

"He followed me out. I couldn't stop him. Trust me, I tried," Nellie said.

A crease formed between Tessa's eyes. "This isn't your place. You could get hurt out here."

She'd told me all about Midnight and what he'd done for her. And by the way she spoke of it, I knew his sacrifice was one of her deepest regrets.

To my surprise, Silver began to transform. His sleek skin shuddered, rippling away to reveal the rough bark underneath. His teeth elongated, sharpening, and his body expanded until he towered over us. He was at least three times as tall as a fae. Spine curved, he leaned down and gently brushed Tessa's cheek with a knobby, branch-like finger.

She had tears in her eyes. "I thought you were stuck, but you can change."

When he spoke, his voice rattled like parchment. "A great deal of power was poured into this chasm once. It gives me strength."

"You should go," she said in a hurry. "Take shelter in the city or escape over the mountains. Get out of here, Silver. I bet you could find someplace in this world where you could be safe for centuries. The gods would never think to come for you."

"I will fight by your side." Creaking, he stood to his full height, the wind and rain battering his thin body. He raised his deadly claw and pointed across the chasm. "They are your enemy, and so they are mine, Daughter of Stars."

"Wait, you know that name?"

"The gods created me ages ago. They accidentally created all of us beasts. In that creation, they passed along the knowledge of their quest and the names of their greatest enemies. So yes, I know about you. I also know what you must do. Use Kalen Denare's power. Channel it. You will defeat her if you do."

"But I can't channel it. Not against the gods. They made certain of that," Tessa whispered.

Deep-throated roars exploded near the bridge. The conversation promptly ended as we all returned our focus to the impending battle. Across the chasm, the beasts hunkered in the mud. Their gleaming eyes pierced the mist. They were watching us.

"Archers, prepare yourselves. We can't be certain what they will do," I ordered, then turned to Gaven. "Get ready by the bridge. You know what to do."

Bows were raised. Strings were pulled taut. Tension drove me to pull my own sword.

Time ticked by in agonizing wait. There was still no sight of the gods. The storm fae weren't moving. Neither were the beasts.

"What do you think they're doing?" Toryn muttered from beside me. "Why aren't they trying to cross the bridge?"

"They're waiting for something," I said.

"I don't like this," Tessa said. "Something's wrong."

Unease churned my gut. We needed the beasts to attempt the crossing. Our plan relied on it. When they tried to reach us, we'd briefly lower the barrier so Gaven could light the bridge on fire. Even in the rain, his flames would rip through the beasts and the waiting fae army, so long as the gods didn't spot him and mute his powers. It would significantly reduce their numbers.

But the beasts stayed put.

I leaned down to speak to Tessa. "Arm yourself. Something's about to happen, and I don't know if—"

Lightning forked through the sky. It shot through the clouds above us, then slammed into the chasm wall. It split the rocks, which rolled forward, tumbling into the chasm below. One of my warriors got caught in the land-slide. His scream filled the air as he plunged into the darkness.

"They're using the storm," Tessa said in a gasp. "They can't breach the barrier themselves, but their power can. We need to get back. We need to find shelter."

She was right, though I hated withdrawing so early.

But before I could shout the order, the ground rumbled.

"Get back from the chasm!" I shouted at my warriors. The barrier was still intact, but the lightning had pierced it. Clearly, it was no match for the power of the gods. Ruari had hoped it could withstand them, but he'd been wrong. Tiger-eyes could not stop the gods. Nothing could.

My warriors fell back, taking several steps away from the chasm edge. The ground continued to shake, and a crack suddenly yawned behind us. A large black talon soared through the dirt and punched down like a hammer from the sky.

Another burst of lightning ripped toward us and slashed the barrier.

Tessa's fingers dug into my arm. "It's one of the scorpions."

I looked at the bridge and the waiting army, feeling more helpless than I'd ever been. We only had one beast to fight, but the barrier would not hold for much longer. We'd be swarmed. And yet, there was nothing else I could do but stay and fight.

I resigned myself to my fate, though I wished I'd had just a bit more time. I'd found my mate, but our time together had been plagued by constant battle, loss, and sorrow. We'd never had a chance to *just live*, to wake up side by side and wander into the Great Hall to break our fast, laughing with our self-made family. The only time we'd ever walked through verdant fields or gazed upon a sky full of stars had been inside our dreams.

I'd wanted it to be real one day. And now it never would be.

I stood tall and addressed the gathered warriors. And as they looked to me, I could see in their eyes they understood. This battle would be our last.

"Ready yourselves to fight the beast," I shouted. "And then stand your ground. Gaven, stay out of sight and prepare to loose your fire on the bridge. The enemy army will be upon us in moments, and we'll take out as many of them as we can."

Tessa slid her hand in mine and squeezed tight before she drew her sword. "There must be something more I can do."

"Just stay with me. And if I fall, flee to the city with your sister."

"I'm not leaving your side, no matter what."

I took her face in my hands and kissed her fiercely. "I love you with everything I am. I hope you remember that when we're nothing but a memory written in the sky."

She shuddered against me, nodding. "Let's make the stars weep."

FORTY-SIX

NIAMH

T he sight of Aesir stirred a breathlessness in me. I paced the deck, wishing I could force the ship to move faster. We'd sailed into the cove along the southern edge of the continent, where the mountains backed up against Albyria and Teine.

I could see the break in the mountains now, along with the empty plains beyond it.

Only they weren't empty.

Val hurried to the wooden railing and gripped it. "Do you see that? When the lightning flashes, look left. There's an army of thousands, and they have...they have lots of shadowfiends."

Her face paled, and she stumbled back. Alastair gently rested his hand on her shoulder.

"What's happening?" Val whispered.

Vera strode to our side. She gazed at the storm-shrouded lands, her hand on the pommel of her sword. "If I were to guess, your people have fled to Albyria, where they are making their final stand against the gods."

"Then we are too late," I said darkly. "There are too few of us on these ships to make a difference. Look at the expanse of them."

"Ah, but look," she said with a smile.

I turned to follow her gaze. Dozens of ships had already converged along the right side of the cove. Their torches illuminated the beach as hundreds of fighters swarmed onto the shore, just outside the path of the storm. A distant flash of lightning revealed the side of the largest ship. I gaped at the familiar symbol. *The Sea Fae's Curse II.*

"I don't understand. That ship got destroyed. We were *on it*," I said, unable to keep the shock from my voice.

"It's a different ship," Vera said. "And it brought the other half of our armada here, rather than returning them to Talaven like we thought."

Alastair grunted. "Bit odd. Did you know about this?"

"Of course not. I would have told you."

I exchanged a knowing glance with Alastair. This made little sense. Even so, now wasn't the time to argue about it. Our king needed us. If the enemy army had gathered around the chasm, that meant they'd backed our people into a corner with nowhere to flee. But I understood why Kalen had made this move. There was only one way into Albyria, and it was across that bridge. The gods could fly, but the fae and beasts could not.

It was a solid strategy, even if it wasn't perfect. Probably the best one they had.

"We'll reach the shore soon," Vera said. "Once we do,

we'll get everyone into formation and go on the offensive. Prepare yourselves as best you can. I left some leathers in your cabin for the human girl."

She moved away, likely to inform the rest of the soldiers on board. Val still clung to the railing, and her emotions were written all over her face. She was scared for her people. And she was likely scared for herself. This was unlike anything she'd ever faced. I hoped if we survived this night, she'd never have to face anything like it again.

"I suppose I better get changed into those fighting leathers," she whispered, turning to go.

"Val, wait." I caught her arm.

Alastair cleared his throat. "I need to polish my sword. It gets to cut through enemy flesh soon, so it should do it looking good."

He wandered off, winking as he went.

I loosened my hold on Val and motioned her to rejoin me by the railing. "There's something I want to talk to you about."

She sighed and leaned against the side of the ship, the wind whipping up her hair. "Are you going to ask me to stay on board during the battle?"

That, in fact, was *not* what I wanted to say, but... "It's not a bad idea, Val."

She swatted aside the hair that blew into her eyes. "I don't think I can do that."

"Do you know how to fight?"

"You take a sword and you swing it at the enemy."

"Yes, well. That's true, but...Val, it takes a lot of prac-tice to get good at it."

Scowling, she turned away. Her jaw worked as she

gazed at the shore we were quickly approaching. My heart clenched. I understand how she felt. I'd never be able to wait on a ship while everyone I knew and loved fought for survival. It was against everything I believed in. And the fact she was brave enough to want to join us in that fight...

I reached out for her hand, but my knuckles barely skimmed hers. Suddenly, I didn't know if I could go through with this. I'd never felt more nervous in my life. I cleared my throat. "That's not what I wanted to talk to you about, though."

She turned back, and her gaze dropped to where our hands brushed. Her eyes swept back up to my face, and my breath nearly caught from the sudden softness in them. She curled a pinky around mine. I didn't know if I could breathe.

"What is it you want to say to me, Niamh?" she asked softly.

That was when I understood, when I realized I'd been such an idiot. Val *knew*. And from the look on her face, she had known for a very long time, and she had been waiting for me to do something about it.

I'd wasted so much time. All these weeks spent together could have been so much more, and yet...and yet, I wouldn't change any of it. Her friendship had become everything to me.

As the wind gusted her hair into her face again, I brushed aside the strands. I didn't think I'd ever touched someone—or *anything*, really—with so much tenderness. The thought of touching so much more of her made me quake.

"You are beautiful," I finally made myself say, with my hand still on her cheek. "You are brave, and you are kind. Before we face what might be the end of our world, I needed you to hear that from me. I need you to know I care for you deeply." My thumb swept down to her full lips. "And I've wanted to kiss you from the moment I saw you, holding that axe of yours."

She stepped closer and tilted back her head in invitation. "I am yours. I have been for weeks. All you have to do is put your mark on me."

I cupped her face with my other hand and pulled her closer. Breath shuddering, I lowered my head and brushed my lips across hers. The longing and wild yearning cascaded through me, and I deepened the kiss, even as I tried to hold my passion at bay. I was scared of overwhelming her, afraid if I did too much, it would frighten her away. But then she grabbed the front of my leathers and tugged me against her.

Her mouth moved against me with a feverish intensity that matched mine. I kissed her fiercely. My hands roamed down the length of her and relished her curves. She was the most beautiful woman I'd ever seen, and she was here in my arms at last. I wanted to spend forever like this.

I did not know how long we kissed and stood there enjoying the feel of each other. But when it ended, all I wanted was more. Val pulled back, gasping. Her face had turned a brilliant pink, and her lips bloomed with color.

She gave me a shy smile. "I've been waiting for you to do that for quite some time."

"I should have done it sooner," I said.

A booming thunder shook through the skies, louder than a moment ago. Val's smile dropped. We both turned toward the shore and the stormy darkness beyond it. We were only moments away now.

"You best go get changed," I told her.

"Into the leathers? I thought you wanted me to stay on this ship."

"I do, but I won't try to stop you if you want to fight. It's your people out there, too, and I know you consider Tessa your family." I pulled a dagger from my side and placed it in her hands. "You're the one who gets to decide what to do. No one else."

Fire sparked in her eyes. I knew it would. "I'll go get changed."

I waited by the railing, watching the rest of the human forces gather on the shore. When Val returned, she brought Alastair with her. He'd found a few extra daggers to attach to his leathers, making him look like the force of nature he always was.

I held out my hand. He wrapped his meaty paw around mine, and we clung tight.

"We go to war together once more, my old friend," I said.

"Always a pleasure." He grinned. "Wouldn't want anyone 'cept your annoying ass beside me."

I gave him a look. "Pretty sure I'm not the annoying one in this friendship."

Chuckling, he gave Val a once-over. "Want some tips?"

"As long as your tip isn't that I should stay on this ship, then by all means," Val said.

I fought back a smile.

"I wouldn't dream of it." He pointed at the dagger she'd sheathed on her hip. "This is a very short-ranged weapon. It won't do you much good until the enemy is right in your face. You'll have your chance to fight. It's inevitable. But you should stay close to me and Niamh in the beginning. Don't rush in unless we need help. Stay back otherwise. Then when chaos descends, channel every ounce of fear and anger and hope and passion into your attacks. Don't go after a fae with a bow and arrow, and stay the fuck away from any elite storm fae. Just be smart about it, eh?"

She nodded emphatically. "Got it."

The ship creaked as it slowed, sand scraping against the bow. I held on to the railing and waited. Val and Alastair followed suit. When the ship had finally stopped, Vera appeared beside us and tossed a ladder rope over the side.

"It's time," she said.

A score of human soldiers rushed past us and scaled down the ladder. Once they were done, Vera motioned for us to go next. Alastair went first. Val followed. I rounded out the rear of our party. Just as my feet hit the beach, another score of humans started their descent. All around us, ships were emptying their forces into the cove. There were hundreds already in formation on the beach. I watched, wishing I could conjure hope, but no matter how many fighters we had, it wouldn't be enough.

Not against the gods.

As the humans gathered in groups, Val, Alastair, and I joined Vera at the front lines.

I almost fell over when I spotted the king, deep in conversation with his closest confidants.

"Well, fuck me," Alastair muttered.

King Duncan Hinde looked tired and haggard. Deep red veins streaked across his face. They wound down the length of his neck and continued into the front of his robe. When he saw me staring, he excused himself from his conversation and walked over.

"I suppose you're wondering how I'm here," he said in a weary voice. "One of my ships found me floating on some debris. I was unconscious. In their worry for me, they thought to return me to Talaven. When I woke and realized what they'd done, I insisted they turn around. Simple mistake, really. They were just doing what they thought was best for their king."

He was lying. His breath reeked of it. And he knew we'd be able to tell.

A warrior mounted his horse, then blew the war horn. All the gathered human soldiers fell silent. The king moved away to join them. I watched, frowning. Why would he lie to us about what had happened to him? He hadn't even tried to hide the falsehoods.

"What's wrong?" Val whispered.

"I'm not certain," I said slowly. "Just...be on your guard around the king. Better yet, let's stay far away from him during the battle. He's hiding something."

I didn't get any more time to ponder. The warrior blew the horn once more, and we were off. The army surged forward, and ranks closed in tight. As soon as we left the beach, the storm crackled overhead. Wind sprayed heavy rain into our faces. We were drenched in seconds.

Our forward motion slowed as mud sloshed around our boots.

In the distance, a contingent of storm fae spotted our approach. Shouts erupted from their company. I tightened my grip on my bow as they charged.

The battle for our world had truly begun.

FORTY-SEVEN
TESSA

Our side of the bridge erupted into chaos. Warriors launched onto the scorpion beast while lightning struck the barrier again. The gods had yet to show themselves, but I could sense them in the skies. They were swirling through the stormy clouds, watching our unit battle helplessly against the inevitable.

As soon as they destroyed the barrier, their army would charge.

Strangled yells erupted from the dying fae. As the scorpion beast slashed the throat of yet another warrior, I grabbed Nellie's arm and pulled her farther from the fray. Angry lightning crashed down from above, burning the grass where we'd just been standing.

"This was not the plan," Nellie whispered, wide-eyed.

"The gods were always going to do something unexpected." I looked around, searching for a place Nellie could find shelter. She noticed what I was doing and pulled away.

"I'm not running, Tessa," she said stubbornly. I could see a reflection of myself in her eyes. Brave and reckless with so much heart. But that heart was edged in anger. Andromeda's power ran through her veins, just as it did in mine, and she was not immune to its call. She felt a desperation to fight. So did I.

"I need to do something," she said. "Don't you?"

I nodded and looked around. I spotted Gaven hiding near the bridge, alone. His part of the plan would begin soon, based on how many bolts of lightning the barrier had endured. I jerked my head toward him.

"We should protect Gaven."

Nellie looked relieved. Together, we circled the fight against the scorpion, then walked toward Gaven at the bridge. He nodded gravely as we both joined him. A group of archers saw what we were doing. They gathered behind us, ready to loose their first volley.

"If this goes according to plan, there's not much you can do without range weapons," he said, indicating the axe in Nellie's hands. Then he smiled. "Though I appreciate the company."

I pointed up at the sky. "It's not the beasts I'm worried about."

"Ah, the gods." He nodded knowingly, but jerked his thumb toward Kalen, Toryn, and Fenella. "They'll have bigger fish to fry than me."

The thought of Andromeda aiming her sights on Kalen again did not provide me with much comfort. But he had Toryn, and he had Fenella. He was surrounded by dozens of other lethal fighters, armed with axes and swords. He'd told me before the battle that many of them had lived through his war against Oberon. They'd stood by his side for centuries.

Still, I watched as he dealt the final, deadly blow to the scorpion. Somehow, he'd leapt on its back. He shoved the blade into its head, killing it instantly. The beast tumbled sideways, and Kalen slid off its back so casually, it was as if he did this every day.

An explosion rocked the ground. A crackling, ear-splitting screech filled the air. Wincing, I turned toward the bridge. The barrier briefly flashed before us, almost as clear as glass. It stretched and bent and shuddered against the force of the lightning. And then it shattered.

Shards of invisible metal sprayed across us. I shielded my face and twisted away, but pain flared through my bare hand. Several pieces thunked into my leathers. Warriors behind me screamed.

The beasts on the other side of the bridge began to charge. They rushed forward in a blur of gray and black, their crimson eyes glowing in the darkness. There were too many to count. And they were moving so fast they were almost on us already.

"Now!" I shouted at Gaven. "Do it now!"

Gaven fell to his knees and palmed the edge of the bridge. With his eyes locked on the enemy, he *shoved* the wood. Light consumed his hands. The heat of it sparked a flame. It grew quickly, building into an inferno. Then he exhaled.

The flames expanded in a fiery burst and surged toward the beasts. The creatures skidded to a stop, and the sudden motion made their bodies collide. A few beasts tumbled over the side. Their shrieks slowly faded into the nothingness below.

Fire swarmed them, engulfing the ones who were still on the bridge. The wood started to burn, erupting into a powerful shield. And still, the creatures kept pressing forward, a slave to the commands of the god above. The scent of charred fur and flesh filled the air.

"Come on." I grabbed Gaven's arm and tugged him back, in case one of the beasts managed to make it across. He seemed dazed, clearly drained from the amount of power he'd poured into the fire.

Nellie wrapped her arm around his back, and together, we helped him hobble away.

He sighed against my shoulder. "It's done. The fire will destroy the bridge. The army won't make it—"

A sudden gust of wind slammed against us. I staggered to the side, shielding my face against the torrential downpour. Hard beads of rain slammed down on our heads, the droplets as large as marbles. Gaven stiffened. He twisted to look over his shoulder, and I had the impulse to do the same.

The rain was putting out the fire. Steam filled the air, blocking our sight of the beasts. Gaven shook his head and moaned.

"No, no, no." He sank to his knees and dropped his head into his hands. "I don't understand."

"It's the gods," Nellie said tightly. "Their power is muting your fae power. They didn't notice you before. But now they have..."

I searched the clouds, my heart pounding. The barrier was gone now. It was only a matter of time before the gods showed themselves. They were already using the power of storms and beasts, but more would come. Perseus could shatter us with fear, even without touching anyone, but Orion and Sirius needed direct contact. Just like Andromeda.

My stomach twisted at the thought of seeing her again. The last time we'd gone head to head, she'd killed me. My neck still ached with phantom pain, and my thoughts were plagued by the memory of my blood pouring from that gaping wound.

I shuddered and helped Gaven to his feet. The thunder of paws on wood grew louder. I withdrew my sword and motioned for Nellie to lift her axe. Kalen called out, having seen what had happened, ordering the warriors to line up around us. Then he came to stand with me, his face grim. Fenella followed, and Toryn stood on Nellie's other side.

Together, we would stand and face the enemy.

Moments ticked by. I held my breath. And then the world exploded into chaos.

Beasts launched toward us from the misty darkness. I held my sword before me and braced myself. Several aimed their sights on us, but their movements were more sluggish than normal, thanks to the mud. As one reached me, I managed to slice through its neck. It joined three others in death that Kalen and Toryn quickly dispatched.

We fell back into formation. Kalen wiped the flesh from his sword and held his weapon at the ready.

We'd survived the first assault easily enough, but I knew not to get too comfortable. Thousands would cross, though the tiny bridge would slow them down, forcing them to come in smaller groups. If they kept up this pace, we might yet have a chance.

Another group of beasts charged off the bridge. Fenella nocked an arrow and shot one in the eye. Other archers did the same, and none missed. The pile of the dead was quickly growing, their large bodies forming a wall of protection between us and the bridge.

"This is going better than I expected," Fenella said with a wicked laugh. "Dumb beasts are just following orders and can't seem to make smart decisions about when and how to attack. Let them keep on coming."

I frowned. It did seem too good to be true, almost as if the gods were hoping to distract us from something else. Heart pounding, I looked up at the city, where the humans were taking refuge in the tower. Surely the gods wouldn't know where we'd hid them.

As if sensing my unease, Silver trudged toward me after another wave of beasts had passed. It still felt impossible he could be here like this, wearing his joint eater form. He looked so much like Midnight it hurt to look at him.

"What is it, Tessa Baran?" he asked in his rattling, papery voice.

"Can you go check on the city? I have a bad feeling."

He huffed, and the gust of his exhale blew back my hood. "No. I swore to stand beside you, and that is what I must do. If you wish to check on the city, I will go with you, but I will not go *without* you."

More beasts stormed across the bridge, but Kalen's archers quickly stopped them. Everything was under control here, at least for now. Swords would not be needed until the fae started to cross. That might be soon, but...where were the gods?

"Nellie, stay close to Toryn. I'll be back in a moment." I turned to Kalen. "I'm going to check on the city. It doesn't feel right that the gods haven't attacked us yet."

His eyes narrowed. "By yourself?"

"Silver is going with me."

"I don't like it. If they're in the sky, they'll see you, especially if you have a towering tree walking beside you. I don't hear anything coming from the city. No screaming. No clanging of steel. Nothing. If the gods had focused their attention there, we'd know about it by now."

Frowning, I gazed up at the hill, taking in the glittering gemstones that shone even now, lighting up the battlements. Everything seemed quiet and still. I just couldn't shake that sense of dread creeping across the back of my neck.

Against my better judgment, I stayed put. The moments stretched by. Beasts continued to swarm, rush after rush, in an endless deluge of blood and guts. The towering pile of bodies stretched from one end of our small unit to the next, so high it now blocked our view of what was coming.

Rain still poured from the sky. I was so wet that I no longer remembered what dry felt like. Mud was up to our ankles, sloshing every time we tried to move.

A body fell from above. It splatted into the mud before us, the neck a ruined, mangled thing. The head landed only a second later. Mykon's unseeing eyes stared back at us. Ruari's brother. I pressed a shaking hand to my lips.

"The gods attacked the battlements like Tessa feared," Toryn said grimly. "And now they're here."

Kalen shifted his body in front of mine. He readied his sword as seven gods landed on the mountain of bodies, their feathery wings free of the rain that plagued the rest of us. Andromeda was in the center. She wore steel plate and a crown embedded with glittering tiger-eye gemstones. It was a statement, a symbol that nothing we could do would stop them. Whatever magic we could find in this world, they were far greater than all of it. And they would crush us beneath their boots.

Hastily, I pulled my hood back over my head. She hadn't yet noticed me. I wanted to keep it that way for as long as possible.

I dragged my gaze away from Andromeda. Sirius and Perseus stood together on her left side. They were armed, but their expressions were downcast. Callisto crouched on the beasts, her hand pressed to the flank of the one nearest to her. She looked different now, with short dark hair and a smaller frame, but her crimson eyes were the same. Orion, Pollux, and a silver-haired woman—who I guessed was the God of Storms—were facing the other way, their focus on the bridge.

That was our only warning.

FORTY-EIGHT

TESSA

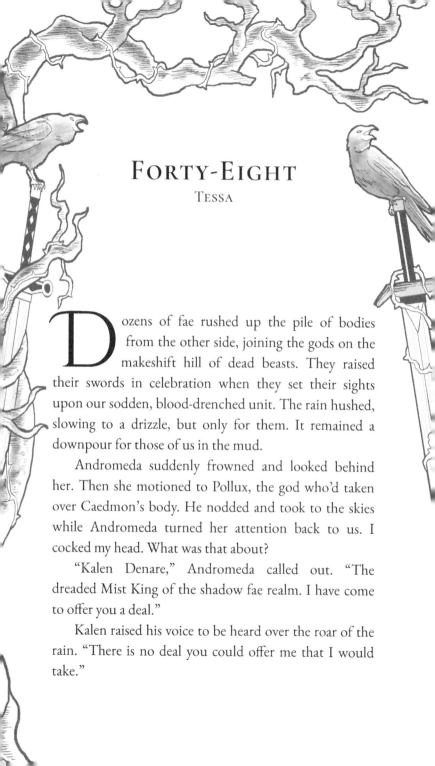

Dozens of fae rushed up the pile of bodies from the other side, joining the gods on the makeshift hill of dead beasts. They raised their swords in celebration when they set their sights upon our sodden, blood-drenched unit. The rain hushed, slowing to a drizzle, but only for them. It remained a downpour for those of us in the mud.

Andromeda suddenly frowned and looked behind her. Then she motioned to Pollux, the god who'd taken over Caedmon's body. He nodded and took to the skies while Andromeda turned her attention back to us. I cocked my head. What was that about?

"Kalen Denare," Andromeda called out. "The dreaded Mist King of the shadow fae realm. I have come to offer you a deal."

Kalen raised his voice to be heard over the roar of the rain. "There is no deal you could offer me that I would take."

She smiled. "You love your people, do you not, king of the shadow fae?"

Kalen didn't answer. He merely stood there gazing up at the gods, his face impassive, though his white-knuckled fist around the hilt of his sword showed his true emotions.

"You have been fighting against me since my return to this world. Even before then, if I take your vow to your mother into consideration," she started.

"Don't you dare speak of my mother," he said, snarling.

She waved his objection away. "And yet here I am, willing to allow you and yours to live. On one condition. Put away your weapons. Stop this madness, this ridiculous fighting. Look at you. You're drenched in mud. Not quite the majestic, powerful fae king that you present yourself as, eh? But I can make all your storms disappear." Andromeda waved at the silver-haired woman named Pandora, the God of Storms. The surrounding rain began to slow. "I can give you everything you've ever dreamed of. A continent to rule. Powerful allies. All you have to do is join us against Talaven. And if you don't, you will prove yourself to be the weak, spineless king everyone has always suspected you to be."

Fenella lifted her bow and shot an arrow at Andromeda. It whistled in the sudden silence, and the arrow struck true. The tip sliced deep into Andromeda's neck.

I couldn't breathe.

A deadly silence pounded down on us. No one moved. Andromeda stared at Fenella with furious hatred boiling in her deep black eyes. Blood dribbled down her neck from the puncture wound. And then she wrapped her long fingers around the arrow and yanked it from her skin.

The wound closed up, healing instantly. Eyes still locked on Fenella, Andromeda dragged her finger across the trail of blood and tasted it.

"Any dissenters will be put to death." Her glittering eyes shifted to Kalen. "Kill her, and I will take that as proof you accept the terms of my deal."

Kalen pulled a dagger from a sheath strapped to his upper thigh. He flipped it in his hands before turning to Fenella. The blue-horned light fae lifted her chin, exposing her neck—her lifeblood—to her king.

"You always were a volatile, violent creature," Kalen murmured to her. "Out of all my Mist Guard, you're the one most difficult to predict. Fortunately, I quite like volatile creatures."

He hauled back his arm and launched the dagger. It spun, end over end, toward Andromeda. She hissed and ducked to the side, though the sharp tip grazed her cheek. Once again, the wound healed instantly, but she looked enraged.

"How dare you?" She leapt from the pile of bodies to land in the mud before us. "Everything I've done is to protect you fucking fae, and this is how you thank me? This is what you do to the one who is trying to save your world?"

Kalen strode toward her, his body a bundle of pent-up rage. I reached out to pull him back, but his cloak slipped through my fingers. When he reached her, he wrapped his hand around the front of her armor and lifted her from the ground. She let him do so.

"You killed my mate," he spat into her face. "I don't care who you think you're saving. Your words mean *nothing* to me. You can take your offer, and you can shove it up your arse."

He released her and shoved her back. Andromeda stumbled slightly, her boots squishing in the mud. Tension throttled me. She wouldn't let him walk away from this. She was too proud to let a lowly fae treat her this way.

A slow smile stretched across her face. She slashed her nails at his cheek. The sharp tips made contact, gorging four deep lines of blood into his skin. Kalen didn't even flinch. He lifted his sword and swung it at her head.

Andromeda sighed when she saw it coming, but she didn't move. Instead, she waited for the contact this time. Her skin suddenly rippled like a sheen of glass passed over the surface of it. The blade hit her neck, bouncing off. Kalen nearly lost his grip on it. A thin line of blood across her throat was the only evidence it had even hit her.

She started to advance on Kalen with fury in her eyes. "Your weapons are useless against us. Your power is useless when we mute it. Your mate was the only one who could wield it against us, and she is dead. Give up, Kalen Denare. Swear your fealty to us, or you will take your final breaths on this muddy battlefield. You will be remembered as the king who could not protect his people because he was too proud to kneel before a god."

Kalen spat at her feet. "You Lamiae are not our gods,

and I will not doom my people to an eternity of serving you."

"Then so be it," she growled.

Just then, Caedmon—Pollux—returned. He thundered to the ground, leaned in close to Andromeda, and whispered something into her ear. I couldn't hear it, but Kalen did. He straightened and returned to the front of our unit while Andromeda was distracted. Her face reddened as she listened to Pollux's report.

He turned toward me and his Mist Guard, mouthing the words. "Talaven has arrived. They're attacking the fae on the other side of the bridge."

His words stole my breath. I gazed up at the wall of bodies, wishing I could see past it, wishing I could search the fields for Val. I hoped she wasn't in the throng of it, but I knew she would be. She'd want to be out there, fighting for those she loved.

"Niamh and Alastair?" Toryn asked quietly.

"Not mentioned, but we can only hope."

"They've come for us," Fenella breathed.

Kalen nodded, still mouthing the words so the gods couldn't hear him. "There could be enough of them to fight the army still on the other side of the bridge. All we need is a way to destroy the go—"

A whistle sounded, then Andromeda roared, "Kill them all!"

Her unit of storm fae warriors shouted, raising their weapons. They charged toward us. Some slid down the hill of bodies. Others leapt. I could feel our own warriors tensing around us. The battle against the beasts had been nothing but a way to lull us into a false sense of security. The real war was upon us now.

"Nock!" Kalen lifted his arm. "Loose!"

A volley of arrows filled the sky, raining death on the enemy fae. Many of the arrows made contact. Blood sprayed and screams erupted as they fell.

"Again!" Kalen shouted. "Nock! Loose!"

More arrows sprayed into the enemy, but there were too many of them for us to slow down their advance. Soon, they were upon us. Bows were cast into the mud. Swords, spears, axes, and daggers quickly replaced them.

We tried to hold a tight formation, but the over-whelming rush of enemy fighters quickly scattered us apart. A storm fae sloshed toward me, his neck tattoo and blank eyes giving him away as one of the fae in the thrall of the gods. I swung my sword at his head. He clashed his steel against mine with impossible force. It threw me back. I slammed into the side of another enemy storm fae.

Out of the corner of my eye, a flash of silver caught my attention. Fenella had her back to the ground, pinned by an enemy fighter who blew wind into her face.

"Fenella!" I started toward her, fear thundering through me.

She managed to kick the fae in the gut. He flinched back, releasing his grip on her, but—

A hand grabbed me by the back of the neck and tossed me into the mud. My sword slipped from my fingers. I rolled over, my cloak sticking to the ground and wrapping wetly around my legs. I tried to scrabble back, but I was stuck there.

Distracted, I looked to where I'd seen Fenella fighting, but a thick press of bodies was in the way.

The storm fae walked toward me. He dragged the end of his bloodied sword in the mud, leaving behind a trail of red. The first one I'd fought now joined him, like a predator drawn to prey. They walked slowly, methodically, circling me as if they were relishing the moment. All around us, chaos reigned.

I pushed against the sucking mud and stood on shaky legs, casting my eyes toward where my sword had fallen. It was gone.

"A human amongst the fae," one of the combatants said, his voice strange and rotten. "We will be greatly rewarded for killing you."

He rushed toward me. I tried to move out of his way, but my boots were too engrained in the mud. He grabbed the back of my head, his fist taking a chunk of hair through my cloak. Pain lanced through my skull as he tugged me toward him. The second storm fae put a dagger to my throat.

I spotted Fenella's horns through the crowd. She was surrounded now. Four against one. And she had a gruesome gash on her neck.

Tears burned my eyes. I ground my teeth, threw out my hand, and touched the fae who held the dagger. Right on the cheek. "Death."

His eyes widened as he fell.

Silver suddenly found me. He sloshed through the mud and yanked the second fae away from me, throwing him toward the chasm. I rubbed my neck and shot him a grateful smile, then started running toward Fenella.

She was still surrounded. Two fae had grabbed her. Each had a shoulder. She kicked and screamed and fought like hell, her beautiful face full of fury.

I screamed, desperately sloshing through the blood-soaked mud, my heartbeat so thunderous I could barely hear anything else. My vision tunneled as the third fae smiled and swung his sword. The fighting around me vanished. A ringing filled my head. I couldn't feel or see anything but my friend.

Fenella felt my eyes on her. She looked at me as the sword hurtled toward her neck, and she smiled.

My queen, she mouthed.

And then the fae chopped off her head.

The world stopped.

My knees buckled.

I fell as if an arrow had shot me in the heart.

"No," I moaned. My voice was still all I could hear. "No, no, no, no, no, no, no, no, no."

Arms wrapped around me, surrounding me like a cocoon. I tried to knock them off, so I could crawl toward Fenella. I had the power of life in my hands. I could bring her back. The wound didn't matter. I could still find a way to fix it. *I had to.*

"Shh, pet, shh," the voice of the woman who held me whispered. "Sometimes death is the only way to protect life."

I froze. It was not Kalen or Gaven or Nellie who had found me crying in the mud. I ripped out of Andromeda's arms and whirled on her. She stood in the midst of battle without a single fleck of mud on her glass-like skin. Her eyes gleamed with hate.

"How curious this is," she said. "I felt your death." She pressed a hand to her heart. "Right here, deep within me. How is it you have regained your life?"

A body fell beside me, the newest casualty in the battle that raged around us. Screams and clashing swords and powerful thunder filled the air in an overwhelming cacophony of pain and death.

"I'm not having this conversation with you." I started to turn back toward Fenella. If I was quick enough, perhaps the magic of my touch could bend the fabric of the world, just enough to weave her broken body back together.

"I understand your pain, but there is nothing you can do for her. The death she endured is final. Not even a god could undo that kind of head trauma."

I hissed, moving toward Fenella despite Andromeda's words. But before I could reach my fallen friend, Andromeda landed before me, blocking my path.

"I don't know how or why you're here, but I cannot let you live," she said. "It ends now between us. And this time, I'll make certain you can't come back."

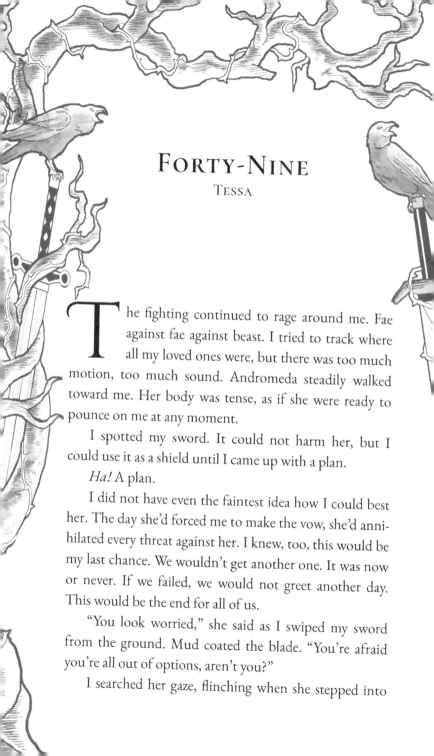

FORTY-NINE
TESSA

The fighting continued to rage around me. Fae against fae against beast. I tried to track where all my loved ones were, but there was too much motion, too much sound. Andromeda steadily walked toward me. Her body was tense, as if she were ready to pounce on me at any moment.

I spotted my sword. It could not harm her, but I could use it as a shield until I came up with a plan.

Ha! A plan.

I did not have even the faintest idea how I could best her. The day she'd forced me to make the vow, she'd annihilated every threat against her. I knew, too, this would be my last chance. We wouldn't get another one. It was now or never. If we failed, we would not greet another day. This would be the end for all of us.

"You look worried," she said as I swiped my sword from the ground. Mud coated the blade. "You're afraid you're all out of options, aren't you?"

I searched her gaze, flinching when she stepped into

the path of my sword. If only this blade could cut her down. "There are always options."

A blur of motion briefly caught my attention. Callisto hurtled by, riding a beast, though she had a different vessel now than before. I only knew it was her by the familiar crimson glow of her eyes. They were the same color of her gemstones. The same color of *all* the gods' eyes, except Andromeda's.

The shock of it punched me in the gut. I returned my attention to Andromeda. Her deep black eyes stared back at me, but they almost glowed from within. Like gemstones. I understood now, the truth of those eyes, even if hers were a different color than the others.

I tried to steady my breathing and keep my face blank. I didn't want Andromeda to realize I'd figured it out. All I had to do was rip out her eyes. Then I'd have her power in my hands. And there would be nothing she could do to stop me.

Slowly, I lowered my sword and dropped it to the ground beside me. "If it's you and me against each other, let's do this properly. No weapons. No powers."

She arched a brow. "You wish to fight me in hand-to-hand combat?"

"You said it yourself. My sword is nothing against you." I cocked my head. "What happens if I snap your neck?"

"You are not strong enough to snap my neck," she said with a laugh.

"Then you won't mind if I try."

Andromeda narrowed her gaze, completely oblivious to the blood that sprayed her steel plate from another gruesome death nearby. She clearly didn't trust me. And she shouldn't. But that tiny flash of uncertainty was all I needed to know I was right. There *was* a way for me to destroy her. I just needed to make sure I didn't hesitate if I got my chance.

"Very well." She started to sheath her own sword, but I shook my head.

"Put it on the ground," I said.

"So demanding for such a small, worthless creature." Still, Andromeda dropped her sword beside her and held up her hands. "Here you are." Then she dug into her pockets and put on her gloves. She waved her leather-clad fingers at me when she was done. "You're next. I know you have a pair of gloves."

I narrowed my eyes.

"You said no powers, so go on then. These are your rules, not mine."

"My powers don't work against you," I said.

"But you've proven they work against the beasts, and I won't have you attacking them as some kind of distraction. Put them on."

Frowning, I pulled on my gloves and moved closer. I sized her up. Andromeda was much taller than me, and her shoulders were broad. I needed to catch her off guard if I had any hope of getting to her eyes. The mud squelched in my slow walk toward her. She remained where she was, making me do all the work.

I stopped when I realized what she was doing. The more I advanced, the sooner I'd tire. Clever. Instead of moving any closer, I anchored my feet, fisted my hands, and waited.

A roar sounded from behind me. My heart leapt. It was Kalen. By instinct, I started to turn, but a flash of movement stopped me. Andromeda had leapt a few steps closer.

"Your people are in trouble, particularly Toryn over there." She nodded to her left.

I tried not to fall into the trap, knowing she wanted to distract me. But Nellie's voice sounded from that direction. She was shouting, her voice almost lost beneath the roar of battle.

I ground my teeth and looked. Toryn was locked in a battle with a fae who could have been his twin, if it weren't for the hollow white eyes and the long, curly brown hair. The enemy, Toryn's brother, jabbed a spear toward Toryn's gut. Nellie dropped the axe and rushed toward them with her claws raised, and my heart jumped into my throat.

I needed to go to her before she got herself killed, but Andromeda had drawn closer in the brief moment I'd glanced away. She was near enough to touch me now, if she tried. My attention felt pulled in a hundred different directions. My friends and family were in danger. Our warriors were struggling to hold the line against the invading army. But I could not look at them. Not if I wanted to end this for all of them.

Fisting my hands, I felt myself snarl, giving in to the darker side of my rage. "You seem awfully cautious, for an immortal god who claims nothing can kill her."

Her hand shot out, and her fingers arched toward my throat. Expecting the attack, I swung my head down and to the side. Her arm passed over my head. Before she could get another shot in, I lifted my mud-caked boot from the ground and kicked her in the gut. She launched back a few steps, nearly losing her balance on the slick ground.

A gurgling sounded beside me. I couldn't help but look, desperate to ensure those I loved were still breathing. A warrior—one of ours—was stuck face-down in the mud. He tried to free himself, his fingers grasping at the mud, but he could not breathe.

I started to reach out to help, but Andromeda swept toward me and knocked me aside. With a growl, she swiped her nails at my face. Pain ruptured in my cheek. Blood now coated her fingers.

"Don't look at them," she hissed. "Don't look at anyone but me."

All around me, people were dying. Out of the corner of my eye, another of our warriors crawled on his hands and knees, heaving. His face was gray and pale. He had the same look that Ruari had after he'd been infected with famine. The sound of wings punched through the roar of battle. Orion was spreading his power through our unit. Even if the warriors didn't die immediately, his famine would weaken our fighters and make it easier to kill them.

It would spread quickly.

We were doomed. Unless I got those gemstones out of Andromeda's eyes.

I fisted my hands. "All right, then. Let's fight."

It had always been meant to come down to this. Everything in my life had led to this moment, when I faced off against the God of Death.

She rushed at me, but this time, I was ready for her. As she swung her arm, I held up my own. My forearm blocked her. The force of her blow felt like a stone crashing against my bones, but I did not break. I did not crack. And I certainly did not back down from it.

As she recovered from the surprise of my block, I threw a punch toward her gut. I wouldn't go for her face. Not yet. Not until I'd weakened her enough so she couldn't stop me. Right now, she didn't know I understood the truth. I'd only have one shot at this. As soon as she knew, she'd do whatever it took to protect the source of her power.

My knuckles crunched when they hit her stomach. Pain flared, ricocheting up my arm. I hissed through my teeth and ducked out of the way when she tried to grab my neck.

Laughing, she bent her knees and curled a finger at me, beckoning me to try again. "Did you truly think your mortal hands could damage the body of a god?"

"Your body is fae or human, just like all the rest of us," I said, stepping sideways to circle her. "You may have strengthened that body, transformed it to your own liking. But you are nothing without it."

She looked at me, surprised.

"What?" I laughed. "Did you think I wouldn't figure it out after what you made me do to Caedmon with that gemstone? You need vessels, or else your tempestuous power can't do a fucking thing."

Growling, she narrowed her eyes. I smiled as she launched toward me in a furious frenzy. I'd been trying to goad her, and it had worked. With rage controlling her, she might just slip up.

She reached for my neck again, but she'd done it enough times that it didn't catch me by surprise. I grabbed her hands and twisted hard. To my surprise, a bone crunched. A hissing scream ripped from her throat as she stumbled away from me.

"How are you doing that?" she spat, her eyes livid. "You're a fucking mortal. You can't harm me."

I lifted my chin, staring her down. "I am the Daughter of Stars."

Her eyes flashed, and her lips parted. But then that fury returned as she licked my blood from her fingers and spat it in my face. It trickled down my cheek. "And yet I am a god. I hold the power of life and death in my hands."

"That's true. But so do I."

Steeling myself, I made my move. My wings shot from my back as I launched toward her. In one powerful beat of them, I was on Andromeda. I collided with her, knocking her onto the muddy ground.

I went for her eye. My fingers dug into her socket. Nausea rolled through me as my fingers slipped around the squishy ball. I pulled it free and fell back.

Shaking, I held it up before me. Confusion ripped through me, tinged with panic. It was nothing but an eyeball. Where was the gemstone?

Andromeda laughed. She rose before me, covered in mud. Her one eye socket was black and empty, leaking blood down her face. The other glowed with brilliant fury.

"Did you truly think that would work? That I would make my stones *that* visible? I'm not like the others." She leaned down, grabbed the front of my leathers, and hoisted me into the air. "You had one way to get your hands on my gemstones, and that was with the Mortal Blade. You squandered that chance, just as you squandered the only way you could destroy me completely—by channeling Kalen Denare's power. You are helpless, Tessa Baran, and it is your own fault." Her smile widened. "If only you were better, stronger, smarter, you could have conquered me."

She pulled me so close I could see a hint of red behind her eyes. "I would have given you an easy death if you hadn't tried to steal my power. But now I'm going to make you watch as I kill everyone you know and love."

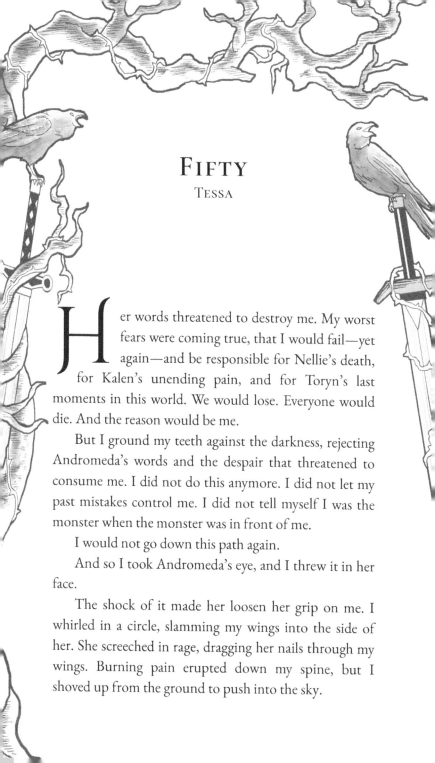

FIFTY

TESSA

Her words threatened to destroy me. My worst fears were coming true, that I would fail—yet again—and be responsible for Nellie's death, for Kalen's unending pain, and for Toryn's last moments in this world. We would lose. Everyone would die. And the reason would be me.

But I ground my teeth against the darkness, rejecting Andromeda's words and the despair that threatened to consume me. I did not do this anymore. I did not let my past mistakes control me. I did not tell myself I was the monster when the monster was in front of me.

I would not go down this path again.

And so I took Andromeda's eye, and I threw it in her face.

The shock of it made her loosen her grip on me. I whirled in a circle, slamming my wings into the side of her. She screeched in rage, dragging her nails through my wings. Burning pain erupted down my spine, but I shoved up from the ground to push into the sky.

Snarling, she called forth her wings and launched toward me. She grabbed for my neck once more, and I rose several more feet. Andromeda followed and darted in close. She got her hands around my arms and pierced my skin with her nails.

She jerked me in close to hiss into my face. "I am going to do everything to you that you've done to me. Every moment you try to fight is another I'll add to all the fear and pain you must suffer, until you're nothing but a broken husk begging for death."

"You can try, but I won't let you lay another hand on those I love," I spit back.

"Oh, no?" A wicked grin curved her lips. "Then enjoy watching this."

She extracted her nails from my skin and shoved me back. My wings caught me before I fell, but Andromeda was already gone. She flew to where Toryn was still locked in a bloody battle with his brother. At least one of them had managed to spear the other, though it was impossible to tell which with all the blood. Both spears were drenched in it.

Nellie had transformed into her wolf form. Snarling, she was fighting off two storm fae who were attempting to come at Toryn from behind. Silver was nearby, but he was locked in his own battle, surrounded by a half a dozen beasts. He couldn't help my sister.

And Andromeda was flying straight for her.

Panic speared my chest. I hurtled after the God of Death, my wings tucked. But Andromeda was fast. She was closing in on her, and Nellie was so focused on the storm fae that she didn't see her coming.

Andromeda slammed into my sister's side. The two of them tumbled onto the ground. It threw them into a chaotic roll through the mud. I tried to steady my breathing as I kept flying. Andromeda was tangled up with Nellie, nothing more a blur of gray fur and deep black wings. I had to get there before she hurt her.

A familiar pain flared in my gut. I would not let this god take her from me.

Andromeda and Nellie finally rolled to a stop. My heart clenched when Andromeda found purchase first. She trapped Nellie's beastly form beneath her with a knee on her neck and another on her chest. Andromeda looked up at me and smiled. She lifted her sharp nails.

"No!" I shouted. I needed two seconds. Just two seconds, and I would be on her.

"Say goodbye to your sister," Andromeda said, laughing up at me.

With a roar, Nellie stabbed her claws into Andromeda's throat.

The God of Death's eyes went wide. Blood gurgled from her neck. Nellie ripped out her claw, watching as the god's body slid sideways, tumbling off her. She quickly shifted back into human form, gathering her cloak around her body.

I landed in front of her only a second later. Her cheeks were drenched in tears, and her face had paled. I held out my hand. She took it and stood on wobbly legs. To our left, Toryn knelt over his dead brother's body, weeping. He had conquered his enemy, but he had lost so much. Nellie put a comforting hand on his shoulder.

"Andromeda made a mistake coming after me,"

Nellie said to me. "I'm the only one here who has a way to wound her."

I looked down at the unconscious god. Already her wound was beginning to heal. "She let her rage cloud her judgment. She wanted to make me hurt as much as possible. That's why she chose you."

"What do we do now? She's not dead."

"No, and taking out her eyes, which I thought would be the gemstones, doesn't work. I tried that."

"Yes, I can see. Disgusting but clever."

"Not clever enough."

I took a brief moment to take in the battle. Somehow, our warriors were still holding strong against the storm fae. There were fewer of them than I would have expected, likely thanks to the human army on the other side of the bridge. The storm had moved that way, and so had a few of the gods. Callisto was nowhere to be seen, and neither was Pollux, Pandora, or Perseus.

But Sirius and Orion were here, flying about on wings. Now and then, they swept down to infect another warrior. All around, faces were pained and gray. The gods did not seem to care if their own fighters got infected.

Andromeda would soon awaken, and she would be vicious.

"I could wound her again while she's still unconscious," Nellie said. "It could give us a bit more time."

But time was not what we needed, not with Orion and Sirius casting pestilence and famine upon our unit. We needed to put an end to this. And if not now, then never.

"Daughter of Stars," a voice whispered raggedly.

I stiffened. I'd heard that voice before. In the sky. Inhaling, I looked up, but the heavy clouds obscured the stars.

"Down here."

Tensing, I looked down at Andromeda. Her lips were pale and cracked, but the wound had nearly closed. Her eye was no longer black but teal. She beckoned me closer.

"Tessa," Nellie warned.

Despite my better judgment, I knelt, called toward her by that achingly familiar voice. Andromeda had never sounded like that, not in any of the conversations we'd shared. Not when she'd been trapped in the onyx gemstone beneath Itchen. Not when she'd tried to draw me over to her side in Malroch. And certainly not when I'd enraged her.

It was as if an entirely different person was speaking to me.

She licked her lips before she began speaking. "My daughter. My stubborn, reckless, passionate daughter. Think about what happened. You died."

I shook my head. "Are you...are you the fae whose body Andromeda stole?"

"That doesn't matter," she said, a little louder now. "You died."

"No, I am alive. Nellie brought me back. But Andromeda—"

"A vow ends with death," she nearly shouted, her chest heaving from the effort.

I sucked in a breath and leapt to my feet. Nellie grabbed my arm. Every possible emotion went through me. Most vows ended when one of the parties died. I *knew* this, and yet I'd been so focused on everything else that it had never occurred to me. I was alive *now*, but that did not matter for the vow. Because for a brief moment in time, I'd been gone.

The vow was broken.

I could use Kalen's power to kill the gods.

That was why Andromeda had acted wary of me. That was why she'd insisted I don my gloves. Not because she feared I'd use my power against the beasts, but because she thought I might try to channel his power *against her*.

I stumbled back. I needed to do this now before too many others died. Curling my hands, I prepared myself for the onslaught of Kalen's terrifying power.

"Wait," the woman croaked out.

I tensed. "My people are dying. I need to do this now. Before Andromeda comes back."

"Kalen's power works two ways," she said between ragged breaths. "Do not fall into the trap of forcing it outward. Chaos. It will cause chaos. Take it in, Daughter of Stars. You have the strength to control it." Her eyelids fluttered. "And just know, I am proud of what you are."

She went still.

Burning tears filled my eyes. I did not know this woman, if she'd been fae or human, young or old, or how long ago she'd lived her own life before Andromeda had stolen it from her. I didn't even know her name. And yet, I felt an aching sense of loss deep in my soul.

Somehow, I understood she would not survive what I needed to do. And she knew it, too.

"Nellie, stand back," I whispered.

But my sister remained by my side and gripped my hand. "I'm here to give you strength. You may need it."

Because I would have to pull the power of the gods into my body. All seven of them, with their vicious rage and terrifying strength. Andromeda had meant to *break* me with this power. She'd thought me using it would shatter my humanity. Maybe it would. But this was the only thing that could save us all.

Shuddering, I put some distant between us and Andromeda, and I closed my eyes.

Blocking out the sounds of battle, I timidly reached through the bond and felt for Kalen's power. It curled deep inside him, pulsing faintly, muted by the other gods. I carefully reached out and touched it. A blast of power slammed into me, eager, yearning, ripping through the bond with a force that always knocked me to the ground.

Distantly, I heard a voice. It sounded panicked. "What is happening?"

I set my jaw. Andromeda had woken, but I couldn't afford to let her distract me again. This ended now.

I heard the rush of wings.

"Tessa, hurry," Nellie said worriedly. "She's coming."

I wrapped my mind around that power and pulled with all my might. Kalen's vicious strength tore through my limbs. It rushed through me, burning me up. My body shuddered. Tears leaked from my eyes. I could feel Kalen's attention shifting to me, curious yet alarmed.

I wished I could warn him.

Exhaling, I felt his mist leak from my skin. I cast that mist around me. It reached Andromeda, caressing her cheek. She was only a few feet away now.

With a deep-throated roar, I lifted my right arm, and I yanked it back to my side, pulling, straining, jerking every ounce of power nearby. Andromeda screamed as her power exploded from her body. It hurtled toward me, a whirlwind of pure death and life.

It almost knocked me off my feet, but I stayed my ground, anchoring myself with the unyielding strength of Kalen's power. Andromeda's essence tried to break free from my hold on her. But I would not relent. I pulled and pulled and pulled. Sweat drenched my neck.

Suddenly, her power consumed me.

My eyes flew open. The world was bright and keening with sound. Rage burned in my veins. Gasping, I tugged out of Nellie's grip and focused on Orion. He'd noticed me now, and he was heading toward Kalen, no doubt to infect him and stop me from channeling his power.

I couldn't do this one by one. It was too slow. They would win if I did not make them all bow at my feet.

A wind rustled my cloak. I tipped back my head to look at the stars. The clouds had cleared now, and the moonlight was almost blinding. I murmured the words of that ancient song.

> *The darkness cries for the light*
> *And comes undone beneath the sky*
> *An old wind blows*
> *With ancient woes*
> *But light will never die*

Closing my eyes, I called upon the power once more, lacing it with the intoxicating rage from Andromeda. The ground beneath my feet began to rumble as the power expanded out of me, desperate for release. I fisted my hands.

And then I ripped the Lamiae from their gemstones. A hurricane of power slammed into me. Angry voices filled my head, shouting for purchase. Storms and shadows, violence and hate, fear and famine. All of it consumed me.

It was too much.

I couldn't think, couldn't breathe.

A storm of black clouded my vision.

I tried to reach for the light, but it was gone.

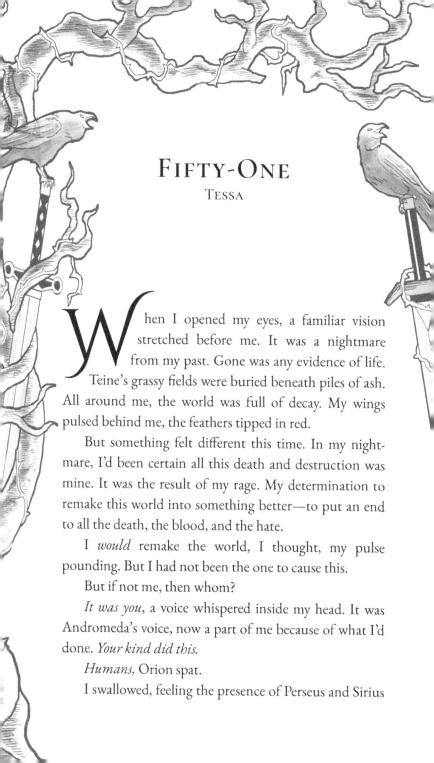

FIFTY-ONE
TESSA

When I opened my eyes, a familiar vision stretched before me. It was a nightmare from my past. Gone was any evidence of life. Teine's grassy fields were buried beneath piles of ash. All around me, the world was full of decay. My wings pulsed behind me, the feathers tipped in red.

But something felt different this time. In my nightmare, I'd been certain all this death and destruction was mine. It was the result of my rage. My determination to remake this world into something better—to put an end to all the death, the blood, and the hate.

I *would* remake the world, I thought, my pulse pounding. But I had not been the one to cause this.

But if not me, then whom?

It was you, a voice whispered inside my head. It was Andromeda's voice, now a part of me because of what I'd done. *Your kind did this.*

Humans, Orion spat.

I swallowed, feeling the presence of Perseus and Sirius

there, too. All of them were there. Inside of me, hearing my every thought. The woman who had whispered my name in the stars had told me I was strong enough to control them, but I could barely think with so many voices desperate to be heard.

"I don't understand," I managed to say, though my voice came out shaky.

Andromeda sighed. *Then it is time to show you.*

The world dropped out from beneath me, and we were spinning through the stars. All around me, bright lights sparkled like diamonds. I wanted to go to them. I wanted to visit every one. But the world rushed in around me once more. We stopped above a plain of blackened dirt. Everything was gray and lifeless, just as before.

This was our world, Andromeda said. *Centuries upon centuries ago, it was full of life. Trees and grass and flowers bloomed. Creatures of all kind flourished. But there was a particular creature that flourished more than most. Humans.*

I started to say something, but I was too dumb-founded to find the right words. There were other worlds, like ours?

Humans eventually did all this. They took and took and took of this world until there was nothing left of it. A short-sighted endeavour, as it resulted in their deaths, too. We wanted to stop them, but we didn't understand how, particularly when they learned how to catch us, encasing us —the essences of nature itself—in gemstones to be used to their liking.

But, near the end, the humans realized our power should not be trifled with, so they cast us into the stars. They hoped it would save them. It did not. For a world cannot exist without the essences of nature. We were lost for a very long time. Then we found your world, where we hoped to survive outside of these stones.

"And you discovered humans here, too," I murmured, starting to understand. These Lamiae, these essences of natures, believed all humans were the same. They'd seen what others did, so they expect the worst from those here, too. That was why they'd fought so hard against them. That was why Andromeda had insisted the 'gods' were not the ones to be feared. The humans were.

The fae were here, too, Andromeda snapped, cutting through my tumbling thoughts. *How excited we were to discover another intelligent species among you. And we saw, with the comet's power of foresight, that the humans would destroy this world, too. They'd already killed off all the dragons. You thought they were only from stories? They were real once. Next, they would destroy the fae. We warned them. We tried to save them. And then they betrayed us. They befriended the ones who would one day be their end.*

I shook my head. This was too much. And then suddenly, we were back above an ash-drenched Teine. A whistling wind was the only sound other than the voices in my head.

Distantly, I understood that perhaps I was dying. None of this was real. It was only happening inside my head. I'd done too much, taken in too much power. My mortal body could not hold it all. In the end, it might break me.

And yet there was nothing I could do but listen.

We saw, do you understand? We saw the future of this world, and we tried to stop it. And so you must stop it now.

"No," I whispered. "These are lies. You're trying to get into my head and make me do what you could not."

Look at it, Andromeda hissed. *Look at Teine and tell me you do not know that this is true. This is the future your world faces. Because of the humans. They saw it coming, too. That's why they cast us out and hid the truth from the fae. Because they knew if you understood why we were here, you would join our cause.*

"Wait," I said. "The other world, you said it died because the humans cast you into the stars. But humans and fae were already here before you arrived. How did they survive without your essences?"

Because you already had your own essences here, separate from us, Tessa Baran. All the wind in your hair, the rain on your face, and the shadows that darken the night. The constant war. The battles and the blood. And the fear you cannot ease. The peace you feel in your sister's arms. It's all here. It always has been. We are merely essences from another world. We were trapped in gemstones and then found a way to physically manifest ourselves. But the humans will destroy this world's essences, too. Nothing will survive here any longer.

"And so you don't belong here. Destroying you would be the best thing for everyone."

You would have to destroy yourself now that you contain us. But just know, it would not save your people. The humans will win, and everyone you know will die. You must use us. You must destroy Duncan Hinde. It is the only way to ensure the survival of this—

Hands shook my shoulders. My eyes flew open. Nellie's face hovered above mine, her long chestnut hair hanging in her face. She looked relieved when I looked at her, but then she blinked and sat back.

She could tell I was not fully myself in here.

"Tessa, what's happening?" she whispered.

The power of the gods swirled through my veins, making it impossible for me to answer. The intoxicating taste of it coated my tongue. Everything was brighter, louder, more vibrant. I noticed for the first time that Nellie's eyes had flecks of teal hidden amongst the brown. They looked like stars, like her face was lit by an ethereal light.

I touched her cheek. That light would die if I did not stop the humans.

Spreading my wings, I lifted myself from the ground. I gazed around at the destruction. The battle had stopped now. Our warriors were corralling the enemy fae, and the beasts were dead. But we had lost so many. There was too much blood. Arms and legs and torsos were caked in gore. It turned my stomach.

Look at what this world was.

Rage filled my chest, fierce and cold. With the combined power of the gods, all I had to do was will it. I could change this world. I could begin it anew. No more humans. No more wicked souls. Anyone who survived would bow at my feet.

Tears filled my eyes. A part of me fought against it. But the power raked through me, breaking down my resistance. It would be so much easier to give in. I wasn't strong enough to fight this.

And the humans...the humans would destroy everyone I loved. They were just across the bridge. If they were not already moving across it, they would be soon.

This was the right thing to do.

I had to unleash it. If I didn't, it would burst free of my control and *force* me to bend to its will.

I pressed a shaking finger to my cheeks, then held it before me. What I'd thought were tears before was blood. It was pouring from my eyes.

Something gentle tugged my soul. Power built on my fingertips, but Kalen's voice whispered in my mind, soothing the frayed edges of my heart. He was speaking through the bond.

I've got you, love.

I ground my teeth. What he didn't understand was that I did not have myself. The power was sizzling on my fingertips. I didn't think I could control it, even if I wanted to. And the rage, that burning rage, made me *want* to give in.

It made me want to destroy them all.

You are not that power. You can control it, he said into my mind, as if he could understand everything I was feeling. Through the bond, perhaps he could. And he had been here before. His power had always been volatile, too.

"It's too much," I said out loud. Pain carved a hole in my chest, through my eyes.

Conquer the power. Control it. Bend it to your will. If you do, we will save this world together, you and I. My power and yours. Our bond. I am your anchor, your tether to yourself. If anyone can master this, it's us.

If anyone could master this, it was us.

We had faced so many hardships. Fate had never been kind. It had kicked us into the mud time and time again, and yet we just kept standing. We freed ourselves from its cruel grip and kept moving. Always toward the light.

Shuddering, I looked down. The ground was miles beneath me. Without knowing, I had flown far above, ready to unleash my wrath upon the unsuspecting humans beyond the bridge. I felt Kalen tug the bond, and my vision sharpened.

Even as far from the ground as I was, I could see him there. He stood at the edge of the bridge, staring up at me. Our gazes locked. He nodded and extended his hand toward me. And somehow, I knew, if I could slide my hand into my mate's, I would make it through this.

The gods screamed. They filled my head with their panic, their fear. They fought against me, desperately trying to gain control of my wings as I began my descent.

I breathed in and breathed out, my eyes locked on Kalen's face. I didn't dare look anywhere but at him. My wings dipped, and the ground drew closer. The gods fought. They shook me from left to right, trying to knock me off course.

But I kept moving. One inch at a time.

When Kalen was no more than a breath away, I held out my hand. My wings trembled beneath me. The gods were trying to flutter them, just once, to toss me away from him. It might be enough to break my concentration, so I would lose control. I clenched my jaw and reached.

Kalen's hand closed around mine.

The gods went silent.

My entire body sighed.

And then I collapsed into his arms, where I knew I would never have to fight again.

I was only unconscious for a moment. When I awoke, I found myself in Kalen's arms. He carried me through the gates of Albyria, surrounded by a weary collection of warriors. Nellie walked beside him. Her hand rested gently on my arm, but she still carried the axe. When she spotted me awake, she winked at me and tossed it onto the ground. A signal of victory.

The battle was over. The war had been won.

Except it hadn't.

I climbed from Kalen's arms, putting a halt to the march into the city. I'd taken control of the power, but I felt woozy from the effort. I stumbled, and Kalen caught my arm.

"Let me carry you, love. You need time to recover from this," Kalen said.

"You don't understand. The humans are going to attack us. Where are they? Where's Val and Niamh?"

"I saw everything you saw. I know about the humans." A muscle in his jaw worked. "I sent Boudica to scout. We've burned the bridge, but the human army brought planks with them, as if they expected us to do that. We're falling back to the city, so what's left of our army can defend from the walls. The gods did attack the battlements earlier, but most of our warriors here were able to take cover. There are enough of us left to put up a good fight."

"And our people who are with them?" I asked.

He shook his head. "Boudica didn't spot Val, Niamh, or Alastair. I can only hope they escaped when they realized what the humans were planning."

"I don't want anyone else to die," I said. "I should go to the bridge and face them myself. I'm what they're here for. They know what power lives inside me now. Everything they've done, it's been to stop *me*."

"Only because they know you will lead to their defeat." He tucked a wayward strand of hair behind my ear. "You and me, together. Just one more enemy. One more battle. One more push for survival, and we're done."

I sighed, so very weary. As I tried to conjure the strength to fight another battle, a cacophony of caws sounded above. I looked up. Hundreds of ravens had stormed the skies. They were swooping in majestic circles, their black wings flared against the moonlight. I watched them, awestruck. The ravens had been gone from these lands for a very long time. And now they were back.

Druid Balfor suddenly appeared before us. He had a bundle of clothes in his hands that he handed to Nellie. Still only in a cloak, she gratefully took them.

"I knew you would need these," he said to her. Then Balfor turned to me, looking nervous. "I have something to tell you. And you might not like what I have to say."

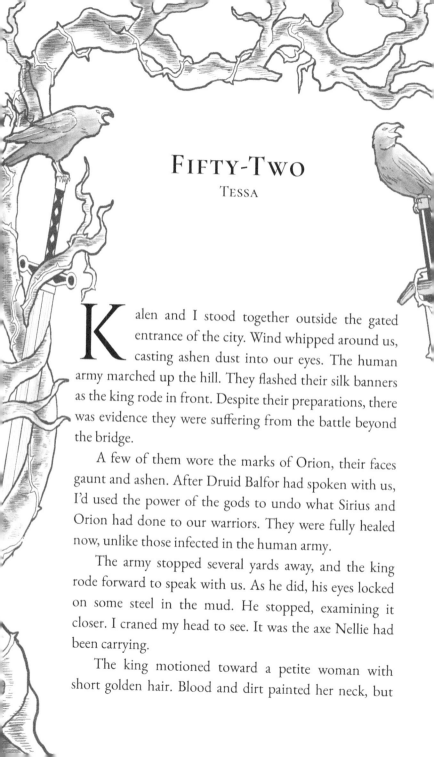

FIFTY-TWO
TESSA

K alen and I stood together outside the gated
entrance of the city. Wind whipped around us,
casting ashen dust into our eyes. The human
army marched up the hill. They flashed their silk banners
as the king rode in front. Despite their preparations, there
was evidence they were suffering from the battle beyond
the bridge.

A few of them wore the marks of Orion, their faces
gaunt and ashen. After Druid Balfor had spoken with us,
I'd used the power of the gods to undo what Sirius and
Orion had done to our warriors. They were fully healed
now, unlike those infected in the human army.

The army stopped several yards away, and the king
rode forward to speak with us. As he did, his eyes locked
on some steel in the mud. He stopped, examining it
closer. I craned my head to see. It was the axe Nellie had
been carrying.

The king motioned toward a petite woman with
short golden hair. Blood and dirt painted her neck, but

there were no visible wounds. Whoever's blood that was wasn't hers, and she carried an impressive broad sword. A good fighter, then. I'd have to keep an eye on her.

"Get the axe, Vera," the king ordered.

She rode forth and collected it before falling back. Strange.

Kalen and I walked forward to meet the king. He looked older than I'd expected. His hair was peppered with gray, and lines stretched around his eyes. Angry veins spiderwebbed across his cheeks. Instead of battle garb, he wore a long, silk robe. His feet were even sandalled. It seemed like a statement to me.

"I take it you're King Duncan Hinde," I said.

He remained on his horse, so he could look down his nose at us. "And you're Tessa Baran and King Kalen Denare."

"*Queen* Tessa Denare," I said.

"Ah yes, of course. You two have wed. I take it you are claiming your place as Queen of the Shadow Fae. I'll admit, I didn't see that in my visions, but I didn't care to look for it. It hardly matters when you will not survive the end of this day."

I smiled. "I understand the confusion. I meant Queen Tessa Denare of Talaven."

Duncan Hinde squinted at me. Then he chuckled, shifting uneasily on his horse. "You do understand you have no hope for survival. I have seen your future and mine. This is the end of the fae, I'm afraid. That includes you, despite your human heritage. Ovalis would not be pleased, but Ovalis has been gone many centuries. What he wanted hardly matters. Not when you threaten the survival of my species."

"His wishes don't matter?" I arched a brow. "I was under the impression he left very clear instructions for you and that you have been following them closely."

"And how would you know that?"

I tapped my head. "I have insight into the visions now, too. And one saw you become a traitor to your own people. Ovalis Hinde wanted to protect Talaven, yes, but he didn't want to doom the world by doing it. But you didn't like that very much, did you? Because it meant handing your reign over to someone who would lead your people toward a better future, a better world. A world where fae and humans coexisted in peace. A world where the Talaven king did not use up every last scrap of their resources until nothing was left but dust. Ovalis tried to save his people from not only the gods but from you. He saw you coming, too, you know."

Duncan barked out a laugh. He swung his gaze from me to Kalen, then back again. "This is ridiculous. None of this is true!"

Kalen sniffed. "Well, I certainly smell a lie, but it's not coming from us."

I smiled. "The knife's edge was a pretty lie. If I had wings tipped in crimson, it meant I'd doom the world. But if they were tipped in sapphire, I'd save you all, yes? That's not exactly true. I would have defeated the gods either way. But the crimson tips mean I defeat you, too. And so you tried everything to prevent it."

"I was protecting my people," he hissed.

"No, you were protecting yourself," I countered. "You were the one who planned to begin a war with the fae once the gods were defeated. You want their gemstones and their mines. You want their land, which bears fruit you cannot grow in Talaven. And you knew our numbers would be severely depleted after all this. Aesir would be ripe for the taking." I paused. "But even so, the fae would have put up a fight. They have elite powers, and your soldiers don't. And they would have retaliated after the first battle, sacking Moonstone. In the end, you would have won, but how many lives would you have lost in your needless war? You know the number. The visions told you."

Vera, the warrior from earlier, rode closer. She'd been listening.

"What's this about?" she asked. "This isn't true, is it, Duncan?"

"Return to the army, Vera," he said sharply. "I didn't call you forward."

She looked affronted. "I see."

Before she could turn her horse around, I raised my voice so she could clearly hear my next words. "Have things been going differently than you thought they would, King Duncan Hinde? Perhaps a beast unexpectedly attacked your ships."

The king narrowed his eyes.

I continued, "Ovalis has been steering you on a path without you knowing it. He knew what you'd do, so he put certain assurances in place. Tricky of him, wasn't it?"

"You speak as though I got all my information from Ovalis's journals. I have my own visions, too. I don't know why things have changed or how this is happening, but it must be something to do with *you*. Because I saw your death today. With my own visions and my own eyes."

"Except they weren't your eyes, were they, Duncan? At least, not most of the time. You used your Druids to see the visions for you." Druid Balfor strode through the castle gates and joined us on the road. He'd explained everything only moments ago. The Druids had been working with Ovalis Hinde's journals for centuries. They'd seen what Duncan would one day try, and they had pretended to help him, following the ancient path they'd all decided upon. Balfor had always been against the gods. He and the other Druids worshiped the essences of *this* world and saw the others as invaders who didn't belong. Those symbols in the cave and at the falls were the symbols of those essences, painted there centuries ago by the Druids of old.

As much as Balfor had wanted to explain everything to me earlier, he couldn't have. Not without risking another fork in the path. I had to make these choices on my own.

And this moment right here needed to happen.

Duncan Hinde paled and jerked the reins of his horse. "What is this? Don't tell me you've sided with them, Balfor. Tessa Baran is one of the gods now. She wants to steal my kingdom."

"I *will* take your kingdom," I said. "But I don't have to steal it to do so. I'm the only heir of your ancient king, Ovalis Hinde. Talaven belongs to me."

He scoffed. "*I* am the heir. Ovalis might be your ancestor, but he is mine, too. Through his *human* lineage, not that of the gods. And I will not let you steal it from me."

I looked at Vera. She hadn't returned to the army, despite her king's orders. Her eyes shifted to Balfor, who nodded solemnly. Then her gaze moved on to the king.

"Did you lie to me, Duncan? You've had another aim all this time?" she asked quietly.

He jerked sideways, only now noticing she was still there. He let out an exasperated sigh. "Yes, all right? But I did it to protect us from *her*. She has the gods inside her now. All seven. And she will flatten this world."

"And you saw her using her great power against us?" she asked.

His lips thinned. He didn't answer, but he didn't need to. He'd never seen any of that.

"You put your reign above your own people. Many of us have died for you. And many more would have died if you got your way." Without another word, Vera swung the axe. The blade cut through flesh and bone, and the King of Talaven's head fell to the ground. His body slid sideways on his horse. The sound of it hitting the mud was the only noise heard for miles.

FIFTY-THREE
TESSA

We welcomed the human army into our city. They seemed timid at first, but when arrows did not rain down from the battlements, they spread through the streets and headed toward the castle. Before anything else, I asked Vera the question I'd been dreading. When she saw the look on my face, she appeared concerned.

"Three of our companions went to your kingdom to treat with the king."

She relaxed. "Ah. Val, Niamh, and Alastair. They're an interesting bunch."

"They are." Did I dare hope? "Do you know what he did with them?"

"When they saw the king order our army to march against you, I was right beside them. They considered trying to kill him, but I rightly pointed out his guards would never let them get close enough. So they ran. To a wall near the river, if I heard them right. They were going to scale it and join your fighting efforts." She laughed. "I let them go. Even then, in my subconscious, I must have sensed something wasn't quite right with Duncan."

I clutched her arm. "They went to scale the wall behind Teine?"

She carefully extracted her arm from my grip. "Goodness. You're quite fond of them."

I glanced over my shoulder at Kalen, my heart throbbing with hope. He'd already whistled for the horses. Toryn handed his spear to a nearby warrior, but Gaven simply remained by the gate, his hands clasped before him.

He met my gaze. His eyes were glazed with tears.

Kalen, Nellie, and Toryn mounted their horses. Silver was nearby, having shifted backed into a steed. To Kalen, I said, "Go ahead. I'll be right behind you."

After a quick glance at Gaven, he urged his horse into a gallop down the hill.

I went over to Gaven. He leaned against the stone wall as he let flames dance across his knuckles. For a moment, I just stood beside him. The weight of the battle pressed down on me. We had won, against all odds, but it had not come without a price.

And if I'd known before what that price would be, I might not have agreed to pay it.

"I don't know how to face the day without her," he eventually said. "We've been together for a very long time. I can't remember a time when we weren't. Friendship is often more powerful than romantic love. More permanent. I never imagined a time when Fenella would not be in my life."

I wound my arm around his back and dropped my

head to his shoulder. I had no words of comfort for him. No hope to provide. Now that I'd consumed Andromeda's power, I understood the full depths of what it could and couldn't do. I would have tried to bring Fenella back to life before I understood. I likely would have spent hours, even days, screaming at the sky, refusing to let her go until I'd wrung every last ounce of my power dry.

But she wasn't coming back. Not from that wound. The only reason it had worked on me was because I'd been born with Life and Death inside me.

Gaven hugged me back, then kissed my brow. "Go. I know you're eager to see Val again. I'll be here waiting."

"You sure you don't want to come with me? Niamh and Alastair will be there, too."

"I'll see them soon enough. I just need a few more moments to grieve before I can truly celebrate their return. Plus, someone needs to find Roisin. She'll be thrilled to see her sister."

"I understand." I started toward Silver, then paused. "Thank you, Gaven."

"For what?"

"For being you."

He smiled.

T followed the others in the distance. They charged toward Teine, where the wooden wall still stood beneath the shadows of the mountains. As we drew closer, three small dots lengthened and widened, revealing my family, my friends.

Niamh led the front. She saw us first. Every inch of her was caked in dirt and blood. She slowed and dropped her empty quiver. Her bow slipped from her hands. Screwing up her face, she screamed and raced across the field.

Kalen leapt from his horse before it stopped. He crashed to the ground but kept on running. When Niamh reached him, they collided into each other so hard I heard the impact from here. She howled, saying his name again and again, with such depth of emotion, it brought me to tears.

Alastair stumbled toward them, a shit-eating grin consuming his face. And beside him was Val.

"Val," I shouted, urging Silver onward. "Val!"

She tensed and jerked her head my way. Her face lit up like a thousand stars. Alastair urged her forward, and she broke out into a run. Silver kept charging, and the distance soon vanished.

I jumped to the ground and threw my arms around my dearest, oldest friend. She clutched me. Her body shook with sobs. I was sobbing, too. Nellie ran over and slid her arms around us both. The three of us just stood there like that, holding on to each other. It had been so long since we'd all been in the same place at the same time. We weren't meant to be apart. We were family, we were blood.

I'd been terrified I would lose them both. So much of my childhood was gone. Life had taken so much from me, but I had not lost them. I squeezed them tighter, understanding just how lucky I was.

I would never take any moment with them for granted.

I pulled back and noticed the blood on Val's leathers. "Don't tell me you were fighting out there."

She smiled. "Of course I was. If you fall, I fall, remember?"

After many, many tearful reunions, we trudged back up the hill, had more tearful reunions with Gaven and Roisin and the humans of Teine. The gods never attacked the tower, but the humans had heard them calling for them, taunting them to come out. Thankfully, they'd waited, just as I'd asked, inside the dark rooms with my daggers clutched in their hands.

The Mist Guard and I gathered in the Great Hall for one last meeting about this lightforsaken war. Niamh and Alastair wanted to get caught up on what had happened, and I was dying to hear their side of things.

It felt like falling into a familiar routine. Kalen tried to keep control while the Mist Guard bickered. Gaven even joined in, though the sadness in his eyes lingered. It would likely linger for a good long while. When Niamh and Alastair looked around and noted Fenella's absence, Gaven was the one who explained.

There were more tears. Not so cheerful ones, this time.

It took hours for us to share our tales. And when we were finally finished, we all sat around the table in stunned silence. We had won. The gods were defeated. The human enemy was gone. We would not have to battle any longer. Just thinking it felt surreal. We'd been fighting for so long. It felt as if I'd been part of this war since my birth. Perhaps somewhere inside me, I'd always known there was more to my life than what I'd been told.

Niamh cleared her throat, breaking through the silence. I noticed she and Val were sitting quite close. Val was almost leaning against her. Interesting. Had they finally told each other how they felt?

"So," Niamh said, "you have the power of...how many, seven? Seven gods. Or whatever you want to call them."

"That's right," I said. "I suppose that makes me immortal now."

"And you're...all right?" She cocked a brow.

"I struggled to handle it when I first consumed the essences, but my bond with Kalen was stronger than anything they could do to me. I have control over them now. Their thoughts, their voices, their wants...it's all gone. I'm all that's left now."

Alastair leaned forward, bracing his arms on the table. "What are you going to do with it? Destroy it somehow?"

I sat up a little straighter. "Oh, I'm going to keep it."

"And that's not dangerous?" Niamh cast a glance at Kalen, who merely shrugged.

"It's dangerous. For anyone who goes against me." I smiled.

Alastair guffawed. "Fuck's sake, little dove. You are a force to be reckoned with now."

"And I'll need to be. For a while, I'm certain this world will live in peace, but there may come a time when I need to put on a show of strength, just to get the point across," I said.

"And you can see all that?" Val asked eagerly. "With this foresight thing?"

"I can only see what Andromeda knew, and she didn't see as much as you'd think. The Lamiae didn't have the power of foresight. That came from the comet, and they could only use it if they went to where it fell."

"So, you're going to keep your new powers." Niamh nodded. "Probably for the best. Just means I'll plan on never pissing you off."

A slow smile spread across my face. I leaned forward and winked at her. "Best not hurt my friend, then."

Val's face flamed. Nellie coughed. Alastair laughed, as he always did. And as I looked around the table at the faces of those I loved, I knew we would make it, even without a vision to tell us everything would be all right. Because even if another enemy arose from the ashes, we would fight them. Together.

We always did.

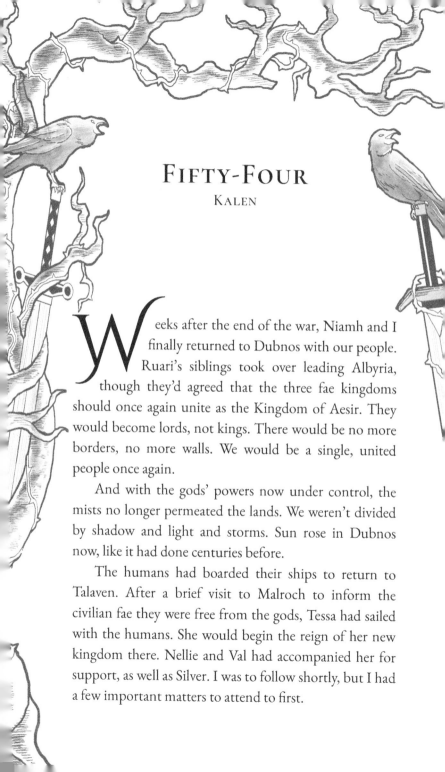

FIFTY-FOUR
KALEN

Weeks after the end of the war, Niamh and I finally returned to Dubnos with our people. Ruari's siblings took over leading Albyria, though they'd agreed that the three fae kingdoms should once again unite as the Kingdom of Aesir. They would become lords, not kings. There would be no more borders, no more walls. We would be a single, united people once again.

And with the gods' powers now under control, the mists no longer permeated the lands. We weren't divided by shadow and light and storms. Sun rose in Dubnos now, like it had done centuries before.

The humans had boarded their ships to return to Talaven. After a brief visit to Malroch to inform the civilian fae they were free from the gods, Tessa had sailed with the humans. She would begin the reign of her new kingdom there. Nellie and Val had accompanied her for support, as well as Silver. I was to follow shortly, but I had a few important matters to attend to first.

"Look at it," Niamh said as she walked into the throne room, her arms spread wide. Empty, cold, and gray, it seemed uninviting at first glance. But it had been home to so many moments of my life. It was where I'd met Niamh, where our friendship had blossomed, and where I'd named her my heir all those years ago.

I smiled and slipped my hands into my pockets. She had always looked so at peace in this room, while most people hated it at first sight.

"Well," she said, turning toward me. "Aren't you going to sit on your throne? It's been a long time."

"You should try it."

Her lips thinned. "Kal."

"I mean it." I nodded to the old chair, lit by a thousand diamonds. "Haven't you always wondered what it felt like to sit there?"

"I'm certain there's not a single fae in this city who hasn't wondered. That doesn't mean I should. It's meant for the king and the king only. That's you, not me."

"What if I told you I'd like to step down?"

"I would say you've gone mad." The muscles around her eyes tightened. "Is this why you left Alastair poking around the barracks and brought me here alone? So you could...what? Tell me you're leaving? Because I know that's what this is truly about. Tessa must reign in Talaven now. You are joining her."

"She is my mate," I said. "And truth be told, I have long wished to hand my reign over to you. I have been king a long time, Niamh. I am done."

She searched my eyes. "You'd be king there, too, though."

"In name only. Tessa will rule, and I will guide her. But she is the one who must lead Talaven to a better world. Druid Balfor was clear."

Niamh began to pace. "I don't know how to rule."

"Yes, you do. You've been with me for nearly four hundred years."

"But what about Alastair and Gaven? What about Toryn? We're your Mist Guard," she said.

"Perhaps they should be *your* Mist Guard," I said with a smile.

She laughed. "I am no Mist King."

"Neither am I. Not anymore."

She stopped pacing then. The expression on her face was one of sudden understanding. I'd stepped in to fight my mother's battle the moment she'd vanished into Oberon's court. And I had not stopped fighting for so very long. I had done what I'd intended to do. I'd found out what had happened to her. I'd avenged her death as best I could. And I'd found a way to stop the gods. With help, of course. I had saved my people.

I'd fulfilled my every goal. Now it was time to move on to another.

Niamh moved to the throne and brushed her finger across the glittering diamonds. "I feel like I'm losing my brother."

Sighing, I crossed the room and palmed her shoulder. "Don't be so dramatic. I'm only going to be across the sea. I can visit any time I'd like, and you can do the same. You know there'll always be a bed for you there."

"You mean that? You won't become a stranger?"

"I could never be a stranger to you, Niamh." Gently, I

shifted her sideways and nudged her onto the throne. Kneeling before her, I took her hand in mine and said, "When my mother vanished, I was a broken man. I couldn't have made it without you. You held this court together, even when I was falling apart. So please. Take my crown and take my throne. The fae deserve someone who is fully committed to them."

She nodded. I knew she understood, even though she hadn't fully processed my request. If I were to stay, my mind and heart would forever be somewhere else. I could visit Dubnos any time I liked, but a ruler needed to be present, especially during the formation of a new kingdom.

"And can I marry Val?" she asked.

"You can marry whoever the fuck you want. You're the queen."

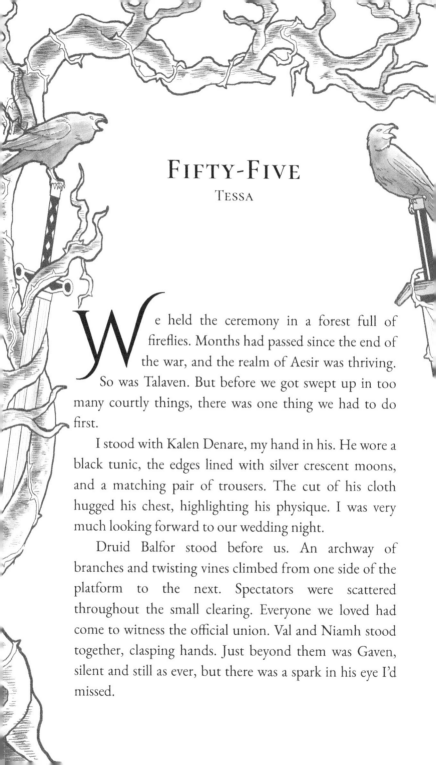

FIFTY-FIVE
TESSA

We held the ceremony in a forest full of fireflies. Months had passed since the end of the war, and the realm of Aesir was thriving. So was Talaven. But before we got swept up in too many courtly things, there was one thing we had to do first.

I stood with Kalen Denare, my hand in his. He wore a black tunic, the edges lined with silver crescent moons, and a matching pair of trousers. The cut of his cloth hugged his chest, highlighting his physique. I was very much looking forward to our wedding night.

Druid Balfor stood before us. An archway of branches and twisting vines climbed from one side of the platform to the next. Spectators were scattered throughout the small clearing. Everyone we loved had come to witness the official union. Val and Niamh stood together, clasping hands. Just beyond them was Gaven, silent and still as ever, but there was a spark in his eye I'd missed.

And then there was Alastair, of course. He spent half of his time in Talaven and half in Aesir. He seemed to like the arrangement. Silver had even asked to come. He couldn't go out in the daylight, still allergic to the moon and the sun, so I'd made certain the ceremony was held under the cover of darkness.

But as I cast a glance over my shoulder at the gathered crowd, it was my sister's smile that caught my eye the most. She was beaming up at Toryn, who had rarely left her side in months. They hadn't said so, but I had a feeling their own wedding would not be far behind ours.

The Druid cleared his throat. "Kalen Denare of the shadow fae realm and Tessa Baran of Teine."

"Tessa *Denare*!" Alastair hooted. A ripple of laughter went through the crowd.

"I'm trying to do this properly," Balfor said with an eye roll. "It is not every day I wed a couple who are...well, *already wed*."

He'd relaxed a great deal since finally revealing everything he knew about the visions and prophecies. It seemed, in reality, Balfor was quite snarky when he had a mind to be. It made me like him so much more.

"Balfor," Kalen said, trying to take control of the situation.

"Yes, yes." He sighed. "Tessa *Denare* of Teine."

"Thank you," I said, grinning. "You may continue."

In truth, Kalen and I did not need a ceremony. Between our previous marriage vows and our mating bond, all legalities were taken care of. But there'd been a time, when the darkness had been pressing in around us, that we'd promised each other we'd one day celebrate our love. It had been a golden thread, leading us toward a future we couldn't see through the cloying mist.

"We will speak the ancient words of the ones who came before us," Balfor said solemnly. "These words are for those who have died and left us for the higher realm. And they are for newborn babes who have only just joined us in this world. It is only fitting we speak them now for the joining of two souls. Everyone, repeat after me:

Grant, O Life, the strength to carry on;

And in that strength, give us understanding;

And in understanding, let us know love;

The love of all existences."

"The love of all existences," I murmured, staring into the depths of Kalen's sapphire eyes.

Kalen tugged me to his chest and kissed me fiercely. I wound my arms around his neck, pressing up onto my toes.

"I am yours, and you are mine," he whispered against my lips. A promise, a vow. One I knew we'd never break. And as our gathered love ones cheered, he took my hand and led me through the forest. King and Queen, husband and wife, fated mates.

He was everything to me and more.

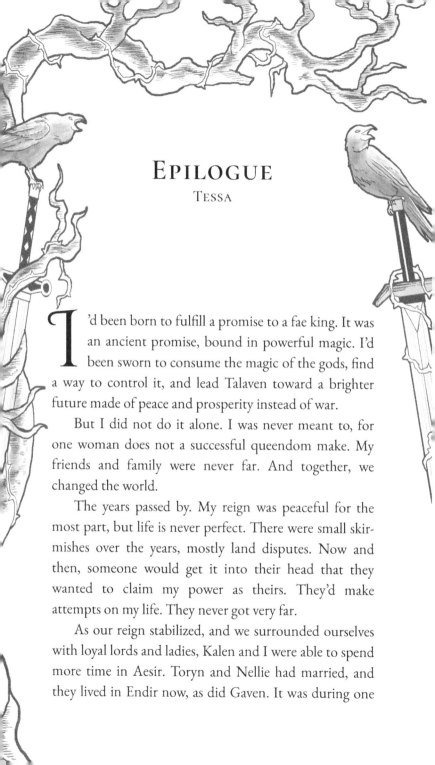

EPILOGUE
TESSA

I'd been born to fulfill a promise to a fae king. It was an ancient promise, bound in powerful magic. I'd been sworn to consume the magic of the gods, find a way to control it, and lead Talaven toward a brighter future made of peace and prosperity instead of war.

But I did not do it alone. I was never meant to, for one woman does not a successful queendom make. My friends and family were never far. And together, we changed the world.

The years passed by. My reign was peaceful for the most part, but life is never perfect. There were small skirmishes over the years, mostly land disputes. Now and then, someone would get it into their head that they wanted to claim my power as theirs. They'd make attempts on my life. They never got very far.

As our reign stabilized, and we surrounded ourselves with loyal lords and ladies, Kalen and I were able to spend more time in Aesir. Toryn and Nellie had married, and they lived in Endir now, as did Gaven. It was during one

of our many visits that Kalen said he had something he
wanted to show me.

He led me across the lush emerald carpet and down
the grand staircase. Candlelit chandeliers splashed light
onto the new portraits that hung along the walls. I smiled
as we passed them. There was Nellie, looking regal in a
green brocade coat and glittering necklace. Toryn's
portrait hung beside hers. The painter had originally
brushed out his scars, but Toryn had insisted he be
captured as he was now, rather than how he used to be.

Just below their portraits hung those of their three
children: Fiadh, Fenella, and Ruari. The portraits had
been painted when they'd been chubby-faced youngsters,
but all three were fully grown now. I'd never seen Nellie
so happy.

And all around them hung the portraits of everyone
we'd lost over the years. Some had to be done by descrip-
tion and memory. Fenella and her brilliant blue horns had
a place of honor high on the wall, where everyone could
see her.

I brushed aside a wayward tear. Even now, after all
these years, I grieved for her. I would have loved to see the
look on her face when I'd taken Talaven from the
corrupted king. She would have laughed so hard.

"What are you thinking about, love?" Kalen said,
noting my silence.

I nodded toward Fenella's portrait as we passed
beneath it. "I wish she'd been there when we won, that's
all. I wish she was here now."

"She probably would have chopped off the king's
head herself."

I smiled at the familiar banter. This wasn't the first time we'd said these very words. Sometimes, I wondered if we repeated them enough we could make them true.

"Come." He tugged me down the corridor. "Let's talk of happy things."

"Like the library?"

"You've noticed where we're going, then."

"I memorized the location of this library the moment Fenella first showed it to me."

"That's right. She was the one who brought you here. Wasn't it after threatening to throw you into the dungeons?" We reached the double oak doors. Before he pushed them open, he paused. "Are you ready?"

I cocked my head. "You're acting very mysterious. Yes, I'm ready to go inside the library. What have you done to it?"

"You'll see." He shoved the doors. They swung wide, and orange light spilled across my face. I gasped. A hundred gemstone lanterns filled the room. All the dust motes and cobwebs that had plagued the stacks for decades were finally gone. Books crammed the towering shelves, and scrolls filled baskets that sat in a row along the far wall. The ceiling was high—shockingly so. But it had always been so dark in here that I had never fully appreciated the vastness of it.

I felt my cheeks ache as I took it all in, trying to count even a fraction of the books. There were thousands of them.

"That was the smile I was hoping to see," Kalen said fondly.

"Books are the boards beneath our feet," I whispered.

"Without them, we risk wading in mud. When did you have this done?"

"I did it myself," he said, surprising me. "The last time I visited. You were busy with some trade route issues, and I thought I'd do something special for you. I know you have the library in Talaven, but—"

"This is my favorite one. It always has been."

"I'll admit, I don't understand. It's never been particularly impressive."

"Because I knew what it could be. It just needed a little love."

He held out his hand once more. "Come. There's one more surprise."

I laughed. "What more could there possibly be?"

He led me through the stacks. Now and then, I stopped to grab a book. By the time we reached the back of the room, I balanced seven volumes in my arms rather precariously. Some space had been cleared, the shelves shifted to stand along the walls. In the center of the floor sat a small, crackling hearth surrounded by several comfortable armchairs.

"Fire in a library?" I asked with a laugh. "Dangerous combination."

"You have the power of seven gods, love. I'm confident the books are safe in your hands." He winked and started to back away. "Enjoy your time reading. You deserve a break from being queen for a day."

"Wait." I motioned to the nearest armchair. "Sit with me. You did all this. Don't you think you should get to enjoy it, too?"

He arched a brow. "I thought you liked utter silence

when you got into one of your books. No distractions. No chatting. Nothing but the words on the page."

"Well, you're just going to have to be a very comfortable pillow, then." Grinning, I tugged him toward me and nudged him into the chair. He opened his arms as I climbed on top of him, curling into his lap and resting my head against his chest. Without another word, I cracked open the first book and inhaled the scent of parchment, ink, and leather. The warmth of the flames caressed my skin, and Kalen's powerful arms encircled me.

I released a full-body sigh. I enjoyed being queen. Ruling had not come naturally to me at first, but I'd settled into it. Helping my people had become my life calling, and I took pride in it. I felt fulfilled and happy, as if I was where I'd always been meant to be.

But ruling was nothing compared to this. To listening to the steady rhythm of my mate's heartbeat. To tasting the remnants of his lips on mine. To smelling the crackling, freshly chopped wood in the roaring hearth.

To feeling the rough parchment between my fingers when I turned another page.

I did not know where the next adventure would lead, but I would embrace whatever the story had in store for me.

Glossary

Druids - religious fae leaders who worship the sky, the earth, and the seas

Familiar - a bonded animal; usually, only shadow fae have this connection

Fion - fae wine that tastes of silver and song

Gemstones - powerful jewels with magical properties

Gods - powerful, immortal beings who once ruled the world with violence, banished when humans and fae joined together to fight them

Joint eaters - monsters of the mist who can transform into any animal

Lamiae - another name for the immortal creatures who call themselves gods

Mortal Blade - a blade only a mortal can wield, and whoever is on the receiving end turns to ash

Pookas - the term shadow fae use for the monsters of the mist who feast on human flesh

Shadowfiends - the term light fae and mortals use for the monsters of the mist who feast on human flesh

The Crones - King Oberon's human wives, who he used as vessels for his true love, Bellicent Denare

The Fell - the time period when the five winged gods first arrived in the world

The Great Rift - the chasm separating the Kingdom of Light from the rest of the world, caused by the clash of powers between King Oberon and the Mist King

The Oidhe - the deal between the mortals of Teine and King Oberon

Tiger-eye gemstones - gemstones found in the human kingdoms; can create a shield

Valerian - a magic-infused herb that causes dreamless sleep

Wraiths - hooded creatures of the mist who leave behind trails of poisonous sand

THE GODS

Andromeda - God of Death (and Life)

Callisto - God of War & Beasts (and Peace)

Pandora - God of Storms (and Tranquility)

Perseus - God of Fear (and Courage)

Pollux - God of Shadows (and Light)

Orion - God of Famine (and Abundance)

Sirius - God of Pestilence (and Healing)

Also by Jenna Wolfhart

The Mist King

Of Mist and Shadow

Of Ash and Embers

Of Night and Chaos

Of Dust and Stars

Falling for Fables (Stand-alone romantasy)

Forged by Magic

The Fallen Fae

Court of Ruins

Kingdom in Exile

Keeper of Storms

Tower of Thorns

Realm of Ashes

ABOUT THE AUTHOR

Jenna Wolfhart spends her days dreaming up stories about swoony fae kings and stabby heroines. When she's not writing, she loves to deadlift, rewatch Game of Thrones, and drink far too much coffee.

Born and raised in America, Jenna now lives in England with her husband and her two dogs.

www.jennawolfhart.com
jenna@jennawolfhart.com
tiktok.com/@jennawolfhart